# BloodVault

## THE DANTONVILLE SERIES - BOOK 3

# TIMA MARIA LACOBA

## Published By
## Tima Maria Lacoba

BloodVault

Book Three of the Dantonville Legacy

Tima Maria Lacoba

ISBN-13: 978-1519486011
ISBN-10: 1519486014

# BOOKS BY TIMA MARIA LACOBA

Laura's Locket: A Dantonville Chronicle

Bloodgifted: Book 1 of the Dantonville Legacy

Bloodpledge: Book 2 of the Dantonville Legacy

Bloodvault: Book 3 of the Dantonville Legacy

BloodWish: Book 4 of the Dantonville Legacy

# CONTENTS

# ACKNOWLEDGMENTS

For my mum,
who's been there for me every step of the way. Your support and encouragement can never be measured. Love you, mum.

A huge thank you to two lovely ladies – my fabulous critique partner, Peita, and my editor, Dionne – who know how to bring out the best in my writing. What would I do without you?

To my dear friend and soul-sister, Claudia, whose boundless enthusiasm for all things Dantonville made writing this series such fun.

Thank you dear Patti, who kept me on track everyday, checking on my word count, and cracking that whip when I needed it.

To my amazing beta readers, Karen, Peita and Susan, who went beyond the call of duty to proofread the entire manuscript for me in less than three days. Ladies, you are amazing.

Thank you to all my facebook friends and followers who've encouraged and supported me in this incredible writing journey.

Thank you for loving the world of the Dantonville Legacy.

# BLOODVAULT

*"So many out-of-the-way things had happened lately, that Alice had begun to think that very few things indeed were really impossible."* Alice in Wonderland by Lewis Carroll

# CHAPTER 1 - DESTINY

**LAURA**

Whoever said we are captains of our own destiny had no idea. Not a clue. Mistakenly, I once believed my life was mine to control, but that illusion has been shattered. Once, I was ordinary Laura Dantonville, primary school teacher, and soon-to-be engaged to Matt Sommers, Detective Inspector and all round nice guy – or so I thought. That was only a few weeks ago. Now….

My pink-diamond engagement ring flashed up at me as I examined the result of my home pregnancy kit. And I had to concede that fate and destiny had control; the strip showed two coloured bands.

I was pregnant.

Nothing unusual in that, except that Alec, my fiancé, is a vampire.

My ex-boyfriend, Matt, hated vampires and wouldn't hesitate to kill them, even if it meant wiping out half my family – the vampire half. I'd had to end our relationship.

Placing the strip of paper on the edge of the sink, I looked down at my flat belly. *Not for much longer.* I rubbed my hands over the spot where, deep within, a little life had been conceived. Soon my warm and fuzzy feeling evaporated, and fear took hold – the birth of our child would mean the end of the curse. For centuries, the firstborn in each generation carried the Ingenii gene, which provided longevity and youthfulness, and gave the chosen Brethren who fed from us the greatest gift of all – the ability to daywalk. That was all about to end, and for many among the Brethren, it meant losing any chance to share in that privilege. Would they be desperate enough to kill my baby? To hinder its birth?

I hugged my arms about me, stepped out of the ensuite into my bedroom and called Alec. 'I need to see you.'

We were still on the *Judy* – Luc's yacht – moored in Double Bay, not far from his Vaucluse mansion. Repairs on the house were only weeks away from completion after the fire that had caused extensive damage to the lower floors but had, thankfully, destroyed nothing major. So for now, *Judy,* was our temporary home.

'Anything wrong, darling?' Alec stood in the doorway, his six-feet-one frame dominating the narrow space. The injuries he'd sustained after being captured by the Rebels had healed, and his lavender eyes sparkled as they surveyed me. Only he could make my body tingle with the slightest glance.

I took a deep breath. 'I'm pregnant.'

His smile faded as his gaze darted from my face to my belly. 'You sure?'

'My period's late, so I did the test – three times with three different kits. Each with the same result.' I gave a nod toward the bathroom. 'It's on the basin.'

Alec stared at me, eyes wide, fists clenched.

Okay, not the reaction I expected. 'What's wrong? I thought….'

He shook his head, closed his eyes and the crease between them deepened. 'No, nothing….' In a blink, he was at my side, holding me close.

I sucked in a breath as I remembered what Alec told me weeks ago – his first wife and baby died in childbirth. Did he fear the same would happen to me? Or, was it something else?

I took his face between my hands. 'Tell me.'

He licked his lips, and his breath came rapidly. 'I can't lose you.'

'I won't die, Alec. Women don't die in childbirth anymore. There are modern—'

'I know, Laura, but you won't be in a hospital. To end the curse, you have to give birth at that damn witch's grave, somewhere,' —he waved his arm— 'in the wilds of Scotland. Do you know what that means?' His pupils dilated.

The curse. I had thought it through; I knew what it meant. Luc had told me the stipulations of the curse the day after the Ritual. At the time I didn't think it applied to me. By the time it did, I had no choice – I was the Child of Light and Darkness who was supposed to mate with the witch's descendant and bear the Child of Promise. Then, and only then, would my father, Luc, and grandfather, Marcus, their men, and all whom they transformed, be given a choice: to return to their human state – and die immediately as age caught up with them – or remain vampire.

Alec had decided on the latter. I wasn't going to die on any witch's grave, nor be transformed into one of the Brethren as a last resort, either. Just as well, as the Ingenii gene I carried prevented it anyway. But, I trusted in my father's – and Alec's – ability to keep me and the baby safe when the time came.

'You'll be there - you're a doctor, and so is Jake.'

'But I'm not an obstetrician, Laura, and neither is he.'

'Well, if other women can give birth in' —I thought of recent incidents on the news— 'parking lots and service stations with no qualified medical people around, and be all right, then so can I.' *I hope.*

It took him a while to answer, the skin around his eyes and mouth tight with anxiety. 'If it came to a choice' —he began slowly— 'between you and the baby, I choose you. I don't give a damn about the curse - that's Luc's obsession. I care about you. Do you understand? I can't lose you…. I can't allow it!'

The passion in his voice, the fear in his eyes, caught at my heart. I placed my finger over his lips. 'Shhh … Don't say that. I love you, and I can't imagine anything more beautiful than having a child with you. I want you both.'

Alec took my hand and kissed the inside of my palm. 'Darling, if there are any complications, even the hint of one, I'll whisk you to the nearest hospital. Luc and the curse be damned!'

I hoped my father didn't hear. He was Alec's sire, and he'd been waiting and planning for the day when the curse would end and our family would no longer be vampire food. In the past, the Brethren had fought battles over us. The most recent rebellion had been defeated here, but a threat still loomed in Europe. My father and his men were in the wheelhouse, on the uppermost deck, trying to intercept a text message and stop an attack on our chateau in France. Alec and I had been with them until I'd been hit by a wave of nausea and excused myself. The sea was particularly choppy tonight, and my sea legs had never been good.

I pulled out of his embrace and stared at him. 'We have no choice. You know that. Unless the curse ends with us, our baby will be the next Ingenii. You want to see our child undergo the Ritual? Will you be princeps … to your own child?'

Alec ran a hand through his hair, and his expression darkened. 'Holy mother of … No! I will not feed from my own child.' The thought of it sickened me, too. 'Now I understand how Luc feels.'

I nodded. My parents faced the same problem when my mother fell pregnant with me. No wonder my father had appointed Alec as princeps instead. He couldn't bear feeding from his own child, just as Alec couldn't face the idea now.

He came towards me and leaned down so our foreheads touched.

'It didn't bother you before,' I said.

'It didn't hit home till now.'

We stood like that as the enormity of it sank in. I silently prayed that when the time came, there would be no unforeseen complications – nothing that would force either of us into making a heart-wrenching choice.

He took a deep breath. 'It's very subtle, but I can smell the hormonal changes on you.'

'Who needs a pregnancy test when you're around?'

He chuckled before sobering and tilting my chin up so I would meet his gaze. 'We won't be able to hide this for long. Others will soon detect your scent.'

'But hasn't the rebellion been defeated here? Who'd attack now? Isn't Rasputin gone?' Rasputin – his name alone made me shiver – a vampire who could mesmerise his own kind into doing his will and who led a rebellion against the Principate. I'd injured him severely to save Kari's life – chopped off his hands. Last I heard, he was on the run.

'As far as we know, he's no longer in the country, but that doesn't mean other Rebels won't swarm here.' His voice dropped. 'They could try to harm the baby … prevent its birth.'

I shuddered. My fears were justified.

'We can't stay here indefinitely, and the residence here is not designed for defence. I'm taking you to France – to the chateau. It's the safest place.' He paused. 'For you both. The security system's one of the best. The sooner we get there the better.'

My heart stuttered. I knew we would have to leave Sydney when the time came, but it had seemed so far away. Now, I wasn't prepared. A million questions rushed through my mind – work, my flat, car … and my passport – who knew where that was? I hadn't used it in years, and I wasn't sure if it was still valid. What if we didn't make it back by the end of January, when the new term began? I hadn't farewelled the kids, parents, other staff at the school. Things were moving too quickly.

'Alec, I'm not ready for this.'

His arm tightened around my waist. 'Laura....' Lines around his eyes creased with concern. 'I know it's sudden, taking you away from all you know—'

'Do I have time to say goodbye?' I thought of John and Eilene. Up until a few weeks ago, I had believed them to be my parents.

He shook his head. 'No time for a personal visit. Call them.'

What a terrible way to say goodbye after everything they had done for me. I could be away for a year, perhaps more. A lump rose in my throat.

He rubbed his thumb gently across my lower lip. 'I know it's hard, but they'll understand. I'm sorry about your teaching job, too.'

So was I. But that didn't compare with having to leave the two beloved people who had raised me, like this. It broke my heart. Yet did I have a choice? 'What about you, the hospital?'

'I have processes in place for such an emergency. I'll let the Board know.'

I sighed and lowered my head onto his chest, fearful of what lay ahead, yet fiercely resolved to see it through.

# CHAPTER 2 – PATH LAID OUT

**LAURA**

My mother, Judy, was at the wheel of the four-deck yacht. Marcus and Luc hunched over the control console as Sam, one of my father's men, clicked away at the onboard computers. Marcus raised his head and smiled at us. I had to keep reminding myself he was my grandfather, as he looked no older than his son, Luc – a young man in the prime of life.

Luc came over and patted Alec on the back. They gave each other a brief nod that expressed more than words. The white-oak serum Alec had created had saved his life tonight. White-oak was the only substance lethal to vampires – reducing their bodies to crystalline ash in minutes. The Principate had outlawed it, but it hadn't stopped the Rebels.

Sam rubbed his nose and switched his attention briefly from the computer screen to us. His lavender eyes crinkled at the corners with his smile. 'Good to see you.'

Kari leapt up from the bench she shared with my best friend, Jenny, and threw her arms around Alec's neck. 'I'm so glad you're okay, Princi. I wanna kill that HH pig!'

Alec looked at me. 'HH?' he mouthed.

'Handless and Hairy,' I mouthed back. 'Rasputin.' She'd given him that nickname after the injury I inflicted on him.

Alec chuckled and prised Kari off. 'Next time I see him, he's all yours.'

Jenny came over and handed me a drink. 'Here, hon, take this. Been holding it for you. Saw your face when they brought him out.'

It had been a shock seeing what the Rebels had done to Alec, and, if I wasn't pregnant, I'd happily down it in one gulp. 'Thanks Jen, but I've drunk a lot of the stuff lately. I think I'll pass.' This wasn't the time to blurt out my "delicate condition."

She shrugged and drank it herself. With a tilt of her chin, she indicated the control console. 'They've been at it the whole time, trying to hack into ... Timur's?' —I nodded— 'mobile to stop Rasputin's message getting through.' Rasputin had learnt of the bloodvault, my father's secret store of Ingenii blood, whose unique qualities enabled vampires to daywalk. He'd sent a message to his master, Timur, who'd scuttled back to Budapest to avoid taking the Pledge.

'That'd be brilliant.'

'That guy's a wiz! I don't think I want to know what satellite he's hacked into.'

'Don't ask.' I linked my arm through hers, and we joined everyone else at the console.

Kari hovered over Sam's shoulder. 'Why's it taking so long?' She combed her fingers through her short, pale hair, until it stuck up like spikes.

'Security system's in place,' Sam muttered. His fingers flew over the keyboard like a concert pianist.

'You can overcome that, right?' she asked.

'Depends on the type of encryption they use.' His gaze darted between the screen, the keyboard and the mobile phone at his right hand. 'Let me try.' A series of numbers and symbols popped up on the computer and phone screens, followed by a loud buzzing. 'Shit!'

'Good or bad?' Kari asked.

'Bad. I triggered the hacker alarm.' His fingers danced across the keyboard again, and the buzzing stopped.

'That's good, right?'

'Kari, do me a favour and zip it!' Sam growled.

She stuck her tongue out at him. I had to bite my lip to stop from laughing.

'Kari, can you double check the navigation charts for me?' Judy asked. 'I don't want us to get lost in the dark.'

I caught the wink Luc sent her. Kari was my mother's best friend, and whereas Judy aged over time, Kari did not. Being a vampire, she would remain twenty forever.

Another ten minutes or so later, Sam cried out, 'Gotcha! Son-of-a-bitch.'

There it was for us all to see – Rasputin's message: "Lebrettan has a hidden cache of Ingenii blood in his castle in France. Attack it now, my lord. Claim the prize and the victory. Your humble and faithful servant, Rasputin."

Luc's face tightened in anger 'Fils de salope! Daring to attack my castle.' Although my family had moved here from France over a century-and-a-half ago, Luc still maintained the D'Antonville Chateau, and it's precious store of Ingenii blood.

Sam looked across at him. 'Wipe it?'

Luc gave a curt nod then added in a grim voice, 'Let's send him one of our own.'

'No, wait.' Marcus placed his hand over the mobile phone. 'Silence might be our best course – keep Timur guessing, unsure whether things are in his favour.'

'Only till that snake of his, Rasputin, shows up,' Sam said.

'Which might take a few days. He's handless and hunted, which gives us a head start.' Marcus's gaze roamed between Luc and Alec.

'Meaning?' Sam frowned.

'Unless we patrol every airport in this country and risk one of our own being mesmerized, we can't stop him making it back to Europe. Once there, he's on home turf. He will reach Timur. Of that I have no doubt,' Marcus said.

No one had to state the obvious – we all knew that once the secret of the bloodvault was out, we'd have Rebels swarming the chateau in France looking for it.

Luc gripped the console and his voice was almost a whisper. 'The chateau – even if he doesn't get that message, Timur'd still want to lay siege to it to make a point: that the Rebels are strong enough to take on the Principate. Yet if we allow that message to reach him he'll head straight there to get his hands on it. No need to come here—'

'When he can get it closer to home. Provence is only a few hours flight from Budapest,' Alec finished for him.

Luc exhaled tersely. 'I doubt he'd do it if I was there – wouldn't have the guts.'

'Timur!' Marcus turned and spat into the water. 'Time I took him on.'

'Time *we* took him on.' Luc's eyes lightened as he gazed at Marcus. They clasped forearms in a poignant moment as father and son came to an agreement.

'Why not empty the bloodvault here and take it back with us to the chateau? No safer place,' Sam suggested.

'It's also remote and the people in the village know about us – know when to stay indoors at night. Here,' —Marcus waved his arm to indicate the city— 'Deus! It's impossible. Imagine asking the neighbours to shelter inside the house till the danger has passed?'

I pictured the well-heeled residents of Vaucluse hammering on Luc's door to be let in, to save them from the vampires outside. Ludicrous.

'It'd be the same with the Paris residence,' Alec said. 'Both are indefensible in an outright attack.'

Judy flicked a glance at the men. 'I think you've all forgotten we need to be there for the New Year's Eve Masquerade Ball anyway. I organised things months ago with the housekeeper and cook.'

'Ah.' Luc raised his eyes heavenward. 'I forgot.'

'A masquerade ball? I've always wanted to go to one of those things.' Fairy tale visions of dazzling gowns and dancing beneath glittery chandeliers flitted through my mind.

'It's *the* event of the year, dear, and I have the organisation down to a fine art now.'

'Ooh, yes.' Kari clapped, her face beaming like a child at Christmas. 'I missed the last few. Not this year … err, next year, I mean. Or is it both?'

Judy chuckled. She touched my cheek, and her eyes glistened. 'This year's will be extra special, because you'll be there.'

Marcus looked pensive, his head bowed. 'It's all coming together, finally, and it will end where it all began.'

Luc placed a hand on his shoulder. 'We leave for France tonight.' He turned his attention to Sam. 'How soon can you get the jet ready?'

'I've had it on standby since the Pledging,' Sam replied.

'When are you coming back?' Jenny had sat silently as the debate carried on around her. Now she set her drink down on the table and rose from the bench, her expression despondent.

'Not until this situation is resolved,' Alec answered.

She sighed. 'Well, I guess my holiday's over.'

I disengaged myself from Alec's embrace and went to her. 'Come with us, Jen. You've said you always wanted to visit France and stay in a chateau. Here's your chance. And there'll be a masked ball.'

She swallowed and glanced around at the others. 'Oh, lawd, I'm so tempted. Would it only be for a few weeks? What about our jobs? If it's for longer, how will I pay the rent on my house, my car...?' She held her hand to her cheek and looked out over the water. Finally she shrugged. 'Thanks for the offer, but I think it's better if I stay.'

My heart dropped.

'I don't believe you're safe yet. Rasputin may be desperate to get back to his master, but he could always send someone after you, later, to use as leverage against us. I'm only offering because you're my daughter's friend,' Luc said.

Jenny gasped, and her face went ashen. She looked at me in desperation.

'Can't some of the Brethren here keep watch over her – just in case?' I asked.

Luc pursed his lips. 'I could ask, but they're not paid bodyguards.' He turned to Jenny. 'What do you value most – those things or your life? It's up to you. Take it or leave it.'

His bluntness affected me, let alone Jenny. Her gaze shot to him, and my throat dried at the fear in her eyes.

Judy placed her hand on Luc's arm. 'Jenny, dear, we can take care of those things. You won't lose your house or car, so rest easy on that count. You never know; we could be back before the end of January.'

'I s'pose then....' Her words came out haltingly, without her usual nervous laugh.

'Settled!' Kari leapt up and threw her arms around us. 'We can have girl time. Go shopping in Lyons.' She nudged Jenny, and, with a wicked twinkle in her eyes, whispered, 'Sexy Terry will be there.'

I assumed Kari referred to Terens. His original Roman name had been Sextus Terentius, so I could see where the "Sexy Terry" came from.

Jenny cracked a smile.

## CHAPTER 3 – IT BEGINS

**ALEC**

Laura's announcement had thrown me. Of course I expected her to fall pregnant – that's why we initially came together. But that moment, the recollection of another birth crashed through the walls in my mind; walls that kept out the memory of my wife's cries. Eclampsia had killed her and my baby son. I shook my head to banish the haunting images. It was not going to happen to Laura. She was not going to die. She couldn't. Yet, how could I prevent it?

A year after my transformation, Luc had taken me to the site of the massacre, where, nearly two-thousand years earlier, Marcus and his men had destroyed the inhabitants of the Pict village in retaliation for the slaughter of Roman captives. They'd heaped together a large pile of stones and placed them as a monument on the witch's grave. Magical wards had then been invoked to keep the site invisible to human eyes. That particular power was contained in the green serpent ring Luc wore, inherited from Marcus. I'd been told the same soothsayer who'd shown them how to summon the witch's spirit had introduced them to another witch powerful enough to create the rings, but not undo the spell.

That site was just as barren when I first saw it in 1919 as it had been after Marcus burned it to the ground. I hadn't been back since. No need. *Must find out the closest city or township with a maternity hospital – just in case.*

'Want to tell me what's bothering you?' Luc's gaze burned into me as we strode through the grounds of the house. 'You look like you drank some bad blood.'

I glanced at him. 'Once we're inside the vault.' These grounds were too open, and Brethren ears too sharp. Laura's pregnancy had to remain a secret to all but our immediate circle.

When he'd had the vault constructed, Luc designed both a soundproof, and bombproof structure. Not even the keenest Brethren hearing would discover what was said within its walls.

I'd left Laura on the yacht with the other women. Kari was on guard, but since there was little chance of an attack, I'd arranged to meet the men at the bloodvault. At least in this part of the world, the rebellion had been quashed, and Jake, Cal and Terens had captured the last remaining Rebels. They'd been on their way to raid the bloodvault. The precious store of Ingenii blood collected by Luc over the years was hidden in the wine cellar, behind the rows of racks that lined the stonewalls disguising the hidden entrance. Unfortunately, it hadn't deterred Rasputin. He'd detected the potent scent of Ingenii blood mingled with the aroma of Luc's finest vintage Bordeaux, and he'd sent in his hounds.

But our men had intercepted the Rebels and brought them back to a secluded part of the walled garden behind the house. Cal and Terens had them on their knees, swords poised at their throats.

'Didn't get anything new out of them,' Jake said. 'You wanna try?' He stood over them, arms folded over his chest.

I didn't have time for this, and I doubted the Rebels could tell me anything new. Knowing what they would've done to Laura had they succeeded and how they'd enjoyed seeing me tortured by Stockton and Rasputin only fuelled my anger. I'd also run out of mercy.

'No. Drop them in the pit. Film it and send it to Timur, with my compliments. Show him who he's dealing with.'

The pit was an old cesspit – the servants' outhouse before the introduction of interior plumbing. The outhouse building had long been demolished, but rather than filling the hole, Luc had found a new use for it, as a type of oubliette – a place of forgetting. The rays of the rising sun gradually reached the bottom before traversing up the other side, leaving it once again in darkness. A titanium grill covered the entrance.

It was a dreaded punishment. Those thrown in died slowly as the sun encroached. There was nowhere to hide, no escape. The Principate reserved this punishment for the worst offenders, whose bloodlust couldn't be satisfied except through killing. I'd seen it used only four times. That had been enough.

I turned my back on the Rebels' pleas and headed for the vault, flanked by Marcus and Luc. Behind me, the men dragged the Rebels away. I blocked whatever sense of compassion I may once have felt. Since becoming princeps, I'd sentenced a few to death, but never like this. Sensing Luc's gaze on me, I stared straight ahead. Explanations could come later.

The cellar reeked of residual smoke and alcohol, but most of the damage caused by Rasputin's fire had been repaired. Fresh paint covered the once wine-splattered walls and ceiling as bottles had exploded in the heat; and new metal wine racks replaced the old.

Luc moved ahead, pulled aside one of the racks exposing a steel door. He inserted his ring into the lock, gave it a twist, and the door swung open. A long, dark corridor lay ahead. Our footsteps echoed on the flagstones until we reached another steel door.

Less than a week ago, I strode down this corridor. Judith, Luc and I had unlocked the vault and extracted several vials of Ingenii blood as a gift to our men – an annual tradition allowing them a chance to enjoy the daylight hours.

'I'll be glad when you're rid of those damned rings.' Marcus's gaze slid to Luc's hand. 'Nothing good comes from a witch.'

I could understand Marcus's loathing of anything associated with witchcraft. It was the cause of his present misery – and that of his progeny. And this attitude had been also reinforced by the centuries he'd spent in a secluded French monastery where all things related to witchcraft and sorcery was of the devil.

I was inclined to agree.

'This one' —Luc raised the green serpent ring— 'has provided us with the protective wards that have kept us safe all these centuries. Don't be too quick to condemn, Father.'

'I stand by what I said, Luc. When this ends, destroy them all.'

Terens and Jake joined us. 'Cal's standing guard,' Jake told Marcus, who had stepped up to stand next to Luc.

They withdrew the key-chains from beneath their shirts – including the third key that belonged to Judith – and simultaneously inserted them into the locking mechanism. It should have been my key in that lock. I seethed knowing Rasputin had stolen it when I was helpless; too weak to stop him taking it, my body poisoned by white-oak.

The door slid open, and we entered the vault. Luc had myriad vials, each the size of a man's thumb, filled with the coveted Ingenii fluid stored in refrigerated glass cases, and slotted into specially designed shelves. The glow from within the vials gave the room a rosy aura. No other light was needed.

I turned and faced the men as the door clicked closed. 'Laura's pregnant.'

Luc blinked. 'Mon Dieu.' His face broke out in a beaming smile, and he slapped me on the back.

Would he still feel the same way when – or if – I told him what I had in mind?

Jake and Sam stared before they, too, grinned. Terens flicked hair back from his eyes and gave me a lopsided grin. 'Good going, man.'

Only Marcus remained grave, eyes closed, head bowed. A mix of sadness and relief emanated from him.

'And so it begins,' he whispered.

I scanned the faces of my friends and sire. They'd waited eighteen-hundred years for this day, and I could destroy it all. Jake, Cal, Terens and Sam would lose the chance to choose their own paths; be their own men. Did I have that right? Could I take away Marcus's choice to die as a human, if that's what he desired? And what of our child? I'd already told Laura should things go badly, it would be her life I'd save. Eight lives were in my hands – people I loved.

Dear God, let there be no complications.

'I know you've waited a long time, but I want Laura to be safe.' I looked at Luc. 'What if there are birth complications? If mother and child are in danger?'

His brow creased. 'Then make sure it doesn't happen.'

Luc's threatening tone angered me. He'd used it many times with others, but never with me, despite our past differences.

I clenched my fists and took a step toward him. 'That's not possible, and you know it!' We glared at each other. 'I'm telling you now, if I think she and the baby are in danger, with or without your permission, I'll be taking her to the nearest hospital.'

'She needs to give birth—' His voice lowered dangerously.

'I know! What means more to you – your daughter's life or ending the damned curse?' Luc's eyes narrowed. 'I love her, and I won't lose her. I've been there before – never again.'

I resisted the urge to bear my fangs, since Luc was my sire, and my friend. Only the respect I felt toward him held me in check, although I didn't know for how long.

Tension swirled between us until Marcus placed his hand on Luc's shoulder. 'Alec's right.' He then addressed me. 'I understand. I wasn't allowed into the room, but I heard my wife Gallia's screams giving birth to Luc and Antonia. It was a hard labour – I nearly lost her. But she was strong.' He smiled. 'I believe Laura may be the same.'

'May or may not. I'm not prepared to risk it.'

A look of stunned silence greeted me. They knew what I was suggesting and how it would affect them all. Jake, who'd been leaning against the door, tensed and gave me a warning shake of the head. I ignored him, wondering how far I could push this, when, like a thunderclap, the answer came to me. 'Luc, you and I were stationed in the field hospital in Abbeville during World War I – in a tent with medical equipment....'

Luc's eyes went round. 'Ha! Brilliant!' He slapped me on the back. 'I'll get you whatever you need.'

'No, let me – I know what to get. I'll make sure she'll have the best care available in any field hospital.' Jake glanced at me. 'She'll be okay.'

I nodded my thanks as relief flooded through me.

Luc smiled. 'I chose well. My daughter couldn't be in better hands.'

We gripped forearms – Roman fashion. I was relieved we were in sync again.

'Good. Now that's sorted, you want us to move this stuff?' Terens stood behind Marcus, arms folded over his chest, the hilts of the crossed swords on his back visible above his shoulders.

'One more thing,' I said. 'Laura's scent's begun to change. We need to get her to the safety of the chateau.' The land around the chateau extended several miles, encompassing forests, vineyards and lakes – easily over twenty miles. No vampire could detect a scent over that distance. She'd be safe there, until the last couple of months, when we'd move her secretly to Scotland. I still had time to work out those logistics. 'Nobody outside our clan, is to know of this. If our child is born in secrecy, the curse will end before anyone finds out. The Principate will maintain power, and no one will be the wiser.'

'And you will remain princeps, as if nothing has changed.' Marcus slammed his fist into the palm of his hand. 'Deus! It just might work.'

If we're really lucky, I thought, and if the Principate supporters remain loyal. There was no guarantee how they would react if they knew of Luc's bloodvault. Another reason to get to the chateau as quickly as possible.

'Want me to start?' With a jerk of his head, Sam indicated the long rows of vials. Luc nodded, and Sam moved past me, down the length of the room, and using the calculator on his mobile, began an inventory.

There were several hundred at least. How was Luc going to transport them all?

'Yeah, it'll all fit. Go ahead, Luc,' Sam said.

'I've been waiting to do this.' Luc palmed his phone, flicked the screen with his thumb, then looked at us and grinned before tapping it. 'Here goes.'

There were nine refrigerated glass cabinets in the room. One by one, the shelves holding the blood vials neatly collapsed; their sides folded down until nine large glass cubes stood in their place. Any of us could lift them easily. The glow of the blood vials indicated no damage.

'Luc, that's ingenious!' I said.

'Had it specially designed, and Sam built it.'

Sam gave a mock bow.

'Impressive, bro.' Terens crouched down and ran his finger along the top edge. 'You know, I can feel it tingling.'

'Magic stuff,' Sam said.

As the men cleared out the vault, I took Luc aside. 'I'll be using the vials from now on … too risky feeding from Laura in her condition. It might stress her and the baby.'

'That's why I've stored them all these years. Time to hand them out to our men as well. From now on, they'll be on guard night and day.'

In minutes, we'd emptied the vault and loaded the cubes, with their priceless cargo, into three separate cars destined for Luc's private jet.

## CHAPTER 4 – UPROOTED

**LAURA**

It was going on four a.m. by the time we strapped on our seatbelts and took off in Luc's private jet. Our exodus from Sydney occurred so fast I didn't have a moment to quiz either Luc or Judy about the chateau. I only knew it was in the Rhone Valley, somewhere in France. When my father decided to relocate, he took the entire household with him, and everything was mobilised with military precision. *Well, he came from a military family.*

With the lights of Sydney disappearing, I thought back over the events of the last couple of weeks, and the way my life had been overturned. Alec was more than enough compensation for those tumultuous events. And now I was expecting our child. A warm thrill coursed through me, yet worries niggled at me, too. The fact I was on my way to the family chateau in France – sight unseen – pretty much summed up the unfamiliar and suddenness of my situation.

My mum, Eilene – I'd never get used to thinking of her as my aunt - cried when I rang and said goodbye. That had been enough to bring me to tears.

'Do you know how long you'll be away?' she'd asked between sniffs.

'Not sure, Mum. At least till the baby's born, is my guess.'

She and Dad had the phone on loudspeaker. 'You'll always be our baby girl, Laura. Remember that,' he'd said, the sadness in his voice breaking my heart.

Dad and I were close. Over the last few brief weeks, I'd come to like and respect Luc – and perhaps in some way, love him – but he would never replace Dad.

I forced down the painful lump in my throat and turned my mind to what lay ahead. My old life gone, there was no use dwelling on it. John and Eilene were safe. Luc had arranged Brethren to guard them, just in case any Rebels remained. I pulled the shutter down over the window – and my old life with it – then folded my legs beneath me and tried to stave off drowsiness. I glanced behind – Jenny had already fallen asleep, her seat fully reclined. I wasn't surprised the emotional exhaustion had caught up with her. It had been a shock for her to find out she could be a target, and she too had had to leave Sydney dramatically. I smiled, knowing my best friend slept deeply and secure.

I was too restless. Sleep wasn't going to happen.

'So, tell me about my new home. What's this chateau look like?' I asked Alec as I whipped out my mobile phone to Google it.

'You won't get Google up here, Laura.' He took out his iPhone, scrolling through his photo gallery. 'It's near Avignon, in an area known as Vaucluse.'

'You're kidding! Same name? Coincidence or did he choose it because of the name?'

'Bit of both.' He passed me his phone, and I gazed in awe at the screen. The chateau was massive, a fairy tale French castle – round towers with small elongated windows, pitched roofs, and embattlements – surrounded by woods and fields on one side, and vine covered hillsides on the other. A long, tree-lined driveway led to the main entrance. One of the conical towers flew a flag, though too distant to determine its markings.

'It's amazing. What's on the flag?'

'Our clan crest.' He pointed to the left side of his chest. I knew he carried a tattoo, as did my father and his men, of a sword and serpent, the symbol of the Dantonvilles.

'Should've guessed.'

'It flies at full mast when the clan's in residence and—'

'Lowered when they're away?' I finished for him in an effort to stifle a yawn. 'That's how it works for the British royal family, isn't it?' Made sense for the Dantonvilles – a royal family, of sorts.

Alec nodded. 'You got it. And when half-mast, it warns the villagers of Brethren visitors. Tells them to stay indoors at night.'

'They know?' I found that unbelievable. How could an entire village keep such a secret, and for so long?

He chuckled. 'They've known for generations. Luc's been good to them, and they've been loyal in return.'

'There's a whole history here I know nothing about.' Generations lived and died in that village knowing – and accepting – that vampires inhabited the chateau. Perhaps there were donsangs among them – humans who voluntarily donated their blood to vampires.

'In time, my darling, you'll learn it all.'

By the time we reached Bangkok to refuel, the adrenaline had worn off and my restlessness had subsided. Craving sleep, I yawned and fully reclined my seat.

\* \* \*

I dozed on and off during the flight, finally waking with a shiver amid the humming of engines and the tap, tap of fingers on a keyboard.

'Good afternoon.' Alec's soothing voice came from the seat next to me. He lowered the lid of his laptop, stowed it, and turned toward me.

'How long was I asleep?'

'About eight hours. Ever since we left Dubai.' He leaned over and adjusted the blanket around me. Part of it had slipped to the floor.

I vaguely remembered the next fuel stopover as I stretched out and relaxed, unwilling to adjust the seat back to its upright position. 'Remind me to always fly in a private jet.'

Alec chuckled, crouched down and smoothed hair from my eyes. 'We'll land in Avignon soon.' His lips brushed mine, and I inhaled his scent – fresh, like a wood after a rain – cinnamon and cedarwood. My body tingled. I tangled my fingers in his hair, and his kiss deepened, taking possession of my mouth and all my senses.

Images of us making love thousands of feet in the air zipped through my mind.

His eyes darkened to a rich and deep purple – he wanted the same. There was no need to read his mind. Warmth crept up from my toes until my cheeks burned. We'd made love many times, and I was expecting our child, yet I still melted under his gaze like a lovestruck teenager.

'How far is the chateau from there?' I asked, breathless.

'About an hour's drive.'

Luc's voice came over the intercom. 'Buckle up, everyone. We land in ten minutes. Adjust your watches. It's seven p.m. here.'

The plane gave a slight shudder as the undercarriage dropped.

I raised my seat and buckled my seatbelt while Alec stored my blanket before sitting.

'Where's Jen?' I asked.

'Playing cards with Kari and the men.' He angled his chin towards the front of the plane. 'She woke up a couple of hours ago.'

Their banter and Jenny's laughter drifted down the aisle. After the shock she'd received from Luc before we'd left Sydney, it was good to hear her laugh. Soon they wandered to their seats.

'Hey, you're awake. You missed dinner, but I saved you this.' Jenny handed me a bread roll wrapped in a serviette. 'Pity it's dark out; the view would be fantastic. Terens said we're flying over the chateau right now.' Her eyes glittered at the mention of his name.

I said a quick prayer that Terens wouldn't break her heart, and another that Jenny wouldn't be rash – my dream of her as a vampire fresh in my mind.

I bit into the buttered roll and lifted the window screen. Far below, all was blackness, but a cluster of bright lights winked ahead. *Must be Avignon.* Our plane descended, and the lights grew larger. Only a few red and white flashing headlights of cars were to be seen along the highway. Most people were probably staying home to celebrate Christmas. Here in France, it was still Christmas night.

A slight bump, skid of tyres and we were taxiing on the runway towards a hanger.

The umbilical cord that had tethered me to Australia snapped, leaving me uprooted in spite of our arrival in the land of my ancestors. It was the original home of the Dantonvilles, or D'Antonvilles to use correct French spelling. Unless we could stop the rebellion and end the curse, this was where our line – and the future of humanity – would end. The Principate was the only barrier to prevent the wholesale slaughter of humans by those who wanted to hunt and kill them for food – the rogues, the Rebels, the true monsters.

Luc's voice came over the intercom again. 'We're home.'

* * *

Compared to the warmth of the plane, outside was freezing. We'd packed for cold weather, but my coat and boots – designed for a Sydney winter – were inadequate. My teeth chattered. Alec placed his arm around me, and I snuggled into him as we made our way down the passenger stairs. He felt warm although he only wore cotton trousers and a long-sleeved T-shirt.

'Aren't you cold?'

'Don't feel it.'

Were the others the same? Beneath leather coats, they wore jeans and light tops, swords strapped to their sides. Kari turned heads in a pink leather mini skirt and matching jacket with black thigh-high boots. Just looking at her made me shiver.

'Plenty of winter gear at the chateau. Luc and Judy had your room restocked,' Alec said.

'They spoil me.'

Alec smiled. 'Let them.'

Terens removed his leather coat, revealing the crossed swords at his back, and placed it over Jenny's shoulders. That simple old-world gesture would be enough to sway Jenny's feelings toward him. If she was undecided beforehand, I had no doubt she'd be in love with him now.

I wasn't sure whether to be happy for her or scared.

Three black limousines awaited us. Before each one stood a green-uniformed man. At first I thought they were human, until I saw their lavender eyes. Brethren. After saluting Alec – Roman style, thumping the right side of their chests with their left fists – they collected and stowed our bags.

I turned questioning eyes toward Alec.

'They're attached to the chateau and volunteer to serve the family,' he said.

'What about during the day?'

'Then human servants take over.'

'Convenient.'

He smiled and, hand about my waist, guided me to one of the limos. 'It makes sense to avoid having humans around at night. We often hold functions, and, with so many Brethren attending, they sometimes mistake the human staff for snacks. Best avoided.'

I glanced up at him to see if he was serious. There was a definite tug at the corners of his mouth. Still, it did have a ring of truth. I would have to keep Jenny locked up at night or at my side in case a fanged visitor mistook her for dinner. It was small consolation that the Brethren were forbidden to kill. Yet, the thought occurred to me that Jenny might even welcome the experience. Again, memory of my dream of her as a vampire skittered through my mind. I shivered.

'You're cold. Let's get you into the car. We'll be there in less than an hour.' Alec climbed in next to me.

'What's in those crates?' Luc, Cal, Sam, Jake and Terens put a large crate inside the other cars before climbing in beside them.

*We emptied the bloodvault and put all the Ingenii vials in those crates,* his voice whispered through my mind. *Only our immediate circle knows.*

Alec and I initially believed the serpent rings allowed us to communicate telepathically only in times of danger. Recently we'd discovered otherwise. *Can't they smell the blood?* With a tilt of my head, I indicated the green-uniformed attendant in the driver's seat.

*Perhaps, but they'll assume it's Judith and Jenny.*

*Is that why Jen's in the other car with Terens?* And Judy, naturally, sat with Luc and Kari in the third car.

Alec nodded.

My father, Luc, had thought of everything.

Our convoy drove out of the city, onto the motorway, and soon the French countryside, with vineyard-covered hillsides, sped past. The half-moon cast eerie shadows over leafless, gnarled and tangled vines, giving them the appearance of endless rows of barbed wire crosses.

Alec glanced at me a few times before he lay his hand on my belly. 'You okay?'

I placed my hand over his. 'I'm fine, and junior's too tiny to know.'

He gave me a dazzling smile. 'I'll have everything in place when the time comes.'

I recalled Judy's reaction when I told her of my pregnancy. While she packed, I had sat her on the bed – Kari was with her – and took her hands in mine. 'You're going to be a grandma.' She had cried happy tears, and Kari squealed, clapping her hands. She placed her ear to my belly.

'It's too early, Kari. It won't have a heartbeat for at least another few weeks.'

Jenny had stared at me as if I'd just smacked her. 'So quick?'

'I can't help it if I'm fertile.'

She'd laughed and hugged me. 'I'll be an aunty!' I loved her perspective.

We drove through a small town, houses hidden behind high stone walls with neatly trimmed hedges and thick trees. Our convoy didn't stop but proceeded through the old town centre. Medieval style buildings rose on our left as we turned toward a stone bridge.

'This is the village of D'Antonville. Most of the household staff live here,' Alec said.

'How many are there?' Luc had several staff at the house in Sydney, but I'd never seen any of them.

'A few: gardeners, cleaners … ruled over by the estate manager and his wife. You'll meet them when we get there.'

Ahead of us, Luc's car turned off the motorway onto a gravelled road that led to a high-walled gateway. Arched wrought-iron gates, the name D'Antonville outlined prominently in scrolled lettering, opened automatically.

Our car followed Luc's.

With my enhanced hearing and sight, I saw the extent of the grounds. Parklands stretched into the distance, the naked branches of trees stretching heavenward like ghostly fingers toward the night sky. Although no snow lay on the ground, a light mist gathered on the base of the car windows and slowly spread upwards. Neither the car heating, nor the occasional swipe of the windscreen wipers, stopped its chilly advance.

Our limo rounded a bend, and I caught my first glimpse of Chateau D'Antonville. More spectacular than the photo, I was left breathless. Perched on a rocky outcrop and illuminated by floodlights, the stone-walled, imposing medieval edifice with its peaked towers and crenulated turrets shone ivory against the inky sky.

From the car behind, Jenny gasped. 'Wow!'

'We'll be within those walls for the next few weeks, sweet Jen,' Terens said.

I turned and glanced out the back window to see him flash a devastating smile at her. She was speechless the rest of the way – not even a giggle. I didn't mean to listen in, but enhanced hearing had some uses, I figured.

'Don't worry about Jen. She's an adult,' Alec remarked. He'd heard their conversation, too.

I gave him a sceptical look. 'You know of any woman who can resist Terens?'

'You can.' He gave me his own killer smile.

'Besides me.'

Alec opened his mouth and closed it again. 'Mmmm.'

I recounted the dream I'd had in hospital, recovering from Maris's attack. In it, Jenny had been lapping at a pool of blood on the ground. She looked at me, and blood dripped from her fangs. I'd woken in fright.

'It was probably caused by trauma, combined with the anaesthetic….' He gazed at me thoughtfully.

'I hope so.'

We drove beneath the entrance archway into a cobblestone courtyard, past a well and up to a massive set of timber double-doors. At the entrance, awaiting our arrival, stood a middle-aged couple – a man and a woman – who greeted Luc as he alighted from the limo. The woman's smile tightened as Judy stepped toward them, and it remained in place on seeing me.

My heart sank.

# CHAPTER 5 – CHATEAU D'ANTONVILLE

**LAURA**

'That's the estate manager and his wife, Madame and Monsieur Thierry.' Alec held the door open for me. 'The Thierrys have served the Dantonvilles for generations. It's regarded as a position of honour among the villagers.'

The woman regarded me through narrowed eyes as we approached, yet they positively sparkled when they alighted on Alec or Luc. Maybe she likes only vampires, I thought. Her immaculately coiffed hair may have been blonde once, but like her husband's, it shone pale silver in the porch light.

Kari bounded out of the car and up to the woman, gave her a hug and spoke too rapidly in French for me to keep up. She can't be too bad if Kari likes her, I thought. The woman's face beamed as she returned the embrace, which convinced me she wasn't fond of humans. Or some humans.

Monsieur Thierry bowed his head. 'Princeps, welcome back. Your rooms have been prepared.'

'Serge, may I introduce our Ingenii, Lady Laura,' Alec said.

Serge Thierry bowed formally to me and directed another group of green-uniformed men to take our luggage. At vampire speed, they had already disappeared through the doorway.

'I'll take you to your rooms. Supper has been prepared.' Madame Thierry's English was as perfect as her appearance. The delicate scent of mandarin, bergamot and myrrh tickled my nostrils. I tried to identify her perfume. Being French, Madame probably used the most expensive.

Jenny came up to me, clutched my arm and whispered, 'Mrs Danvers.'

The demented housekeeper was from the novel, *Rebecca*, Jenny's favourite book. 'Please not,' I whispered back.

We followed her into the grand entrance hall. The scent of burning wax filled the air, as did the hiss of a thousand tiny flames hit by the draught from the open door.

A magnificent marble staircase curved up to another level, its porcelain finish sliced through with fine, dark grey and black veins. Wrought-iron handrails, accentuated with scrolls and fleur-de-lils, divided at the top and ringed the first floor. At the base of the stairs, atop the endrails, were two black candelabras. The soft flickering light of their candles made the dark red crystals dangling from their base resemble great drops of blood.

Similar candelabras hung suspended from wall fittings, their shadows clothing the entrance hall – spooky but comforting at the same time. Was it a trick of the light or my enhanced vision, that caused a myriad of dazzling, shifting colours to appear within the heart of the flames?

Jenny squeezed my arm. 'I can just imagine Dracula coming down those stairs.' Her voice rang out in the vast space, and everyone's head turned.

Alec chuckled, and I suppressed a giggle when Madame Thierry glared at us.

'Shhh, Jen.' I didn't want to upset Mrs Danvers, err, Thierry. She was responsible for the entire household while Luc and Judy were in Australia. Perhaps she resented our presence, worried we'd intrude on her control? I glanced at Judy, and her tight-lipped expression confirmed there was tension between them. But this wasn't the time to ask.

We traipsed after her when Luc passed us, his arms full with one of the large crates containing the precious Ingenii blood. Jake, Cal, Terens and Sam followed and disappeared behind a set of black enamelled doors to the right of the staircase.

'What's behind there?'

'The Great Hall, milady. I would be happy to show you around later.' I hadn't expected Madame Thierry to answer, nor call me "milady."

'Please, call me Laura.'

'It's best to maintain the standards, milady.' She turned and continued up the stairs.

I made a mental note to explore – without her – after we'd settled in our rooms.

As I trod up the stairs, I resisted running my hand along the marble inlays on the silver-grey walls, to discover whether they were real or trompe l'oeuil. Knowing Luc, they were probably genuine.

At the half-landing, I caught my breath as I glanced up to see the outline of a lead-lined window that spanned the height and length of the wall. Even though it was dark outside, I could identify the silhouette of a Roman soldier with his shield and spear – Marcus Antonius. Around him in full military gear were the familiar figures of his men. It was a grander version of the same window in the Sydney house.

I leaned over to Alec and whispered, 'Vaucluse a copy?'

'He couldn't take it with him, so he had it reconstructed.'

'Was he homesick?' It had never occurred to me that a powerful man like Luc could feel like this. His outward appearance was so confident, so self-assured … content.

'From what I've heard, it was a wrench for him when your ancestor decided to leave.'

My father … vulnerable?

Alec's gaze went from me to the doors of the Great Hall, then back to me. 'I have to leave you here, darling.' A slight crease marred his brow, and he ran his hand down my arm. 'There's something we need to discuss, but' —he glanced at the others— 'not here. I'll join you in our suite as soon as I can.'

A tight knot developed in my stomach. 'Discuss what? Where are you going?'

'Vault. And there's nothing to worry about. We'll talk later.' He kissed me and disappeared down the stairs, leaving his delicious musky taste on my lips.

Jenny nudged me in the ribs with her elbow. 'What have we got ourselves into?'

'What do you—'

'Lion's den or gilded cage?' Her eyes were wide, and her heart thumped loudly in her chest.

Kari spoke with Madame, their heads together and giggling like a couple of conspirators. It was so at odds from the severe impression Madame Thierry conveyed. Kari was obviously her favourite.

'Gilded cage … for now. The lions are out there. We're safe here. Remember what Luc told us?'

'I know, I know.' She tapped her temple. 'I was excited, thrilled even, when you told me everything. But, things have changed, and I'm not sure I want….' She chewed the inside of her lip then blurted out, 'Right now I wish we were back at the café in Coogee, enjoying a drink. I wish none of this had happened. Just being two ordinary Sydney girls … not chased by anyone.'

I didn't have to be half-vampire to sense her fear. And she had every right to be afraid, especially as I had inadvertently dragged her into this. Yet, what other choice was there?

'We still can be ordinary, once this is over.'

She shook her head and pulled Terens's jacket closer around her shoulders. 'You reckon? Look at you, hon; you're changing. You really believe you can return to your old life and your job? Nah uh. You've got a baby coming ... there's danger out there....' She waved her hand in the air.

'Look, I'm not naïve. I don't know what to expect, but I've been told once the baby's born, the curse is lifted, and my family will be human again. I might just lose all this super sight and hearing stuff. I don't know, and neither does Alec. But one thing I do know is we're going to win, Jen. We have to. I won't believe otherwise. Besides,' I added as Jenny's brow crinkled. 'You think the bad guys could beat our guys?' I flicked the collar of Terens's jacket and smiled.

Her mouth curved slightly. 'You're still going to be a mum.'

'And you're going to be aunty and godmother.'

'Coming up?' Kari leaned her head over the railing. 'Goodies waiting for you in your suites.' She clapped excitedly. 'C'mon.'

Jenny and I gazed up at her then smiled at each other. 'I'd say we're in the best of hands, Jen.'

We bumped foreheads and it was a relief listening to her giggle. 'I gotta find out where his room is.'

'Then we'd better move.' We quickened our pace to catch up with the others.

Madame Thierry led us along a wide hallway, where crystal chandeliers caught the glint of cream and gold marbling on the walls that were interspersed with in-set fluted half-columns. Plain white doors on either side of the corridor broke up the pattern. She looked at Jenny as she opened the first door on the left. 'This is your room, mademoiselle. I hope you'll be comfortable.'

Jenny gasped. 'I ... I'm sure I will.' Her eyes wide, she stood for a moment as if unsure whether to enter.

Sweet rose scent wafted out from the candle on the coffee table, which melded with the rose pink of the soft furnishings in the suite.

I gave her a gentle nudge and whispered, 'Go in.'

'Milady, this is your room.' Madame Thierry opened a door directly opposite Jenny's to reveal an enormous room with pearl-grey and green furnishings, infused with the subtle scent of mint.

On a small glass coffee table by the window sat a stunning duck-egg blue Faberge egg. I'd read enough about them to know they were the favourite jeweller of the Russian Tsars, and sent out of business by the revolution. Anything with the name Faberge was priceless. One bump and I had visions of it crashing to the floor. I made a mental note to avoid that coffee table.

'Thank you, Madame. Everything is as I expected,' Judy said.

With a tight-lipped smile, the housekeeper bowed her head and click-clacked down the hallway, her heels a noisy staccato on the heavily lacquered parquetry.

Judy exhaled. 'Let's have supper, dear.'

'Is there some tension between you and her?'

'She's an excellent housekeeper. I can't fault her that.'

'But?' I closed the door and moved to the small round table in the lounge area of my suite. A covered tray lay in the centre, and my mouth watered at the aroma of delicacies she'd prepared. I'd slept through my last meal.

Judy wandered into another room, to the right of the sitting area. I heard her opening and closing doors, muttering, 'Good. Everything I ordered. Even unpacked for you.'

I chose a delicious-looking mini baguette and followed her. 'What did you order—' My breath left me as I gazed around the spacious room. A king-size bed with a plush, silvery-coloured, padded bedhead rested against the wall, and at its feet, a mint-coloured Louis XIV ottoman.

'Bathroom's through there.' Judy pointed. 'In the tower.'

*Tower?* My boots sank into the soft cream carpet as I peeked into the bathroom. Perched serenely atop two stepped platforms, their sides decorated with Roman carvings of acanthus leaves and vines, sat a full-length marble bathtub with gold tap fittings. A curved, ivory-lacquered dresser hugged one side of the wall, while a series of gilded mirrors were moulded into the other. A bronze teardrop chandelier hung from the ceiling, its light bouncing off the mirrors, giving the enclosed tower an illusion of space.

Behind me I heard a whistle. 'Not bad.' Kari surveyed the room. I must have worn a blank look, for she added. 'They refurbished your suite in time for your homecoming.'

'It's fabulous.' I blinked and then smiled as I imagined Alec sharing that bath with me.

Judy joined us and linked her arm through mine. 'Do you like your room?'

'Of course I do. It's beautiful. Thank you.' I kissed her cheek.

Her eyes became wistful. 'Oh, Laura, if you only knew how many times I'd wanted to bring you here. But we simply couldn't; the risk was too great. The servants would have taken one look at your eyes and....' She didn't need to finish – my lavender eyes were the sign of a Bloodgifted.

My life would've been in danger, for apart from our immediate circle, no one at the time knew I was Luc's daughter. That secret had to be maintained until I came of age – the time of the Ritual. Even I hadn't known.

'I'm here now.' I covered her hand with mine as she brushed away a tear. Again I was reminded of the sacrifice my parents made for my safety, and I thought of the little one growing in my womb. What wouldn't I do to protect my child?

Judy's smile was watery. 'I'll show you the rest of the chateau tomorrow. Goodnight dear.'

I stared at the door after she'd gone, when a strange, keening sort of sound had me looking out of one of the three narrow windows. 'Hear that?' I asked Kari, sure her vampire hearing had caught the strange noise too.

'Hear what?'

'A weird sound. How can I hear it and you can't?'

She sniffed then shrugged. 'You're probably developing the same enhanced senses as Luc. This chateau's at least nine kilometres in from the boundary wall, which is double the distance of our normal hearing range. Luc did it deliberately, so none of our kind could sense whether he and Princi were here or not. Keeps everyone on their toes. But it also means I can't tell if there's someone out there.'

'Alec and Luc hear that far?'

'Yep. Great stuff, your family's blood.' She flashed me a grin. 'So what's this sound like, the one you can hear and I can't?'

For a moment I lost track of her question as I processed her last comment. I can hear up to nine kilometres? That was about six miles away. 'Um … high pitched, like someone's keening, or some kind of night bird.'

Her brows were drawn, eyes narrowed. It was the same expression as the day I met Rasputin. Surely he couldn't have beaten us to France? I dismissed the idea. No way, unless he could fly. 'Kari, can vampires fly?'

She burst out laughing. 'Only in movies.'

That allayed my silly suspicions. I had slept restlessly on the plane, and the bed looked inviting. I kicked off my boots and lay down; the firmness of the mattress was perfect. I closed my eyes … the chateau is secure – nothing nasty can get in … scrolled through my mind like a mantra.

# CHAPTER 6 - BLOODVAULT

**ALEC**

I raced to the far end of the Great Hall just as Luc and the men disappeared through the secret passageway behind the princep's throne. I squeezed through, and the panel closed behind me.

Luc turned to me. 'Ah, Alec. Good.' He strode ahead, our footsteps echoing on the stone steps that led down to the subterranean caverns beneath the chateau. The scurrying sound of thousands of tiny creatures carried in the darkness as we moved deeper toward our goal. The walls were damp from moisture trickling down the limestone to add to the stalagmites rising from the cavern floor.

The chateau had been built some distance from Antonius's original villa, on a rocky outcrop peppered with subterranean caverns. A system of labyrinthine passageways, false doors and sheer drops would confuse anyone who managed to find their way down here. A mere human would be lost forever.

'Yep, working nicely,' Cal muttered. Every thirty yards, a click went off on his mobile. He'd recently updated the security system so no one could access this area without him knowing.

'It's only us here,' Terens said. 'Why leave it on? It's getting on my nerves.'

Cal chuckled. 'Haven't been down here in a year. Got to test it. What's bugging you?'

'Nothing.'

I glanced at Jake. He shrugged. Terens was usually the most casual, least fazed member of the group. But I had something else on my mind, and although I didn't need Jake's permission for what I was about to ask, I wanted his okay.

'I'd like Kari to share in the blood vials. With this rebellion going on, I need her to be with Laura round the clock.' Kari could go places with Laura I couldn't, plus I wouldn't be able to be with her always. Nor could I keep her locked in the chateau for the entire term of her pregnancy, no matter how appealing the thought.

Jake's head swivelled toward me. 'She's no longer—'

'Just wanted you to know first.' Jake had sired Kari then spent a century training her before setting her up in her new life.

'Appreciate that. She's a good kid. Yeah, go ahead.' He jerked his head in Luc's direction. 'What about him? He's got to okay it.'

I slapped Jake on the back. 'Doubt that'll be a problem.' I left him and joined Luc.

We skirted the edge of the subterranean lake when the ruby glow from the cubes the men carried glowed more brightly. And from the pattern of stalactites hanging from the cavern roof, I knew we neared the vault. My hunch was confirmed when the eyes of the serpent ring on my hand flared.

Luc held up his arm, and we halted before a wall of polished stone.

'Let me take Judith's key. You need both hands,' I said. Three keys inserted simultaneously were needed to unlock the vault. Luc, Marcus, Judith and I each possessed one – three and a spare. Until my transformation, Luc had kept the spare key in the library safe, hidden discretely behind Marcus's decaying armour. It was later entrusted to me … until Rasputin stole it.

I would get it back, if it was the last thing I did.

Luc nodded, pressed Judith's key into my palm and slid aside a camouflaged panel hiding three locks.

Marcus joined us. 'How many centuries since I've done this?'

'Too long,' Luc answered.

We inserted our keys into the locks as Luc thrust his own green-eyed serpent ring into the stone. Silently the door swung open, and the intoxicating scent of Ingenii blood hit us in a powerful wave. We inhaled; nostrils flared, and the tips of our fangs protruded beneath our upper lips. I swallowed and sheathed mine, aware of my growing hunger and that I'd be living off those vials for the next nine months.

'Unload.' Luc stepped aside to allow the men to pass. We followed, and the door automatically sealed behind us.

Marcus whistled. 'Deus! I'd forgotten the scale of this place.'

Thousands of thumb-size, ruby vials lay line-upon-line within recessed stone bays, illuminating the cavernous space in a haze of red. Like a wine cellar, Luc had grouped the vials according to name and numerical order of Ingenii. Those closest to the entrance were the oldest. Engraved bronze plaques above each group identified the subject, from Paulus in the early fourth century until now. Judith's bay was the last. Beyond her, the stone wall was blank, for Laura was the last Ingenii, and the curse would end with her. Being pregnant also meant her blood couldn't be collected and stored. It appeared Luc had thought of everything, and I didn't doubt Fate had played her hand, as well.

'Line them up against that wall.' Luc pointed to the furthest end of the cavern, where the once-smooth rock face was pockmarked with a series of small indentations, ready to receive the new stock of vials.

He pressed a button on his mobile, and each cube unfolded and resumed its previous cabinet size. As the men unpacked each one and placed the contents into their assigned recesses, I strode along the length of one collection of blood vials, choosing my supply for the months ahead. First Blood was what I wanted. It was the most potent, infused with strength and energy unmatched later in an Ingenii's life, and I'd only need to feed twice a week. Seventy-two vials would see me through Laura's pregnancy. Over the centuries, Luc had collected thousands of vials – at least a hundred from each Bloodgifted – but only ten each of First Blood. Since there had been thirty-three Ingenii before Laura, I would have more than enough.

'You've added to the supply since I was here last.' Marcus strolled down the other side.

'There've been at least twenty Ingenii in that time,' Luc answered.

'I'll take all the First Bloods. Only need about seventy-two. That okay with you?' I glanced at Luc and noticed Marcus peering at one particular bay. The name on the plaque read, *Primus Paulus* – his grandson.

'Ah....' Luc's gaze surveyed the chamber.

'Paulus.' Marcus continued to stare at the vials as if they were the only ones here. 'His blood is stronger than all the others and will boost the First Bloods. It's all you'll need, my boy.'

'How is that possible?' I asked. 'Isn't all Ingenii blood the same?'

Marcus finally turned. 'It's closer to the source – stronger, more powerful. Luc'll explain. He knows more.'

Before I could ask anything further, Marcus strode away.

Luc rubbed his face. 'It's odd, but over the years I've noticed the blood's strength slowly declining. I mean, it's miniscule, yet it's there. Each generation of Bloodgifted is progressively weaker than the previous one. I was going to ask you how Laura's blood compares to Judy's?'

'Impossible to tell. Laura's half-vampire, so naturally her blood's far more powerful.'

He nodded. 'Well … I guess it's no matter now. We're nearing the end anyway.'

His observation intrigued me, though. I recalled Marcus describing the curse as a living entity. Did that mean it had a limited life-span, using the Bloodgifted as a type of countdown to the end? 'You think it's signalling its own demise?'

'I have no doubt about it.'

'Then the longer we keep Laura's condition a secret, the better.' Let the Brethren believe Laura has no romantic attachments and that I am as infertile as the rest of my kind. That way, our child could be born in secrecy and hopefully we could transition into the post-Bloodgifted era without anyone being the wiser. The Principate would continue, and with blood vials to sustain us – giving us the daylight advantage – we could end the rebellion. And prove to our Brethren the Principate can exist and function without the Bloodgifted.

But in the meantime, we would need the help of our allies. Rasputin knew of the bloodvault, and if he made it back to Timur, we'd only have days before his army would reach us.

# CHAPTER 7 – ON THE ROOF

**LAURA**

I woke with a start. My hand flew to my belly as my gaze darted about the unfamiliar room. Whether it was a dream or something else, I couldn't recall, but my heart beat a rapid staccato. For a split second I forgot where I was, our speedy relocation from Sydney causing a strange disorientation.

'Deep breaths, Laura.' I rubbed my still flat-stomach, the tiny life growing inside. 'It's okay. We're safe here. Mummy only had a bad dream.' For the first time, I'd used "we".

I reached out my hand over the cold sheets to the other side of the bed. 'Where's Daddy?' I giggled at what I'd just called Alec. Was this the new me, adjusting to impending motherhood? A rush of warmth coursed through me, and I smiled as I tried to imagine what our baby would look like. He or she would not have lavender eyes; of that I was sure. They'd be … I had no idea what colour Alec's eyes must have been before his transformation. Grey, brown, blue? My hand caressed the sheets, wishing he was here to warm them. My body longed for him. Any time apart seemed like torture, even if it was only a few hours. Was he still with Luc and the other men in the bloodvault? The serpent ring on my finger glowed a dull red, so wherever he was, he was safe.

Although the room was dark, I saw everything clearly – the delicate scroll pattern along the top of the walls, a tiny spider nestled in the corner of the ceiling, even the gossamers of dust that whirled on the air currents in the room. Before my coming-of-age these things would have been invisible to my human eyes. But in the last few days, everything about me was changing, and not just because of my pregnancy. The sound of a moth's wings fluttering around a light bulb was loud to me, as were the human voices several kilometres away.

Before we'd left Sydney, despite Luc training me to tune out the noise, it had still been sensory overload. By contrast, this place seemed quieter – few human voices could be heard. Perhaps that was why Luc had placed the perimeter wall at such a distance from the chateau, not only for protection, but to create a distance between himself and the incessant chatter of thousands of human voices. Brethren servants, too, must welcome the break from the babble outside the walls.

My stomach growled. Through the open door, I spied the tray of delicacies Madame Thierry had prepared. The mini baguette I had earlier had been delicious.

The bed bounced as I bounded toward the tray. That's when I heard it – a shrill keening, like a soul in torment. It made the hairs on my arms stand on end. It didn't seem to be coming from anywhere within the chateau. A night bird? I stuffed another mini-baguette into my mouth and padded to the window. Tree branches obscured most of my view, but there appeared to be a solitary figure, in white, standing on the boundary wall at the far end of the estate.

Mesmerised, I watched. Was it a ghost, or some local nutter who liked to climb walls in the dead of night to wail at the half moon? I peered closer, but the wind whipped up the tree branches, and I lost sight of the figure. When the wind dropped, the figure was gone. Every nerve ending tingled. If vampires existed – I'd only learnt of their existence a couple of weeks ago – then why not ghosts? This chateau was hundreds of years old, maybe more. Who knows how many people had died here in that time? Vampires weren't the only inhabitants.

I continued to stare out the window. There it was again – arms upraised, the same high-pitched wailing. A chill shot through me, and I jumped back drawing the curtains together, tightly bunching the folds of fabric.

The serpent ring on my finger glowed scarlet. Whatever the figure was, it posed no threat. I took a deep breath and slowly peered through the curtain again. The ghostly form was still there.

I slipped on my boots, threw on a coat and stepped out into the empty hallway. All the lights were on and unfamiliar voices drifted around me. It was probably the Brethren servants. I paused at Jenny's door. She slept, her slow heartbeat and steady breathing were quiet and peaceful. I didn't have the heart to wake her. Another human heartbeat came from the other end of the house. Presumably that was the estate manager. I assumed the sleeping one, directly above my room, belonged to Judy. But there was another, slightly faster, heartbeat also coming from above, so close to Judy's they could've been in the same room. Who? One of the staff? But there were no human staff on duty yet.

I went to the end of the corridor and peered up at the stairs. The heartbeat moved, coming closer to where I stood. Madame Thierry appeared. She started and her hand flew to her breast.

'Milady, I didn't expect to see you up at this late hour.'

'Nor I you, madame. Is everything all right with my mother?'

'Yes, yes. I … always do the rounds of the house before retiring. Make sure everything's secure. It's my responsibility.' Madame

Thierry's heart thumped louder and faster, and she looked down at me with a haughty air.

Why did she make me feel as if I were the intruder? It made my hackles rise. I had to remember she was only doing her job – she was the housekeeper, after all. So why did her checking my parent's suite bother me? 'Thank you, madame. I won't keep you.'

Her eyes narrowed, and with a slight bow of her head, hands folded primly in front of her, Madame Thierry walked past me and down the other end of the corridor, keys dangling from the belt at her waist. She glanced back at me then checked one or two locks before striding to the tower door at the far end.

I dismissed the feeling of unease. Kari liked her, so she must be okay. It's Jenny's fault! Her and her Mrs Danvers quip. It's screwing with my mind.

I shook my head and dismissed the housekeeper from my thoughts.

Whatever part of the chateau Alec was in must be soundproof, as his familiar slow heartbeat wasn't detectable. Besides, if he and Luc were busy I didn't want to disturb him.

'Now what?' I wanted a better look at that weird apparition, but wandering alone in the chateau at night, no matter how secure the place was, probably wasn't a good idea. Besides, I didn't fancy bumping into Madame Thierry again. When did that woman sleep?

A silvery laugh tinkled from somewhere a few levels down. 'Kari, are you busy?'

'What's up?'

I loved my newly enhanced hearing. 'I think I saw a ghost.'

'Really? Where?'

'Outside, on the boundary wall.'

A second later, she stood before me, wiping the back of her mouth with her hand where a few drops of blood lingered. She'd been feeding. 'No ghosts here, Laura. I should know; I've lived here a long time.'

I knew Kari had been a little girl when her family moved here from Finland in the late eighteenth century. Her father had been a stonemason, and Luc had employed him to oversee extensions to the chateau. Later, a cholera epidemic killed her family, and she, too, would have died had Jake not transformed her.

'Okay, you tell me.' I took her hand, led her back to my room and pointed out the window. 'There.'

Kari drew the curtains aside and peered out. 'Too far for me. Sure it wasn't just moonlight on the trees?'

'My imagination isn't that wild. And it doesn't come with sound effects.' She shot me a look. 'It's wailing or moaning – definitely not wind. Kari, there's someone, or something, out there.'

Her eyes narrowed in concentration. 'Okey-dokey. Binoculars needed. How embarrassing – never had to use them before.'

'Sorry.' I shrugged. At least she believed me. 'Too many trees here. Is there a better view of that end of the estate?'

She pursed her lips, and the red stain on them deepened. 'There's the rooftop.' Her brow crinkled. 'Not sure if I should take you up there … but I'm dyin' to see whatever you saw, too.'

We grinned at each other, and she turned to dash from the room.

'Hey!' I yelled. 'Too fast! I've only got vampire hearing and sight, not the speed!'

'Wait here … I'll be back with the binocs.'

While she was gone, I located a scarf, woollen hat and gloves in the closet and shoved them in my coat pocket. Although the chateau was centrally heated – for the benefit of humans – I had to adapt to the icy cold of a northern hemisphere December.

I stepped out into the hallway just as Kari reappeared. Apart from the binoculars, she wore the same outfit from the plane – hot-pink leather mini-skirt and jacket. 'You're not cold at all, are you?'

She grinned. 'Nope'

We strode down the hallway, the heels of our boots clicking on the parquetry flooring. Another set of stairs led to the next level where the walls were decorated in jade marbling. I was reminded of the green-eyed serpent ring Luc wore. 'Kari, Judy and Luc's suite is on this level, isn't it?'

'It takes up most of this wing of the house.' With a jerk of her head she indicated a set of white double doors to our left. 'It's over there.' I'd guessed right. It had been Judy's breathing and heartbeat I'd heard.

We went through a single door at the other end of the corridor, which led to a curved, narrow stone stairwell set into a conical tower.

'This leads straight up to the roof.' Kari took the steps two at a time.

With a click, the door closed behind us. The air was freezing. Warm breath streamed from my mouth, causing crystals of condensation to form as I followed her. I pulled on my woollens and noticed how clear my sight was in the pitch dark – my fingers, hairline cracks in the wall, light-grey polished indentations in the stone steps made by thousands of footsteps over the centuries.

'Nearly there,' Kari called back.

After fifty steps, she stopped and pushed open a rusty door, hinges groaning. A rush of frosty air bit my face and sucked the air from my lungs. Above, the inky sky swirled with a galaxy of stars, each with their own dance of colours.

'Here, gimme your arm,' Kari said. 'It's a bit dicey up here.'

She was right. The night frost on the metal roof made it slippery, and the heels of my boots didn't help. Kari was sure-footed, despite her killer stiletto heels.

The flat roof provided an unhindered view of the entire estate. A raised ledge with a series of crenulations ran the length of the perimeter. I silently thanked the builder when a powerful gust nearly threw me off my feet. If not for Kari's grip I could've slid across the icy edge.

I had second thoughts as I steadied myself, but the faint wailing sounded again. I held my breath and concentrated on that noise alone. I was not mistaken – a solitary keening rent the air.

'Over there.' My heart pounded as I pointed beyond the tree line. The figure appeared. From this height, I could see it was a woman, stunning, in a ghostly sort of way. She was atop the wall, on her knees, ebony hair blowing wildly in the wind, an anguished look on her beautiful face.

We leant against a crenulation, which sheltered us from the wind, and stared at the apparition. 'The ghost of someone's mad wife?'

Kari chuckled as she raised the binoculars to her eyes. 'That I'd like to see!'

The apparition's wail became a plea, as she extended her arms toward the chateau. A scatter of incoherent words reached me. 'She's saying something, but my French is hopeless.'

Kari breathed out.

'Who is she?'

'Uh huh. Not a ghost.' She scanned the horizon before lowering the binoculars. 'It's Lucinda Ortiz.'

I didn't like her worried frown. 'What's she doing here?'

'Good question.' Kari turned to me. 'Laura, she's Jean's damme, his creator.'

I felt the blood drain from my face. 'Jean-Philippe?'

Kari nodded.

My stomach churned on hearing his name, the horror of the night still fresh when he'd tried to kill Alec to get to me. I'd only known Jean-Philippe for a few brief days, while holidaying in Italy after my eighteenth birthday, before he abruptly and mysteriously disappeared. For years I'd heard nothing from him, until a few weeks ago, when he'd suddenly re-entered my life in a crazy attempt to seduce me away from Alec. How could he expect me to rekindle a long-dead adolescent crush? When I refused, he tried to rape and kill me.

'It's the only way I can be free of you,' he had said.

Those dreadful words still burned in my memory, and I struggled to swallow the bile that rose in my throat. To save me, Alec had been forced to kill him – they'd been friends. I never wanted to hear his name again.

'Why is she here?' I could barely get the words out as a shiver racked my body, and not only from the biting cold.

'Has either Princi or Luc told you about the sire-juvy bond?'

I tore my gaze from Lucinda and stared at Kari. Her pet name for Alec's position as Princeps usually made me giggle. The serious note in her voice, and my own horrific memories, killed any thought of that. I shook my head.

'There probably hasn't been time, I s'pose.' She sighed and placed her arm around my shoulders. 'You're freezing to death. C'mon let's get you inside.'

'Not yet.' I leaned closer into Kari's warmth as the wind whistled around us. 'Tell me about this sire-juvy bond.'

'Okay, here's the gist. There's a close bond between all vampires and their sires and dames – kinda like a sixth sense. If one's in trouble or dead, the other's gonna know it.' She raised her eyebrows knowingly at me.

My heart gave a sickening jolt. Kari knew about Jean-Philippe's death, and by the looks of things, so did Lucinda. 'You know … about what happened?'

Kari chewed on her lower lip and gazed at me. 'Judy told me everything. Thought it was best I knew.' She looked at me, possibly gauging how I was going to react.

I nodded. 'Fair enough, I guess.'

'If I waited for Jake to tell me anything, the world'd be ended.' She shrugged. 'You wanna know more about her?' Kari's eyes shone. 'Jean wouldn't have been like that except for her. She changed him while she was still a juvenile, and that's a big no-no in our world. It can cause complications, because the whole transformation process takes about a century … or so. Everyone's different, but that's the general time. The Elders locked her away for a while as punishment. She must've only recently been released.'

'And Jean-Philippe?'

'He should've been terminated, but Luc intervened. Nobody could work out why.' She raised her eyebrows knowingly at me. 'He asked permission for Jean to be moved into his household – finish his servitude with him – so he could observe him, and if he showed signs of insanity then he would give the termination order.'

I groaned. It all made sense: Luc was protecting a man he believed was his son, even though he wasn't sure. What a mess. 'And no one saw anything odd in him?' I shook my head.

'Nah, he appeared okay. I left a few years later and didn't see him again till the Ritual – alive and out of servitude.'

I turned and stared at the lone figure of Lucinda. 'What does she want?'

'I can lip read.' She raised the binoculars to her eyes.

'You can?'

'Uh, huh. Had to learn so I could find out what the guys were saying when they whispered stuff to each other I wasn't supposed to hear.'

'Sneaky.'

She gave me a cheeky grin, and then looked through the binoculars. A hiss escaped her lips. 'Not good. She's demanding justice.'

I opened my mouth and closed it again. Justice? For what? She'd sired a monster! Images flashed through my mind of that dreadful night when he'd broken into Alec's apartment and attacked us. My fisted hands shook with horror and suppressed rage. The words finally spilled out. 'Jean staked Alec then tried to rape and murder me. He knew I was his half-sister, yet that didn't stop him. Alec killed him trying to protect me. What justice could she want? That's insane!'

'Yup, that's about it. Everyone reckons she must've been changed by a juvy as well coz she's not all right in the head either.' She lowered the binoculars again and lightly touched me on the shoulder, adding in a soft voice, 'He deserved what happened to him – coming after you like that. He should've been terminated when the Elders said.'

I exhaled tersely. 'How did she know we're here?'

'Dunno. Maybe she's been here a while … waiting, and that's not good. C'mon.' She took my arm. 'Luc needs to know so he can get her off the wall before the locals notice.'

If they haven't already. 'Why doesn't she come to the door?'

'Can't. There are magical wards around the place. None of our kind can enter without permission – it's like an invisible shield that keeps 'em out.'

'So she's been stalking the place all this time?' I shook my head at the absurdity of it.

'Looks that way.' Kari tugged on my arm.

I searched my pockets for my mobile phone when I remembered I'd left it sitting on my bedside table. 'Got your mobile on you? I'll ring Alec.'

'He's down in the vault, and it's soundproof. No mobile reception.'

'We need to let him know.' I shivered again.

'Okay, inside,' Kari said, arm around my shoulders, and guided me toward the roof door.

I'd seen enough. I took a long last look at the pathetic figure of Lucinda, her bedraggled hair whipping about her face as she pounded into the stone with her fists. How long could that part of the wall last under her relentless assault? Would the magical wards hold? I considered the possibility and, rather than fear, a sense of pity overcame me. She was mourning and probably didn't know the circumstances surrounding Jean-Philippe's death. I'd loved him once too, but the memory of our brief time together was marred forever by the terror of that night.

Kari secured the door, and we descended the stairs.

'You said she may have been transformed by a juvy? You're not sure?'

'No one is. She showed up out of nowhere at the prefect's palace – a huge sensation at the time. No one had ever heard of her.' She halted to think. '1836 I think it was …a big Elders' meeting in

Madrid. Our whole clan was there. Luc was presiding.' Kari started walking again. 'Everyone stopped when she called out from the doorway, "I'm Lucinda Ortiz, and I and my son, Jean-Philippe Louis Auguste Reynard, wish to present ourselves to the prefect."' She rolled her eyes. 'Everyone just stared then laughed … except Luc, as I remember. He went white and still. Now we know why.'

'Said he hadn't seen Jean since his adolescence. It must have been a shock to him.'

'He sure as hell knows how to keep a secret. I would've blabbed it.'

Me too. I was hopeless at keeping secrets. I had blurted my family secret to my ex-boyfriend, Matt, the same night I had learnt of it, which has caused nothing but problems since. 'Maybe that's why Jake won't tell you anything.'

Kari snorted.

'Did Lucinda say her sire was a juvenile?'

'She named him, but nobody had heard of him. Said he'd died soon after changing her.'

'Leaving her alone … to fend for herself?' A rush of sympathy came over me as I thought of her solitary figure striding along that boundary wall. It wasn't her fault she'd been mentally affected. Being in such a situation would send anyone off the rails. Poor thing….

'Yeah, well, the guys need to know.' Kari turned and gave me a mischievous smile. 'Since there's no other way to contact them, we'll have to go down to the vault.'

'You know the way?'

'Kinda.' She paused. 'I know the way into the tunnels but not into the vault itself.'

Her comment didn't exactly inspire confidence, but it appeared I had little choice if it was the only way to reach Alec. On the other hand, I could wait for Alec: surely he wouldn't be too long? Yet, the thought of checking out some secret tunnels and the bloodvault itself was almost irresistible. I could put my newly developed senses to good use and track Alec's scent to the vault.

'Lead on, Kari.'

The deserted ground floor reception area was dark apart from the light coming from the two candelabras atop the endrails at the bottom of the stairs. It would have been quiet, too, if not for the rustling of the trees outside and the soft, melodic voices of the Brethren staff scattered about the chateau.

Kari opened one of the lacquered, black double doors and ushered me into a magnificent hall. Several-hundred people could have filled it. Chairs lined the walls, the gold thread in their upholstered covers picked out by spotlights centred on the line of portraits above them. As in the Sydney residence, it was a gallery of Dantonvilles – every Bloodgifted since the curse's genesis.

Did each house Luc owned have the same setup, mini reflections of here?

A massive stone fireplace commanded attention on the left side of the wall. Above it, the dominating family escutcheon – the bronze image of two serpents coiled around a sword. Kari hurried to the far end of the hall, to a kind of throne beneath a marble canopied roof supported by four pillars in the shape of two twisted serpents. It took my breath away.

'Luc's throne?'

Kari nodded. 'It's called the Alabaster Throne.' She disappeared behind one of the pillars. Seconds later, the entire assemblage silently slid to the side, revealing a narrow door set into the wall.

'Is this one of the things you're not supposed to know about?'

Her broad smile confirmed my suspicion when she reappeared and interlocked her arm through mine. 'You up for some exploring?' I squeezed her arm in reply.

Kari opened the door, and we peered into a musty tunnel that stretched several metres before curving off to the right. As we took a few steps in, the door slid closed behind us.

# CHAPTER 8 – THE BLOOD CONFIRMS

**ALEC**

A loud beeping reverberated from the chamber walls. It came from the other end of the vault, where the men still stacked the Ingenii blood into their respective bays.

'Shit!' From his back pocket, Sam retrieved his mobile phone. 'We've got a breach. Someone's in the tunnel.'

Metal scraped against metal as the men unsheathed their swords. Unlike me, they rarely parted with their weapons. Even here.

Luc's head swivelled toward Sam. 'Can you tell how many?'

'No, only location,' he answered.

I glanced at the serpent ring. It's eyes were red – no sign of danger. Yet the beeping on Sam's phone continued.

'Cal, any chance it was triggered by a bat?' There was a colony of them in the caves.

'Unlikely.' The beeping increased. 'Whoever it is, they're headed straight for the fire trap.'

It was the first of the booby traps Luc and Sam had installed toward the centre of the tunnel system. An incendiary device planted into the ceiling would set off a flamethrower when the trip wire was activated. The confined space in the tunnel would intensify the ferocity of the fire yet isolate it from the chateau above. Anyone caught within ten feet would be incinerated. No vampire could survive it, let alone a human.

My serpent ring flashed. Its eyes had turned black. My gut clenched and I spun around – all appeared normal. Luc's gaze darted between me and the ring – he'd seen it, too.

A hard, cold lump settled in my stomach – it could be Laura. The vault was soundproof and I had no choice but to use the telepathic powers of the ring. *Laura, are you okay?*

*Alec? I'm fine.* Her voice in my mind was calm, almost carefree.

*Where are you?*

She hesitated. *Um, in the tunnel. It's supposed to lead to the bloodvault.*

My blood froze. *Stop! Don't move! It's booby trapped. You're directly below one now.*

'Oh, Lord!'

'It's Laura! She's in the tunnel,' I said. Luc's eyes widened and he swore. 'Deactivate the firetrap!' I called out to Sam. 'Laura's right under it.'

An expression of horror crossed his face, and he shook his head. 'The wires have to be manually pulled.'

In an instant he, Marcus, Cal, Jake and Terens had joined us, all speaking at once.

'Deus! Get her out of there!'

'How the hell—?'

'Why is she down—?'

Terens grabbed my arm. 'Anyone else with her?'

'Don't know.' I sprinted from the vault. *Laura?*

*I'm here. You said not to move.* There was fear in her voice.

*Are you alone?*

*Kari's here.*

'Kari's with her,' I called back over my shoulder. Luc and Sam were right behind me. Jake uttered a curse, and in less than a second was sprinting by my side.

Sam pulled out his mobile and pressed buttons. 'I've deactivated security. But there's nothing I can do about the traps.'

Blood roared in my ears, almost drowning out the thud of our footsteps on the cavern floor. Only the crunch of insects, too slow to escape, sounded beneath my feet. I spied the tunnel entrance in the distance. Nearly there. I caught her unique scent – the sweetness of honey, peach and jasmine.

She and Kari were in the third chamber, well away from the house. Behind me, the men's hot breath was on my neck. Sam took the lead, and we sped through a series of narrow chambers. 'Shit!'

Laura and Kari stood with linked arms, the toe of Kari's boot touching the trip wire. The pulse in my throat drummed wildly – so close. So damn close!

'Alec!'

'Stand absolutely still, honey,' I said. 'There are four flamethrowers aimed at you. Sam going's to deactivate the main trigger.'

'Flamethrowers? You guys never said—' Kari spluttered.

'Kari, your toe's on the trip wire. Shut up and listen!' Jake growled.

Kari paled, eyes widening into two luminescent orbs then narrowing. 'Well it's your fault. Should've told me. I wouldn't have come this way.'

Jake growled again.

'Kari, shush!' Laura turned frightened eyes on me. 'We came to tell you Lucinda's wandering the boundary wall.'

Lucinda? What was she doing here? 'You could've used the ring.'

She and Kari exchanged glances. This venture had more to do with curiosity than a sense of urgency.

'I don't give a damn about Lucinda! It could've waited. You've put yourselves in mortal danger.' Luc's knuckles were white. He jerked his head to Sam, indicating to pull the wiring.

'Sorry, Papa.' Laura's eyes glistened.

Luc sighed and in a gentler tone said, 'Ma petite, step over the wire. Come here.'

'Not without Kari.'

'No, Laura. You should go,' Kari urged her.

Laura shook her head and stubbornly remained in place.

Damn this! While Sam scaled the wall and began the deactivation process, I had to shield Laura from any potential fiery blast. I stepped over the wire and took her into my arms. Jake did the same with Kari, careful so as not to dislodge her foot on the trip wire.

'Alec, no.' Laura trembled.

'Don't argue.' My voice was gentle. 'I won't stand by and watch something go wrong.'

Sam protested. 'Nothing's going to go wrong. I designed it, and I can take it apart.' He pulled out several wires and held them up. 'See? Easy. Oh ye of little faith.'

There was a collective sigh of relief. The danger was over, but I didn't want to release Laura just yet. She felt good. Strands of her rich copper-coloured hair peeked out from beneath her woollen cap. My fingers twitched to touch them.

'Kari, I should put you over my knee for that,' Jake said.

'It's my fault.' Laura sucked in her lower lip. 'I asked her to take me here.'

'And how did you learn that, Kari?' Luc asked. His slow, deep tone meant danger. Surely he'd do nothing to hurt Kari, but he could be unpredictable.

Jake tensed and tucked her behind him. 'Leave that to me, Luc.'

Kari popped her head out from behind him. 'He never tells me anything. So I learnt to lip-read. I know what you guys are saying when you don't think I'm watching.'

There was a split second of silence before Jake and I burst out laughing. Sam cracked a smile and glanced at Luc. 'That's a hint if ever I heard one.'

Luc's expression remained impassive. Only the narrowing of his eyes and his scent – that of ozone during a thunderstorm – revealed his anger. Muttering to himself in French, he turned on his heel and strode from the tunnel.

'He's angry, isn't he?' Laura's soft voice interrupted my thoughts. I sensed disappointment in herself and concern that she'd let him down.

'He'll get over it. He was worried about you, and now with Kari knowing the way down here, he feels he's losing control.'

She let out a pent-up breath. 'I'm too curious. It's getting me into trouble.'

I remembered another, more recent time, when she'd wandered up to the ballroom in the Sydney residence and discovered Jean's makeshift studio. It had endangered her life. 'Yes, it is. But that's one of the things I love about you. Never a dull moment.'

Her frown gave way to a radiant smile that sent a wave of desire through me, which I intended sating as soon as we were done here. It'd been several days since we'd had sex, and I saw the longing in her eyes, too. The subtle change in her scent confirmed it.

'Judith trusted me with knowing about Laura. Why couldn't you trust me with this? It's just as important,' Kari protested as she skipped alongside Jake in effort keep up with his long strides. He headed in the direction of the vault, rather than back to the chateau.

Laura glanced at me with raised eyebrows, the same question on her mind, it seemed.

'For your protection. The less you know the better,' he answered.

'I can handle myself. And besides, I have this.' She hopped in front of Jake and pulled a cord from around her neck from which dangled a wolf's-head ring.

The men and I had retrieved several from the fingers of dead Rebels. Each ring carried a concealed, deadly white-oak spike, a substance outlawed by the Principate. Anyone found in possession was executed. Luc had taken and stored most of them, but I had kept one for myself, as had Marcus.

Jake stopped. 'Where did you get that?'

She pursed her lips and avoided Jake's gaze. 'Found it.'

'Where?'

'On the drinks counter, the night you and Princi fought the Rebels under the boat. I only took one ... to look at, and' —she shrugged— 'forgot to put it back.'

Kari was enterprising, which made her a perfect bodyguard for Laura. Even I hadn't seen her take it. I struggled not to smile when Jake closed his eyes and pinched the bridge of his nose. 'You know the penalty for possessing white-oak.'

'It's not like I'm dealing or anything. And since I'm Laura's bodyguard, shouldn't I have the best weapons for her protection?'

'She makes sense, you know,' Laura said. 'Why should only the Rebels have them?'

Kari grinned and tucked the ring back into her jacket. 'That means I can keep it, right?'

Jake scratched his head and looked at me. 'You're head of the Principate. Your call.'

'Keep it, Kari.' Enforcing the white-oak ban was no longer going to work. It only gave the Rebels an advantage. I'd managed to immunise our clan against its fatal effects, but since the tests were still in the early stages, we didn't know how long the protection would last. Would the vampire virus eliminate it from our system? Only time would tell. In the meantime, we needed to capture as many of the wolf's-head rings as possible and keep the existence of the serum from the Rebels. 'Jake, I want you all to carry the captured wolf's-heads. Every one we seize, we use.'

One of his eyebrows shot up, and he tilted his head in the direction Luc had taken. If Luc objected, as princeps I could overrule him, although I hoped that wouldn't be necessary. 'Leave it with me,' I said.

He nodded and strode out of the tunnel, Kari at his heels. 'C'mon, kiddo, since you want to know everything.'

'I'm no kid!'

'To me you are.'

She looked back over her shoulder at Laura and rolled her eyes. Laura sighed and shook her head. 'Men!' she muttered.

'Am I missing something here?' I whispered.

'Tell you later.'

It appeared we both had things to tell each other – alone. Thankfully that would come sooner rather than later, since she and Kari had wandered down here. Luck or providence? Whichever, it now meant I could give Kari a few vials of Ingenii blood, in the security of the vault, rather than later, up in the chateau. The staff were loyal, but it wasn't worth the risk of any of them overhearing.

'This is amazing! Like something from a fairy tale.' Laura waved her arm and gazed at the calcite formations in wide-eyed wonder. 'Angel's wings … miniature castles … and a lake. It's so Arthurian. I almost expect the Lady of the Lake to pop up.'

It'd been a long time since I appreciated the beauty of these caves. Now, through her eyes, I saw it once again: the faint shimmer of pink in the otherwise pure white calcite structures, and the silver sheen on the helictites, which hung from the roof like lengths of ribbon. Some formations had long, jagged edges, which, to the romantic minded, could pass for dragon's teeth.

'I didn't know you like Arthurian romance.'

'There's a lot about me you don't know, Alec Munro.' Her impish smile dazzled me, and behind it I sensed the promise of more delightful discovery to come.

'Then I'm happy to spend the rest of my life finding out.' I brought our clasped hands to my lips and kissed her soft skin.

Laura blushed. That small reaction never ceased to thrill me.

'Will you two quit with the lovey-dovey.' Kari's grin belied her words. She glanced up at Jake and slipped her hand in his. He smiled back and ruffled her hair.

*Dumb move, Jake, mate.*

Laura groaned and dug her elbow into my ribs. 'See?' she mouthed.

'What?'

She pointed toward Jake and Kari, and her sweet voice whispered through my mind. *Kari's in love with Jake. And he doesn't see it.*

*He does. Just doing his best not to encourage it.*

*Why? Kari's lovely.* Laura turned questioning eyes on me.

*He has his reasons.* And it was time he was over them.

She shook her head. *Then he should tell her. It's sad seeing her hanging onto to him like this. He's breaking her heart.*

I squeezed Laura's hand. *They'll have to work that out. Nothing we can do.* I liked Kari. Yes, she could annoy the hell out of all of us, but she was also a charmer. And she and Laura had bonded. That was good. It would make things easier for her, having Kari as her shadow. Which reminded me.... 'Kari, I have a surprise for you at the vault.'

'You do?' She clapped and grinned. 'What is it?'

'Ahem!' Jake cleared his throat.

He rarely did that, and it meant he was concerned about Luc's reaction. I hadn't checked it with him yet. 'It can wait till we get there.'

'See what I mean? He never tells me anything.' Her exasperated tone only served to make him laugh.

Marcus, Terens and Cal stood at the entrance to the vault. As we neared, Marcus strode forward and enveloped Laura in a fierce hug. 'Deus! Don't scare us like that.'

'I didn't mean to.' His shoulder muffled her voice, her delicate form swamped by his massive one.

Terens lounged against the door, arms folded across his chest, a half-smile on his face. 'Something tells me you've got a knack for trouble, pet.'

'It's a gift.' She shrugged, and he chuckled. 'So this is it? The bloodvault?' Laura stared past Marcus, at the light streaming through the open door.

'Come, it's time to meet your ancestors,' Marcus replied, and with one arm around her shoulders, led her in.

'I met them in the Great Hall – on the walls,' she said with a smile, swivelling her head to the panorama before her. 'Wow. How many are there?'

'Thousands, ma petite.' Luc approached and took both her hands in his. The scent of thunderstorm no longer clung to him. 'Forgive my anger.'

Her smile would have melted the coldest heart. 'There's nothing to forgive, Papa. You had every right—'

'Shhh!' He placed a finger over her lips. 'It's past. You're safe, and that's all that matters.'

Sam jogged up to me. 'Reset everything. No harm done.'

My gut wrenched when I thought what may have happened if he hadn't set the security alarms. Inside the soundproof vault, we would've heard nothing. 'Good.'

Terens joined us and slapped Sam on the back. 'Look, that, ah, earlier crack I made about the beeping. Just wanna say … I was wrong, okay?'

Sam shrugged. 'Sure, man. Forget it.'

Terens nodded. 'Glad it worked, bro.'

'This feels hot. Is it supposed to?' Laura dug inside her coat to withdraw the crystal ruby pendant vial Luc had given her. It contained three drops of his, Antonia's and Marcus's blood, an elixir powerful enough to render her immortal. She'd promised me – and him – she'd drink it should her blood revert to human after the lifting of the curse. As she dangled it before her face, the vial's contents began to glow a deep scarlet, which intensified around her like a halo.

Cal whistled. 'Will you look at that?'

Around us, the miniature vials began to flare, and a soft, deep hum filled the chamber and increased 'til the walls vibrated with the sound.

'Deus! I knew she was the one. Knew it the moment I saw her as a babe. My blood burned then as it does now.' Marcus's eyes blazed as he looked at Laura.

Luc gave a great shout of triumph and pumped his fist. 'All the confirmation I need!'

She clapped her hands over her ears. The din of the humming was deafening. Her eyes widened as she looked at her father.

'Your ancestors just announced our arrival, affirming we're the ones the prophecy spoke of.' I could think of no other reason for the humming.

Luc had been right all along. Now more than ever, we had to be ready. If the Rebels do come, they'll see the chateau occupied and ready for battle: give our allies confidence and hopefully make our enemies think twice before attempting an attack. And I very much doubted Count Timur would want to share that secret of the bloodvault – once he learnt of it. Otherwise he'd have to fight every other vampire on the planet to get to it first. But then again, I could be wrong. He was a shrewd and cunning bastard. If anyone could turn it around to his advantage, he could.

I turned to Marcus. 'I don't remember reading this in your Chronicle.'

Marcus spread his hands wide. 'What can I say? Everything the witch told me I wrote down.'

'Looks like the bitch left something out. But I'm ready for a fight.' Luc's eyes blazed, and the tips of his fangs protruded from his upper lip. The scent of a thunderstorm clung about him. He slammed his fist into the rock face. It gave way like soft putty.

Laura came to my side and slid her hand into mine. I gave it a gentle squeeze. Her other hand nervously touched the ruby crystal vial at her breast. 'Well, that doubly confirms it then. Still think the rebels will come? Timur and Rasputin?'

'We have to expect it, ma petite. They want this.' He spread his hands to indicate the vault. 'But they're not getting it. They won't get through our defences.'

'He's right, Laura. That's why I wanted you here.'

She looked at me, and a faint smile graced her lips. 'Looks like Kari's going to be busy with those sword lessons, 'cause I'm certainly not going to be the helpless damsel when an attack does come. Unless you want to take over the role of teacher?'

Hell, I'd forgotten. I did mention that. 'We'll discuss it.'

Laura gazed about the chamber. 'The humming's stopping.'

This was true, and with it the unnatural glow of the blood vials. In the calm that accompanied it, all I heard was the blood roaring in my ears and the loud thump of Laura's heartbeat.

For a few seconds no one spoke, until Luc sprang across to Paulus's bay, grabbed a fistful of vials and tossed them, two at time, to me. 'That should be enough for several months.' With a jerk of his head, he indicated the other bays. 'The rest of you grab a supply for yourselves – start with Linus and work your way down. You're permanently on daylight duty from now on. Hurry, we don't have much time.'

The men leapt to help themselves, stuffing their pockets with the precious substance from Paulus's son, Linus. It could be hours, maybe days, before we could expect company – if the Rebels were determined to get their hands on the blood vials. It was Brethren protocol for the European prefects to present themselves whenever the family was in residence at the chateau. I was hoping the rebellion wouldn't interfere with that. Would Timur attack when all the Principate delegates were assembled here? Would he be that bold?

Marcus threw back his coat, exposing the Roman sword at his side – his weapon of choice. Unlike his men, he'd never taken to using a broadsword, except for executions. He chose the next bay down from Linus, and began tucking the thumb-size containers into a pouch at his belt.

'Kari, you too,' I said. 'I want you with Laura when I can't be, and that includes the daytime.'

Kari's mouth dropped open, and her eyes went round. For a rare split second, she was speechless. I glanced at Luc, who gave me an approving nod – not that I needed it.

'Well, go on. That's your surprise,' I said to her.

With a squeal, she threw her arms around my neck and kissed my cheek. 'You're the best Princi ever!' She rushed to Jake's side, leaving the scent of lilacs and peppermint in her wake.

Laura gazed at me, eyebrows creased in a slight frown. She pointed to the vials. 'Why do you need those?'

Damn, I'd forgotten.

I took a deep breath and lowered my voice. 'That's another thing I wanted to discuss with you. I'll be feeding from these.' I tapped my pocket and hastily added as her eyes flared, 'For the duration of your pregnancy, to avoid distress to you and the baby.'

'But—'

'Laura, why do you think pregnant women aren't allowed to give blood? There's a chance you'll get anaemia, and my drinking from you will only make it worse. Plus, you might lose a lot of blood giving birth. You want to risk our baby's health, and yours?'

Her beautiful features softened. 'No ... I didn't think.'

'We haven't had much time to talk about it, have we?' I ran my thumb along her lower lip, savouring the silken feel of it beneath my skin. My mouth tingled to taste her again.

'What about ... um.' She blushed and her eyes darted to the side.

The men were busy picking through the Ingenii vials. I'm sure they weren't listening. I leant down and murmured into her ear, 'As soon as we're alone.'

'Add a few more little bottles to your supply, Doctor Munro,' she murmured back. 'You'll be needing them.'

The subtle change in her scent was unmistakable, amplified by her pregnancy. Arousal. I liked it.

Within minutes, our pockets were filled, and we exited the vault. Sam, Cal and Luc led the way with Marcus, Terens and Jake the rear. Laura warily scanned the tops of the walls and ceiling when we re-entered the firetrap tunnel.

'Any other booby traps I should know about?'

'None in the house or grounds, only here,' I replied.

'Are there other secret tunnels?'

'Don't even try.'

Her low, throaty laugh made me hard. If not for Lucinda outside on the boundary wall, I'd sweep Laura up to our bedroom this minute. But as princeps, I had another type of duty to perform – a far less pleasant one.

# CHAPTER 9 - LUCINDA

**LAURA**

Once back inside the house, Luc sent Cal to fetch Lucinda. He then issued instructions to the servants to prepare the Great Hall. Lights were switched on, and soon a roaring fire was sending sparks shooting up through the chimney, its light casting flickering shadows along the walls and ceiling.

Alec had asked me to stay. 'You're part of the Principate, and I'd like you by my side.' He'd even had a servant move one of the antique upholstered chairs that stood by the wall over to the Alabaster Throne.

My heart swelled. I'd hoped he would ask me but was uncertain about this Principate business, and the extent of my involvement. There hadn't been much time to explain it to me. I made a mental note to ask either Alec or Judy exactly what the duties of an Ingenii included, besides being the private blood bank of the princeps.

There was also Lucinda. Having only seen her from afar, my curiosity was piqued. What kind of a woman was she? And what exactly did she mean by wanting justice?

As the hall heated up, I removed my coat and scarf, to drape it around the back of my chair. Alec instructed a servant to return it to our suite. Did the queen of England ever sling her coat, gloves and hat over her throne? Not a good look, perhaps?

He then took his place on the Alabaster Throne, his navy-blue shirt a striking contrast to the snow-white stone on which he sat. I sat to his right, Luc stood to his left, his back against one of the pillars. Alec leaned forward as Cal ushered in Lucinda. Her long, dark hair streamed about her shoulders, her eyes wary as she scanned the hall. What I had assumed to be a white dress turned out to be a sleeved cloak. It parted as she entered, to reveal black leather pants and bustier.

'My Lord Princeps. My Lord Dominus.' Lucinda sank to her knees in a curtsey.

*Dominus?* My thoughts whispered to Alec.

*Ancient term, something like … Master of the House.'*

*Oh.*

Cal closed the double doors with a boom. She hissed and spun around, nails extended into claws as if expecting an attack.

'You have nothing to fear here, doña,' Alec assured her.

She pointed at Cal. 'Then why is he here, armed with a sword?' Her voice was melodic and deep, with a strong Spanish accent.

'Protocol. Would you expect the Ingenii to be without her guard?'

Her eyes never strayed from Cal as he picked up another of the antique upholstered chairs and placed it in the centre of the hall, facing Alec and myself. He then returned to the doors, leant back against them and crossed his arms over his chest.

'Please, be seated.' Alec indicated the chair.

Again, her gaze darted about the hall before she sat on the edge of the seat. Her cat-like gaze locked on me. 'So, you are the Ingenii?'

Her question startled me. She phrased it almost like an accusation as her cold gaze swept over me.

'You've requested an audience, Doña Lucinda,' Alec addressed her, and she turned to him. 'What can I do for you?'

She lifted her chin and glared at him. 'My son is dead.'

A sickly coldness crept over me as if all the warmth had been sucked from the room. I clutched the arms of the chair. *Alec, she knows!*

*Say nothing,* he whispered telepathically back to me. 'Which son are you referring to?'

'Jean-Philippe. My Jean.' Her voice rose in pitch. 'How could you ask? He was taken into my Lord Dominus's household.' She pointed to Luc. 'Why are you not avenging him?'

Her wild gaze darted from Luc to Alec. A dead weight settled in my stomach. From what I'd recently learnt, vampires cannot lie to one another – they'd instantly know. But then again, why hide it? She should know what Jean-Philippe had done. Flushed with heat, I wanted to stride down from the dais and tell her exactly what he'd tried to do to me. It was only Alec's sideways glance, his hand on mine, and the subtle shake of his head, that stopped me.

Luc snorted. 'He's not your son, Doña Lucinda. You're his damme, not his mother.'

Her nostrils flared, and the wooden arms of the chair on which she sat creaked under the strength of her grip. 'He is my son! I gave him life.'

'His second life, but his birth mother was Adelaide, daughter of the Duke D'Orleans. Otherwise I could call the princeps my son. How ludicrous!'

Which would make Alec my half-brother. No way! My skin crawled at her twisted thinking. Alec and I are no more related than anyone who has had a blood transfusion.

'No! No! No!' She sprang from the chair, and it banged on the floor. 'He has my blood. My blood.'

Luc growled. Alec rose and took a step forward. 'Doña, we do not deny that your blood saved him, and if you wish to regard him as your son, then I have no objection. Lord Luc only reminds us that Jean also had a human mother; as did we all.'

Alec's soothing voice calmed her. Slowly she sat, and her gaze travelled to a spot above our heads. Nodding her head slowly, she said, 'Yes, yes true. She gave him birth, but I gave him eternal life – a far greater gift. And she is dead. I strive to look after my children.' Lucinda looked about the hall. 'I see no Adelaide here, no Duke's daughter. Where is she? Point her out to me – I'll tell her who his true mother is.'

Was she nuts, as Kari had hinted, or was she being facetious? Somehow I wanted to believe it was the latter. Lucinda's lavender eyes were luminous against her olive skin. Could someone so beautiful be out of her mind?

Luc quietly swore, and from the way his fists were clenched, this meeting was about to be terminated.

My hands slid to my belly. My child. I would do anything to protect it, and the thought of anyone hurting my babe sparked a fire deep within me. Did all vampire women feel the same way about their "children"? Or was it only Lucinda?

Alec glanced at Luc, and his lips thinned. 'Doña Lucinda, we all know how much you loved Jean, how close the bond between you was.'

'Was? So you know he's dead. Tell me!' She strained to remain seated, her body like a tiger ready to spring as she leant forward on the chair.

'There is no easy way to tell you this.' Alec's voice remained neutral. 'I was forced to terminate Jean. He had attempted to kill Lady Laura and me.'

It was blunt and cruel, but it had to be said.

'No!' She shrieked and flew at Alec.

Cal leapt forward, picked her up and thrust her back in the chair, holding her down by the shoulders. She kicked, spat and scratched at him until Luc stepped in.

'Be still,' he said, his voice dangerously low. 'Or I will tie you to that chair and move you closer to the fire.'

She stilled instantly. Her face ashen and eyes bulging, she stared back at Luc. My father could make anyone cringe in fear, and Lucinda's lips and chin trembled as her gaze darted in the direction of the fireplace.

What could induce such terror? Had someone attempted to burn her in the past? The horror of it made me shudder and softened my heart toward her. Whatever it was, my father knew how to exploit it. He nodded to Cal then resumed his place next to me, hands folded over his chest. Alec placed his hands on his hips and glared at Luc before dropping his head. I doubted either of them knew how to handle this.

Lucinda whimpered. My heart thumping, I left my seat – ignoring the men's protests – and stood before her. Cal still gripped her shoulders.

'Lucinda, I'm Laura. I knew Jean.'

Her eyes flared. 'He was in love with a girl of that name.'

'Me,' I said simply. 'We knew each other a long time ago, and only for three days. I knew him as Philippe. Then he disappeared from my life and only reappeared a couple of weeks ago, at the Ritual. He wanted me to love him again, but it was impossible. I loved another. He couldn't accept it. That's when he tried to kill me, and the princeps.' She sucked in a breath. I carefully phrased the next words. 'Philippe said the only way he could be free of me was if I were dead.'

Her gaze shot to Alec, who'd come to stand next to me, then back to me. 'Madness.' All I could do was nod, hoping my words were sinking into her muddled mind. Her expression changed to a smile. 'He liked that name better than Jean. Said every commoner was called "Jean,"' she whispered.

I had liked the name, Philippe, too, but now it would be forever associated with fear and insanity. The horror of that night still loomed in my mind. Alec's face came to view to help quell those memories.

Like flicking a switch, her mood swung quickly again. 'No! My Jean would never attack the princeps. He was his friend.' She tried to rise, but Cal held her down.

'Judge for yourself if I'm lying.' I peered into her eyes. No matter how much it sickened me to recall that event, I steeled my mind to replay it all. And although I knew she couldn't read my mind, perhaps she could see it in my eyes.

Lucinda reached out, and Cal restrained her. 'No, it's okay,' I said. Somehow I knew she wouldn't hurt me, and my hunch proved right.

Lucinda touched my cheek. 'He always spoke of you. How he sees you everyday; the sound of your voice; what you and he did....' She shook her head. 'I don't understand.'

'Jean-Philippe stalked her. Laura knew nothing of it. He made up lies,' Alec said.

Lucinda's face crumpled and soon her shoulders heaved as deep sobs wracked her body, and tears of blood spilled down her cheeks. She banged her fists against her thighs. 'Mea culpa! Mea culpa!' Alec crouched down so his face was level with hers. She lifted blood-rimmed eyes to his. 'I did this to him; changed him when I should not have. But he was so young ... and handsome. I couldn't let him die. I took the risk and....'

She hugged her sides and slumped to the floor, her deep keening filling that great empty room. It was a cry of deep pain and unimaginable loss. Were all sire-juvy bonds this strong? Would Luc feel the same toward Alec...? Fear clutched my heart, and I turned my mind from that thought.

Alec rose and whispered something to Luc, who had joined us. My father nodded, and then he and Cal headed for the door. 'Let's leave Lucinda to mourn. Give her some time alone,' Alec said.

We left as well, the sound of Lucinda's wails following us out.

'Will she be all right on her own?'

'She won't hurt herself, if that's what you're worried about. More likely she'll destroy some of the furniture, crack the stone – nothing that can't be replaced or repaired,' Alec replied.

I thought about the antique upholstered chairs. Surely they were irreplaceable?

We gave Lucinda an hour. Her wailing had eased, and I'd heard no banging or crashing of furniture. Cal opened the door. Lucinda sat in a crumpled heap on the floor, shoulders heaving, her ebony hair hiding her face, her once-white cloak now bespattered with drops of blood. She didn't look up as we entered.

Cal helped her up and eased her into the chair. She was almost lifeless in his arms, as if her grief had drained it all from her.

Alec placed a handkerchief into her hands. 'Wipe your face, doña.'

She didn't move, except for the slight, jerky rise and fall of her chest from muted sobs.

'Here, let me help you.' When I reached out for her hand, Cal hissed and shook his head.

'I would never hurt her.' Lucinda raised her head and blinked at me through the matted strands of her hair, the dark tendrils stuck to her face by bloody tracks. 'You are kind, lady.'

Alec strode to the door and called for a bowl of water. Within seconds, he was placing it on the floor by her chair. He took the handkerchief, dipped it in the water and handed it back to her.

As she cleared her face of hair, Alec said gently, 'Doña, I don't wish to cause you further distress, but we need to know about your sire.'

'It does not matter now. He is dead,' she said, her voice hollow.

He leant down and touched Lucinda's upper arm. 'Tell me everything you know about him.'

'Why? What difference does it make?'

'Tell me anyway.'

'Rodriquez,' she mumbled as she wiped her face. Her hands shook, and soon the rest of her body trembled violently.

'When was the last time you fed?' I asked. The thought had sprung into my mind, and I followed my instincts.

She raised her head and inhaled deeply, nostrils flared, eyes boring into mine. Was she trying to mesmerise me, like a snake does with a potential meal?

'Lucinda!' Alec's voice rent the air. Her head snapped up. I blinked. 'We'll get you some blood.' He jerked his head to Cal, who promptly left the hall. 'Concentrate on me. Tell me about Rodriguez.'

'He was kind to me. Taught me how to survive, and then they killed him.'

'Who killed him?' Alec asked.

Cal came back with a goblet of blood and placed it in her hands. As she drank, some of it spilt onto her chin and down onto her clothing in her haste. I tried not to gag. She ran her finger along the bottom to scrape up the last droplet.

'Thank you.' She held it out to him.

'More?' he asked.

She nodded, and Cal sped from the room. Colour returned to her cheeks and her hands no longer shook.

'My question, doña, is who killed him?' Alec straightened, hands behind his back as he waited.

'I do not know. I think it was his sire. Rodriguez said he had ordered his termination for disobedience. He was meant to deliver me to his master as a blood slave. But he could not do it.' Her words became clearer, her eyes more alert. 'Instead, he changed me to keep me safe, and we went into hiding. Five years we were together. He taught me what he could. One night he went out to hunt and never came back. I knew they had found him.' She gulped down the second goblet of blood from Cal, who took up his position behind her chair again.

'He mentioned no other name besides Rodriguez?' Alec asked.

'No. He did not want me to know. He told me if anything happened to him, to stay in hiding until I came of age, then go and present myself to you, Lord Lucien. He said that once I was recognised as one of the Brethren, the Principate would protect me; his sire could not touch me. When I heard you were in Madrid, I went there.'

That's what Kari saw. Lucinda had only been following her sire's orders and ensuring her own protection. 'Why bring Jean-Philippe with you? Didn't your sire tell you the penalty for transforming a human while still a juvenile?' Alec looked at me with raised brows. 'Kari told me,' I said.

Luc sighed. 'What that girl doesn't know, she doesn't tell.' Alec and Cal both stifled a smile. 'Why come to me? Wouldn't it have been easier to go to your prefect?'

'He told me not to; some of the prefects are in his master's pay.'

Luc barked out a sardonic laugh and shook his head.

'I think we know whom: those who ran from the Pledging. I have their names.' Alec's voice was grim.

I could taste the tension in the room.

He gave a barely perceptible nod and resumed his position on the Alabaster Throne. Luc perched on the arm of my chair. 'Could you answer Lady Laura's question, doña? Why did you transform Jean?'

Lucinda closed her eyes and bent her head. 'I know I should not have. Rodriguez warned me. But there was a terrible battle near my hiding place. So many young men dying, many dead. I was hungry, and I thought ... they were almost dead anyway. Then I saw him.' Her eyes flew open, and they were filled with pity. 'He was so handsome. Too young to die ... calling for his mother.'

Luc stood and paced toward the fireplace. Her gaze followed him.

'Pray continue, doña.' Alec leaned forward, arms on his knees, hands clasped in front of him.

Lucinda dropped her empty goblet to the floor where a solitary bead of blood trickled from the rim. It held me mesmerised, as the light from the crackling fire played about its smooth surface, making it appear molten gold. I swallowed.

'You should have let him die.' Luc's hands were braced against the mantelpiece, and he kicked one of the logs, sending sparks shooting up the chimney.

Lucinda paled and shrank back into the chair. 'I've paid for it,' she murmured.

'Can you recall him mentioning his master at all, or a clan name, or perhaps even a kingdom?' Alec asked.

She shook her head. 'He was very careful.'

'Describe him to me.'

Lucinda lifted her head, and a faint smile appeared. 'He liked to laugh, and his moustache used to curl up when he did. He wasn't a big man – we could see eye to eye. His features were fine, handsome. I liked to touch his hair. It came down to here' —she touched her shoulders— 'and curled up, too. Brown hair that shone in the moonlight.' Her voice trailed off, and a single red tear slid down her cheek. She let it splash onto her cloak.

'Luc, sound like anyone you know, or knew?' Alec wouldn't have known Rodriguez – the man had lived and died a few hundred years before he was born.

My father kept his back to us. 'No.'

Alec sighed and turned back to Lucinda. 'Where did you meet? It might give us a clue.'

'Does it matter? He's dead.'

'Doña!' Lucinda and I both jumped at Luc's sharp tone. 'We need to know whether he was a juvenile to account for your condition.'

She cocked her head to look at him, scrunching the ends of the cloak in her fists. 'I know I am … different. He told me I might be…. I don't remember how I was before he changed me.'

'Where?' Alec repeated.

'Barcelona.' She pronounced it with a slight lisp. 'Rodriguez came to my father's house and took me away.'

'Barcelona. The prefect there is Alonzo. He might have an idea who—'

'If we're dealing with a juvenile, he would go unnoticed. Does anyone pay attention to a knight's squire?' Luc continued to stare at the flames.

'Did you ever see your family again?' Her story had me intrigued. It had happened so long ago, yet to her it was probably as clear as yesterday – as were knights and squires to my father.

Lucinda's eyes clouded. 'No, lady.'

'Can you recall anything else about him? A birthmark, or a particular piece of jewellery, like a ring or amulet...?' Alec spread his hands. Once again she shook her head and then lowered her gaze. Alec slumped back in his seat and ran his hand through his hair, a gap opening in his shirt as he did so.

I glimpsed the sword-and-serpent tattoo on his left breast – the symbol of my family's clan. An idea occurred to me – a long shot – but worth a try. 'Lucinda, did your sire have a tattoo, perhaps?'

Her head shot up. 'Yes. I remember now. Here.' She tapped the side of her neck. 'It looked like the head of a wolf. When I asked him about it, he became angry and told me never to mention it again. After that, he kept it covered and warned me to stay away from any who bore that mark.'

Luc spun around, eyes ablaze. Alec sat forward and thrust out his hand, the wolf's-head ring he'd taken from a dead Rebel on his little finger. 'Like this?'

Her eyes flashed in recognition. 'Yes. But he had no ring. How—'

'Timur!' Luc's lip curled up into a sneer. He came toward Lucinda and placed both hands on the arms of her chair. 'Rodriguez never mentioned that name?'

She shrank further into her chair, pulling the cloak tightly around herself as if to hide. 'No,' she whispered, her eyes wide. 'Count Timur! If he finds me….'

'He won't,' I replied. 'You're safe with us.' I nodded to Alec and Luc who exchanged glances.

Count Timur, the Hungarian prefect, was leader of the Rebels and Rasputin's creator, planning Alec's assassination and my kidnapping. It was only the quick action by the Czech prefect, Karl, which foiled his plans. And it seemed he was involved in blood slavery. I didn't have to guess what that must entail.

'Timur's juveniles carry his mark, but when they come of age, they're given a smaller version of his ring,' Luc said.

'The fact he wasn't wearing one….' Alec didn't have to finish. It probably meant Lucinda's sire had been a juvenile. 'His name should be in the archives.' Alec rose and stepped down from the platform. 'How many males named Rodriguez can there be? Unless it was a pseudonym.'

'Are all juvenile names recorded?' I still had so much to learn.

'Supposed to be – juveniles and fully fledged – and the records are sent here to the Principate archives,' Alec replied. 'No wonder Timur was after him and the girl. One of his own not only hid her from him, but changed her while still a juvenile himself. And by law, he would have been held responsible.'

Luc bent over and looked at Lucinda intently, so much so, she tried to hide her face in her cloak. 'I misjudged you, doña. It's not your fault you are this way.' Large eyes peeked at him from the folds of her cloak. 'Accept my apology.'

Poor brave Lucinda. How she feared my father, yet she had dared to come here alone and present her case.

'Gracias, Dominus.' The cloak slipped from her face, and she sat upright, her scarlet tears drying, leaving a track down her cheek.

I rose and joined Alec and Luc. The nasty count was already on the Principate's hit list. Any extra charges against him would make no difference. 'If it turns out Timur is her grandsire – I take it that's the right term?' Alec nodded. 'What then? He's already at war with us.'

'It could give us an advantage. Those Brethren who had been punished for not controlling their juveniles, and seeing Timur get away with it, might change their allegiance – weaken his side,' Alec said.

'And the blood slaves? Are they what I think they are?' I glanced at Lucinda.

'Exactly, ma petite. Mesmerised humans forced into bondage, especially those with a rare blood type, or the very young.' My brows shot up. 'Those who are too young to smoke or take drugs … whose blood is still pure.'

My whole being tensed in revulsion, for I knew Luc referred to children. How many hundreds went missing in different parts of the world every day, taken by monsters like Timur to satisfy their blood lusts? My revulsion turned to anger. 'Let's find out for sure. We check the archives. Then, with Lucinda as witness that Timur intended her for a blood slave, use that against him, too.'

Luc shook his head. 'Vampires will only react when they see a perceived injustice or threat against themselves. Otherwise they won't interfere in another vampire's *indiscretions*.' A muscle ticked in his jaw.

'Just like the human world,' I said.

Luc snorted. 'True. And you may just be right.' He glanced at Cal. 'Library. Bring her.' He turned on his heel and strode from the room.

'Doña?' Cal offered Lucinda his arm. She looked at me, and when I nodded and smiled, she reluctantly laid her hand on Cal's arm and let him lead her from the hall.

Alec drew me to him. 'Would you prefer to get some sleep?'

'No, I'll sleep in tomorrow.' I twirled the hair at the back of his neck around my fingers. 'You know, I was angry with Lucinda for coming here. It interrupted our time alone together. But now … I kind of feel sorry for her.'

'So do I. She's had it hard. I had no idea.' His lips grazed mine, which drew a sigh from me, and his kiss grew insistent. Even through my closed eyes, I was aware of the glow of the serpent rings, which reflected the burning desire Alec and I had for each other. I stood on tiptoe and pressed myself closer to him, willing our kiss to intensify. Slowly, his mouth lifted from mine. I ached at the loss. His hand stroked my cheek. 'If this wasn't so important....'

'I know.'

Hand in hand, we left the Great Hall and crossed the entrance hall. Alec's thumb caressed my palm, sending tingly sparks shooting through me. The double doors were ajar, allowing light to stream into the dimly lit entrance, and I caught a glimpse of the interior. But nothing could have prepared me for the sumptuous visual feast that awaited. When he pulled the door open, I gasped.

# CHAPTER 10 – THE LIBRARY

**LAURA**

Row upon row of bookcases lined the walls, but it was the magnificent vaulted ceiling that made me catch my breath. Like artful icing on a wedding cake, rich stuccowork shaped like scrolls, acanthus leaves, fruits and vines swirled around frescoes of images taken from classical mythology. Gods, goddesses, satyrs and centaurs paraded across the ceiling in all their naked glory.

Dark blue carpet ran the length of the room. In the centre stood a small table with a raised platform, like a lectern, covered with a sheet of glass. I drew closer. Beneath the glass lay an open book, and from the illuminated Latin lettering and slight yellowing of the pages, I guessed it was Marcus's original chronicle. I glanced to my right, and there sat Marcus, at one of the few tables in the room, writing in a book.

He looked up and smiled. 'This will be the last of my journals. Once the curse is lifted, there'll be no need for me to add any more.'

'How many have you written?' I asked.

Marcus pointed to a set of shelves containing red-leather volumes. There were several hundred, at least. 'I've kept a meticulous record of events from the beginning. Here's your account.' He spun the book toward me. It was written in Latin, French and English. *"On this day, in the Year of Our Lord ... my granddaughter, Laura Anne Dantonville, announced she was with child – the Child of Promise."*

Warmth crept into my cheeks as images of Alec and I making love flitted through my mind, and the muscles of my inner thigh tingled at the memory. Alec squeezed my fingers.

From another table, at the farther end of the room, came Luc's voice. 'This is the right volume.' He, Cal and Lucinda were huddled over a large tome that spanned the width of the table. Luc flicked through a few pages. 'Ah! Here it is.'

'You found Lucinda's sire?' I strode toward them.

'No. The record of Timur's registrations three-hundred years ago.' Luc ran his finger down the page.

It contained a list of hand-written names, with dates beneath. Next to some names was the outline of a wolf's-head. Others were blank, and yet others had seemingly simplistic drawings: a large nose here, a crudely drawn face with a mole on a cheek. I pointed to one. 'What's that?'

'A butterfly,' Alec replied. 'If these others are any indication, it could be a birthmark. Looks like Timur was adding his own identifying marks.'

'He drew these?' If so, he wasn't a bad cartoonist.

'Not exactly. The archivist copied them from the original letters. And those are stored in a folder.' I followed Alec's gaze to another bookcase crowded with box files.

'You have an archivist?'

'Adeline, the head librarian at D'Antonville. She's happy to do it, since Luc gives her unlimited access to all the rare manuscripts.'

I was sure there were many. My father had an impressive library in his Sydney residence, filled with first-edition books he'd collected during one-hundred-and-fifty years there. I couldn't begin to imagine the treasures hidden here.

'She's in seventh heaven, ma petite. Especially when I let her read the Carolingian texts.' Luc turned another page of the manuscript. 'She didn't believe me when I told her Charlemagne was a lousy poet.'

Would I ever be accustomed to the way my father so casually referred to great historical figures of the past? It was easy to forget he'd known them, and perhaps had even fought alongside them. They were long gone, but he was still here. Did he miss them?

'Rodriguez,' Marcus murmured, pulling me from my thoughts. 'Deus! There's a few of them. We need something more to go on.'

There were so many names; so many Timur had transformed, all from different nationalities. It was as though he were building an army. Perhaps he was. Perhaps he'd been planning it a long time. I shuddered.

As Alec placed his arm around my shoulders, his voice whispered through my mind. *He won't succeed.* I hadn't consciously done so, yet Alec had heard my thoughts. Seems there were to be no secrets in our relationship.

Lucinda sucked in a breath. Her finger hovered over a particular name. 'It's him. It's him!'

The name Jose Luis Rodriguez Gonzalez stared up at us. From the half-dozen or so other Rodriguez's on the previous page, this was the only one with the scrawled picture of a curled moustache. But there was no sketch of a wolf's-head. Perhaps that meant he never completed his servitude, and that Lucinda was right – he'd been killed.

'What year did he transform you?' Luc asked her.

'It was the second-last year of his majesty, Philip V. Seventeen-thirty-six.'

Luc jabbed at Rodriguez's name. 'Timur changed him in seventeen-o-one.'

We could all do the maths – he had been a juvenile when he transformed Lucinda. Here was the tangible proof we could use against the Hungarian prefect. Even the Rebels might take exception to one of their own unpunished for something others had been disciplined for. If it was sheer self-interest that drove them to rebel, then the same self-interest could be used to turn them against their leader.

Marcus took the phone from his pocket. 'Time to sow some dissension among the Rebels, I believe. But first, let's put Doña Lucinda's name where it belongs.' He picked up a pen, and in a beautiful flowing script, added her name below her sire's before closing the book and passing it to Cal, who returned it to the shelf. 'I'll leave a note for Adeline telling her about my addition.'

'Marcus, wait.' Alec's brows were drawn, as if in concentration. 'As I see it, we have three advantages—' He stopped and looked at Lucinda. 'I'm sorry, doña, but these are private matters that—'

'No, I understand. Please do not apologise.' She raised her hand, palm outwards.

'You're welcome to stay here with us for as long as you like. Cal will escort you to one of the guest rooms.' Marcus indicated the door.

'That is most kind of you, my lord Marcus.' She bowed her head. 'But I cannot stay. I must return to my home.'

'Where is home?' I asked.

'Uruguay, my lady. That is where Rodriquez told me to go should anything happen to him. He had holdings there he never told his sire about. I am safe there.' Her smile was sad. 'But before I go….' She held her hand out to Cal. 'Please, Señor, return to me my dagger.'

Cal glanced at Marcus before gingerly placing an ivory-handled blade with a blue-jewelled pommel into Lucinda's palm. Light glinted on the decorative swirls that ran the length of the blade.

'Gracias, Señor.' She was about to slip it into a concealed sheath in her belt, when she stopped, flicked the blade around and handed it to me. 'Please, take this, my lady. I know it is but a small compensation for what my son did to you.'

Her gesture caught me by surprise. What would I do with a dagger? Then I remembered the corkscrew I had used against Rasputin. I'd smeared a bit of my blood on the end and threatened him with it. A dagger would be a far more effective weapon and more portable than a sword. Lucinda's gift was exactly what I needed.

'Thank you.' The ivory handle fit snugly in my hand as I searched for someplace to conceal it.

'Use this.' Lucinda removed her belt and tied it around my waist.

I slid the dagger into a narrow slit beneath the buckle, which made the protruding blue pommel look like a piece of jewellery. Who knows if it wasn't a priceless gem – perhaps a sapphire? 'Thank you again. This is a generous gift,' I said.

Luc stood and bowed. Marcus kissed Lucinda's fingertips. 'You have but to call, doña, and our swords will be at your service.' He and Cal escorted her out while I withdrew the dagger to examine it more closely. The quillon, just above the blade, was shaped to resemble a naked cherub with outstretched wings. Was it gold? 'This has to be a rare antique.'

'May I?' Alec balanced it on his palm then on the tip of his finger. A tiny bead of blood appeared. 'Spanish steel – blade heavy, single edge.' He handed it back to me. 'It's a very valuable gift.'

I nodded. 'I didn't know what to expect when Cal brought her in … I thought I'd dislike her – and at first I was angry she came here at all. But meeting her, hearing her story….' I looked at Luc. 'I misjudged her, too.'

Luc stroked his chin as he gazed at my dagger. 'Very nice. Keep it on you at all times, ma petite. Alec, whatever you were about to say, wait until we reach my office. It's more secure.'

'Wise move,' Marcus said as he returned, his long strides clicking on the polished floor.

I could only assume he was thinking of the night household staff. Being vampires, they were capable of listening in to every conversation anywhere in the house. Although loyal, it seemed my father and grandfather didn't want to test their fealty by discussing secrets openly.

Alec nodded. Fingers entwined, we followed them to Luc's office at the far end of the library. While the walls of his office in the Sydney house were hung with pictures of me, here was a series of gold-framed photographs. Each had its own spotlight, and occupying the spaces between bookcases. I coughed at floating dust particles not only covering the books, but on the small mounds of yellowing scrolls, which sat on the shelves.

Luc seated himself behind a large greyish-green-marble desk, hands folded behind his head, his sharp lavender eyes on Alec. 'What do you have in mind?'

Alec leaned forward on the leather sofa we occupied. 'Use what we've got to crush the rebellion. One.' He raised one finger at a time. 'We have the white-oak serum. Two: we have two magical rings, which prevent mesmerisation by Rasputin. And three: a supply of Ingenii blood.'

Marcus perched on the edge of Luc's desk. 'You confident about the serum?'

'It stood up to the punishment Stockton meted out on me. That's as good as a clinical trial.'

'Could you use that as a bargaining chip? Offer to vaccinate loyal Principate followers then maybe add one free vial of Ingenii blood as a bonus,' I suggested. The slogan, *buy one get one free*, perversely flitted through my mind. I had visions of Brethren stampeding to Team Principate to get their hands on the coveted vials.

Alec turned to me and smiled. 'You read my mind.'

The blank expression on Luc's face didn't bode well. 'Those are only for the clan.' He stared at me unblinking. 'Not to be shared with anyone!'

I chilled at the cold rasp in his voice.

Alec stood. 'Laura's right. I have a feeling we'll need to do exactly that. Rasputin already knows, and it's only a matter of time before he's able to contact Timur – if he hasn't already.'

'And once Timur has that knowledge, he has two choices: either keep it secret and grab it all for himself, or broadcast it and promote his cause as the righteous one,' Marcus said. 'And if I guess correctly, he'll take the second option, the cunning bastard. Deus! He could turn our allies against us.'

'Exactly,' Alec said. 'Luc, you need to offer it first, as a show of faith.'

The seconds ticked by as my father slowly lowered his arms and placed both hands on the desk. A muscle pulsed in the side of his jaw, his lips thinning to a gash as he looked from Alec to Marcus and me. 'No.'

Alec slowly clenched his fists. Marcus stood and leaned on the desk to face his son. 'Those vials will not sustain us indefinitely. Not if we have to stand alone, which could happen if our allies learn of it.'

'Luc, please see reason,' Alec said.

My father's eyes began to change as his gaze leapt from Marcus to Alec. Although his mouth was closed, I saw the minute bulge above his upper lip and knew his incisors had slid down. Marcus moved to stand in front of Alec. He was shielding him! I knew my father had a temper – I'd witnessed it only once: when Russell had tried to abduct me. His anger had been justified then, but there was no reason for him to lose it this time, and especially not with Alec.

I rose from the sofa and went to him. 'Papa, you've been saving those blood vials for this very time. There are so many. Couldn't you spare a few for your most trusted prefects, like Karl and Milena? They'd be indebted to you for eternity.'

As he gazed at me, his eyes resumed their normal colour. He sighed and rose. 'Ma petite, that blood was collected to ensure your protection. Our men will need all of it in the coming days.'

'Then think of Karl and Milena, and' —I thought of other loyal Principate prefects who I'd met at the Pledging— 'O'Toole, as our men. They're loyal to you and the Principate. You know that. They didn't have to stay behind when Rasputin disrupted the Pledging ceremony, but they did. They were ready to take the Pledge. And it was Karl who'd warned you about Timur. Risked his life to tell you.'

A wry smile lifted the corners of his mouth. 'You'd make an excellent diplomat.'

'Does that mean you agree?' I smiled. Had I swayed him?

One eyebrow shot upwards, and his smile widened. 'Let's say I may reconsider.'

Just then I heard Sam's voice. Seems the security of Luc's office didn't include those with Ingenii blood. 'Luc, get on the laptop and open the Principate website. You need to see this. It's bad.'

# CHAPTER 11 - FIRST OFFENSIVE AND COUNTER OFFENSIVE

## LAURA

Alec, Marcus and I sprinted to Luc's desk as he logged on.

'The Principate has a website?' Somehow I couldn't picture centuries-old vampires in tune with modern-day technology, especially running their own website.

'It's a secret site. Only Brethren can log in,' Alec replied.

What kind of information would there be on a vampire site? Local gossip, best place to hunt, who's been outlawed this week, executions, rebellions? I suppressed a giggle.

The screen showed the coiled golden serpent and sword symbol of the Dantonvilles on a red background, and as Luc clicked the comments link, the screen showed a video picture of Count Timur.

*"Brethren, you have been told to regard me as the enemy. You have been lied to. The Principate has kept secrets from us all, and I'm about to reveal its greatest one."* Marcus sucked in a breath. Alec's hand tensed in mine. *"I have it from a reliable source that our illustrious leader, Prime Elder Lord Lucien, has a hidden cache of precious Ingenii blood in the French Residence. He's been collecting it for centuries. Why, I ask, is it that only he and the princeps feel it's their right to daywalk, and the rest of us must be content with the dark? Surely he could have shared some of it?"* Timur smiled benevolently, his dark moustache curling up at the ends, as he continued describing the double standards of the Principate and the privileges accorded to the few.

It sounded so reasonable that had I not known his true purpose, I could've been persuaded. I checked the stats and saw that the video had only been viewed a few times. But by whom?

*"I call on our Brethren to join me and demand a share of the Ingenii blood. Lord Lucien has kept it all for himself for too long. Rise up with me, my Brethren, and together we will walk into the light."*

Luc swore and banged the desktop. The laptop bounced, and a large crack appeared on the desk. 'That son of a bitch! Rasputin must have got a message to him.'

In spite of losing his hands, Rasputin had somehow managed to get word back to his master. Who knew how many messages he'd sent to make sure his information got through? We'd only intercepted one. I imagined him mesmerising some poor human into using his phone, for there was no way he could've reached Europe before us.

'Sempronius, can you delete it?' Marcus asked.

'Working on it. The bastard's used some type of….' He swore then whooped in triumph. Timur's face suddenly disappeared as the screen cleared. 'Done it. Give me a few minutes, and I'll tell you who logged on and saw it.'

'No matter who saw it, it's going to get around. What worries me is if it were Principate supporters, why didn't they let us know?'

Alec's face wore a deep frown. He licked his lips as he stared at the computer screen. 'It's just as I feared.'

Sam's voice came again. 'More than a dozen prefects saw it, along with eleven others. The majority were Principate supporters.'

'Merde!' Luc kicked his chair aside and turned to face the window behind his desk. 'Which ones, Sam?'

Sam rattled off a list of names, a few of which I recognised.

'Marcus, you need to get on there and save the Principate. They won't listen to me—' Alec's phone rang. He checked the screen and took a deep breath. 'Karl.'

I held my breath, too. Would Karl understand? Of all the prefects I'd met, he was my favourite. Marcus went to Luc's side. As they conferred, I listened in to Alec's call. I heard Karl's voice just as clearly as if Alec had the phone on speaker.

'Is it true, what Timur alleged? You've got a stash of the stuff you could've easily shared with the rest of us?'

Alec briefly closed his eyes. 'It's true.'

'The fucker's right! And here I was believing we were friends. If I'd known—'

'Karl, how soon can you get here?' Alec's gaze was fierce on Luc's back.

'What? What for?'

'So you can hear the truth from me.' There was silence on Karl's end. I wouldn't let myself believe he would join the Rebels.

'Not tonight, if that's what you mean. Earliest I can make it is night after tomorrow.'

'Good. Contact the other Principate prefects privately. I'll explain everything – why the Ingenii blood has been stored, and why the secrecy.'

Silence again. I held my breath.

'I'm asking you to trust me, Karl, for our old friendship's sake.'

'All right.' He released a long exhalation. 'But only because of that.'

Alec and I released our pent-up breaths. 'Thanks.' He tucked the phone back in his pocket and wrapped me in his arms. 'Promise me you won't leave the chateau grounds for anything. Until we get this sorted, not even daytime is safe. No telling how many Timur has swayed to his side.'

I smoothed the hair back from his brow. 'You think the Rebels' donsangs might try something?'

'The wards around this place only keep Brethren out, not humans. The estate's patrolled. Should anyone trespass, they'll get caught. But outside … it's risky.'

'Poor Kari, there goes our shopping expedition.' Jen, Kari and I had planned to visit either Avignon or Lyons. I sighed as I thought of everything I'd have to tell Jen in the morning. Wherever Kari was, I was sure she'd hear these latest developments – if she had already consumed the blood vial. 'I'll have to keep her occupied, get her to teach me some more sword moves. And now that I have the dagger' —I tapped my belt buckle— 'maybe she could show me a few tricks there, too.'

Alec's eyes were serious. 'I hope it never comes to that.' My mood matched his. But I knew I wouldn't hesitate if I needed to use it.

There was a knock on the door. Alec called out, 'Come in, Kari.'

Her pixie face appeared, a wary look in her eyes as she glanced from Luc to Marcus. 'I heard my name.'

'Then you know?' I asked.

She nodded. 'We were in the Games Room. Sam's on the computer. Terens nearly punched the screen when he saw Timur's face.' She giggled and skipped to my side.

'Kari, you're to be with Laura at all times. Now that you can daywalk, where she goes, you go.'

She winked at me. 'Understood. I overheard something about more sword lessons and a dagger?'

'Show you later,' I whispered.

Marcus called for his men, and less than a second later, Jake, Cal, Terens and Sam strode into the room. Sam went straight to Luc's desk, flopped into his chair and took over the laptop.

Terens glowered as he came to Alec and me. 'I'm going to get that piece of shit if it's the last thing I do.' His personal vendetta against Timur wouldn't be resolved until one of them was dead. Timur had been responsible for Terens losing an arm. He looked at me and tugged at the diamond stud in his ear. 'Sorry, pet. Didn't mean to swear in front of you.'

'If that's swearing, Terens, then you've got nothing on the language I hear from kids in the playground.'

He grinned and shook his head. 'Beats me how you put up with those little sh—'

'You all know what's happened.' Marcus's voice boomed out. 'Timur's hoping to gain ground by revealing the bloodvault. First offensive goes to him. Now we need to counter that.'

Luc turned from the window. 'My hand's been forced in this. One prefect's already pissed off, and I'm sure he's not alone. Alec's summoned all the prefects here, and they'll arrive within forty-eight hours. Marcus has contacted the Elders.' He grimaced. 'I've no choice in this. Perhaps ... it's for the best. As I was informed' —he eyed Alec— 'it'll keep our allies loyal.'

'We haven't had a chance to discuss this yet,' Marcus added. 'But I was also considering asking you, Alec, to use the serpent ring to protect our allies from mesmerisation.'

Alec nodded. 'Good idea. I'm surprised Timur hadn't used Rasputin's talents to force the prefects to his side before now.'

'Maybe he couldn't,' Jake said. He was leaning against one of the bookcases, one foot resting on a lower shelf. 'The more I think about it, the more I'm convinced his power is just developing. Rasputin's coming to the end of his juvenile stage, and when he does, that's when I reckon his power will mature.'

'Like Ingenii blood, which doesn't kick in 'til we're fifty?' I asked.

'Something like it. We know he used hypnotism on humans before he was turned, but I believe it's only now beginning to work on Brethren. It's the only explanation. Timur's an opportunist. He wouldn't waste a valuable resource like Rasputin.'

Marcus's face was a study in concentration – brows drawn, gaze fixing on each of us intermittently. 'Then there's no time to waste. Who knows, maybe Timur has done us a favour? Because now we know how to prepare. And rather than waste our resources going after him—'

'Apart from us, no Brethren can approach him without being mesmerised. Too damn dangerous. We'd be outnumbered,' Jake said.

'Which is why we need to neutralise him instead.' Marcus smiled grimly. I was elated to see my grandfather take charge as the soldier he once was. 'Luc, give me your and Judith's key. I'll take Terentius, Justinius and Calixtus with me to the vault and bring up a pouch full of vials for the prefects. Sempronius, give us a couple of minutes then deactivate the booby traps. I'll let you know when we're back in the tunnels so you can reactivate them.'

Luc removed the bloodvault key from around his neck and handed it to Marcus, with his green serpent ring, and took Judith's key from his pocket. 'You'll need this, too.'

Marcus squeezed Luc's shoulder before leaving with his men.

I glanced at my watch. Dawn was still a few hours away, but in the winter, the sun rose later. My body hadn't had a chance to readjust to the time difference yet, and I was wide-awake. Back in Australia, it was lunchtime. Jenny had been smart to get to bed soon after our adventure in the bloodvault. Her jetlag wouldn't last long. But my body clock was completely out of whack. Regardless, I needed to get at least a few hours sleep so I could join Jenny in the morning. It wouldn't be fair for her to be on her own in this place. My head drummed – there was also so much to tell her, and I wanted to protect her. There was the impending arrival of the prefects in less than two days, and if my guess was right, they wouldn't wait to consume the Ingenii blood in those vials. They'd want to be sure they were given the genuine stuff. I was sure that, like lizards on a rock, we'd be seeing several dozen prefects basking in the early sunshine. Who knows how long it was since they'd felt the sun on their faces.

Jenny must be prepared to meet them.

'Alec, I need some sleep. I want to be with Jen when she wakes up.'

'You've been amazing; you know that?' He brought my hand to his lips and kissed it.

'When I'm not setting off booby traps.'

He chuckled. 'I'll escort you.'

'It's okay. I know the way, and Kari's with me.' I glanced at Luc, who hadn't moved from the window, head down, fingers digging into the wooden frame. 'Stay here with Papa. He needs you.' As I turned and headed for the door, Luc cleared his throat.

'You were right.' We both turned to him. 'It's hard for me to admit I'm wrong. I should've acted sooner. All my plans....' he shook his head.

I crossed the room and kissed his cheek. 'Will work out. I know they will. You've been right in everything up until now.'

'This thing with Rasputin, no one could've predicted,' Alec said.

'I've blocked both Timur and Rasputin. They won't be using our website again,' Sam said, then added under his breath, 'Unless they create their own. I'll put a Google alert out for them.'

'Go to sleep, ma petite.' Luc hugged me, and Kari and I left.

Kari nudged me as we climbed the stairs. 'Show me this dagger.' I removed it from my belt, and she whistled, examining it from all angles. 'Nice. I'll show you how to use it tomorrow.' Suddenly she stopped, and I turned to see a huge grin on her face, eyes alight. She gripped my shoulder. 'Daylight. Laura! I haven't seen it in over two-hundred years.' She clapped her hands and then clamped them over her mouth. Two large red blood drops welled in her eyes and slid slowly down her cheek. 'It only just hit me,' she mumbled behind her fingers.

I winked away the stinging behind my own eyes. 'We'll spend the whole day outside.' Hopefully Jenny and I wouldn't freeze to death.

Kari wiped the tears with her sleeve, leaving scarlet smears on her pink jacket. 'Promise you won't sleep in?'

'Promise.'

I laughed as, in her excitement, she half-dragged me up the stairs. 'The sooner you get to sleep, the sooner you'll wake and be ready in the morning.'

* * *

I recited a relaxing mantra, counted sheep, and even imagined myself floating on a fluffy cloud – the mattress was certainly soft enough. Nothing worked. My body refused to sleep. Niggling thoughts itched my brain. Were all the Principate prefects loyal? Who's to say they wouldn't use the blood vials to betray us? Just like humans, vampires were treacherous: I'd witnessed that in Russell.

Argh! I gave up and stared at the stuccoed ceiling. Nice cherubs. Their fat, rosy faces reminded me of the little one growing in my womb. A thrill coursed through me, and I splayed my fingers over my still-flat tummy.

At the sound of pages of a magazine being turned in the next room, I remembered Kari was in there. My bodyguard.

I sighed, threw the covers aside and walked to the window. At least this time I knew I wouldn't be confronted by a spectre on the boundary wall. My ring flared a bright scarlet. Alec was near. The deep, rich timbre of his voice came from the living room, and my heart leapt. The door opened and closed as Kari left.

His dark silhouette appeared in the bedroom doorway. My eyes drank him in.

'Can't sleep?' he asked.

'No.'

'Some exercise might help – vigorous exercise.' He stalked toward me, and my inner thighs clenched in anticipation.

# CHAPTER 12 – VIGOROUS EXERCISE

## LAURA

The slow, rhythmic thud … thud …thud of Alec's heart beneath my cheek woke me. I must have dozed off soon after our last bout of sex, as it was still dark outside. I sighed contentedly and angled my head to look up at him. 'I like your idea of "vigorous exercise."'

He chuckled, and my head bounced on his chest. 'Have I tired you out enough?'

'Perfectly.' How was it possible that whenever we had sex, he was able to bring me to new heights? Angle his hips in such a way that he hit my G-spot every time, making me cry out in bliss? And just as I floated back from my own personal nirvana, he'd do it again? How much pleasure could a girl take? A lot. I smiled.

He had drunk one of the blood vials before he'd climbed into bed. I knew he did it to avoid taking my blood during sex, but oddly enough, I missed his bite. Had it been my imagination, or did it induce more powerful orgasms? Still, I was wonderfully sated.

Alec smoothed the hair from my face and kissed the tip of my nose. 'You should be asleep.'

I kissed his warm, firm lips, revelling in his taste, his scent: musk, cinnamon and cedarwood. 'It's probably the jetlag. I'll try to stay awake all day and get to bed early tonight. Since everyone's daywalking now, I don't need to be a night owl. Besides, I promised to see daylight with Kari. She's so excited.'

His eyes warmed. 'She deserves to be. And how else could I have her with you when I can't be?'

A thought occurred to me. 'What about the servants?'

His eyebrows shot upwards. 'How do you mean?'

'Well, what if, somehow … Rasputin's able to get to them? Mesmerise them.'

'We would know if any one of them posed a danger. Did you notice the rings the Brethren staff wear?' I shook my head. 'They're identical to Luc's – green serpent eyes. He had them made soon after the First Rebellion in the tenth century. They swear an oath of fealty on the ring. Should any prove disloyal, the ring betrays them – its eyes light up. On Luc's ring, too. That way he knows there's a traitor in our midst.'

'But he still has to find who it is. Does he … what? … round them all up and check which one of them has a glowing green hand?'

'Yes. But I would hope the others would notice and inform either Luc or me first.' He threw one arm behind his head while with the other played with the strands of my hair.

'What about the human servants? They come and go from the village. He could mesmerise them into attacking the chateau. And what about the Thierrys?'

'The Thierrys are loyal. The family fought with Luc in the Crusades and have faithfully stood by our clan in both rebellions.'

'But they're still human. Do they visit the village often?'

His brows wrinkled. 'I suppose they do. Judith would know about that kind of thing.' For a second or two, he nibbled on his lower lip. 'Good point, though. Rasputin can't get into the chateau, but the village.... There are two-thousand souls in D'Antonville. Even using both our rings, we couldn't get through the whole population in time. And the other problem is, only a handful of families know about us.'

'We have to do something.'

'Let me think.' He brought a lock of my hair to his mouth and ran it along his lips, gaze on my face.

I sat up. 'I may know a way.' Alec dropped my hair and cupped my breasts, his thumbs circling my nipples, sending ripples of desire shooting through me. 'You're distracting.'

'It's mutual.' His eyes darkened.

I needed to get him back on track and ignore the delicious sensations rising in me. 'Jen, Kari and I will go down to the village to shop, and I could casually start a conversation about Rasputin. If I raised my ring, like this' —I wriggled my hand in front of my face— 'after I've got their attention and say something like, "Whatever Rasputin tells you, do not do it". In French, of course.'

'Laura, even trying that, you wouldn't get through more than a dozen or so people. Although, saying that has given me an idea.'

'I thought of it first.'

His mouth twitched. 'All credit's yours, darling.' He leaned forward and kissed me, long and deep, his tongue teasing mine as his thumb and forefingers pinched my taut nipples. In a blink, he'd rolled me beneath him. '*If* Rasputin makes it here,' —he dropped a kiss on my breast—'which I doubt' —he kissed my other breast— 'he'd choose the most important people to mesmerise; those in authority, like the police, the mayor, local councillors. That's what I'd do.' He dipped his tongue into my navel.

It was getting harder to concentrate. 'Luc probably knows them. Could we invite them to dinner and do it then?'

He looked up through hooded eyes. 'Too short notice. I'll need to go to them.'

'Why not the both of us? Two rings would work faster than one.'

'Too dangerous.' He smiled, and, moving further down, lowered his head between my legs.

'But … oh!' After that, any argument became impossible.

# CHAPTER 13 - NIGHT FORAY

**ALEC**

Laura slept, eyes fluttering in a dream, breasts slowly rising and falling in rhythm with her breathing. I longed to lie here, just listening and watching her sleep. But there wasn't time. Her idea to use the serpent ring to protect the villagers from Rasputin's mind control was inspired. I needed to test it. If I could do so tonight and it worked, there'd be no need for her to accompany me later. She was safer in the chateau.

Inhaling her honey and jasmine scent, I dropped a kiss on her brow. I dressed and then called Kari to watch over Laura until I got back. I left Kari curled up on the sofa leafing through a magazine. Laura was the most important thing in my life – the reason for my existence – and I felt better knowing Kari was with her.

Luc and Marcus were still in Luc's office when I walked in.

'Did you manage to contact everyone?' I asked.

'Yep.' Luc stretched back in his chair and rubbed his face. 'Everyone's coming. If only for the blood vials.'

Marcus sat on the leather sofa, one leg crossed over the other. 'So close. So damn close and this happens.'

I sat next to him. 'Laura reminded me of something – the villagers.'

'What about them?' He turned toward me, an eyebrow raised.

'How safe are they? You considered that?' I knew I had Luc's attention, too. 'Either Rasputin uses them against us, or he slaughters them all in reprisal.'

'Unfortunately, gone are the days when they could run here for safety. The population's grown.' Luc stood and paced. 'Even so, how long could we protect them here?'

He had a point. There was no way the chateau could accommodate the whole village, not even the original D'Antonville families, of whom there were a few hundred. We had no idea when an attack would come. Could we ask them to desert their shops, businesses or employment till the danger passed? It wasn't feasible.

'I doubt Rasputin will even get this far. His master needs him,' Marcus said, then added, 'Terentius has asked my permission to go after Timur. I said, yes.'

Terens was good, but not infallible. 'We can't rely on Terens. Anything can go wrong. We need our own plan. Listen to Laura's good suggestion,' I said as I went over to the computer to locate the list of the original D'Antonville inhabitants. 'To use the serpent ring to guard their minds from mesmerisation.'

Luc stopped pacing and came toward me. 'On several-thousand people? That's impossible! You know how long that would take?'

'I believe Alec has something else in mind.' Marcus leaned forward and clasped his hands on his knees. 'Am I right?' I admired his keen perception.

'Look at this list of names.' I pointed to the screen. 'D'Antonville's leading citizens and all descended from the First Families.'

Beneath the list lay a map of the village with the location of each original D'Antonvilles highlighted: the Mayor, police chief, school principal, the local Catholic priest and a few business owners.

Marcus stood and joined us. 'Their fathers served on my estate when this land was known as Gaul. Never once has their loyalty failed. Damned if I leave them to Timur and his minions.'

'That's what I thought.'

'So what's your idea?' Marcus looked at me keenly, although I had the notion he knew exactly what I was about to suggest. His soldier's mind would already be weighing up the pros and cons of the situation.

'How do you feel about a little night reconnaissance?'

He smiled. Luc didn't. 'The ring worked for us, but humans?'

'We don't try, we'll never know,' I said. 'And it's not just the ring I want to use, but white-oak. Get them to carry it in some form – bullets, daggers, splinters hidden in jewellery.' I thought of Timur's wolf's-head rings. 'Things kids can carry around their neck or in their pockets.' At least they could defend themselves, and since our clan was immune to its dangers, it posed no threat to us.

'And then what? Play Santa Claus, visit each one, wake them from sleep and tell them to look into the eyes of the serpent? And where would we get all that white oak? Those Rebels' rings we confiscated are for our use alone. Ahhh!' He waved his hand in the air and strode to the other end of the room. He stood, hands behind his back staring at a photograph on the wall. It was the hospital at Abbeville where we'd been stationed during The Great War. I remembered him taking it – a few weeks before he'd turned me.

Then the idea came to me. It was so simple, and it could possibly work. 'Let's scatter powdered white-oak into the village water supply.'

A sufficient amount emptied into the village reservoir would be diluted as to be almost tasteless to humans, but still deadly to vampires. The only problem I could see was with the Brethren staff.

Until this emergency passed, they would have to feed either from blood-bags or outside the village.

Luc looked back over his shoulder at me. 'How much wood would you need to grind down?'

I did a quick mental calculation. 'A kilo should do.'

'What about the staff?'

'Feed in the next town or stick to blood-bags. There's an ample supply here.'

He turned, a faint smile on his lips. 'That could work. But … I want to know for sure before we go contaminating the water supply. We need to test it first.'

Not on anyone here, I hoped. 'There mightn't be time for that, Luc, and I don't want to send any of the men out to hunt down a Rebel. I reckon a small amount of powered white-oak scattered into the reservoir will do the trick. That way we can protect not only the First Families, but the whole village.'

'What say you?' he turned toward Marcus.

'Only wish I'd thought of it myself.' Marcus grinned and slapped me on the back.

I hoped the villagers would be as agreeable. 'Let's start with the mayor. That way we only scare one person tonight. Get him to contact the others to assemble at his house. Once we explain the situation—'

'They'll probably be only too happy to head out into the woods and collect the stuff for us,' Marcus added.

Luc rubbed his chin. 'Short notice, isn't it?'

'We've done it before. June 1940. Remember?'

Luc smiled grimly. 'Ah, yes. The German staff officers.'

I'd been living in Paris when the Germans invaded. Luc had flown out from Sydney, worried about the threat to the chateau. The Nazis had planned on confiscating it for their own use. I was with the Resistance at the time and couldn't join him. It was later I'd found out that he'd killed the Nazi delegation and placed extra wards around the estate to hide the villagers in case of a German reprisal. It had remained in place until after the war.

'All right. Let's do it,' he said.

* * *

The three of us stood outside the mayor's house. I'd never met the man, or any heads of the First Families since becoming princeps, and that had been more than a generation ago.

At this time of night, we didn't expect anyone to be about, especially in the dead of winter. There were no shops at this end of the village, only high dry-stone walls hiding private gardens and two-to-three storey houses. A light frost covered the ground, amplifying the crunch of our footsteps.

We leapt up and over the balcony. Luc peered through the glass doors. 'That man's snores would wake the dead. No wonder his wife sleeps in a separate room.'

I heard only one heartbeat coming from the room, and since I didn't really know the man, assumed he was either widowed or divorced. Extending my senses, I heard two different heartbeats coming from the other end of the house. His wife and child?

'Sure this is the right room?' I asked Luc. Men weren't the only ones who snored.

'Know his scent: garlic and Camembert.'

I tried not to chortle. What other scent would one expect from a rural Frenchman?

Luc pried the door open. Marcus touched his shoulder. 'Let me. It's been a long time, and I need to get back into the habit.' He smiled at his pun. Having lived in a monastery for over a millennia hadn't dulled his sense of humour, nor his soldierly skills.

Luc stepped aside as Marcus went to the man's bedside. Leaning down, he whispered in his ear, 'Wake up. Seigneur needs you.'

'His servant answers,' the man slurred in his sleep.

A summons. Is that what he'd used in 1940? I glanced at Luc. Why hadn't he told me about this? Obviously it was important enough to be passed down from generation to generation among the First Families, until it was ingrained into their subconscious, but not important enough to tell me? My hands clenched.

The man stirred and slowly opened his eyes then jerked back in shock. 'Sieur Marcus?'

'Be calm, Bouchard. Get dressed and summon the others,' Marcus said.

He groped around his bedside table and found his glasses. 'Has something happened? Is something wrong?'

'All will be revealed when the others get here.'

Bouchard switched on the light, rose hastily and threw on his dressing gown. He stopped, eyes wide behind his spectacles, on seeing Luc and me. 'Milord Lucien?' For an instant his gaze dropped to my hand. 'Milord Princeps?'

I nodded and extended my hand. 'Alec Munro.'

He bowed his head in deference. 'An honour to meet you, milord. We knew the family had returned, from the flag. But to see Sieur Marcus....' He sat on the edge of the bed, mouth open, staring up at him without blinking.

'There's not much time.' Luc grabbed the phone from the bedside table and handed it to him. 'We'll be in the living room.'

'Don't take too long, Bouchard.' Marcus clapped him on the shoulder.

The man blinked. 'Of course, of course … my house is yours!'

Luc seemed to know his way around and led us into the living room. While we waited, he poured himself a glass of brandy. 'Bouchard's collection is almost as good as mine. Must commend him.'

Marcus perused Bouchard's books and took one down from the shelf.

I sat in one armchair; Luc took another. 'Why didn't you tell me about the Summons?' I asked.

He held the brandy glass at eye level and gazed at me through the amber liquid. 'My apologies. It was an oversight. Hadn't been used in years, and I ... forgot.'

I took a deep breath. Luc rarely admitted to any wrong doing, let alone a so-called oversight. Had it been deliberate? I was meant to be princeps, yet in reality, Luc still ruled. He'd turned me to save my life, but it had also been a lucky break for him. Only I could help end the family curse – lucky me. If he hadn't transformed me when he did, he would have had to eventually. As a human, I wouldn't have lived long enough to give Laura the long-awaited child. So making me princeps was for his convenience, not mine. I'd still been a juvenile. I shouldn't have held any office.

The Brethren knew who the real power behind the throne was.

'From now on, Luc, I want to know everything. So while we're waiting, is there anything else you may have forgotten to tell me?'

Over the rim of the glass, his eyes narrowed. Not that I cared. 'No,' he said.

'The lad's got a point.' Marcus placed the book he'd been reading back on the shelf. 'He's princeps in is his own right now. Has been since the Pledging. He should know these things.'

Luc downed the rest of his brandy. 'I said it was an oversight.'

'I hope so.' He was my sire, and I respected him for that, but Luc had been princeps for more than a millennia and a half before I was born. It must be hard for him to let go, especially as Laura was his child.

He slammed the empty glass onto the coffee table. 'Are you saying I'm hiding something from you?' To my surprise, the glass didn't shatter.

'No, Luc. What I'm saying is, it's time you let me in on everything. Let me do the job on my own. I can't do that if you conceal things from me and continue to call the shots. I'm not a juvenile ... nor your puppet.'

'You were never my puppet.' He sat back again and turned his face toward the window.

'No? If I'd refused to take the office, what would you have done? Punished me for defying my sire?'

Luc's gaze pierced me. 'I have too much respect for you to have done anything of the sort. You know that.' He stabbed the air with his finger. 'But without me, you would never have been accepted by the Elders or leading Brethren. I had to be there, behind you.'

'Of course you did. You engineered the whole damn thing! I never wanted it. But that's beside the point now. Your intervention is no longer necessary.'

Luc exhaled and dropped his hand, rose and strode to the window. I waited for some response – an argument even – but he stood there, hands in pockets, and stared out. The muscle in his jaw ticked. Luc was so used to being in control that even a hint about him relinquishing any part was seen as a challenge to his authority. Yes, he made me princeps and I'd claimed it at the Pledging. Seems I needed to make it clearer.

Marcus folded his arms across his chest and glanced from me to Luc. 'The finest commander is the one who leads in battle and trusts his men to win the war. It's time you learnt to trust, Luc.'

'I trust my men,' he threw back over his shoulder.

'When you place one in a position of power, trust him to execute the office.'

The silence between us stretched. I heard Bouchard speaking on the phone to the heads of the First Families, and the opening and closing of cabinet doors. Presumably he was dressing at the same time. The other two occupants of the house slept on.

Luc nodded and turned to face me. 'You've earned it. I won't interfere again.' I stood and extended my hand. We shook. It was a hell of a concession for him to make. But it was about time. 'I'll ask first.'

Marcus smiled.

Bouchard's scent tickled my nostrils before I heard the heavy thud of his footsteps coming down the carpeted stairs. His silhouette appeared on the other side of the frosted glass doors that closed off the living room from the hallway. He knocked – a few light taps.

'Bouchard, it's your house. You don't need to knock,' Marcus said.

He came in, a nervous grin on his face. 'Milords, this is an honour. Can I get you … ah, I see you have sampled my Janneau Armagnac, Milord Lucien.'

'An excellent drop. I commend you. May I?' Luc poured another glass.

Bouchard had dressed in a suit. He adjusted his tie and several times smoothed down his bed-ruffled hair. As Marcus indicated for him to be seated, a number of cars pulled up outside.

'They're here,' I said. 'Best if you opened the door, Bouchard.' Surely they knew we could hear their whispered greetings and hushed questions between them?

'Yes, yes. Please excuse me.' He jumped up and bumped into the glass on his way out.

'Poor bugger's scared shitless,' Luc said.

'Do you blame him?' I added.

A group of about eight men and two women filed into the room. Sleep still shadowed their faces; a few yawned, others tried to rub the tiredness from their eyes. All were dressed in suits, except for one – Morrel, the Police Chief. He was in uniform. It showed the honour they accorded us. Each inclined their heads in greeting.

I glanced at Marcus and Luc. Both gave me a barely perceptible nod. 'Ladies and gentlemen, please excuse the late hour, and thank you for coming at such short notice.'

'It must be an emergency, milord,' Morrel said as he removed his cap and tucked it under his arm. Keen blue eyes surveyed us. 'Last occasion we received such a summons was in my grandfather's time, during the war.'

'Let's hope this is the last.' I indicated for them to be seated. 'I assume you're aware of what's been happening in our world?'

They exchanged glances before Bouchard spoke. 'We know of the proscriptions. It's on the website … and the staff keep us informed. I also saw Count Timur's video before it was taken down, and I alerted the others.'

'Good man,' Marcus muttered.

'You've been collecting Ingenii blood?' Madame Giscard, the principal of the local school, was the last of her family line. She'd never married or had children. With her eventual death, another one of the First Families would be extinguished.

'For an emergency such as this,' I answered before Luc could. The muscle ticked in the side of his jaw again.

'How much danger are we in?' Morrel asked.

'At this stage, it's hard to know.' I explained the situation with Rasputin. Their eyes widened on hearing his name. One or two repeated it several times and shook their heads.

'Incredible,' one of them muttered.

'In that case, wouldn't it be sensible to move the Ingenii blood somewhere else, if that's what they're after?' another suggested.

'Impossible.' Luc poured himself yet another glass.

'We can't relocate the entire village, and we certainly wouldn't all fit into the chateau.' Morrel stood and took a step toward me. 'That's why you called us, isn't it? What's the plan?'

I liked Morrel. Taking his cue, I addressed each one in turn. 'You are the most prominent people in the village. You have influence that Rasputin can use to his advantage. That's why you need to be protected. There's a chance he may come here – unless our men get to him first.' I raised the serpent ring. 'You all know what this is. It has the ability to protect your minds from mesmerisation.'

'How?' One of them asked.

'A brief flash of light from the serpent's eyes.'

'Is it safe?' another asked.

I didn't blame him for his caution. 'I've used it on myself and our men. It won't hurt you.'

'Milord Luc, couldn't you place wards around the village again, as you did during the war?' Bouchard asked.

Luc shook his head. 'Times were different. The town was much smaller and mostly made up of First Families. Not anymore.'

'True. The village has grown. More outsiders.' Morrel twirled the cap in his hands.

'Most of the school's enrolment come from these. The parents travel to Orange or Avignon for work. Any type of magical protective ward would be impractical, but we must protect the children.' Madame Giscard rose and helped herself to Bouchard's brandy. 'I need a drop myself.'

'You can't protect the village ... at all?' Bouchard spread his hands in appeal.

There was no hiding the scent of fear in the room. Even without Rasputin, the Rebels could wipe out the entire village just for the sake of it, but at least we could ensure the villagers were armed against the Rebels.

'I believe we can. Firstly we need to guard your minds from a Rebel attack, and secondly to arm you with the only effective weapon against our kind: white-oak.'

Bouchard's eyebrows shot upwards. 'Isn't that outlawed?'

'We're re-examining that. The Rebels are in possession of white-oak hidden within a ring.' I removed the wolf's-head ring from my finger and triggered the deadly spike.

'Very clever,' Morrel said and held out his hand. I dropped the ring into his palm. He examined it from all sides with the others crowding around for a closer look. 'How soon are we to expect an attack?' he asked before handing it back.

'Difficult to say. They may not even come to the village.'

'Pray God they don't,' Bouchard whispered and wiped his brow with a handkerchief.

The others nodded.

'There are several white oaks in the forest outside the estate. I could easily organise the children to gather up fallen twigs and branches.' Madame Giscard's eyes lit up at the prospect. 'We could make it a craft project: fairy wands for the girls … swords for the boys? Let me work on it.' I sensed she felt the need to maintain a semblance of control, to avoid the impression of helplessness.

'Good idea,' I said. 'Make sure all the First Families are given a supply. Until this emergency passes, you need to protect yourselves.'

'What about outsiders?' Bouchard asked.

What I was about to tell them might not sit well with some. But it was the best hope they had. 'I intend spreading a small amount of powdered white-oak into the village water supply. It's harmless to humans and tasteless. But to any vampire who tries to take a bite out of you, it'll be lethal.'

After a moment's silence, they began to argue among themselves.

'What if someone has a nasty reaction to the stuff?' one asked.

'If they die, they'll sue the council!' Bouchard buried his head in his hands.

Maybe I should've just dumped the stuff into the water without telling them. 'It's the best solution.' I stared at each in turn. 'Take it or leave it.'

'We'll take it,' Morrel said. 'It's easier to blame it on accidental water contamination – there are always bits of branches and twigs falling into the canal – than it is to explain away deaths caused by vampire attack.'

'It's settled then. Now, look up here.' I raised the serpent ring.

'Wait!' Bouchard called out. 'When will you pour the white-oak powder into the canal?'

There wasn't much left of tonight. 'Later today.'

'What if someone sees you?'

Morrel sighed loudly. 'I'll put up a roadblock to stop any cars. Besides' —he turned to face Bouchard— 'who goes there at this time of year?'

Good thing it was winter and the temperature rarely dropped low enough to freeze the water – no ice-skaters as witnesses. 'Ready?' I asked again.

Several pairs of human eyes focused on the ring. As before, a warm sensation ran the length of my finger. There was a brief flash of red light. They blinked and gazed around at one another.

'How do we know if it's worked?' Morrel asked.

'Let's test it, shall we?' Marcus approached Bouchard and tilted his face toward his own.

Good choice. He appeared the most susceptible to mesmerisation. A smile tugged at Marcus's mouth. 'Bouchard, you are to remove all your clothes and stand naked in front of us.'

Morrel snorted, and Madame Giscard slapped him on the upper arm.

Bouchard's eyes widened, his ruddy cheeks turning an even brighter shade of red. 'Milord Marcus! Certainly not!'

'See? It works.' Marcus leant against the bookshelf again.

'Then I'm satisfied.' Morrel rose from the sofa he'd been sharing with the others and placed the cap on his head. 'I'll have that roadblock set up as soon as I get to work.'

We shook hands, and he left, the others following. Luc, Marcus and I did the same. My last glimpse of Bouchard was of him trudging up the stairs muttering to himself and clutching his bottle of Janneau Armagnac.

## CHAPTER 14 – SUNSHINE AND BATHTUBS

**LAURA**

I jumped. Kari sat cross-legged on the end of my bed. 'Did I wake you? Princi told me not to.' She was certainly taking her role as my bodyguard seriously.

Alec's side of the bed was barely cold, so she couldn't have been waiting long. The heavy drapes blocked out the light, but from the way Kari kept glancing at them, I guessed it must be dawn or close to it.

'Is it daylight?' I asked. She smiled and clapped. She was waiting for me rather than go out on her own. I was touched. 'Pass me my robe.' It was draped over a chair. I flung it on and went to the closet. 'Give me a minute, Kari. It's freezing out there.'

It didn't take me long to dress warmly. Kari hopped from foot to foot, her eyes wide and bright. 'Ready?'

She nodded, and together we opened the drapes.

Light flooded the room and alighted on Kari. She tensed and stepped back. I took her hand and placed it in the path of a sunbeam. 'Look, no burns.'

She twirled her hand and turned it palm upwards. 'It's warm.' A grin lit her pixie face.

'C'mon.' I led her onto the balcony. The entire estate spread out before us. Frost covered the ground and glistened like crystal in the sharp morning light.

Step-by-step, Kari came out into the light. As if in prayer, she closed her eyes and raised her arms and face toward the sun. 'Look at me, Laura. I'm in the sun. I'm in the sun!'

I stood back as she spun and twirled and laughed. The short-sleeved, knee-length dress she wore made me shiver just to look at it. But I'm sure the only thing Kari felt was elation. She grabbed my hands and spun me around with her on the balcony in the freezing morning air. We probably looked like a couple of loonies, yet how could I not laugh along?

Next instant, Kari vaulted over the railing. 'See you after breakfast,' I called after her and turned to go back into the warmth of my suite when a small movement in the garden caught my eye. It wasn't any of the prefects. Madame Thierry stood there, smiling after Kari. That woman must exist on only a few hours sleep! How did she know to be here at just this time?

Kari saw her and skipped to her side. 'Regardez-moi madame!' She grasped her hands and twirled her around.

'Comment-est ce possible, mon chouchou?' If I hadn't heard her use such a sweet term of endearment for Kari, I would've never guessed Madame Thierry had a soft side.

'Il est un cadeau du princeps. Est-il pas marveilleux?' Kari's excitement was infectious, and madame laughed, too.

She gave her a wave as Kari disappeared into the distance then stood watching before turning on her heel to re-enter the house. I was about to step back into the warmth of my suite when Judy appeared. The beatific smile Madame Thierry had worn only a second before dissolved, and her eyes took on a hard, cold edge, as icy as the frost on the ground. The change was astonishing, disconcerting even.

Rugged up in coat, boots and walking cane, Judy looked set for a morning stroll. 'Bonne matin, madame….' Her rapid burst of French was too quick for me, but she passed a sheet of paper to the housekeeper before continuing down the drive.

Madame Thierry stood there, lips thinned. She crushed the paper in her hand and threw it into the bushes as she re-entered the house.

I shook my head, amazed. Madame Thierry's actions were nothing short of contemptuous. *Must tell Judy when I see her.* I stepped back into the warmth of my suite and closed the doors when a strong pair of arms encircled me from behind.

'You smell delicious in the morning.' Alec's lips grazed the side of my neck. 'Taste delicious, too.'

Madame Thierry was forgotten.

I leaned back into him and just as quickly lurched out of his arms. 'You're cold. Where've you been?'

'A hot bath might remedy that.' His eyes darkened, and a wolfish grin appeared on his face.

I'd never showered, let alone bathed, with a man before, and the idea of doing so with Alec sent warm ripples of pleasure through me. The humungous Roman bath in our suite really should be experienced.

'With bubbles or without?' I smiled, and turning in the direction of the ensuite, slowly shed my clothes on the way.

I heard his quick intake of breath. Next minute, I was whisked off my feet and carried into the magnificent bathroom. Early morning sunshine bathed the room, but it wasn't strong enough to melt the lacy frame of frost etched around the outside of the windows. Some of the ice crystals caught the sun, creating tiny rainbows that danced on the corner of the ceiling and along the walls.

The indoor heating warmed both floor and bath, making it more magical.

Alec lowered me to my feet, removed his shirt – which had warmed up a little –and wrapped it around me. Before I had a chance to admire his muscled torso, he lowered his head and kissed me. The delectable sensation of his lips on mine, his tongue exploring, teasing and ravishing mine, made my toes curl, let alone what it did to the rest of me. I inhaled his scent, letting it suffuse my senses and merge into every cell in my body until I felt I was drowning in him.

His heart beat strongly against my breasts, faster than usual. He gripped my buttocks and squeezed. A sigh escaped his lips. 'I can't get enough of you,' he breathed. 'You're like a drug.'

I tightened my arms around his neck and pressed myself even closer. My lips were going numb, my tongue so sensitive, every nerve ending was on fire, yet I couldn't stop either. I was lost in him, and the next time I opened my eyes, Alec's eyes were so dark, I saw my own reflection in them. He was breathing hard, and the frost on the windows had melted.

'You still want bubbles?' he asked. It was the last thing I expected him to say.

'Um....'

'Because I want to see all of you, not that frothy stuff.'

'Okay. It's fine by me.'

He released me long enough to turn on the taps and strip down. I would never tire of admiring his body – firm, taut muscles; strong thighs, and every accoutrement any woman could possibly want in a man. And he was all mine.

Steam rose from the Roman-style bathtub. Alec lowered his shirt from my shoulders, picked me up, trod the two steps up to the tub and gently lowered me into it. He climbed in behind me and pulled me back against his chest. The tub was long enough for us both to stretch out comfortably. With one arm, he covered my breasts; his other hand rubbed my belly where our baby grew. Slowly he moved downwards, parted my thighs and massaged my core. I threw my head back against his chest and revelled in my growing pleasure. His arm about me tightened as his fingers increased their rhythm. Soon I was moaning and whimpering, causing the water to slosh around us as I rode his fingers to my climax.

I cried aloud as I came and slumped back against him as the blissful wave washed over me. Still floating on my cloud, I felt Alec kiss the top of my head. I went to turn around and straddle him, but he stopped me. 'No. That's my thanks for your idea. It worked.'

'To use the ring? Of course it would.' I smiled smugly up at him.

'You sound just like your father.'

'I'll take that as a compliment.'

He chuckled. 'It is, my darling.' I loved to hear the Scottish lilt in his speech. He'd been only fifteen when his family had emigrated from Scotland to Australia, and although his accent was now Australian, the occasional Scottish burr reappeared.

The water temperature was perfect. As the steam wafted around us, I leaned my head against his chest and closed my eyes – and felt his hardness push into my back. Alec hadn't had his own release.

Turning around, I straddled him before he could stop me.

'No, it's okay.' It was obvious it wasn't, from the way he gritted his teeth. I could almost hear them grinding.

I eyed him suspiciously. 'Is this in any way related to you taking my brilliant idea and running off with it on your own?'

'No ... not entirely.'

'I should make you suffer for that.' I rubbed myself along his swollen length, enjoying the way he sucked in a shaky breath. How long should I make him squirm? I rubbed against him again and languidly traced the outline of his sword and serpent tattoo on his chest with the tip of my tongue. Did he just moan?

'Isn't that what you're doing?' he groaned.

'Lucky for you I can't stand to see a creature in pain.' I wasn't about to tell him how desperately I wanted him inside me. I lowered myself onto his hardness, clasped his face between my hands and kissed him deeply.

His hands gripped my hips as he thrust into me, spilling more water from the tub, sending it cascading down over the marble steps.

He closed his eyes and grunted as my body took all of him. My muscles tingled, tightened. I only needed ... one more ... thrust.... Ah! I threw my head back as the glorious release shuddered through me.

Alec let out a long sigh and then relaxed. I collapsed on top of him, his chest heaving in time with my own.

'Don't think this lets you off the hook,' I said.

He chuckled and turned on the hot tap. Just as well. Half the water was gone, and my butt was getting cold. Alec eased me off him and pulled me back against his chest. He cupped my breasts to keep them warm as the tub slowly filled with steaming water.

'Tell me how it all went. Who'd you use the serpent ring on?'

'The heads of all the First Families.'

'First Families?'

'Descendants of Marcus's household – former slaves he'd freed. They chose to remain on his estate as paid servants. When he later joined the monastery, their children and grandchildren down the line stuck with Luc. It was they who founded the village.'

'So how many of them are there?' After nearly two-thousand years in the same place and with the same people, wouldn't there be a problem with inbreeding?

'Only about eight families are left. The others either left or died out. They tend to hold the official positions – passed down from father to son, or daughters nowadays. Some of them still work on the estate.' He mentioned names and their standing in the village, and their reaction to having white-oak dust sprinkled into the village water supply.

I laughed when he mentioned the mayor's fear about being sued. 'Poor guy. I can kind of understand his worry.'

'It won't happen,' Alec said.

'So that's why you felt so cold when you came in – you were out in the open dumping stuff into the water supply.' His clothes were almost frozen, but of course he hadn't felt it. Since my coming-of-age, I'd begun to develop some vampire characteristics, such as extra hearing and sight. Whether immunity to hot and cold would be one of them, I would have to wait and see. Fangs and a taste for human blood? Luc assured me I wouldn't, though he wasn't always right.

'It was still dark enough not to be seen,' he said. 'But it's done. Luc's notified the staff not to feed from the locals until this rebellion is put down.'

'Nice to know others have brilliant ideas, not just me.' I had visions of little mounds of crystalline dust decorating street corners and dark alleys should the Rebels try feeding from people in the village – if and when the attack actually came.

He chuckled again, closed his eyes and lay back, arms resting on the sides of the tub. I scooted to the opposite side so I could get a full view of him. Our toes just touched. I wriggled mine against his. He cracked a smile from full lips that always left me trembling. Water glistened on his tattoo, and I followed the trail of one drop as it slid languidly down his body. I swallowed. He was, indeed, the most beautiful man I had ever seen.

Light climbed higher on the windows and slanted along the walls. My mind floated. Soon Jenny would be awake – if she wasn't already. And what valleys and forests was Kari roaming? Another image popped into my head – Alec and I on the beach; he was bouncing a beautiful little baby girl on his knee. She had dark hair, like him, and blue eyes. He laughed as she giggled. And there was I, the sun behind me casting a golden halo around my head. I, too, was laughing. It was so perfect, and so anticipated – the curse lifted and our child, free. I sighed.

Alec's eyes flicked open, and the vision dissolved. 'I know.'

I glanced at my ring. Yep, it was glowing, as it always did whenever we were together. And it was sharing my thoughts more and more. 'How is the ring doing that when I'm not actively trying?'

'What did you see?' he asked. I described the beach scene. 'Those were my thoughts.'

That's why it popped into my head from nowhere! I must have grinned from ear to ear. Who would've thought this big, bad vampire was such a family man, who looked forward to playing with his baby? A blue-eyed little girl. How could I not love this man?

I surged forward, wrapped my arms around his neck and kissed him. From the other room, came a knock on the door.

'Petite dejeuner, milord et milady,' said a woman's voice.

Breakfast. It must be the day staff. They were human. 'Room service?'

'Judith must have organised it. Stay here. I'll get it.' He climbed out, went to one of the wall cabinets and pulled out a bathrobe.

I leaned my elbows on the side of the tub and enjoyed the view. What a shame to cover up such a delectable derriere.

He laughed, looked back at me and shook his head. 'As I remember, I promised I'd teach you how to use that dagger Lucinda gave you,' he said as he walked out.

And more sword lessons, too. I heard him thanking the household staff, and then the rattle of a trolley being wheeled in. I was out of the tub within a second then draped a robe around me from the same cabinet and walked into our bedroom.

It was indeed a trolley, and the aromas that rose from beneath the covered plates were mouthwatering – warm croissants, berry jam, a mix of cheeses, and hot coffee.

Alec enjoyed the coffee, and, while I ate, he outlined the plans for the day. 'I'll be ordering an ultrasound machine so I can monitor the baby's progress from here. I don't want you in a hospital. Jake's going to help out.'

Okay, I could handle that. I had complete trust in Alec. And it still felt so far away. It'd be another two to three months before I would even start to show. When the time came, I knew I'd be in good hands. Right now there were other concerns, a key one being my friend across the hall.

'Right after breakfast, I'll go see Jen.' Was she over jetlag? Well, I would soon find out.

I knocked on her door. No answer. I knocked again. Still no answer. She can't still be asleep, can she? I checked my watch. It was after eight.

'Jen?' Silence. 'Jen, it's me. Open up.' The door was locked.

Alec came up behind me and knocked more loudly. Nothing. 'Want me to open it?'

He would have to break the lock to do that, but I didn't care. Was Jenny okay? Did she have an accident in the bath? Was she lying unconscious…? My mouth went dry.

'Yes.'

Alec forced the door. Her suite was a similar layout to ours. The bed was made and had not been slept in. My stomach dropped. I ran into the bathroom and breathed a temporary sigh of relief to find she wasn't lying on the floor unconscious. Or fallen asleep in the bath and drowned. And the balcony doors were locked from the inside.

My heart raced.

# CHAPTER 15 – DAGGERS

**LAURA**

'Alec, where is she?' I spun around, expecting her to appear.

He checked the cabinets. 'Her clothes are here, so she can't have gone. She has to be somewhere in the chateau.'

I stood in the centre of the suite, hands on hips, completely at a loss. 'If she hasn't slept here...?

Alec went to the door and sniffed. His brow creased. 'You know her better that I do.' That was an interesting statement. 'Does she ... easily form attachments?'

I had a suspicion. 'You mean does she fall in love easily? Yeah.'

Her last attachment left her for another woman. I was there to pick up the pieces. Took her ages to get over him. And now it looked like she'd fallen for Terens.

'Mmm.... In that case you need to know that Terens has gone. Went after Timur.'

'Oh no.' I briefly closed my eyes. Knowing that Terens would be here was probably one of the factors that swayed her into coming with us, besides her own danger, of course. And he'd left to chase after his enemy.

'Let's find her, then,' he said.

'How?' This place was huge. I could listen out for her heartbeat, but it would simply merge with all the others, since the human staff were on duty.

'I think I may know where she is. This way.' He took my hand, and we walked down the corridor.

'That's right, I forgot. You can follow her scent.'

'It wasn't her scent I picked up.'

My stomach dropped, and, as always, the worst-case scenario raced through my mind – she had been taken. But how would an enemy get in? Weren't we meant to be safe here? 'Please don't tell me—'

'She's safe.'

We went past the grand staircase to the other wing of the house, until we reached the end of the hall. He stopped in front of a white door, with a bronze plaque on which was engraved a pair of crossed swords. My stomach did a sharp twist as I guessed to whom this room belonged.

Alec closed his eyes and inhaled. 'She's in there.'

'Terens's room?'

He didn't say anything. He didn't have to.

I knocked. Silence. She was probably still asleep. Regardless, I needed to make sure she was okay. The door was unlocked when I turned the handle. The room was dark, yet I could see clearly, and her steady heartbeat came from the bedroom. When I tiptoed in, she was curled up in Terens's bed, the evidence of shed tears in the red circles beneath her eyes. A half-screwed up sheet of paper stuck out from beneath the fold of the feather quilt.

It was a note. Should I, shouldn't I read it? Was this the cause of Jenny's distress? I read it and passed it to Alec. It was from Terens.

Either he'd handed it to her, or he'd slipped it under her door. My guess was the latter, and she'd gone looking for him.

'I'll go. She'll be needing you when she wakes.' He kissed my cheek and left. So much for emotional support.

'Jen,' I whispered.

The note I placed on the bedside table, while I sat in a chair and waited for her to wake. It wasn't long. She stirred and opened her eyes, blinked a few times before closing them again.

'Jen?'

'I'm an idiot,' she mumbled from beneath the covers.

'No, you're not.'

She released a long breath. 'Only an idiot falls for the wrong guy.'

I rose from the seat. 'Move over.'

Three people could have slept comfortably in Terens's bed, and I recalled that Kari occasionally referred to him as Sexy Terry. I could imagine how many women had occupied this bed. And now Jenny lay in it.

She wriggled slowly to one side. 'How did you know I was here?'

'Alec picked up Terens's scent at your door.'

She made a sniffling noise. Her back faced me as I scooted alongside. 'He didn't have the guts to tell me personally. Shoved a note under my door.' Her hand reached out, groping for it. 'Where is it? I had it with me.'

'It's on the bedside table, Jen. I … uh … saw it.'

She rolled around to face me. 'Okay, fine. Saves me repeating it.'

This was going to be tricky. 'It was considerate of him to leave you a note. He didn't have to, you know. I mean, you've only known each other a few days, and he's….' He had a reputation as a playboy and had had two, maybe three, women in bed with him – at the same time. No, I wasn't going to mention any of that.

'He's what?'

I squirmed. 'Nothing. I was just thinking … he's got a job to do. We're in a war, and he's trying to keep you safe by finding Rasputin and Timur so they don't end up coming here.'

Her eyes misted over as she gazed up at me. 'I guess….' Her lip trembled. 'Or it's just a handy excuse to get away from me. Why do I always fall for the wrong guy? What's *wrong* with me?'

That moment I was angry with Terens for doing this to my best friend. Maybe he realised his flirting had gone too far? He was probably used to women like himself, who enjoyed the fun but didn't take it seriously. Jenny wasn't like that. Maybe he knew he'd made a mistake there. So to avoid the situation, he left. 'There's nothing wrong with you, Jen. Any man should consider himself lucky to be loved by you.'

Her tears fell onto the pillow, and soon her shoulders heaved in heartbreaking sobs. I wrapped my arms around her and held her for as long as it took. It wasn't Jenny's fault she gave her heart so freely and unconditionally. Was it Terens's? On the yacht, on the plane, and even on the drive here, he gave her the impression he cared. And being Jenny, she fell for him. But then, I recalled, he'd expressed a desire at Christmas to hunt Timur. If he hadn't intended on staying, why did he encourage her? My brain went round in circles, trying to figure it out.

Her weeping soon subsided. 'I'm thirty-four years old, and look at me – blabbering like some love-struck teen. Gawd, I'm pathetic.'

'You are not. You're human, and I wouldn't have you any other way.'

She sniffed and sighed.

There was something I wanted to know. 'Jen, how did you end up in here?'

I looked around at the display of weapons – swords mostly – arranged on the walls. Animal skins served as rugs. Maybe he liked hunting – beasts as well as men.

She pulled away from me and turned to face the other side. 'It's embarrassing.'

'Tell me anyway.'

'I saw the note being slipped under my door. Picked it up, read it … and raced out the door looking for him. I ran after him, hon. Ugh!' She pulled the feather quilt over her head. It took a few minutes before she spoke again. 'Caught up with him this end of the corridor. He led me back here so we wouldn't be overheard.'

'You talked?'

She nodded then shook her head. 'I wanted—'

'I don't need to know all the particulars, Jen.'

'We didn't have sex, if that's what you're thinking. He didn't even kiss me, except on the cheek.' She fought back tears. 'Told me he had to go. Not sure when he'll be back.'

I took a deep breath. At least he hadn't taken advantage of her. In the short time I had known him, Terens had come across as a decent man. I liked him, but he had his faults, and I had a feeling Jenny had found them.

'He'll be back.' I hoped she'd be over him by then. 'In the meantime, don't mope or wallow. We're going to enjoy ourselves, Jen. We're in France. We're going to go shopping and exploring and … I want you to be happy.'

Jenny rolled back to face me, a small, sad smile tugging at the corners of her mouth.

'C'mon, out of bed.' I pulled at the covers.

Jenny climbed out, still fully dressed from the night before. She tried to smooth down her dishevelled hair, but there was nothing she could do about the smudged makeup and crumpled clothes. 'I hope no one sees me. I look like shit,' she said as we traipsed down the hall back to her room.

'A shower and breakfast will work wonders. After that, I'll be doing something which'll probably make you laugh – Alec's giving me knife-throwing lessons.'

'What for?'

'You wouldn't believe who I met.' Back in her suite, I showed her the jewelled knife, told her about Lucinda and the booby-trapped tunnels below the chateau. 'The caverns are incredible.' And since they were no longer a secret, I told her about the bloodvault, too. 'The place glows. Honestly, it's like an Aladdin's Cave without the genie.'

'You're the genie, hon.'

She had a point – this current war was about me. Yet I was no one's genie, no slave existing only for another's bidding. If Count Timur had his way, that's exactly what I would be. All the more reason for me to perfect my fledgling sword skills, and now, dagger throwing. I may not be a warrior princess, but if that's what it took to protect myself, and the ones I loved, then so be it. I touched the dagger hilt at my waist, surprised at how natural it felt having it there – and how comforting.

I stayed with Jen the rest of the morning, doing my best to keep her mind off Terens. A knock on the door and Alec's smiling face reminded me it was time for my new lessons.

\* \* \*

'Take a half step forward and aim a little higher,' Alec said as I pointed my dagger at the target he and Cal had set up for me. I'd missed on my first attempt – it landed handle first on the wall and bounced off.

Embarrassing.

Cal covered his mouth with his hand, but I caught the smirk. 'This might take a while.'

We were in the games room on the first floor, located between the two wings of the chateau. Part of one wall sported a wooden board and several dartboards. On the wooden board, Alec had placed a mock paper dummy, to which Cal had added Rasputin's face. 'More tempting target,' Cal explained.

'Watch me, Laura.' Alec demonstrated the proper stance as I, once again, took aim. 'This dagger is blade heavy. See?' Alec balanced it on his finger, and the blade dipped. It was surprising considering the handle looked to be weightier. 'It's been designed to be thrown using the handle.' With a flick of his wrist, he embedded the dagger right between Rasputin's eyes.

'Nice,' Cal said. He was leaning back against the edge of the dark-green billiard table. 'Good to know you haven't lost all your military skills.'

'How's yours?' Faster than a blink, Alec withdrew the blade and threw it at Cal – who laughed and caught it deftly by the hilt.

'Always good, my man, always good.'

Alec grinned and caught the return throw then turned to me. 'This dagger's perfect for you – less chance of you cutting yourself on the blade if it happened to be handle heavy. The heavy part is what you aim at your target.'

Ohhh! That made sense; the heavy part gave the object velocity and strength. I was glad I didn't have to throw it using the blade – something I'd seen in the movies. Knowing me, I'd end up accidently nicking myself. It was one of the reasons I'd always hated sharp and pointy objects. Ironic that I now carried one around with me all the time.

My next two attempts were somewhat more successful – the dagger landed handle first, but at least it hit the target rather than the wall.

Cal chuckled. 'Getting there. I guess you could always try and knock him unconscious.'

'Hey, give her a chance. Laura's doing great. Aren't you Laura?' Kari's enthusiasm buoyed me. She'd spent most of the morning out in the sunshine, and her cheeks had a rosy glow in spite of the weak winter sun. She and Jenny were spinning around on a pair of bar stools, calling out encouragement.

'I'm trying.' I took my position, gripped the hilt of the dagger, curling my thumb and fingers as Alec had shown me – not too tight, nor too lose so it wouldn't slip from my grip. Bending my arm toward my ear, I let go with a flick of my wrist.

Please, please land blade first. It spun twice and thudded blade first into the wood, just outside the figure's outline.

'Good.' Alec smiled, his lavender eyes sparking. 'Right way in, and you didn't miss the board.'

Kari and Jenny cheered. Even Cal grinned.

'Remember, every half step is a full rotation of the dagger. Use that as your guide when aiming at an opponent. You want the blade to end up there,' —he pointed at the target— 'not the hilt.'

'Sure it wasn't a fluke?' Cal was obviously enjoying himself.

His doubts only served to make me more determined. 'Keep it up, Cal. I'm going to prove you wrong.'

'You do that, angel.' This time he wasn't teasing. The smile he gave was genuine. Cal really did want to see me succeed.

'Isn't there somewhere else you have to be?' Alec asked as he pulled my dagger from the target and brought it back to me.

'Nope.' Just as well he was on the opposite side of the room from the girls. Wise move. I was sure he knew Kari well enough to know how far to tease me, and by extension, her, before she would react. That would be fun to watch.

'Okay, let's try again. Ignore Cal.' Alec placed the dagger in my hand and whispered, 'Pretend it's his face on the dummy.'

I resisted a laugh, took aim, concentrated and threw the knife. Bullseye, bullseye, bullseye, I silently chanted. 'Yes!' I pumped my fist in the air when the blade embedded itself in Rasputin's heart.

Alec winked at me.

Kari and Jenny whooped and spun their stools before Kari leapt up and thumped Cal in the arm. 'Ha! Told ya!'

'Knew you could do it, angel.' Cal smiled, and I gave him a mock salute.

We practised for another hour, until the number of times I missed the paper target steadily diminished. Alec shifted the target either closer or farther until I judged the distance accurately to get a hit. Only once did I thump the target handle first.

'The further your opponent is from you, the higher your throw angle. The nearer your opponent, the lower the angle – closer to your ear. And use your wrist, Laura. You're not throwing a softball.'

Hey, I was good a softball! But following Alec's directions once more, I aimed and hurled my dagger. With a satisfactory thud, it buried itself in Rasputin's nose.

'Great shot. If only it were for real,' Kari said.

'He gives me the creeps. Don't ever want to see him.' Jenny grimaced and pulled her coat more tightly about herself.

'You and me both, Jen.' But some sixth sense told me I would. I hoped my sixth sense was wrong, that Terens would find and despatch him before Rasputin could even set foot in this country.

'You've got the impact correct, now let's try for accuracy. After that we'll call it quits for today.' Alec marked the target in specific places for me to throw, with an X marks the spot.

I'd developed a powerful forearm, thanks to all those years playing tennis and softball, but my accuracy had always been a hit and miss affair. This time, my life would depend on it. I took aim, held my breath and hurled the dagger. It missed the mark by a few centimetres, but it was close enough.

'Not bad,' Alec remarked. 'For someone who's never thrown a knife before, you've done pretty well.'

I couldn't help grinning at Alec's compliment. It was important that I prove myself and contribute to my own defence. Not that I would ever be some kick-arse street fighter, but I wasn't the helpless damsel in distress either.

After another few throws, he seemed satisfied with my progress. 'We'll do a bit more tomorrow, and then maybe some sword play.'

I rubbed my arm, unsure whether I'd be able to lift anything tomorrow. My muscles ached from today's exertions.

He retrieved my dagger, wiped it clean of wood dust and handed it to me. 'I hope it never happens, but if you find yourself in a threatening situation against a Brethren, don't hesitate to use your blood. Smear a drop of it on the blade. It might even work as a deterrent.'

I'd used that tactic before, and I'd been armed with only a corkscrew. But it had worked. Even a scratch with my blood on it would kill any vampire. 'I will.'

I tucked it back into my belt, secure in the knowledge it was there. Thank you, Lucinda.

'Okay, Jenny, it's your turn now,' Alec said.

'Huh?' She looked at him like a rabbit caught in a trap. 'Me?'

Brilliant. I could've kissed Alec for suggesting it. Keep her occupied, and preferably keep her mind off Terens. Kari was helping too.

'It won't do you any harm to learn a few basic throws.' Alec tore the old target from the board and threw it in the bin before pinning a new one in place.

'But, but … I'm really not in the mood.'

Kari gave her a push. 'Oh, go on. If Laura can do it, so can you. Let's see if you can do better.'

'I doubt it.'

Cal angled his head to face her. 'If I promise not to tease, will you try?'

With a deep sigh, she rose and removed her coat. 'Use Laura's dagger?'

'No. I'll find you one.' Cal strode to a large, ceiling-to-floor cabinet located near the dartboard. Both sides of the door, and the interior, were lined with daggers, knives and pointy objects galore. What an arsenal! He hefted several before selecting one. 'This should do nicely.'

'You fine to do this?' Alec asked him.

'Yeah. Got nothing else to do.'

The new target didn't have a face attached. I was about to say that she could pretend it was Terens but stopped. The less people who knew about that attachment the better.

I sat next to Kari at the bar. Alec joined us. 'Thanks for including Jenny,' I whispered.

He winked at me and interlaced my fingers with his.

Jenny inched back when Cal handed her the knife. Was she nervous around him, or was it the dagger? Since she hadn't shown any reticence around the men, I assumed it had to be the latter. Then I remembered her once telling me she'd cut herself badly as a child and had to get stitches. She'd shown me the scar on her palm.

'You'll be okay. Pretend we're playing darts.' Cal smiled at her, highlighting the dimples in both his cheeks.

She took it from his hands. 'Haven't played darts in years.'

'Bet you were good.' Cal was putting her at ease, saying just what Jenny needed to hear right now – something positive about herself. With a nod, he indicated the dagger she held. 'I picked one similar to Laura's: a lady's blade. Check its weight. Can you feel it in the handle?' She nodded. 'Okay, get a firm grip. Not too tight. Take aim – and don't worry if you miss the first couple of times – and … throw!'

Jenny let go. The dagger bounced off the target. Her shoulders slumped. 'Can't even get that right.'

'Let me show you.' Cal stepped behind her, his six-foot frame dwarfing her. 'Take a half step forward.' She did. He then placed one hand on her shoulder, wrapped his other hand around hers and pulled her arm back behind her head. 'Like this. Now take aim and … throw.'

With a thud, the dagger embedded itself into the target. She gasped, and a smile appeared. Kari and I let out a whoop.

'Try again?' Cal pulled the dagger out and handed it to her.

'All right.'

He stood quite close as she took aim. 'Remember, light but firm, and aim just above the spot you want to hit.'

She did as he directed, and the dagger landed squarely in the target. Jenny laughed and turned to me. 'I did it!'

'Yay!' Kari and I high-fived as our stools whirled.

Cal's dimpled smile was focused on Jenny as, this time, she retrieved the dagger and twirled it in her hand. She had her confidence back, and I couldn't be happier. Thank you, Cal.

'I'll do it myself this time. Straight to the heart … I hope.' Jenny took the proper stance, sucked in her lower lip as she aimed and threw. The knife landed exactly where she wanted.

Alec clapped, and Cal gave her an encouraging nod.

'You're a natural, Jen. Two goes and you're hitting the target. Took me ages.'

'Hit the heart again and the dagger's yours.' Cal stood in front of the dartboard, hands crossed over his chest. So close to the target, he must have confidence in Jenny's ability.

Jenny's mouth dropped open. She gazed at the slender blade in her hand, turned it over and examined it more closely. 'There are markings on this. You know what they mean?'

'Tell you after the throw.'

'Okay. You're on.' She took her time, aimed it several times before the dagger left her hand and landed squarely in the dummy's heart. She squealed then placed both hands over her mouth.

Kari whistled, and I cheered. 'Looks like you lost part of your collection, Cal,' chuckled Alec.

Cal shrugged as he retrieved the dagger and, with a theatrical flourish, handed it to Jenny. 'All yours, my lady.'

She blushed. I couldn't remember the last time I'd seen her cheeks flame like that. Apart from Alec, I also couldn't remember when I'd last seen a man behave so gallantly.

I leapt off the stool to check out her shiny new dagger. A simple, brown leather band wove around the handle, topped with a smooth gold pommel. Jenny turned it so the blade caught the light, bringing the markings into better view. It appeared to be a flower – a lily perhaps? – and beautiful cursive writing.

'Now you have to tell me what it means.' Jenny looked at Cal.

Cal ran his thumb over the blade's surface. 'It's a golden lily, and the words say "Forever Faithful".' He gazed at her a moment, a half smile on his lips. 'You'll need the cover that goes with it.'

As Cal went to the cabinet, Jenny repeated the words. 'Forever Faithful. How romantic. You think there's a story with it?'

'Possible. Ask him.'

Cal returned with, what looked like, a gold sheath attached to a circular pin. 'This is a barette and meant to be worn like a brooch or a hairpin.' At Jenny's stunned look he added, 'Well I did say it was for a lady.'

'This, I've got to see.' When Jenny slid the dagger into its sheath, it passed for a dress brooch, although the pin was clearly designed to be worn in the hair. Perhaps in a bun, or gathered in the back where it could be quickly and easily retrieved? She pulled back a few strands and clipped them in place with the barette. It was lovely against her dark hair, and no one would ever know what lay concealed within the sheath. Cal was right; it was the perfect lady's weapon.

'Try pulling it out,' I said.

Jenny reached behind her head and easily unsheathed the dagger, but it would take a bit of practice getting it back in without having to unclip the whole thing. Nonetheless, she was thrilled with it. 'Thanks, Cal.'

He smiled. 'My pleasure.'

She left the barette secured in her hair as we left the games room, her hand straying to it as we walked away.

Did we need some special weapons licence to carry these daggers? But then again, why worry? The men in my family could mesmerise any nosey government official. I inwardly laughed at the way I had become so complacent and accepting of the supernatural in my life. Yet, I knew it was all coming to an end. Then what? Would Alec be strong enough to maintain the Principate alone should Luc and Marcus choose death over eternity in vampire form? How long would the bottled Ingenii blood last? Would our allies remain faithful now that Luc's secret was out?

I sighed. So many questions to which there were no answers – at this stage. I could only trust to Providence that Alec and our baby would be safe.

# CHAPTER 16 - ALLIES OR REBELS?

**ALEC**

Luc was brooding. Dangerously so. He stood next to me as I took my seat on the Alabaster Throne in the Great Hall, and casually draped one arm across the top of it. Marcus stood to attention to my right. The sun had set an hour ago. The hall had been prepared and the Great Table brought out. It was only ever used for prefect gatherings. Bronze tags were set into the timber, inscribed with the names of individual prefectures. Next to each one, three vials of blood had been laid out. Marcus believed that was enough as a goodwill gesture. I agreed. Luc had made no comment.

Along one wall, a refreshments table had been set up. Bottles of Luc's best wine and other liquors, along with goblets of blood, waited. Those who preferred to imbibe from a fresher source would have to wait till after the meeting and do their hunting in Avignon.

I rose from the throne as Cal, clutching the Spear of Office, ushered in Karl and several other European prefects. Naturally, they arrived first, Europe being a small continent. Most of the capitals were only a few hours flying distance from each other.

'Welcome, Brethren.'

They knelt before Marcus and bowed their heads in deference to me. O'Toole, the Prefect from Hibernia, inhaled and smiled. 'It *is* the real thing. Ingenii blood. Told you it would be.' He grinned, swatted Karl on the upper arm and strode ahead of the others to the table. Each of them knew where to find their place since the bronze tags were arranged in order of importance – the most ancient prefectures having the pre-eminence.

O'Toole's was four spaces down from the head of the table. Karl's was opposite his. Although Luc was prefect of Viennensis – this province – being Chief Elder, he took position at the head of the table.

I found it odd that Marcus and the Elders still maintained the ancient Roman provincial boundaries – and names – between some European nations. But then again, France, like Germany and a few others, was geographically too large for one prefect to manage. I guess it made sense. Still, I had to think twice before addressing O'Toole as Prefect from Hibernia instead of Ireland. Only those nations outside the Empire were addressed by their modern names and boundaries.

Karl hadn't moved from the doorway. The scowl on his face told me I had a battle on my hands to win back his trust. The others filed past him into the room, nostrils flared, each with their gaze fixed on the blood vials before them.

Marcus stepped down to greet the Elders and ushered them to the head of the Great Table. They were responsible for the world's oldest provinces. The prefects turned to them and bowed but kept their distance. While Marcus conversed with them, I went to Karl.

'I couldn't tell you.' I kept my voice low.

He retrieved a gold cigarette case from his pocket, took one out and lit it. 'Yeah, Principate business, huh?'

'There are some things I can't divulge, regardless of how I feel about it.'

His gaze slanted past me, to Luc. 'Looks like he drank blood from a rat.'

'Wouldn't you?'

His lip curled up into a half smile as he blew smoke from the side of his mouth. 'His dirty little secret is out.'

'It's not what you think.'

'No? Can't wait to hear it.'

There was no talking to him in his current mood. I strode back to the throne when the rest of the prefects arrived. Luc's eyes were hooded as he watched them enter. This was going to be a hell of a meeting.

Sam and Jake entered and took positions on either side of the entrance. Jake carried an antique medicine chest where we'd stored the precious anti-white-oak serum. We didn't have much, but enough to inoculate everyone here – if they chose.

Cal closed the doors and banged the base of the iron spear three times onto the stone floor. The meeting had begun.

I rose. 'Thank you for coming at such short notice, Brethren.'

Luc stepped down from the dais. 'I know all you want are the vials in front of you, and you don't care who gives it to you – me or the prefect from Hungary.'

Marcus and I exchanged anxious glances. This was not the time for Luc to display his displeasure. We could not afford to antagonise our allies.

'Speaking for myself,' Karl said, 'I'd prefer it as a gift from the Principate … My Lord.'

My scalp prickled at Karl's tone, and I couldn't entirely blame him. I could taste the tension in the room. It burned like acid on my tongue. 'You deserve to know the truth behind Count Timur's—' I began.

'He's a rebel,' Luc snarled. 'Let's name him for what he is!'

'Maybe he has a reason,' Alonso, the Spanish Prefect called out. How much did he know about Lucinda and her connection to Timur? I'd quiz him later.

Luc growled and took a step forward. Damn! He needed to calm down. Marcus placed a hand on his shoulder. Some prefects backed away. A small group began to argue among themselves, while casting accusing glances at Luc and me.

I couldn't allow that. 'Ladies and gentlemen, you've come here in good faith, and you will not be disappointed. As you can see' —I pointed to the vials on the table— 'you are about to receive an incomparable gift.'

'Why didn't we know about this before?' one asked. Several 'Ayes' echoed around the hall. I saw Karl's upraised eyebrow as he stood toward the back, near Jake.

'You didn't need to know … at the time.' Luc strode forward, touched my shoulder and whispered, 'Let me do this this. It's my skin they're after.'

'We're in this together.'

His smile was faint. We had reached an understanding. I faced the gathered prefects again, when one of the Elders raised his hand for silence. Kwome, one of the oldest Brethren on the planet, stepped up to the dais. His tall, black frame towered above the rest of us. Only a few weeks before, he and the other Elders had officiated at Laura's coming-of-age ceremony.

'Marcus Antonius Pulcher, we have known each other a long time – nearly two-thousand years. We have seen much together. You are my brother, and I have always trusted your word. Tell me now, did you know your son had been collecting Ingenii blood all these centuries?'

Marcus stepped down and approached him. 'Yes, I did.'

Kwome held up his hand again for silence as mutterings and hushed whispers echoed around the hall. 'Did you partake of them?'

I caught Jake's eye as an oath escaped his lips. Whatever way Marcus answered, he'd be perjuring himself. If he said no, he'd be caught in a lie although he'd taken a vial for the first time only a few days ago – at Christmas. If he answered yes, he might not be given a chance to explain. It could mean the end of the Principate.

Marcus drew in a breath. 'Three days ago, for the first time, I tasted First Blood. After which, I resumed command of my men, to lead them against the enemy.'

'You were never tempted to share in the Gift before that?'

'No.'

Kwome's gaze burned into Marcus's. A small smile appeared. 'I would not have been as strong as you, my friend.'

My hands unclenched. Next to me, Luc released a breath. Marcus and Kwome gripped forearms – Roman style. 'It's your turn, old comrade. We fight together in this,' Marcus said.

The other Elders clapped, and the prefects followed their lead.

Marcus stepped back onto the dais. 'You all know the prophecy, that a time is coming when the Bloodgifted will be no more. Without the benefit of Ingenii blood, how long do you think the Principate will survive?' He paused as his gaze settled on each prefect. 'For that very reason, Lord Luc has been storing the blood vials, knowing that one day we would need them, that as the curse nears its end, there will arise those who would prevent it. They would take and use the Ingenii to daywalk themselves, annihilate the Principate and create more Bloodgifted. They would enslave my family for eternity. This I cannot allow.'

'Then your secrecy was justified,' Kwome said.

Some bought it, sensing the truth in Marcus's words. But not all. 'More like you didn't trust us,' one called out.

'Can you blame me? Or is it my imagination that nine prefects are missing? Gone on holidays perhaps?' Luc's gaze swept the gathering. His sarcasm wasn't lost on them. Heads swerved as they glanced around at each other.

'He's got a point. I wouldn't trust us either,' O'Toole said. 'I'd've kept it a secret too.'

Good on O'Toole. So far we had the backing of the Elders and the leading prefects. We had to win the rest.

'But now the Rebels know, and they'll be swarming here,' I added.

'Not just for the blood vials, but for my daughter.' Luc's hands clenched as he stood before them. It had caused quite a stir when Luc had revealed Laura was his daughter, at the Pledging ceremony. Nine prefects had defected.

'You need us,' another voice said. 'That's the only reason you're sharing the Ingenii blood.'

'Just as much as we need the Principate to protect our lands. Let's not delude ourselves. Isn't that why we're here?' Karl strode to the front and turned to face his fellow prefects. 'I hate the fact Lord Luc kept this from us, too. Yet, maybe I can see the sense in it. How many of us would've thought of preparing for the future like that? Hell of an idea, if you ask me. Now we can share in it.'

'How'd the Rebels find out?' another asked.

I was expecting this. 'One of their donsangs saw our men during the day. Knew they couldn't have received the lady Judith's blood, since it's no longer potent. Nor Lady Laura's, as it's lethal to our kind. He told Rasputin who … guessed the rest and sent word to his master.' My ambush and capture could remain a secret.

'And that fucker goes and releases it on the Principate website.' Karl swore again, marched to the Great Table and picked up one of the blood vials. 'Mind if I take this now? I can be in Budapest by sunrise ripping Timur's head off! He'll never know how he lost it.'

'Count von Czernin, I believe the Elders should have the privilege of imbibing first.' Marcus motioned with his hand for the Elders to approach the table.

'Forgive me, my Lord. I was too eager.' Karl lowered his vial and knelt before him.

Marcus smiled. 'No harm in that. But the proprieties must be respected.'

The prefects all went down on one knee as Kwome, Zhou, Maiara and Grey Bear made their way to the Great Table. It wasn't only out of respect and reverence for their great ages, but that they'd survived so long without seeking self-destruction. Marcus watched it happen to two of his men. He could do nothing.

How long since any of them had seen daylight? Compared to these ancient beings, I was but a babe. Yet I was the one who'd been privileged to daywalk while still a juvenile. How Luc had gotten away with appointing me Princeps, I can only guess. Marcus drew respect, but Luc was feared.

Grey Bear's eyes blazed as he brought the blood vial to his lips. He hesitated, then threw his head back and drank it in one go. The stained-glass windows of the Great Hall shook as he released a roar.

Marcus clapped him on the shoulder. 'Welcome to the light.'

Grey Bear and Maiara had been appointed to the Eldership recently, following Maris's death. Not that she did such a magnificent job it needed two to replace her. On the contrary. The Americas were simply too great to be under the control of one Elder. By their age, Maiara and Grey Bear should've been in the Eldership, but neither had expressed interest – until now. Perhaps it was the current rebellion. More likely, it had to do with Marcus's own return to the Principate, which had prompted it.

At a nod from Marcus, I addressed the prefects. 'Ladies and gentlemen, daylight awaits.' They rushed to the Great Table. 'Each vial lasts four days. You have twelve days to find and annihilate the Rebels in your prefectures.'

'And after that?' one asked. 'You can't expect to give us a taste of daylight then take it away again.'

'The supply is limited. If we continue to share it out indefinitely, it'll be gone within a year,' Luc said. 'We'll all be walking in the dark again.'

Luc was right. Judith's blood had lost its potency. After living nearly eighteen-hundred years on Ingenii blood, Luc was about to re-enter the world of the nightwalkers. If that wasn't hard enough, he was also dealing with the effect of withdrawal. Ingenii blood is addictive, and Luc had been on it a long time. His sudden mood swings and display of temper would only worsen until his system was clear of it.

It was interesting how the prefects consumed their first lot of vials. Some downed it on one go. Others savoured every drop, eyes closed, slowly sipping and licking the inside of the tiny glass. Their withdrawal would be far less dramatic, but it would be there nonetheless. And if Laura's blood lost its power after the lifting of the curse, I could expect the same. Yet we had little choice. The rebellion had to be quashed.

Karl licked his lips. 'Holy fuck! Is this what you experience every time? The rush is something else.'

'Every time.'

'Lucky bastard.' He grinned.

I was – I had Laura. Personally I couldn't care less about the properties her blood bestowed. She was all that mattered to me.

Jake signalled me and pointed to the medicine chest at his feet.

I leaned over and whispered in Luc's ear. 'Now might be time to tell them about the serum.' He nodded. I beckoned for Jake to come forward. 'Ladies and gentlemen, may I have your attention again? I have something else for you, something the Rebels know nothing about.' I took the chest from Jake's hands, opened it and removed a stoppered test tube. 'You all know me to be a doctor. I'm also a medical researcher. In the last few days, Jake and I have been manufacturing a serum to combat the effect of white oak.'

'Bloody hell! You haven't!' Karl's jaw hung.

I grinned and held the test tube aloft. 'It's been well tested' — although not in the clinical sense. But they didn't need to know that— 'on ourselves.'

Gasps came from the gathering. 'Holy virgin … What a fool thing to do! Why couldn't you have used one of the Rebels to experiment on,' O'Toole blurted out.

'It's not how I work, O'Toole. If I did that, I'd be no better than the Rebels.'

He scratched his head and looked down. 'Fair enough. I still say it was foolhardy.'

'Maybe so, but I had complete confidence in my serum, and as you can see' —I spread my arms wide— 'I'm still here, and so is Jake.'

Jake grinned.

'Some of you may not know that Count Timur has created a set of rings based on his family crest.' I held up the wolf's-head ring and activated the deadly white-oak spike. 'The spike you see here is white-oak. On the night of the Pledging, he scratched Tribune Terens with it. Thanks to Jake's quick action, he only lost an arm.'

I couldn't help but see Baroness Milena smile and wink at Jake. None of my business. Stick to the topic, I told myself.

'What's the point of the Principate outlawing white-oak when the Rebels are now using it?' one of the prefects said.

I held up the test tube again. 'Why do you think we made this? One jab and you're immune to white-oak. Doesn't matter if the Rebels have a forest full of the stuff. It won't have any effect on you. The downside is, you'll experience flu-like symptoms that last for about an hour – general weakness and muscle aches and pains. Small price to pay. I'm planning on making enough to inoculate every Brethren Principate supporter.'

Seconds ticked by as they conversed among themselves, glancing around to see who'd be the first to step forward. Luc circulated among the prefects as Marcus did among the Elders.

'You'd think they'd jump at the chance,' Jake whispered to me.

'It's a lot to take in. Wait till I tell them about the Rings.' If they were concerned about the inoculation, how would they respond to me using the serpent ring on their minds?

'Can't wait,' Jake whispered back.

It occurred to me then whether the ring was powerful enough to project simultaneously into over two-hundred Brethren minds. I knew it worked on half-a-dozen human ones, but … I should've asked Laura to be here. Our rings combined would be more effective. And doing this one-Brethren-at-a-time would take too long. Dawn wasn't far off. I listened out for Laura's heartbeat. Slow and steady. She slept. I couldn't wake her. I pictured her golden hair splashed over the pillow, full lips partly open, lush and inviting. …

'I'll take it.' Karl stood before me.

'What?' Damn, I'd switched off.

'Jab me first. I trust you.' He rolled his sleeve up.

Looks like I was back in his good books. 'Thanks, Karl.'

'You owe me big time for this.' His grin belied his words. Jake retrieved the syringe and prepared to inject it into his arm. 'Be gentle with me.' Karl winked at him. I tried not to laugh. Jake rolled his eyes and stuck the syringe all the way in. 'Shiiiit! If I didn't know better, I'd say you enjoyed that.'

Jake smiled, and without looking away from Karl, called out, 'Next.'

'Go grab a goblet and sit down till the side effect passes. It won't take long,' I told him. 'I'll join you as soon as I can.'

The Elders lined up first followed by the prefects. It was almost sunrise by the time we'd injected everyone. Slivers of light slanted through the stained-glass windows and rested on groups of moaning and groaning vampires.

'It's like being human, again,' one complained.

'Watch your language,' another retorted.

One or two still shied away from the light. 'Don't be afraid. Look.' I grasped their shaking hands in mine and placed both in the path of a beam of light. No dreaded smoke; no stink of burnt flesh. 'When you're fully recovered, go enjoy the morning.'

They kissed my hand. A red tear rolled down the cheek of another.

I rose and went to sit next to Karl. He'd begun to recover; had lit a cigarette and was watching Milena. She was sitting on one of the chairs by the wall, Jake next to her. Her head rested on his shoulder.

'She would choose him.' He sighed, and a puff of smoke escaped his nostrils.

'Did you tell her it was you who's been keeping her lands safe?'

'Nah.'

'Maybe you should. It might give her a different perspective of you.' Milena, like the other prefects, had learnt the dangerous game Karl had played with the Rebels to keep her and the other Principate leaders safe. It'd been revealed at the Pledging. As for Jake's intentions, I had no idea. None of my business.

'Anything on the grapevine about Rasputin's whereabouts?'

'Heard something about him losing his….' He wriggled his hands.

I couldn't help but smile when I recalled how it had happened. 'Laura did it. Used Sam's sword.'

He laughed when I filled him in on the details. 'Spunky little thing, isn't she. What I would've given to see that.' He drew on his cigarette.

'I want to know if he's made it back to Europe.'

He shook his head. 'Haven't heard, but that mesmerisation thing bugs me. If he can do that to Sam…? Why hadn't I heard of it?'

'Jake reckons he's only now developing it – as he's leaving the juvenile stage.'

My comment prompted him to turn and stare at Jake and Milena again. He stubbed the cigarette to mash on the stone floor before taking out another one.

'What if I told you the serpent ring has the power to overcome that?'

Karl's gaze slid from Milena to me. 'How?'

'It emits a harmless beam into your eyes.'

He turned fully toward me. 'You've tested that, too, huh?'

'Had to.'

He eyed me a few long seconds then nodded. 'And now you want me to volunteer my services as first guinea pig again, huh?'

I smiled.

Karl huffed and shook his head. 'You know you're going to owe me so much you won't be able to repay.'

'We'll work something out.'

He took a slow drag of his cigarette as his gaze roamed the room, settling on groups of prefects before refocusing on Milena. I would've loved to know what was going through his mind. 'Harmless?'

'Completely.'

'Definitely works?'

'I can guarantee it.'

He swivelled toward me again, brow creased. 'How could you know it works unless you—'

I angled my body to face the wall and told him about the ambush and my capture by the Rebels. His pupils narrowed when I mentioned Stockton's torture method. 'Prokleta svine!' It must have been a particularly bad swear word if he had to say it in Czech.

'Marcus dealt with him. But Rasputin got away.'

'That snake always does.'

We sat like that for another few minutes while Karl finished his cigarette. Me? I rehearsed the words in my mind to convince everyone to let me flash the ring into their eyes. And it had to be now, while they were still too weak to run away.

'Now or never.'

'Good luck,' I heard him murmur as I left to find Luc.

He, Marcus and Kwome stood by the fireplace discussing the Principate's response to Timur and his cronies. The Elders were among the first to recover from the inoculation. Great age has its advantages. Marcus extended his hand when he saw me approach.

'Well done, Alec.'

'One more thing to go.' I displayed the serpent ring on my hand.

'Marcus has just been telling me about that.' Kwome took my hand and peered at the ring as if expecting it to reveal its secrets. He then lifted his gaze to me, and in those depths I recognised the sage-like seriousness of an ancient one who perceives a truth to which others are blind. I'd seen it in Marcus. 'All these centuries, and only now we learn what else it can do. Perhaps it was waiting for you...? Perhaps we were all waiting for you.'

My scalp tingled, especially when he raised my hand to sniff. Surely he couldn't detect the witch's blood in me? Only Ingenii blood enhanced the senses to such a degree. A muscle ticked in Luc's jaw. He gave Marcus a sideways glance. Some understanding must have passed between them, for Marcus grasped Kwome by the upper arm and guided him to a secluded corner, presumably to explain what we had planned next.

'You think he suspects?' I asked Luc.

'If he does ... I'd rather him than any of the others.'

I'd worry about that another time. 'Time to introduce Phase 3 – the ring.'

He gave me a nod and I stepped back up to the dais. Some prefects had already recovered and were helping themselves to the refreshments. A few still lounged on chairs or reclined on the floor. How to do this? Try it out on small groups? Or take them by surprise? As I thought about the best approach, a warm sensation spread along my finger. The serpent's eyes glowed brightly. I raised my hand ... and found myself suffused in a deep red glow. Faces turned toward me, and, in that instant a flash of brilliant light lit up the Great Hall. Every eye reflected back scarlet. Seconds later, it was gone. They all blinked, and once more, lavender eyes stared at me.

Problem solved.

'What the hell was that?' one asked, and soon more questions were thrown at me.

'Ladies and gentlemen, there's nothing to worry about.' I wracked my brain for an explanation. Did they need to know their minds were now as immune to Rasputin's psychic attack as they were to the fatal affects of white-oak? Best they didn't. That way, should they encounter him, Rasputin may think his powers not as effective as he would like to believe. If I could put a dent in his ego, even make him doubt himself, then all the better. 'The ring is displaying its power. You know all is well when the eyes glow red. Now that many of you have recovered, please help yourselves to the refreshments provided. Those of you who prefer to feed directly, you know the house rules – do not feed from the staff or the villagers. You may now be immune to white-oak, but the water supply here is laced with it. Avignon is a far better hunting ground.'

I signalled Cal to open the doors. Human servants carried in fresh blood supplies and left immediately. Many among them were donsangs who, on this occasion, were instructed not to donate.

By now, sharp winter light had filled the hall. Men and women, who had neither seen nor felt the sun in centuries, turned their faces toward the windows. Expressions of fear gave way to ecstasy. One by one they bowed to me and the Elders, before tentatively making their way out into the sunshine.

A new era had begun. Who knew how long it would last.

## CHAPTER 17 – MADAME THIERRY

**CONSTANS THIERRY**

Commuters jostled her as she hurried from the train station at Avignon to her pre-arranged meeting at the café a few shops down from the entrance to the station. She'd made all the necessary preparations for the Elders and prefects' meeting tonight. Her husband, Serge, could handle the rest. He loved his job at the chateau – his vocation, as he called it.

Poor stupid Serge. If only he knew she'd married him so she could be the wife of the Steward of D'Antonville, so she could be close to *him*.

'Pardon, madame.' A man bumped her in his hurry to get past, breaking into her thoughts and almost knocking the bag from her shoulder.

Five pm. It was already dark, and people wanted to get home. Over the years, she'd taught herself to embrace these long winter nights, when the sun set so early – a prelude of things to come, she reminded herself. And time was running out. She'd waited long enough. It would have to be now, while she was still on the good side of fifty.

The icy wind whipped around her face, taking small bites of her cheeks and nose that weren't protected by her scarf. One day I won't feel this, she thought.

She passed a small boutique, an antiques shop and … there it was, a glass-fronted, cosy little place with dark, green awnings – *Café D'Or*. She stopped and took a deep breath. There was still time to change her mind. In spite of the biting cold, her hands began to sweat as she rehearsed in her mind the bargain she was about to make. It wasn't like she was betraying *him*. She would make sure of that. No. No backing out now.

The exquisite aroma of coffee and warm croissants greeted her as she walked in. She inhaled. Will I miss this? Can I really leave this behind? In the far corner of the room someone cleared their throat. She glanced at the man sitting there. His pale, almost luminous skin set him apart as Brethren.

He beckoned to her.

Constans Thierry wove her way through the tables, past the unwary humans absorbed in either their newspapers or each other. He raised an eyebrow when she sat next to him on the padded bench, rather than in the chair he indicated.

'I don't want anyone to overhear us,' she said by way of explanation.

He shrugged and leant back against the corner wall. 'That's easily taken care of.'

Ah, he could mesmerise them, she thought. What an extraordinary skill; her mind was already envisioning ways she could put it to use. But first, she needed to become one of them. Since it was forbidden for the stewards of D'Antonville to be transformed, she knew it was hopeless asking one of the Brethren staff to do the honours. Besides, she had no desire to be a servant's juvenile. In her dreams, it was *he* who gave her immortality. But dreams were just that. If Count Timur kept his side of the bargain, then he would send her someone appropriate to do it. Perhaps even this man who sat eyeing her curiously.

'I was told you have something to offer us.'

'In return for a favour.'

His mouth creased in a sardonic smile. 'Isn't that always the case?'

The way he perused her made her wonder how much he knew. No doubt he could see the whisks of grey in the hair peeking out from beneath her cap, the deepening lines around her mouth and eyes. 'Have you been told … of my request?'

Another sardonic smile. Did he think her too old? Her composure slipped under his scrutiny, and she automatically tucked the stray hairs back beneath her woollen cap.

'You've left it a little late.'

She straightened her back and glared at him. That wasn't her fault, she wanted to shout at him. She'd waited so long, hoped the relationship between *him* and Judith had been based solely on the feeding bond, until she'd learnt that the new Ingenii was their daughter! The Brethren were sterile; everyone knew that. Yet *he* could have children, and it had taken everyone by surprise. How she hated that woman. But she refused to give up hope. If her plans worked out, that woman would soon be gone, and *he*, being an immortal, would not mourn her forever. He'd lived for nearly two-thousand years before she existed, and he would do so again. When he was ready, she would be there.

'No, monsieur, I'm not too late.'

'Very well, shall we talk terms?'

'I can bring your master two valuable items. The first is Milord Lucien's ward ring – the green-eyed serpent. Were he to lose it, the protective wards around the chateau would fall. And the second is a key that opens a treasure vault—'

He sat forward, his eyes burning into hers. 'The one with his secret blood stash?'

She didn't know. Only guessed. There are some secrets not even the stewards knew about. *He* wore the key around his neck. She'd glimpsed its outline beneath his shirt on the rare occasions he'd visited – how she relished those times – so it had to be special. And she'd made it her business to find out by listening at keyholes and befriending the Brethren servants until they felt comfortable sharing what they knew. 'Yes.'

'Do you have it with you?'

'Certainly not.' Did he take her for a fool? How easy it would be for him to take the items and either kill her or leave her to face *his* wrath. 'Render the service first then I'll pay you. The ring in return for destroying the chateau and all the D'Antonvilles, and the key once I'm transformed.' She thrust her chin out at him.

'Very well.'

'I will remove his ring and lift the wards so you can attack. I don't care if you kill everyone there, but Milord Lucien must be taken alive. He is not to be killed or tortured....' Another face swam before her eyes; a sweet pixie face she'd come to love. She didn't deserve the fate she'd planned for the rest of that family. 'Nor Kari – Karelia. She is not to be harmed, either.'

He eyed her again, and that sardonic smile returned. She was beginning to hate it. 'Any other requests?'

She sat tight-lipped.

'I see. I suppose we can spare the girl. Milord Lucien is another matter. I can't promise—'

'You must or there's no deal.'

He steepled his fingers beneath his chin, and she could almost see his mind working. She knew she was asking for a high price, but then surely they'd see the reward was worth it. 'The only one of concern to us is the current Ingenii. We need her alive. But, Milord Lucien … perhaps we can accede to your request.'

She stared at him. 'You do, or we have no deal. Why do you need the young woman – Milady Laura? You cannot feed from her. Of what use is she to you?'

His eyebrows rose. He looked at her intently before a smug half-smile crinkled his lips as if he knew something she didn't. That wasn't possible. How she wanted to slap that horrid smile away.

'We have plans for her.'

They could do with her whatever they wanted so long as Milord Lucien was unharmed. She shrugged. 'Do with her whatever you want.'

He leant back against the wall. 'I'm curious. How are going to accomplish obtaining Lord Luc's ring and key? He's not going to hand it over to you.'

This time it was her turn to give a smug smile. He didn't need to know her secrets. Being a child of one of the First Families, and having grown up playing on the estate grounds, she knew every tree, every pathway, room and hidden passageway. As a child she'd often snuck into Milady Judith's room, borrowed one of her shawls to drape over herself to disguise her scent. If her presence were detected they'd assume Milady had been checking the passageways. Oh, the things she'd gleaned from her clandestine forays through the chateau's walls.

'That's my business.' She pulled a folded paper from her bag and handed it to him. 'It's a layout of the chateau and grounds.' She'd made sure to omit the secret passageways – for now. 'I'll contact you when the protective wards are down and where you can find the Ingenii. The rest is up to you.' She rose to leave.

He angled his head, his eyes narrowing as they perused her. 'You really believe Lucien will accept you in place of Milady Judith?'

Here was the crux of her plan. 'He need never know my part in all this. All he'll see is a grieving widow, turned against her will. That's the final condition of my side of the bargain – Lord Timur is to take all the credit. My name is not to be mentioned.'

He laughed then stood and extended his hand. 'Lady Macchiavelli, we have a deal.'

# CHAPTER 18 – ROOM OF RAINBOWS

**LAURA**

'This is incredible!' Jenny gazed at the stunning frescoes on the ceiling in the library and ran her fingers along some of the books' spines. 'What a treasure. How old are some of these books?'

'Very.'

After Jenny and I had slept-in, it was later in the afternoon before Kari could take us on a tour of the chateau. Judy had given us a map of the place the night before. While Luc, Alec and the men had been with the Elders and prefects, we'd watched DVDs in the games room. We'd all sung along to a whole bunch of old musicals Kari had chosen. It was a joy to see Jenny laughing, her mind on something else other than Terens. Was it too much to hope her infatuation could be wearing off?

She peered into the glass case holding Marcus's chronicle. 'This is beautiful. How comes it's under glass when the others aren't?'

I explained.

'Holy crap!' She angled her head to get a better view, the cleverly disguised dagger Cal had given her pinned at the back of her head. 'He's drawn the witch and the men's faces.' Her finger hovered over one illustration. I didn't have to guess whose face it was. 'He hasn't changed....'

'C'mon, we've got lots more to see.' I linked her arm through mine and tugged her away.

'Any secret passageways here?' Jenny asked.

Kari smiled, and I shook my head. 'Don't know and not interested – not after my last experience! Judy said we're free to go anywhere. Except the servants' quarters below stairs where the Brethren servants sleep.'

'That's fine with me,' Jenny said.

I pulled the map out of my pocket just to be sure. Though Judy hadn't indicated at any secret passageways, it wouldn't have been surprising. All castles had secret tunnels, used as escape routes in times of siege or to connect lovers to each other's bedrooms.

Judy had suggested we avoid Luc's office and the Great Hall. Some of the prefects might still be in there. I had no intention of exposing my best friend to a horde of vampires, benign though they may be. I'd glimpsed them roaming the grounds, almost as if in a daze. Most had their faces turned to the sun, while others had removed their coats and were sunning themselves like lizards on a rock. I shivered just watching them. It was freezing out there. But then, I'd recently learnt how little they felt the cold ... or the heat. I only had to look at Kari – jeans, red turtleneck sweater and matching ankle boots.

'Okay, lead on, Kari. Where next?'

She held out her hand. 'Let's see Judy's map. What's she indicate on there.'

I pointed to the room labelled *conservatory*. Judy had highlighted it, and underneath she'd written *my garden room of rainbows*. That alone was enough to rouse my curiosity. 'I'm dying to see that.'

'Let's go then.'

We re-entered the entrance hallway and walked behind the grand staircase to the other side of the chateau, where the gardens and maze were located. Those were next on my list; perhaps tomorrow.

Jutting out from the stone wall at the rear of the chateau was a jewel – a steel and glass enclosure that captured and transformed light from the weak winter sun into a dazzling kaleidoscope of colours that seduced the senses. Thousands upon thousands of panels of stained glass splashed rainbows onto a mirrored-tile floor so smooth it appeared to undulate like ripples in a pond.

Fluted stone pillars supported a vaulted ceiling from which hung delicate gossamer strands of a fibre optic chandelier in the form of a swarm of butterflies.

Jenny and I gasped.

'This is so much more than a conservatory,' I said.

'It's like being at the end of the rainbow.' Jenny's eyes were like saucers.

I took a tentative step onto the mirrored floor, almost expecting to slide across its surface. But the rubber soles of my boots provided a sturdy grip, and I stood in the centre of one splash of colour.

'You look like the genie in the bottle,' Jenny said. She'd used that same word earlier.

'Why do you say that?'

She shrugged. 'You remember that old TV series about the genie in her pink bottle? You kind of remind me of that with' —she pointed to the windows— 'the light shining on you, making your hair glow.'

I relaxed and guessed this room did resemble the inside of a jewelled bottle. I clasped my hands in front of me, prayer fashion, and tried wriggling my head from side to side.

Jenny laughed. 'Pity you don't give three wishes. I know what I'd wish for.' She winked at me.

I rolled my eyes and plonked onto one of the plump cushions of a wicker armchair. Several sofas were grouped around a coffee table, and cane palms and other greenery were scattered around the room. I glanced at Kari to see her staring wistfully up at the ceiling. It was the only part of the structure with clear glass panes, and through it I glimpsed patches of blue sky.

*She probably wishes she was out there.* I hadn't planned on going out of doors today, but seeing the longing in her eyes changed my mind. No one said we couldn't go out, and since all the Elders and prefects were around, I couldn't be safer.

Decision made.

Unfortunately, my cashmere dress wouldn't be warm enough to go outside. It would only take a minute to run back to my room and grab a coat.

'Kari, what's this maze here?' I pointed on the map pulled from my pocket. 'I'd love to see it.'

A warm smile lit her face. 'Okey-dokey. It's fun. Lost a few donsangs in there over the years. They couldn't find their way out. We had to fish 'em out.'

Great. My sense of direction wasn't the best, either. But Kari could guide us.

'Thought we were indoors today?' Jenny laughed as she twisted and turned, checking her reflection in the mirrored floor tiles. 'You wouldn't want to wear a miniskirt in here. You can see everything – in multicolour!'

'Then just as well you're wearing jeans.'

'We going out then?' Kari clapped her hands. It confirmed to me she wanted to be outdoors but had held back because of me.

Jenny knew Kari had been given Ingenii blood. 'Well I'm not going out like this. It's freezing out there. We'll need our coats.'

'There's a cabinet with guest coats and jackets at the back-entrance door.' Madame Thierry stood in the doorway, hands clasped in front of her, a smile on her face. I jumped when I heard her voice, feeling like a schoolgirl caught in some trespass. Why did she have such an effect on me? This was my family home, after all. And how the heck did she know we were here? 'I'm sure Mademoiselle Kari knows where it is. Saves you time running upstairs.'

Jenny and I exchanged glances. 'She's psychic,' Jenny whispered to me.

Or she'd been following us. Now, more than ever, I was convinced she saw us as intruders. Was she making sure we wouldn't touch or damage anything? Perhaps that was the reason for the tension between her and Judy – the ever-present housekeeper and the frequently absent landlady.

Only Kari appeared pleased to see her. 'You think of everything, madame.'

When she turned to me, madame's smile reminded me of a stalking cat. 'I have the perfect coat for you, milady. Come.'

She led the way and withdrew a deep-blue, double-breasted, hooded coat with large black buttons. The smell of mothballs and camphor clung to the fabric. I wrinkled my nose. But it was the one next to it which caught my eye – a black-and-white check with toggle buttons. 'I like this one.'

I reached out to remove it from its hanger when madame snatched it away. 'I'm sorry, milady, this one needs to be cleaned. I'll send it off today.' She threw it on the ground and held the blue one for me to slip on. It fitted perfectly. 'There. I knew it would look good on you.' She beamed.

The coat on the ground didn't look dirty, but then I didn't have a chance to examine the collar and sleeves.

To Jenny she handed a duffle coat. 'Parfait.' She turned to Kari. 'Mademoiselle Kari, I doubt you need anything.'

Kari laughed, pecked her cheek and skipped out the door. 'You two coming?'

The cold pinched my cheeks as soon as we stepped outside, and I raised the hood. Yet it was invigorating, and I was seized by the urge to run. Pity my boots had high heels, which sank into the moist lawn, making it impossible to move faster. Behind me, Jenny laughed.

She had the same problem. Every time she took a step, a clump of grass would cling to her heels.

We could see the maze ahead of us, on the other side of the lawn. Kari stood there, hands on hips, tapping her foot. 'Slow coaches!'

Jenny and I giggled so hard we had to prop each other up every time our heels disappeared into the soft soil. It was a great way to keep warm.

'I hope the ground's a bit firmer where you are,' I called out to Kari.

From a distance, the hedge didn't look imposing, but up close it was at least two metres over our heads. Thank goodness the ground was packed earth: nice and solid. I grabbed a few leaves and scraped the dirt from my heels.

'See? Better.' She stomped her feet to prove it. Kari's boot heels were higher and pointier then mine. How she managed not to get stuck was beyond me. 'Want me to give you a hint how to get to the pavilion at the centre?' she asked.

'Let's stick together.' I looked at the stretch of green ahead, and a strange uneasiness seized me. The laughter of the last few minutes faded, and I turned to see Madam Thierry pocket her phone and wave at us. Nothing odd in that. I smiled and waved back, tucked my hands into the coat's pockets and followed Jenny and Kari in.

# CHAPTER 19 – THE EMERALD RING

**ALEC**

'Alec, come quick. I can't wake Luc. Something's wrong.' Judy's voice came from somewhere on the ground floor of the chateau.

'Where are you?'

'Library.'

I'd been talking with Karl on the front lawn when she called me. His brow creased. He'd heard. 'What does she mean; she can't wake him up?'

My scalp prickled, and I automatically glanced at my serpent ring. The eyes were red. No danger. I listened for Laura's voice. She was with friends. All good there. Yet why…? Luc had excused himself around midday. That was more than three hours ago.

Her face was pale, hands shaking when she met Karl and me at the entrance to the library. 'He's in his office. He's not moving. Why can't I wake him?'

'Let me look.'

Luc was splayed out on the sofa, an empty bag of blood on the ground next to his hand. His pulse was strong. I checked his eyes – he'd been drugged. When I sniffed the bag there was no noticeable scent or residue, or taste either. Only one drug I knew that fitted – Rohypnol. It would've taken effect within twenty minutes of ingesting, but another two-to-three hours before he would've fallen unconscious.

'The blood bag was spiked. There's a chance the others might be, too.' I checked the mini-fridge. There was only one other. Good chance it was spiked, as well.

Judith's hands flew to her mouth. 'He's going to be all right, isn't he?'

'He'll recover in about eight-to-ten hours.' Not even vampires were immune to the drug, it seems.

'Who did this?'

'And how? How did anyone get in here to drug those bags?' Karl inhaled deeply and looked about. 'Can't pick up any other scent.'

Judith gasped. 'But someone had to have been in here! Unless….' She spun around and rushed past Luc's desk, to push against one of the bookcases. 'There's a passageway behind here. An old escape tunnel. It leads to the servants' gate at the other end of the wood. I don't know when it was last used.'

I knew of the tunnel, and all the other secret passageways in the chateau. Luc had led me through them in my early juvenile days. He'd rightly insisted I be familiar with every corner of the estate. Although the family had moved to Australia in the mid nineteenth century, Luc had always seen to it that the passageways were maintained.

'Let me.' She moved aside as I shifted the bookcase to reveal an iron door. No sign of dust when I opened it. I sniffed. Judith's scent again. Yet she said she hadn't been anywhere near this passage. I had no reason to doubt her word.

'Sense anything?' Karl was at my back.

I shook my head. 'Stay here. I'm going to check out the other end.' It only took me a few seconds to run the length of the passageway and open the trap door that led to the surface. The servants' gate faced me. I took another whiff, and there to my right, in a crumpled heap, lay a pale blue jacket and pants. Judith had worn it on the flight from Sydney. Whoever spiked Luc's blood supply used her clothing to disguise their scent. It may have been either a woman or man And why discard it where it could be so easily found? Unless they were sure it wouldn't be traced back to them?

My mind swarmed with questions as I raced back to Luc's office.

'Those are my things!' Judith took the clothes from my hands. 'I sent it to the laundry when we arrived. Where did you find it?'

'Dumped at the exit to the tunnel.'

She looked from me to Karl and back again. 'What's going on?'

'I don't know yet. Is there anything missing?' Whoever was here must have come for something, and it wasn't to kill Luc. Why drug him? What the hell were they after? And how did they know about the secret passageway? One of the servants?

Judith scanned the room and shook her head. She went to Luc, knelt, took his hand and placed it against her cheek. As she did so, she gasped, dropped his hand and pulled open his shirt. Her face went pallid. 'It's gone! His ring and the bloodvault key.'

Her words were greeted with stunned silence.

Without Luc's green serpent ring, not only would the wards guarding the chateau disappear, but also those around the witch's gravesite in Scotland. What had been hidden for centuries would now be visible to all. If the Rebels wanted to prevent the curse from ending, all they now had to do was find and destroy the site. And that wasn't all. Without the ring and Luc's key, there was no way to unlock the bloodvault once our current stock of Ingenii blood vials ran out. Mine would last the length of Laura's pregnancy, and that was cutting it fine.

Whoever took the ring and key must have known exactly what they were for.

This was a disaster. My gut churned. I spun around as Marcus entered. 'What's happened to Luc? He should be—'

'Close the door behind you. This can't get out.'

His brows drew together, and he rushed to Luc's side.

'He's been drugged. The ward ring and bloodvault key have been taken.' I paced the room trying to get the slightest trace of any other scent.

'Deus! How?'

'I don't know!'

'Can someone please explain to me what the hell Luc's ring and key actually do?' Karl asked. He stood by the desk, his gaze darting between Marcus and me, and Luc's unconscious form on the sofa.

'Ever wondered why none of the Brethren could enter these grounds without permission?' His eyes bored into mine. 'Luc's ring contains a spell, which prevents any Brethren from entering. It also shields the site of the curse – the witch's grave – and' —I knew I could trust Karl with this knowledge— 'together with the key, opens the bloodvault.'

'Holy shit!'

'That's about right. We can't enter the vault now, and when the blood vials run out....'

Karl's mouth dropped open. No words came out. Judith brushed Luc's hair back off his face and kissed his brow.

Marcus strode to the door, opened it and called for Jake and Cal. Mingled expressions of horror and anger greeted his words. 'Line up all the servants in the Great Hall. I want to know who did this.'

'Wait. May I make a suggestion, my Lord Marcus?' Karl moved away from the desk, where he'd been standing.

'You may,' Marcus said.

'If there's a damn Rebel spy here, summoning all the staff like that just might make them suspicious. They could do a runner, especially if they know all your not-so-secret passageways.'

'Hate to admit it, but he has a point,' Jake said.

'Who's your oldest, most loyal servant? They usually know everything that's going on. Ask him … or her.'

We exchanged glances and nodded. For all his cockiness and easy-going nature, Karl often made good sense. His perceived flippancy masked a sharp mind.

Marcus sent Cal to fetch Serge Thierry, the estate manager.

'What about the Elders and prefects?' Jake asked.

'Keep them occupied till they leave. Show them the maze.'

Jake and Cal sped off.

'What makes you think it's one of servants?' I had my doubts. The human staff had nothing to gain by siding with the Rebels, and Timur was certainly behind this.

'Who else could it be? They have full access.' Marcus's neck muscles were corded to breaking point. He needed someone to blame – and punish. This wasn't just an attack against the Principate. This was personal – it was his son.

But it would also be pointless punishing the wrong individual. It would only allow the real culprit to get away. 'I don't believe it's anyone among the human staff. Makes no sense.'

'It has to be, Alec. The Brethren staff are prevented from disloyalty by their rings. Luc would know straight away if….'

'If his ward ring had warned him. Which we don't know because it's missing.'

'Deus! What a situation.' He rubbed his face then looked at Luc, lying pale and still. Judith hadn't moved from the floor by his side. He grabbed a chair and placed it next to the sofa on which Luc lay. 'Come, Judith, sit.'

It took a while before Cal ushered Serge Thierry through the door. The man bowed. 'Please excuse the wait Sieur Marcus, but my wife just returned from her weekly shop in Avignon.'

'Yes, I remember her telling me,' Judith said. Although her expression was neutral, I sensed an undercurrent of tension when she mentioned Madame Thierry's name. I'd known Judith for over fifty years, and she'd rarely displayed animosity toward anyone.

Serge Thierry sucked in a breath on seeing his unconscious employer. His wide gaze flicked to Marcus then back to me. 'Milord Lucien….'

'Serge, we—' I began.

The whirr of rotor blades came from the back garden. Since when did helicopters fly over the estate? The serpent ring on my finger began to burn, and its eyes had turned black. My throat went dry.

*Laura, where are you?* I sent my thoughts to her.

*In the maze. Does Luc own a huge black helicopter?*

*Get back to the house!* I tore out of the room.

*Oh my stars! It looks like….*

Shouts, Laura yelling at Jenny to run … gunfire.

# CHAPTER 20 - TAKEN BY THE WOLF

**LAURA**

'Run, Jen!' The ring burned on my finger, and I didn't have to look to know the serpent's eyes were black.

We'd only just entered the maze when whirring rotor blades hovered directly above us. The noise and power of the helicopter made the upper branches of the hedge sway violently showering us with leaves and bits of twigs.

Two men – clad in black, masked by balaclavas – were lowered on ropes and swung toward us. Kari threw me to the ground and covered me with her body as they swooped, just missing us.

'No, don't go out! Stay in the maze.' Kari grabbed Jenny and shoved her into a gap in the hedge. 'They'll snatch you more easily if you're out in the open.'

Rebels! They had to be Rebels, and I knew who they were after. My heart raced like a runaway train as they attempted another swoop.

Kari and I rolled aside in time, but the hedge was too thick to crawl under. I heard the man swear as he missed us yet again.

Above the noise of the engine and rotor blades were yells from the other side of the lawn, and gunfire. My hands shook, and sharp branches dug into my face, but we dared not move. The Rebels in the helicopter aimed their guns at others because no bullets strayed near us.

'Laura, stay down.' Alec yelled. They were shooting at him.

'We're under the hedge. They can't reach us,' I called out to him.

Then came a sound I didn't recognise. Kari clawed away some branches so we could see – a wall of flame between our hiding place and the chateau. Kari gasped. They were using flamethrowers to prevent a rescue. My heart hammered enough to make me nauseous. 'We can't stay here, Kari. We're sitting ducks!' I shouted above the noise of the chopper.

Two pairs of black-booted feet ran towards us. Kari stood and snarled at them, and they shot her twice in the chest at point blank range. All I could do was stare in horror as the impact sent her sprawling. Blood oozed from the wounds in her chest. I knew the bullets wouldn't kill her, but the blood loss could if she didn't get immediate help.

Jenny screamed, and one of the masked gunmen aimed at her.

'No! Don't hurt her!' I tried to crawl out from under the hedge but got caught in the branches.

An arm wrapped around me and hauled me up, tied a harness around my waist and I was whisked into the air. Jenny's tear-stained face was below me.

I was thrust inside the helicopter, strapped down to a seat and surrounded by half-a-dozen-or-so steely-eyed commando types.

'Target achieved. Let's go,' one of them said. He gave the thumbs-up sign to the pilot then strapped himself into the seat beside me. We moved at high speed, the chateau receding further into the distance.

I shook, and my throat dried as the shock hit me. The thunder of the rotors was nothing compared to the roaring in my head as my mind envisioned every imaginable fear. And again and again, my mind replayed the horrid scene of Kari being shot. Hot tears spilled down my cheeks.

*Laura!* Alec's voice resounded in my mind. *Talk to me. Are you hurt?*

Alec was okay! An image of him staring up at the sky surfaced in my mind. I closed my eyes so his face was all I'd see, his voice the only sound I'd hear. *Alec! I'm okay. They haven't hurt me.* I'm terrified, I wanted to say. *They shot Kari!* I wiped my eyes with my sleeve.

I felt rather than heard him release a pent up breath. *She's alright and as angry as a hornet.*

I let out a sob of thanks. *Oh thank Providence! Jen?*

*She's unhurt. Laura, do whatever they say. Don't give them any reason to harm you. Do you hear me?*

*Yes.*

*I'm coming for you, darling.*

I nodded, for whether I liked it or not, I was in no position to save myself. How could I possibly fight a bunch of commandos? *I know. I'm counting on that.*

*Laura, honey, take a look at the men who took you. Can you see any identifying marks on their clothing? Check their hands. Any rings?* Alec only ever called me "honey" when he was worried.

I didn't want to look at my kidnappers. The one to my right, next to the window, had shot Kari. Did he know she was a vampire, and shooting her probably wouldn't kill her? Or was he simply a cold-blooded killer? If anything, I wanted to remove my dagger and stab him with it.

I took a few deep breaths. As long as I could hear Alec's voice, I would get through this. Apart from the two men between whom I was wedged, there were three others who sat directly opposite. They stared straight ahead rather than at me. That bothered me – didn't they have the decency to look me in the eyes after what they'd done?

Equal measures of fear and anger swirled through me. Given the chance, I would have delighted in staring them down.

I pretended to stretch my neck and angled my head in a way to give me a better view of the cockpit. Two pilots. Nothing about their black uniforms gave them away, and since they all wore gloves, it was impossible to identify any wolf's-head rings. Who else could have sent them other than sleazy Count Timur?

*Five men, two pilots. No insignias or wolf's-head rings. They look like commandos – all black uniforms, balaclavas … no way to identify them.*

*Can you see out the window? What do you see?*

I turned to face the window, and the man closest to it pulled the shutter down. I bit my tongue. *They pulled the shutters down.*

Alec swore. *Laura, you're going to have to use your other senses. Close your eyes and concentrate on sound and smell. Take in the scents of the men around you. Remember them. Now try to relax and let your senses work. If I'm right they're not taking you very far. Helicopters don't travel fast.*

Alec was right. Within thirty minutes we were touching down. It had to be Avignon airport. I was escorted off the chopper – sandwiched between two of my guards – and to a waiting jet. It too was black, like the guards' uniforms. A wolf's-head image was painted in silver on the side. No doubt now who'd ordered my abduction.

*We've landed at Avignon airport and they're taking me to a private jet. It has Timur's insignia – a wolf's head.*

*Son of a bitch! I knew it! Darling, we won't make it to the airport in time, but our jet'll be right behind. They're probably taking you to his place in Budapest.*

*Can you intercept us?* Alec didn't answer straight away. Either he was talking to the others, or he was avoiding giving me bad news. I didn't care which as long I continued to hear his voice.

*We can't do anything while you're in the air, but once you land, I expect Timur will have a car waiting to take you to his castle. We don't have allies in Hungary, and Timur's men will be on the lookout for us. Karl's on the phone to his contacts as we speak. They're going to try something … as long as it doesn't endanger your life.*

I understood what he meant. A car chase through the streets of a crowded city was dangerous. I automatically placed my hands over my belly afraid for the tiny life growing within me, grateful my abductors hadn't tied my hands. Maybe they didn't see me as a threat, as they hadn't searched me. My fingers traced the outline of my belt buckle, which hid my dagger.

The flight to Budapest took a little over two hours – at least I assumed that's where we were. My guards lowered the shutters when we boarded the jet at Avignon. Why? Didn't they want me knowing where we were headed? Or was it an intimidation tactic meant to keep me docile? Whichever, it was dark by the time we landed anyway. My heart gave a jolt when I saw no limousines waiting for us on the tarmac. We hadn't landed at the airport, but on a private airstrip outside the city. Directly in front loomed a massive snow-covered castle, its dark grey stone appearing as cold and forbidding as the being that inhabited it.

*Alec, we landed right in front of … I think it's Timur's castle. He has a private runway.*

*Describe the building. I want to be sure they haven't taken you somewhere else.*

*Grey stone, one tall tower with black tiles, lots of buttresses and smaller tower rooms set into them. Many statues set into the wall… looks a bit like a cathedral … stone bridge across a frozen creek….* I tried to send a mental image as my description seemed so inadequate. I felt the warmth of the serpent ring on my finger.

*I can see it! That's the place. Hell, when did he build a private runway?*

*Where are you?* He didn't answer, so I assumed he must be informing the others.

*About to land at Ferenc Liszt airport. Changing course now.*

Was Alec piloting Luc's jet? Where was Luc? Suddenly, the castle doors opened. Timur stood there, dressed in a royal-blue, heavily gold-braided jacket with red, gold-braided pants, and black boots. It looked to be some sort of military uniform – an old Hungarian cavalry uniform? I'd seen similar in museums. Hands on his hips, his moustached smile curling one end of his mouth, he looked like the proverbial cat who got the cream.

I wanted to shove his face into it.

The snowy ground crunched beneath my boots as I was led from the plane. I tried to look up into the sky, hoping to see the lights from Luc's jet, but was prevented by the guards who grabbed my arms and marched me forward.

Timur gave a mock bow. 'Welcome to my humble abode, my lady. I hope your journey was a comfortable one?'

'Why don't you ask your henchmen?'

He laughed, and with a jerk of his head indicated for them to take me inside. 'My private chambers.'

Timur's castle had none of the elegance and beauty of Chateau D'Antonville. There were no lights, not even candles. Cobwebs hung from stained chandeliers, and dust clung to moulding furniture. Faded and threadbare tapestries barely clung to the walls. Who knew how old they were and what other priceless treasures were slowly decaying in this place?

Movement caught my eye. One vampire, then another and another emerged from the shadows. They said nothing. Just stood, watching me. Their lavender eyes glowed in the darkness. One of them bared their fangs, hissed at me and slunk back into the shadows.

Alec was right to call this place a lair – a true vampire lair. I shivered from a combination of fear and cold. It was as chilly within as outside – maybe more so. He probably didn't feel the cold, but what about his human staff? Perhaps he had none, judging by the castle's dilapidated state. Or he ate them. The thought slipped into my mind, and I had to swallow the bitter taste in my mouth.

Up a flight of stairs we went, and more vampires emerged – from within doorways, behind columns, and some, acting like a group of gargoyles, stared down at me from the ceiling rafters. Only the unnatural twist of their heads as I passed and their lavender eyes gave them away.

My feet almost slipped on the damp stone as we strode up to the first landing, so it was a surprise to be led into a well-lit, warm and comfortably furnished room. What a striking contrast. A fire roared in the grate, and the aroma of scented wood mingled with the scent of ham and cheese. A coffee table was set with a tray laden with sandwiches and a decanter of red wine. My stomach rumbled as I hadn't eaten for several hours. The food looked, and smelled, good. Two dark brown Chesterfield sofas were positioned on either side. On one of them sat the last person I wanted to see – Rasputin.

I instantly lost my appetite.

He rose and came toward me. I fought the urge to take a step back.

'Didn't I tell you we would meet again, my lady? Please, come.' He indicated for me to sit.

The door closed behind me as Timur, and my guards, stepped into the room. He snapped his fingers. 'Your coat.'

A sickening shiver snaked through me. Was there a sinister implication? He held out his hand and waited. 'The room is quite warm. You have no need of it.'

Give them no reason to hurt you, Alec had said. I undid the buttons and handed it to him. Rather than hang it on the coat rack near the door, he turned it inside out and tore out the lining. A smug smile smeared his face as he dug his hand into the cavity and pulled out an object hidden within. My heart stopped when he opened his palm to reveal the green serpent ring and the bloodvault key Luc always wore around his neck.

The only way they could have obtained both was if Luc were dead. And Madame Thierry had handed me that coat. She had to be involved.

He slipped it on his finger. I felt the blood drain from my face.

# CHAPTER 21 – RACE AGAINST TIME

**ALEC**

*Laura! Answer me, darling.* My fists clenched over the plane's controls. Laura still hadn't responded. A third time now. She had to be okay. I wouldn't let myself consider otherwise.

I circled the area over the Rebel stronghold trying to locate a suitable place to land. It worried me that Timur had taken her here, knowing we'd follow. Was it his extreme arrogance, or something else? A niggling thought took hold – did Timur already have Luc's ring? That would certainly make him bold enough, knowing the protective wards on our estate would vanish only to reappear on his. Yet I couldn't fathom how the ring could have passed to him so quickly?

If what I feared was true, we couldn't enter – the protective wards would keep us out. Laura would be in there on her own. I swallowed to ease the dry thickness in my throat.

'Over there.' Cal pointed to a road at the far end of the estate. 'Let's try setting her down there.'

I could barely concentrate as we began our descent.

I'd wanted to come alone, but Cal and Karl insisted on coming. The others stayed behind in case of attack. Marcus was sure, that with the wards down, a Rebel assault on the chateau was inevitable. The brazenness of Laura's kidnapping astounded me, especially as they seemed to know exactly where she'd be.

No doubt now; it had to be one of the human staff. Heaven help the culprit when Luc and I find him.

I landed the jet on the icy roadway. A line of trees on one side hid it from the fortress's view. Regardless, we knew the Rebels would sense our presence and be waiting for us. In the dark, with no humans about, we didn't need to conceal our weapons. I threw open my black coat and pulled my sword from its scabbard. My gloved hand tightened around the hilt. We leapt from the plane.

Almost immediately, we were set upon. They lunged at us with the deadly white-oak spiked rings, aiming for any exposed skin. Despite our immunity to the venom, none of us could dare be weakened by even the tiniest scratch.

Most of them were kids: seventeen or eighteen years old at the most. Many were thin, even emaciated, their hair dirty and matted, clothing in tatters. Had they been like that before they'd fallen into Timur's clutches, or had he done that to them?

One or two looked no more than fourteen or fifteen. Girls as well as boys, and all newly turned, maybe only in the last few days. There were about twenty, and they were scared. My blood boiled. I didn't want to kill them. If Timur was their sire, they had no choice but do as he commanded. Karl had said that bastard was involved in the illegal blood-slave racket. These kids, I was certain, were the victims of that.

From the collective curses around me, Cal and Karl felt the same. 'Fuck! They're kids. And look at them!'

'That rat catcher! He knows we won't kill them. It's a delaying tactic.' Cal grabbed a couple and twisted their necks to knock them out. Their companions gazed at them in horror. Weren't they told that breaking a vampire's neck didn't kill them, only rendered them unconscious?

'And it's working,' Karl added.

Some retreated, others surged forward to avenge their companions. We grabbed them, twisted their necks until nearly a dozen lay unconscious at our feet. How could these kids overcome seasoned warriors? My hands itched to relieve Timur of his head. Cal was right. It had to be a delaying tactic.

He pointed his sword at the youngsters. 'Stand aside and let us pass. I don't want to have to kill you.' His Hungarian was more fluent than mine – he'd been around longer.

'Liars! Look what you've done,' one called out. Blood red tears smeared her face and trickled down onto her bedraggled clothing.

They were so newly turned they hadn't yet developed the capacity to smell truth. 'They're not dead. Didn't your sire explain this?' I pointed to the unconscious youngsters. 'They're only temporarily knocked out.'

'Don't listen! Remember what Lord Timur said,' another deeper voice called out. 'These men hold the secret to daywalking. Kill them and it'll be ours.'

One or two moved, but their companions stopped them. They wavered. I grabbed the nearest one by the collar – scrawny little fella who squealed – and hoisted him into the air. 'Wanna die?'

'No,' he squeaked. 'BBBut … you'll kill me anyway.'

'Who told you that?'

'LLL… Lord Timur.' Poor kid was terrified.

'Then he's the one who lied. Listen to me, all of you. I'm the princeps, leader of the Principate – our vampire government, in case none of you have heard of it – and I'm the only one who's allowed to daywalk.' I was simplifying it, but time was running out. 'We keep the rogues in order to protect all of you and safeguard our world.'

'Is that like a president or somethin'?' One blonde-haired lad called out.

'Yes.'

They exchanged glances. I clenched my sword tighter, wishing it were against Timur's neck. One of the unconscious youngsters stirred and sat up, his wide-eyed gaze on me. I jerked my head in his direction. 'What more proof do you want that I'm telling the truth?'

'No! Attack! Your sire has commanded you.' It was the same deep voice as before, from the back of the crowd. He looked older, and he urged the juveniles towards us.

Cal sped past me and threw him to the ground, sword poised at his throat. 'You want to attack? Do it yourself. Don't hide behind a bunch of kids.'

The youngsters hesitated, and I seized the opportunity. 'I have the power to assign you to a new sire; one who won't send you to your deaths. You don't have to obey Count Timur – I can release you. All you have to do is consent.'

A murmur arose as they glanced at each other, unsure whether to accept my offer. I could smell their fear

'I … I consent.' The kid I held by the collar squirmed in my grip. 'If you promise to be my sire.'

'I accept.'

He grinned as I lowered him. 'Juvy to the president. Cool!'

'Princeps,' I corrected him.

Karl slapped me on the back. 'Congratulations! You're a daddy.'

I gave him a sidelong glance. Thanks, Karl.

The rest of them surged forward with the same request, their hollow-eyed gazes turned on me expectantly. A few others slunk back into the trees and ran off. When they warned Timur that his ex-blood-slave juveniles had defected, all the better. Yet how on earth was I going to be responsible for the ones who faced me now? Not only was it was against principate laws – as a safeguard to the human population – but it was impossible for one individual to be responsible for so many over the required period.

'I'm sorry.' I shrugged. 'It's against all our rules for any Brethren to care for more than one juvenile at a time. The principate will look after you till we assign you new sires.'

There were groans of disappointment. They shuffled their feet forming a tight knot of bodies. I didn't have time for this. Every muscle in me strained to run and break into that fortress – to free Laura, to rip Timur apart, to crush to powder every stone of that building until nothing remained. But as princeps, I also had a responsibility to these kids. It was killing me.

'So where do we go?' A red-haired girl with creamy skin asked.

Cal whistled and tilted his chin in Karl's direction. I smiled and nodded. 'Go to Count Karl von Czernin's residence in Prague. You'll find sanctuary there and be assigned new sires.'

'What?' Just to see Karl's incredulous stare was worth it. Thank you, Cal.

I continued. 'It's not far. You should make it long before sunrise.' It then occurred to me, being so newly turned, they might not know his residence. 'Hands up those of you know where it is?' About four hands shot up. 'Good. You lead the rest.'

I angled my head toward Karl. 'Yours is the nearest Principate safehouse. This makes sense. Besides,' I quickly added, as I sensed he was about to protest. 'I reckon quite a few of these kids could be Czech.'

He raised an eyebrow, turned to the waiting youngsters and rapidly fired questions in Czech. Several hands shot up, including the scrawny youngster I'd held. 'Sacra! How'd you know?'

'Guessed. From what I know of Timur, he'd do that just to get back at you.'

'The fucker! You're right.' He took out a cigarette and lit it. 'Fine, as long as you arrange for the Elders to sort this mess out soon.'

'You have my word on it.' I thumped him lightly on the chest then turned toward the youngster I'd accepted as my juvenile. 'What's your name, son?'

The boy turned wide eyes toward me. 'Dominik … uh, sir.'

'What do you want done with this one?' Cal dragged the ringleader forward.

He sneered and shielded his head when some of the youngsters spat at him.

'He kidnapped us….'

'Used us as blood slaves.'

'… never wanted to be vampire.'

Another confirmation – Timur had turned these kids against their will, and the one Cal held procured them. I was tempted to throw him to them. 'That true?' I asked him. He looked at me through hooded eyes. No answer. 'I'll take that as a yes.' I nodded to Cal who beheaded him before digging the spike of a white-oak ring into the remains.

The youngsters gasped and stared wide-eyed at the crystalline remains. Son of a bitch! These kids had no idea…. I glanced at the fortress and dug my nails into my palm.

It was time to move. Only one thing remained to be done. 'You're no longer under Lord Timur's power. Get rid of his insignia. Hand over those wolf's-head rings.'

One by one, they removed them and placed them into our hands. I passed one to Karl. He nodded his thanks as he slipped it on.

'You want us to help you attack?' several eager voices asked.

As far as I was concerned, these youngsters wouldn't be doing any attacking anywhere, anytime soon. I wanted them safe in Karl's castle. But their knowledge of the layout of the castle and entry points could be helpful. They may even know where Laura was being held. Time was ticking, but these juveniles could now well be an advantage to us.

'No. But tell us entry points.' I pointed to the fortress with my sword. 'Hidden passageways, tunnels….'

They all spoke at one.

'Didn't see much. He kept us locked up.'

'In the dungeons.'

'Only took us out when he and the others needed to feed—'

'—Or have their fun.' The youngster who said it turned hollow eyes to me. He was no more than fourteen.

Bile rose in my throat.

Dominik stepped forward. 'There's an old conduit … empties into the moat.' His face paled as he said it. 'Me and few others' —he turned and glanced at six youngsters who stood huddled together— 'had to chuck out the remains….'

I pressed his shoulder. He didn't need to elaborate. Somewhere beneath that fortress was a drain filled with dead kids' bodies. 'Where?'

'Under the bridge,' he whispered.

I stared at Timur's fortress. The stench of death floated on the mist to me. I would batter it down and rip the place apart stone by stone. The thought of Laura there, alone, and probably scared, chilled my blood. I squeezed the hilt of my sword hard, nearly crushing it.

'He's got more men inside – waiting for you,' the youngster added.

I expected this. I grasped Dominik by his thin shoulders. 'Listen carefully. Wait till these kids wake up' —I flicked my head in the direction of the group of unconscious youngsters— 'then go straight to Count Karl von Czernin's castle. Do not feed until you get there. Understood?'

He nodded, and as I conferred with the men, Dominik did as I asked. I watched as the group speed off, ensuring no one made a last-minute turn towards Timur's fortress.

Finally.

'Let's go.' Cal, Karl and I raced toward the fortress and were met by a group of eight sneering men. Each held aloft a wolf's-head ring and a sword in their other hand.

These were seasoned fighters, unrepentant rogues. I swung my sword and beckoned them toward me, itching to avenge those youngsters. 'This is for Dominik.'

With a yell, Cal, Karl and I charged. We leapt upwards to land behind them. The Ingenii blood increased our speed. Before they'd turned, we cut them down. Another group appeared to bar our way. As we leapt upwards, again, so did they. I grunted as we crashed. One blade missed me by inches, but mine found its mark. I landed, dropped to a crouch and rolled into the feet of another who ran at me – my action almost a blur to him. As he bowled over, I rose and sliced off his head. His blood seeped sluggishly into the pristine snow, it's metallic tang rising to my nostrils.

More Rebels appeared. My blade dripped with blood and coated my hand as I hacked my way closer to the fortress.

Next to me, Karl took out another four, the spiked tip of one Rebel's ring barely missing his cheek as the man somersaulted over him and ran off.

The rest scattered. Cal gave chase.

I pocketed the dead Rebels' rings and raced towards the moat bridge. A dozen-or-so Rebels came at us from three sides. Something whistled past my ear. It wasn't a bullet.

'Pull your lapel up. They're using white-oak darts!' Karl pulled one out of his sleeve and showed it to me before turning and aiming it back. A barrage of darts followed, missing us by inches. We dove beneath the bridge.

'There.' I pointed to a metal door. Was this the entrance to the conduit? As more darts landed around us and embedded into our leather coats, I pulled open the door and slammed it shut behind us.

An overpowering stench had me doubling over, wanting to retch.

'Holy shit!' Karl covered his nose with his sleeve.

I did the same, then extended my senses to get an idea how far this tunnel led. No Rebel presence. The only living things down here were the rats and cockroaches.

'I'm not surprised they aren't hammering to get in after us.' Karl indicated the door with a jerk of his head. 'That reek'd kill anything!'

How many rotting bodies were down here? Since we couldn't leave the way we came, there was no choice but to endure the smell and follow to where it led. 'Let's keep moving. It should lead us into the dungeons.'

I took two steps and found myself slammed backwards into Karl.

'Hey! What's up?'

'I don't know.' But I suspected. I stood and moved forward again. It was invisible, but it was there nonetheless. My hand tingled as I touched the unseen barrier, feeling my way along its length. It stretched from floor to roof, barring our way into the Rebel fortress. Dead end. I banged my fist into it only to be thrown back again against Karl.

'Stop doing that!'

'We can't get in. Timur's using the ward ring.'

Karl swore and rushed shoulder first into the barrier. He was thrown back against the concrete wall. 'Oh yeah, we're fucked!' He slid to the ground and remained sitting, sleeve against his nose. 'If the stench doesn't kill us starvation might. No way am I feeding from rats.'

I crouched next to Karl, closed my eyes and leant my head back against the wall. My mind filtered options of escape. 'Cal, where are you?'

'Heading your way. You in the conduit?'

'It's a bloody stench-infected drain!' Karl answered.

'Timur's got the ward ring – the barrier's up. We can't get in—'

'Or out,' Karl added.

'Over a dozen Rebels waiting outside.' One of the perks of ingesting Ingenii blood was the ability to not only communicate over longer distances but to speak at a lower decibel even other Brethren couldn't hear.

'On my way.'

Within seconds, yells and the clash of metal came from outside. I nudged Karl, and wrenching the steel door off its hinges to use as a shield against the Rebel darts, we charged out.

Many Rebels already lay dead, heads separated from their bodies. Cal's speed and military expertise deflected every dart with the flat of his sword.

I saw a flash of silver as moonlight caught the edge of the wolf's-head ring. A Rebel jumped down from the branch above me. I swerved and spun around, my sword slicing cleanly through his neck. Four others encircled me. I threw the metal door at one and bounded over their heads, cutting down another as I did so.

Karl sliced down the other two. Those who were left leapt up and over the outer wall into the safety of the fortress.

Cal followed and was thrown to the ground. 'Yup, you're right. That rat catcher's got Luc's ring.'

I roared, picked up a dead Rebel's head and hurled it at the wall. It smashed against the stone rather than bounce against the barrier.

We stood staring.

Karl grinned. 'I have a brilliant idea.'

# CHAPTER 22 – IN THE LAIR OF THE WOLF

**LAURA**

For a split second, the room swam before my eyes and blackness descended. Alec's voice whispered through my mind, yet I couldn't respond. I reached for the wall as my knees buckled. Timur gripped my elbow and led me to the sofa.

'Wine.'

A cup was placed to my lips. 'Nnn… no, nn…not wine.' My body trembled.

Timur snapped his fingers and pointed at the teapot. 'Pour. Give it to her,' he grunted to one of the guards.

The man avoided eye contact as he placed a cup of hot tea into my hands.

My palms shook, nearly spilling the contents, but I managed to get it to my mouth.

'In spite of what you may think of me, I am still a gentleman, Lady Laura. It's obvious you received a profound shock seeing me in possession of this.' He lifted his hand, revealing Luc's green serpent ring. It looked wrong sitting on his finger. It didn't belong there. It was Luc's. I took a deep gulp of tea to swallow the lump in my throat. Luc can't be dead. He can't be dead.

'Much to my disappointment, but a relief to yours – I'm sure – Lord Lucien is very much alive. My little bird in your household retrieved his ward ring and key for me in return for … a special favour.'

Luc was alive! My father was okay! A sob of relief escaped my lips before I could clamp them shut.

'Yes, I thought that was it.' He rose, took my cup and refilled it, and handed it to me. 'Drink, since you prefer it to the wine.'

The tea was good, and the cup warmed my hands. I drank slowly, to give myself time to think, to process what he'd just said – there was a traitor in my family's household. I was guessing Madame Thierry. Somehow she'd managed to remove Luc's ring and bloodvault key. I was stunned at the failure of our security. Luc was so careful.

'I don't believe you.'

He eyed the ring on his little finger. 'Well, it didn't jump here by itself! Lucien is too trusting of his family and household. That's his weakness. I, on the other hand, trust no one. Which is why I now possess this.'

Not for long, I wanted to say, when I saw his gaze stray to my hand – my serpent ring. I slid my hand beneath my thigh, out of his sight.

'You won't be needing that soon.' He and Rasputin exchanged a glance, and they both laughed as if sharing a secret joke. It sent a chill through me.

What did he mean by that?

Timur stood before me, one hand in his pocket the other smoothing down his moustache. While I sipped my tea, he pulled out a chain from his jacket pocket. Alec's gold crucifix and key dangled from the end. He'd shown it to me the first time we made love. I needed to take it back. It belonged to Alec. I itched to slice Luc's ring from his finger and hoped I'd get the opportunity. I sipped my tea. Timur removed Luc's key from another pocket and slipped it on the chain. It clinked as it joined Alec's. Only one more key, either Judy's or Marcus's, and he would have access to the bloodvault.

But he has no idea where it is, and I certainly wasn't going to reveal its hiding place. I imagined him and Rasputin walking straight into Sam's booby traps. Was it worth the risk?

Although my hands had stopped shaking, I clutched the teacup as a comforter and took stock of my surroundings. If there was one thing I'd leant from my ex-boyfriend, Matt, it was to look for exits, and any object to use as a weapon, if ever I found myself in a dangerous situation. Okay, exits first. Apart from the door I came through, there was one other, set into a bookcase, to my right. There was the fireplace. Rule that one out. But on one side of the fireplace was the usual collection of iron pokers, shovels, brushes and tongs. All had nice long, heavy-looking handles. Pity they weren't made of white oak.

Rasputin stood next to them, hands in his pockets – or rather the knobbly stumps that would eventually become his hands – staring at me as a snake does at its potential meal. 'I must say, I'm puzzled.' His voice was caressing.

I shrugged and feigned disinterest, but his comment had every one of my senses on alert. From what Alec had told me – including my own limited experience – Rasputin was unnaturally perceptive. Although Alec had said nothing, Rasputin had worked out the existence of the bloodvault in Sydney and in France. Could he possibly perceive that I was pregnant – even at this early stage?

'Why did you reject the wine? Surely it would've been better for you than tea?'

Rasputin's eyes bored into mine. This time his attempt at mesmerisation wouldn't work – my serpent ring would prevent it. I planned to lie. But I always hiccupped when I lied, which was why over the years I'd learnt the art of evasion – although it didn't always work. 'Mesmerisation doesn't work on me. The serpent ring prevents it. Give up.'

His eyes narrowed, and his lips curled into a sneer. 'Thank you for the reminder. I have—'

I didn't want to hear anything he had to say. 'What do you want with me, Lord Timur?'

Timur sucked his teeth. 'We come to the crux of it.' He sat on the other sofa, leaned back and crossed one leg over the other, the smooth black polish of his boots catching the light from the fire. 'Originally I had thought to keep you all to myself until one of our ex-Elders fatally discovered your hidden secret.' No one had known my blood was toxic – not even me – until Maris had tried to feed from me. He grinned, and my stomach turned. 'As it is,' he played with the chain, deliberately dangling the keys, 'I may have something just as valuable, and I won't have to wait fifty years.'

Crap. I knew what he had in mind. Since none of the Brethren could feed from me, I was only good as a breeder of future Ingenii. But that would mean having to wait half-a-century to enjoy the benefits of the Bloodgifted, as our blood doesn't mature till we reach fifty. As Timur wasn't willing to wait that long, his only recourse was to kidnap me and hold me for ransom. The price? All the contents of the bloodvault, I'd bet.

'I'm sure you recognise these.'

'They look like keys and a crucifix to me. I didn't know you were religious?' I raised my eyebrows and feigned ignorance.

His gaze flicked to Rasputin then back to me. 'I don't like being taken for the fool.' Timur's eyes narrowed. 'What do these keys unlock?'

'Which particular key? Or is it the crucifix you're referring to? You really need to be specific.'

Rasputin laughed. 'She likes to play games.'

Timur stared at me, long and hard. I poured myself another cup of tea. Not that I needed one, but it gave me time to compose myself and something to focus on, other than his cold lavender stare. Like all his kind, Timur could sniff out a lie, literally smell the undercurrent of emotions humans produced when they tried to cover the truth.

'One of them,' he flicked Alec's key. 'This one, I believe, hung around your guardian's neck. You must have noticed him wearing it.'

My imagination went into overdrive – falling leaves in autumn, waves on a beach, ice-cream cones – any image other than the one his words evoked. The chemical signals my body would produce would betray me immediately. Better still, I focused on the memory of Alec's bleeding and bruised body after the torture inflicted on him by Rasputin and his henchmen. Anger laced my words. 'If I did, it was none of my business.'

He sucked through his teeth, again. 'Come, Lady. You expect me to believe he didn't share such knowledge with you, when you're obviously intimate. I smelled him all over you the night of the Pledge.'

My stomach sank like a stone. There was no point in denial, so I had to play it out. I took a deep breath and smiled. 'Do you tell your lovers everything?'

His lip curled up as he pocketed the chain. 'They don't leave my bed alive.'

How I wanted to throw the hot tea in his face, then hurl the pot. How many young women had he murdered in his long lifetime? And he'd continue to do so. Could I stop him? All it would take was one drop of my blood smeared on his lips, and he'd burn to ash. It wouldn't be hard to slide my finger on the edge of the blade of my dagger. But how to do so without being seen?

'Does that technique work for you? Get many takers? Or do you have to stoop to mesmerisation?'

That wiped the sleazy grin from his face. Timur rose and upended the coffee table. Everything crashed to the floor. I jumped and grabbed the side of the sofa for support as he lunged toward me. 'No more games, now. I know those two keys unlock the secret blood stash Lucien has been hoarding for years. And I know that you know. And I'm sure you also know exactly where it's located.'

I swallowed, staring back at him, defiant. But my heart thumped out a staccato I couldn't calm when he sniffed, bared his fangs and leant in to my neck. His eyes glazed over and became reptilian. I fought my instincts, the repulsion rising in me, and angled my head to the side, baring my throat. If he had just one little taste....

'My lord!' Rasputin yelled, grabbing Timur's shoulder. 'Don't. That's what the little witch wants.'

Damn!

Timur snapped upright, eyes wide, breathing laboured as he stared back at me. 'Her blood's like a frickin' magnet. Lock her in the north tower. It's far enough away from the servants, and the cold will dampen her scent.'

I resisted growing panic. The north tower didn't sound good.

'An hour is all I need, my lord,' Rasputin said.

I dreaded what this meant.

Timur eyed Luc's ring. 'Take your time. Do what you want. Enjoy yourself. While I have this, not even a Principate army can enter.' He grabbed a small black box from the mantelpiece. 'Show her the instruments first. It may induce her to tell us what we want, and then bring both to me in this. I'll send it to Lucien, with my compliments. Unless he reveals the location of his blood stash, this is how he'll get her back – piece by piece.'

Both men grinned. My stomach plummeted.

Rasputin whistled, and two other men entered – the same commandos who had kidnapped me. 'Take the box and escort the Ingenii to the north tower.'

'May I have my coat?' I was shivering.

'You won't be needing it.' Timur turned and walked towards the other door.

'I thought you said you were a gentleman.'

'When I choose to be.' To Rasputin he added, 'Muffle her screams. I don't want to excite our guests.' He slammed the door.

The guards grasped my arms and led me into the cold corridor. One guard walked in front, the other behind. Rasputin followed.

Iciness, that had nothing to do with the temperature in the hallway, spread through my body. *Alec? Where are you?* No answer. Why? *Alec? They're taking me to the north tower. They're going to torture me! Please answer. Talk to me! Alec!* I dug my nails into my thighs as my limbs began shook.

My legs were leaden as we climbed a set of narrow, winding stairs, which ended at a tall metal door. I was pushed through it and stumbled across the freezing stone floor. I regained my balance and wrapped my arms around me for warmth, but even my boots couldn't keep the chill of the damp floor from seeping through to my feet. Moss-covered stonewalls surrounded me. About two metres up, a narrow slit had been cut into the wall through which I was able to peek at the moon. Even if I could jump that high, there was no way I'd be able to squeeze through.

A biting blast of wind hit me. My teeth chattered. It was like being in a refrigerator. But worse still was the writhing of my stomach anticipating what was to come.

Cold laughter made me spin around. Rasputin stood framed in the doorway, a threatening presence in the dark. 'I've been counting the hours for this moment. And here we are.'

I rewarded him with no comment or show of fear. I turned my back.

'Have you ever experienced agonising pain? Such that you begged for death?' His voice held a menacing edge. 'This night, both of your hands will be cut off. Slowly.'

*Oh god!* I recoiled, hitting the wall. *Alec! Alec!* The serpent ring felt cold on my finger, and its eyes were black. A violent tremor racked my body. I stared at a chip in the wall, trying to even my breathing, as dread took hold of me.

'Face me!' His voice was louder.

My hands were sweaty, heart pounding when I turned. Rasputin whistled, and two guards stepped into the room. One carried a jagged saw and wooden block. The other held a thick leather strap, a bucket, and a flaming torch. The door closed behind them.

His lip curled, and he thrust his handless arms toward me. Black gloves covered the stumps where his hands should have been. 'I promised myself to reciprocate, to savour your agony as the torturous pain slices through your body.' He indicated for the man holding the bucket to drop it at his feet. 'I'm sure you've been wondering about this? I hate waste, and that poisonous blood of yours is too valuable to let seep into the ground. Instead, I'll collect it and use it to coat our weapons.' He sniggered. 'Looks like the Principate's about to go up in smoke.' His henchmen laughed. 'And since we can't have you dying on us, the fire here' —he indicated with a jerk of his head— 'will burn into your flesh and sear the open wounds to stop further bleeding.'

My chest constricted, my breath coming in gasps.

Rasputin smiled. 'Yes, that's what I want to see – the terror in your eyes. You knowing what's coming and you can't stop it. Splendid! Now, where is Lucien hiding his blood stash?'

I swallowed. 'Even if I were to tell you, it'd make no difference. You'd still....' I couldn't even mouth the words. I clasped my trembling hands behind my back.

'No, you're right. Nothing will prevent *that*. Perhaps I could reward you by slicing your hands off more quickly.' He glanced at one of the guards. 'You, show her.' The man pulled out a long knife from inside his jacket, and then a piece of paper, which he sliced cleanly down the middle. 'See?' Rasputin said. 'The edge is so much sharper. One chop and it's all over.'

'Some incentive.' My throat had dried, so I could barely get the words out. What a choice. Yet, something in his tone belied his words. The hunger staring back at me demanded pain.

'Personally, I prefer you don't tell me.' He rose from the block. 'My master told me to show you the instruments. Let's have a demonstration to put us in the mood. After which we shall begin.' He addressed the other guard. 'Show her.'

The man took the block of wood and slowly sawed through it, his eyes gleaming as he stared at me. Rasputin grinned. 'Imagine it cutting through flesh and bone.'

My chin and lips trembled. If his aim was to produce mental torture first, it was working. I swallowed hard, closed my eyes and bit down on my lip, but nothing could prevent me imagining the horror to come.

Rasputin laughed. 'Perfect! Now strip. I want you naked and shivering. It will intensify your pain.' He grinned.

My eyes shot open. The guards leered at me and licked their lips – no hope of rescue, no hope of mercy in their cold stares. My knees buckled, and I slid down onto the chilly floor, my eyes squeezed shut so I couldn't see the dreadful blade in the guard's hand.

I'd faced evil before, but never on such a scale. A scream built in the back of my throat. It was exactly what a sadist like Rasputin thrived on. I didn't want to give him the satisfaction, yet how would I be able to bite back my screams once the excruciating torture began? My thoughts turned to my baby. The pain, the shock, the blood loss … neither of us would survive it. I would never see my baby.

'You're a monster!' A sob broke from me.

'Am I? Thank your father's kind for making me one. Stand up and remove your clothes or one of these guards will do it for you.'

'I… I can't.' Should I reveal my pregnancy?

'Lift her up.' He motioned to one of the guards.

'No!' Bracing my hands against the wall, I slowly drew myself up, but the trembling in my legs remained and spread to the rest of my body, joining the sickening hammering of my heart.

I had no choice.

'Tell him you're pregnant! Tell him you're pregnant!' my mind screamed at me.

My hands shook, fingers icy cold, and I reached for my belt – my dagger! A tiny spark of hope flared within me. God bless you,

Lucinda. Rasputin sneered. Let him think I was about to remove my clothes. I would fight, kick, claw, stab and tear at them, scream and yell than succumb like a lamb to the slaughter. And if that failed, I would stab myself in the heart rather than suffer the horror he had prepared for me.

Sweat beaded on my brow. The guards were between me and the door. How to get out? The cell was small. Rasputin was no more than four steps from me, the guards on either side of him. I needed a momentary distraction. Would they fall for what I had in mind? Gut churning, and swallowing the lump in my throat, I glanced at the door behind them, then screamed as loud as I could.

They whirled around. I lunged forward, withdrew my knife and slashed Rasputin deep across the side and back of his neck. He grunted and clutched at the deep cut with his sleeve as he staggered backwards.

One of the guards grabbed me, and I stabbed his hand. He howled and let go. The other caught both my wrists but I managed to knee him in the groin.

The door crashed open. A figure appeared in the doorway, the light catching the glint of the diamond stud in his ear. In a blur, both guards lay dead, and Rasputin found himself pinned to the ground, a sword only centimetres from his bloody throat.

'You okay, pet?' Terens asked.

# CHAPTER 23 – OUR TICKET OUT

**LAURA**

'Oh, Terens!' A sob broke free from me. 'I've never been happier to see anyone in my life.'

'My pleasure, pet. I heard everything.' His eyes blazed as he looked down at Rasputin, and he dug the point of the sword into the wound I'd already given him. 'I'm so tempted to end this piece of shit, right here and now.' He exhaled. 'But unfortunately we need him.' Then under his breath he uttered, 'I need him.'

'Is Alec with you?' My legs leaden, I stumbled past him and stuck my head out the door. The corridor was empty. My heart sank.

'He can't get in, just like we can't get out. That's why, for now, I've got to keep this thing' —he kicked Rasputin— 'alive.'

Rasputin laughed – a strangled gurgle that turned my stomach. The cut I gave him was beginning to heal. Bugger.

Terens grinned down at Rasputin. 'I deliberately snapped those humans' necks to make it look like you did it. So, when you and she disappear, guess what your shit of a master's gonna think?' Before Rasputin could respond, Terens stomped on his neck. The bone snapped. Pity it didn't kill him. A broken neck would only keep him unconscious for the next fifteen to twenty minutes. Terens hoisted Rasputin's limp form over his shoulder and pulled a wicked-looking dagger from his boot. 'Let's get you out of here. There are other things in this place you don't wanna meet.'

'How? Timur's got Luc's ring and the power that comes with it.'

He stabbed Rasputin's rump with his dagger, wiping the blood on his pants. 'He's our ticket. He had permission to come and go before the ward came down. We'll use him to get us out.'

We ran from the cell, down the narrow steps, our boots clicking on the worn stone. His other comment had me intrigued. 'What other things are here?'

'Lamiae. Nasty creatures.' I detected disgust in his voice.

Before I could ask anything further, he lifted his sword. We halted mid-step. Listening. My heart beat triple time. Voices drifted through the walls. They hadn't discovered our escape, yet.

We ran.

'Where'd you get the dagger?' Terens asked.

'Long story.'

'Can't wait to hear it.'

We went through a side passage into another corridor. He indicated for me to be silent as we crept into a room. It was furnished sparsely with a red-velvet-canopied four-poster bed, a mirrored dressing table and chair, and an old-fashioned, carved wooden wardrobe. He dumped Rasputin's body onto the floor, strode to the wardrobe and pulled out a coat, which he threw to me. 'Put this on. It'll keep you warm and disguise your scent.'

I slipped it on and snuggled into its woollen warmth. It was a man's coat, the sleeves long enough to cover my hands like a pair of mittens.

He rummaged around until he withdrew a couple of ties. One he fastened around Rasputin's mouth, the other he used to secure his arms to his body. Then he checked the exits and the window before sitting on the edge of the bed, letting his feet rest on Rasputin's unconscious form. 'We should be safe here for a while until I figure out what to do.'

I sat on the dresser chair. 'How did you know where to find me?'

'Didn't. Only snuck in an hour or so before I saw you being dragged out from the chopper. Came here to kill that bastard, Timur. Had to change my plans in a hurry. So what the hell's been going on?'

Terens's expression remained neutral as I recounted my kidnapping, until I mentioned Timur retrieving Luc's ring from a hole in the lining of my coat. His brow furrowed. 'Yeah, I heard Timur say that – his "little bird" in the chateau. Madame Thierry specifically handed you that coat?'

'Yes.'

He leant his elbow on his knee and rubbed his chin. 'For someone else to have placed the coat there in the hope you'd pick it….' He shook his head. 'I don't believe in coincidences. Has to be her.'

'I agree. Alec said her family had been faithful for years, centuries even. Why would she turn? And there is tension between her and Judy.'

He grimaced. 'Jealousy? I dunno. Maybe. Whatever … the bitch has betrayed us.'

'Can you ring Marcus?'

'Nah. Battery's dead. Can you contact Alec with that telepathy thing?'

'No, I've tried.'

'It's Luc's ring – blocks everything, and now it's keeping us stuck in here and Alec and Cal out there. I'd love to know how the hell she got hold of it.' He chewed his lower lip, brow drawn in concentration as he twirled and flicked the dagger about in his hands.

My heart leapt. 'Alec's here? Where?'

He flicked his head toward the window. 'Jet landed less than thirty minutes ago. Managed to glance out a window. Saw it was ours as it flew over. He's probably in the wood trying to figure a way in.'

I raced to the window, but Terens caught me round the waist before I reached it. 'Hey, there are Rebels out there. Want 'em to see you? We gotta stay hidden, pet.'

'Sorry, I ... wasn't thinking.' I sat back down. My hands ached with the cold, and I tucked them – grateful I still had hands – into the coat's pockets to stop them going numb. The room was icy, and to light a fire in the grate was out of the question – we'd be discovered immediately. Yet, knowing Alec was somewhere out there caused a flame of hope to burn within me.

'We don't have many options. Either we hide here till daylight, find where his master's holed up, stake him and take back Luc's ring. Or, I find a way to get you out of here then go back and finish the job.' He rubbed his chin and eyed the door.

'How long can we stay here?' I didn't want to remain in this horrid castle, but if there was no other choice....

'Reckon we've got four, maybe five hours before the bastard will send his hounds to check on you.'

A tremor racked my body as I thought of what Rasputin was planning to do to me. 'He wasn't going to torture me for information, but for pleasure.' I pointed at Rasputin. 'It would've killed me. I guess I'm not the prize asset I thought myself to be.'

Terens shook his head. 'Wrong, pet. Ingenii are incredibly resilient. It's your vampire heritage. All Brethren know that. You'd survive ... damaged but alive. Seems Timur allows his monkey here' —he kicked Rasputin again— 'to do what he likes.'

I buried my head in my hands. How close had I come to losing them, and maybe my sanity, from the agonising pain? And I still wasn't out of danger. Tears rolled down my face.

'Hey, hey, hey, Uncle Terens is here.' His arms came around me. 'It's gonna be okay, pet. I'm getting you outta here. I promise you on my life; I won't let that stinking piece of shit ever touch you again.'

He cradled me as I cried, even as I wanted to laugh at the "Uncle Terens" title. Then again, he'd watched over me since I was a baby.

A roar tore through the silence, followed by shouts, yells and swearing.

'Shit! He's checked on you earlier than I thought. Gotta run.' He scooped Rasputin from the floor, dumped him over his shoulder and unsheathed his sword. 'Keep your dagger handy.'

I wiped my eyes and palmed my dagger, silently thanking Lucinda, yet again. 'Where to?'

'Dungeons. There's a conduit, which empties into the moat. Didn't want to take you back that way.' He stopped and looked hard at me. 'Stay close.'

Dungeons. The word conjured the worst images – pain, horror, torture. Who'd expect anyone to flee there? And what was so bad about the conduit that he didn't want to take me that way? But with the shouts getting louder, I had no time to let my imagination free. Terens checked the corridor before we slipped from the room, Rasputin's upper body dangling down his back as we ran. I winced as the stone floor amplified the thud of our boots as we made for a door at the other end. Stairs led downwards. So far we hadn't met anyone – no weird gargoyle vampires stepping out from the shadows. Would our luck hold?

Terens halted and placed his finger to his lips. We both listened for voices, or the tramp of feet headed in our direction. I dared not breathe. My palms sweated, and the dagger slipped. I caught it before it clanged to the floor. Terens rolled his eyes. A minute later we were running again, our boots stomping on the stone steps. Down, down where the cold pinched my cheeks and stale air assaulted my nostrils.

He kicked open a metal door. A long, dark hallway lay ahead with a set of stairs descending ever downward. My stomach somersaulted at the stench.

'What is that?'

'Human remains.'

Oh, my Lord! I covered my nose and mouth with my sleeve as we reached the bottom. A series of caged cells stood on either side of a dank corridor. Their doors were open. Bowls of water, and what looked like food, lay spilt on the dirt floor. The place smelled of fear and death. I didn't have to imagine the poor unfortunates who'd been imprisoned here.

At our feet, a narrow channel that reeked of human excrement and blood ran down the centre of the floor to a metal grill at the other end. I had a feeling that's where Terens intended to go.

He glanced back at me. 'Those cages have been emptied recently.' He lifted the grill to reveal a narrow opening wide enough for a man to slip through. But Terens was a big guy with a big burden. How on earth was he going to get through?

'Worse to come, pet.' Terens dropped Rasputin's body down the manhole with a thud and jumped down after.

Gripping my dagger and ignoring the tight knot in my stomach, I climbed down after him – and stepped onto something soft. The stench was overpowering. I dry wretched.

'Don't look down. Stay close. Eyes ahead.'

Terens's sword glinted in the darkness as he held it out. There was no speck of light to signal the end of the tunnel, and I fought the urge to vomit every step of the way. My peripheral vision revealed layers of human bodies piled one on top of the other, each in different stages of decay. My boots sank into putrefying flesh and kicked against skulls. A couple of times I nearly tripped.

Terens grabbed my arm. 'Hold onto me.'

I repeated his words in my mind. Eyes ahead. Don't look down. Don't look down. But nothing could alleviate the dreadful smell. It was burnt into my nostrils forever. My thoughts strayed to the young people, perhaps even children, whose murdered remains lay here. They had been preyed on by a monster who had demanded all their blood. How different from my father's household. I blinked away tears.

How long is this tunnel? Eventually the artificial softness of the ground gave way. Here were dried skeletal remains, human as well as animal. Who knew how old they were? They crumbled like rotted wood beneath our feet. I glanced at Terens. His face was pallid, lips curled back in a grimace. Even a seasoned warrior like him was disgusted by what we'd seen.

'Once I've killed Timur, I'm going to burn this place down!'

'Let me light the match.'

'You got it.'

In spite of the darkness, I saw the outline of a door. We were almost there when Terens's sword hit an invisible barrier. It bounced back, nearly smacking him in the face.

'This is it – the protective ward.' He adjusted Rasputin's weight on his shoulder and held him in place with one hand. 'Okay, pet, you can help out here. Grab this thing's leg and hold it out. We might be able to get through as one entity.'

'Fingers crossed.' We strode to the barrier, me holding Rasputin's leg in front of us so it would be the first object to make contact. Hopefully it would let him through – and us. Rasputin's leg bent as the protective shield held. 'Not letting us through.'

'Try again.'

We took a step forward. Again the barrier obstructed us.

Terens threw his head back. 'Bastard could've waited another hour. Shit!' He nearly wrenched my arm from its socket when he threw Rasputin's body against the wall.

'Why won't it let us through?' My gut churned. We were at a dead end. If the Rebels discovered us we were trapped.

'My ruse worked all right. Would've gone perfectly if that bastard, Timur, hadn't decided to check on you.' He kicked the unconscious Rasputin. 'Now he's stuck in here as well. Timur doesn't want his monkey to leave, and as long as he wears the ward ring, he controls who comes and goes.'

'Oh no!' Terens had carried him all this way for nothing.

Heaped against the wall, Rasputin's leg twitched. 'He's coming to.'

I made a small incision in my palm and smeared my blood over the blade. If Rasputin came anywhere near me, I wouldn't hesitate to strike. It would give me no pleasure seeing him die in such a horrible way, but it was my life or his. And after what he had planned to do to me, he deserved no compassion.

Terens lurched forward and snapped Rasputin's neck again. He'd be out for another twenty minutes. I sheathed my dagger. 'How many times can you do that?'

'Infinitum. Now let me think.' Terens dug the point of his sword into the ground and slid down onto his haunches, head bowed.

We hadn't come all this way for nothing. So close, only to be stopped.... An idea popped into my head. Did that rule refer only to Brethren? I was human ... well, half-human. Would the barrier keep me in? I stretched out my hand.

'What are you doing, pet?'

'See if it'll let me through. I'm not vampire.'

He rubbed the diamond stud in his ear. 'Worth a try. Go ahead.'

Taking a deep breath, I moved forward, the metal door to the outside so cruelly close. Although I could see nothing, my fingers tingled, and the sensation spread up my arm as I touched the invisible wall. Like a piece of transparent plastic, the barrier stretched under the pressure of my hand, until it finally burst, and I stepped through.

Terens blew out a breath. 'Well, what do you know!'

I held my hand out to him. 'Take it and come through.'

He shook his head. 'No, pet. It doesn't work that way. Your human side is stronger, which is why you can get through.'

'Try.'

He sighed, grasped my hand and took a step forward, only to crash into an unseen wall. No matter how I tried, the barrier on his side held.

'It's no use. You go. Run into the woods. Alec'll find you. Tell him ... Lamiae.'

'What about you?'

'Do what I came here for – kill Timur and take back Luc's ring. Without it, we're stuffed.' He hoisted Rasputin's body over his shoulder again. 'Going to use Timur's monkey here as leverage. Either we trade or I kill them both. Or, I trade and still kill them both.' He grinned. 'Yeah, that sounds better.'

'Be careful. Rasputin's cunning.'

'Don't worry about me. Now go. Don't waste anymore time.'

I tore open the heavy, rust-encrusted door. A delicious draught of fresh air hit me. I inhaled deeply to rid myself of the nauseous stench in my nostrils and turned to take a last look at Terens.

'Run!'

The dagger in my sweaty palm, I raced up a set of steps leading to a bridge that spanned the frozen moat. I prayed no guard would spring into sight. Surely the crunch of my boots on the snow would give me away? Where were the woods? Terens said to make for the woods. A whistle split the silence. My heart leapt into my throat and like a startled rabbit, I ran for the nearest clump of trees.

*Alec, where are you?* I didn't dare call out for fear of Timur's guards. The woods could be full of them.

Ahead of me, a figure loomed. *Laura?*

My heart beat so wildly it nearly broke through my ribcage. I ran towards him, caught my heel on a rock, my ankle turned and I went down. Blood thrummed in my ears as I scrambled to my feet.

Someone grabbed my arm. I screamed, withdrew my knife and stabbed out wildly.

## CHAPTER 24 – THE WOLF LOSES HIS BITE

**LAURA**

The Rebel howled and released me as my dagger found its mark in his eye. A second later his head rolled in the snow. Alec's sword dripped with blood as he caught me to him. I threw my arms around his neck, my heart fluttering like a freed bird.

'I thought I'd go mad.' After a moment, he pulled back and caught my face between his hands. 'Did they hurt you? How did you get out?'

'No, I'm okay, and through the conduit. But if Terens hadn't got to me in time....'

'He's in there?' Cal stood next to Alec, his brow creased, eyes fierce as his gaze darted between me and the conduit.

I nodded. 'He got me out—'

'The conduit? I was in there earlier. Laura, there are things—' Alec's brows knitted.

'I know. It's filled with human remains. Horrible.' I closed my eyes, turned my head from Alec's shoulder to draw in more fresh air. Would that stink ever leave my nostrils?

Yet another sweet, coppery tang rose from the ground. The ground was littered with disembodied corpses. Blood stained the snow. My stomach heaved.

'What do you mean if he hadn't got to you in time?' Alec asked.

I concentrated on Alec's face, trying to block out the grisly scene around me, and recounted what Rasputin had planned to do to me. His expression darkened, his eyes paled, and although his mouth was closed, I could tell from the tiny bulge above his top lip that his fangs had slid down. Cal swore. Karl sucked in a breath and then spat onto the ground. 'I'm going to kill that ape!'

'I used my dagger and sliced his neck, but there's no way I would've gotten out without Terens.' I shivered.

Alec pulled me closer. 'We need to get you somewhere warm.'

'I'll be all right, but Terens can't get out. Timur's got Luc's ring and he's going after it – alone.'

'Terens can handle himself.'

'I know he can, but there are a lot of vamps in there and some of them are strange ... like statues ... gargoyles even, and perched in the rafters. Weird. He said to tell you "lamiae"'.

Cal and Karl exchanged glances. 'Then he's in danger,' Cal said. 'How many did you see?'

'The gargoyle things?' Cal nodded tersely. 'Maybe three ... four at the most. "Lamiae"?'

'I'd forgotten about them. It's been so long....' Cal looked at Alec. 'How much do you know?'

Alec shook his head. 'Apart from the name, not much. Luc only mentioned them being wild, uncontrollable and powerful. I found out more about them in Marcus's chronicle. They can't be killed. Not even arrows and spears made from white-oak can penetrate their leather-like skin. If the images are anything to go by, they're more animal than human. Marcus said it took you guys years to catch them then imprison them in separate fortresses, each under the control of a prefect.'

Cal nodded. 'They're the most ancient of our kind. How old exactly, no one knows. Possibly Babylonian by their speech – those who could still speak. Like us, they can mesmerise their prey, but what makes them really bad is they can do that to us, too –their own kind. They project an image of peace and tranquillity … you know, like a favourite place you want to be. Once you let them into your head….' He drew his finger across his throat. 'Had a hell of a time locking them away. Keeping them starved's the only way to stop them.'

'Timur's probably fed them by now. So how do we stop those things getting into our heads?' Alec asked.

Cal scratched his head. 'You can't. Just keep telling yourself it's not normal. Fight it all the way.'

'Wonderful!' Karl lit a cigarette and sat on a stump.

I guess it didn't matter if his light would attract unwanted attention. From the litter of corpses around us, the Rebels already knew they were here.

'Who turned the lamiae?' Were they gargoyles transformed by a vampire? Why on earth would anyone do that? My head swam at the possibility that another creature of legend existed.

'No one. Plague killed most of the Babylonian population. Of the survivors, a few became lamiae – the first vampires.'

'The virus mutated their DNA,' Alec added.

'That's it. Every vampire on the planet is descended from them – except us, of course.'

'Then why don't all other vampires look like them?' I was relieved that gargoyles didn't exist, except as decorative drainpipes. It was odd, though, that the progenitors of all vampires were so different in appearance from their descendants. What had happened? And when?

Cal shrugged, braced an arm against the tree and stared at the fortress. 'Don't know. The worst of them we locked away in separate fortresses. This one' —he pointed with his sword— 'wasn't one of them.'

'He's gathered them.' Somehow Timur had managed to collect the most vicious creatures on this planet to use against the Principate. But, how was he controlling them?

Cal nodded. 'Of the nine prefects who defected, four were Keepers of the Lamiae.' Cal shook his head. 'I thought I knew those guys. How the hell did Timur get to them?'

'Rasputin,' Alec said. 'It had to be him. Too much of a coincidence that of all the prefects, those four – the most loyal Principate supporters – should defect. He mesmerised them into releasing the lamiae to Timur.'

'Rasputin!' Karl spun around and kicked one of the decapitated Rebels' heads, sending it soaring over the treetops.

Cal's earlier words nudged an idea. Nothing is indestructible – the lamiae must have a weakness, a vulnerability somewhere. If they were the first vampires, then … 'Could my blood kill them?' All three turned to stare at me. 'It killed Maris, why not them? I mean, they're still only vampires, right?'

Alec's brow creased. 'Don't see why not, but it means—'

'—Taking some of my blood, I know. But if you only take a bit – enough to kill those things….'

Alec's jaw tightened. I knew that sign. 'No. We'll find another way. I'm not risking you.'

I sighed. Taking a syringe-full was not what I had in mind. I withdrew my dagger. 'My blood's smeared on it.' I'm sure they could smell it. 'All I did was my cut my palm.' I held that up next. The cut had already healed. His eyes widened in understanding. 'Show me your swords, gentlemen!'

Alec smiled. 'That I can do.'

Once again, I gritted my teeth, ignoring the sting, and sliced open my palm. I wiped my hand along the flat of Alec's blade then pumped my fist to encourage more bloodflow to smear along Cal's and finally Karl's swords. I did the same with their daggers.

'What if it doesn't work?' Cal eyed the tips of his weapons warily. My blood was just as deadly to him and Karl. Both knew how to handle dangerous blades, so I didn't have to fear for them.

'Then we've lost nothing,' Alec replied as he licked clean the wound, kissed my palm and tied a handkerchief around it.

Despite everything around us, when our eyes met, it was impossible to look away. I was drawn into those lavender depths and filled with a strength and courage I never knew I possessed. Did Alec feel the same?

Our rings glowed, bathing our faces in a ruby aura.

'Yes,' he whispered and kissed my knuckles.

'Happy to test for you, Cal, right into that fucker's face!' Karl's voice broke the spell. He growled and pointed his sword as if plunging it into Timur.

I blinked and refocused. My blood would no longer be fresh by the time they entered the fortress. It would have dried on their blades. Would it be just as effective? Perhaps the threat of coming into contact with my blood may be inducement enough for Timur to surrender Luc's ring and the two bloodvault keys. I could only hope.

'You need to know that Luc's ring and bloodvault were hidden in the lining of the coat I wore when I was kidnapped. Madame Thierry handed it to me. She got it from the storage cupboard at the back of the chateau.'

Cal's brow furrowed as he looked at the coat I wore.

'Not this one.' I pulled the lapel of my coat. 'Terens found this one for me. Timur's got the coat Madame Thierry handed me.'

His expression changed to an incredulous stare. 'What are you saying, Laura?'

'Timur boasted he had a contact in the chateau. The first thing he did was take my coat and search it. He knew exactly where to look. And it was Madame Thierry who insisted I take it when I preferred another one. I doubt someone else hid it there hoping I'd put it on.' I recounted what I'd witnessed earlier that morning. 'Terens reckons it's her, too.'

For a moment no one spoke. Cal kept shaking his head. 'I can't believe it. The Thierry's have been the most loyal....'

Even Alec looked shocked. 'Luc was drugged. Anyone in the household....' His eyes widened. 'Cal, it has to be her. Only she has access to every room in the chateau – she holds the keys, and if she has something against Judith and Luc....'

'But what? What possible motive can she have?' Cal spread his arms and shrugged.

'I don't know, but until we do....' Alec pulled out his mobile phone and dialled. 'Jake, confine Madame Thierry to her room. She may be our culprit.' On the other side, Jake gasped. 'Look, I don't have time to explain. Trust me. Lock her up.' Jake asked after me. 'Yes, we have her. She's safe.' Alec pocketed the phone and looked at Cal. 'You know I had to do that.'

Cal dipped his head, face crestfallen. I could understand his shock, his disappointment. What if I was wrong? What if I'd misinterpreted everything and falsely accused an innocent woman based on circumstantial evidence? My stomach churned. I'd dropped a bombshell. Yet, something deep within me said I was right.

Karl squeezed his shoulder. 'The sooner we get Terens out, the sooner we can get back. We question her – we must know the truth.'

Cal's eyes were steel as he looked up at the fortress. 'Laura, is he laying low?'

I shook my head. 'Said he's going after the ring ... wants to kill Timur.'

Cal swore. 'Idiot will get himself killed! Why can't he wait? We know a way in.'

He turned, and plucking a round object from the ground, quietly stalked toward the fortress. Only then I recognised it as a human head.

Alec grabbed Cal's arm. 'Wait! You're not going in there alone. Let me get Laura to safety, and we'll go in together.'

'There isn't time. If they catch his sent.... The lamiae remember us.' Cal's body tensed; his knuckles white as he clenched his sword.

Howls and shrieks emanated from the fortress. Cal's gaze darted to the forbidding buildings. The wind had picked up and whistled through the branches, joining in the unholy chorus. Had those things found Terens? I prayed they hadn't.

'Go. I'll take Laura to my place in Prague. I promise to keep her safe.' Karl placed his hand on Alec's shoulder.

Alec's chest rose and fell as his gaze burned into mine.

I knew he was torn. 'I'll be fine. Go. Terens is in there. He needs you.' I reached up and kissed him. 'Go!'

His kiss in reply was fierce, pressing his lips to mine, drawing the breath from me. He nodded to Karl and, grasping a rebel head, sped towards the fortress.

My warrior.

Karl tugged on my hand. 'We must go.'

'No, wait, please.' I watched as they scaled the outer walls and disappeared into a window, praying he'd come back to me, praying all three would come out alive.

'They're in!' He grinned then taking my hand, led the way through the forest.

The temperature plummeted the further we travelled. Pine branches whipped my face and pulled at my hair. Once or twice I stumbled, my boot catching on exposed tree roots. We stopped at the edge of a dirt road. The snow had been ploughed and salted to keep the road free of ice.

Karl withdrew his phone and called his contacts. The utter silence of the woods was unnerving. I kept my ears trained for the slightest sound, anything to indicate the proximity of Rebels hunting us.

As the night wore on, the cold deepened. I rubbed my arms, wriggled my toes and stomped my feet to keep my blood circulating. My teeth chattered so hard I could barely speak. 'W-w-w-where are w-w-we going?'

Karl's gaze roamed the woods, his sword at the ready. We moved off again. 'Luc's plane. It's on the other side of that crop of trees.'

I stumbled again, trying to keep up with him. Karl sheathed his sword and swung me onto his back. We sped through the night. In the distance, the jet's dark shape stood silhouetted against the moonlit sky.

Within minutes, I was strapped into my seat, a blanket wrapped around me. Karl taxied the plane down the empty road. Soon we were airborne. I stared from the window as the fortress receded from view.

'Stay alive, my love,' I whispered and with every ounce of will sent it winging to Alec, hoping somehow he'd hear, wherever he was within those nightmarish walls.

The eyes of my serpent ring alternated between dark red and black. Since the rings didn't differentiate between wearer, sometimes it was hard to know who was in danger. It could be either of us, or both. Yet deep down, I knew it was Alec.

# CHAPTER 25 - LAMIAE

**ALEC**

We'd leapt in through a partially open window. I inhaled and nearly sneezed. Dust and mould. No whiff of Brethren, though, except for the Rebel's head in my hand. I let it drop and strained my senses to catch the slightest sound of movement on the other side of the door. Carpet muffled our footsteps.

Cal searched the room for exits. 'Terens, where the hell are you?'

Voices all around us. I concentrated on one alone.

'Cal? How'd you get in?' Terens – he was alive.

'Rebels' bodies.'

I cracked open the door and glimpsed a wide corridor with a set of stairs. Above rose a vaulted ceiling criss-crossed with rafters. Laura said she'd seen the lamiae perched in them. I'd never seen the creatures, except for the images in Marcus's chronicle.

'Mid-level, green carpet, moving toward the staircase,' Terens replied.

'I see it,' I whispered to Cal. 'Terens, any lamiae?'

'Plenty. They caught my scent. They're onto me. You got Laura?'

'With Karl. On her way to Prague.'

'Good.'

If the lamiae were after him, we didn't have much time. Tightening my grip on my sword, we ran into the corridor.

'Stay where you are,' Cal said. 'We're coming.'

There was a short silence. Then a breathless, 'They found me, bro.'

We hurried through the building unopposed. I sensed Brethren all around me, drawn by the smell of the Ingenii blood. Yet not one confronted us. A few hissed as we passed, their eyes fixed on our blades. I bared my fangs. They retreated and slunk into murky corners.

I inhaled. Amidst the number of Brethren, Terens's scent was difficult to isolate. Another masked it … one I recognised. Rasputin. He was a fearsome opponent.

Terens grunted. We sped toward the sound, passed endless corridors and doors, the sickly smell of decay all around. Ahead loomed a grand staircase overlaid with fraying red carpet. Below us, on the next level, his back against the wall stood Terens, the edge of his sword at Rasputin's neck. Several dead Brethren lay at his feet. Four snarling creatures inched their way toward him. Tough, leathery skin covered their grotesque features, and a foul stench surrounded them. They appeared more bat-like than human with their long pointy ears and flat snouts. These were the vampires of nightmare, the original nosferatu.

'I know you,' one of them said, each word hissed out on foul breath. 'Terentuisssss.'

Timur stood behind them, his back to me. 'I'm pleased to see my servant hasn't betrayed me.'

'Yeah? How much is he worth to you?' Terens pulled Rasputin's head back. But his movement was slow, almost drowsy. He shook his head and blinked rapidly a few times as if warding sleep from his eyes.

Damn! The lamiae were getting to him. His gaze whipped to us, and he smiled. We leapt over the railing. Cal landed next to Terens.

I jumped on Timur and forced him to his knees before he could sense my presence, the edge of my sword a hair's breadth from his throat. 'Smell the Ingenii blood? Just a tiny nick and you burn.'

'Do it!' Terens ground out. I knew he'd come here to kill Timur.

Timur let out a loud growl. 'How did you get in?'

'Hitched a ride.'

'Calixtusssss. Sssssuch a long time,' another of the lamiae hissed. Long talons extended from almost-reptilian fingers, and he swiped at Cal, who swung his sword in a wide arc to keep them at bay.

'Kill them! Kill them!' Timur screeched.

'Another sound and I cut slowly. Let the Ingenii blood do its work.' I twisted his head to the side, the cold edge of my blade tickling his skin.

A sweet calm fell over me as I imagined myself holding Laura, her beautiful smiling face gazing at me....

'What the hell are you waiting for? Do it!' Terens's voice pierced through the haze. Sweat glistened on his brow, but his eyes blazed as he glared at Timur.

I gritted my teeth and brought to mind whatever I loathed, whatever made me edgy ... whatever made me want to kill.

The fog cleared, and adrenaline surged through my blood. 'I want him alive and brought before the Elders for trial and public execution. We could end this rebellion with one blow – cut off the snake's head, and the body dies.'

'Why the shit do you think I came here for?' Terens snarled.

'You imprisssssoned ussss. Sssstarved ussss. No blood for ccccenturiessss!' The lamiae grinned and fanned out, encircling us.

Again, that debilitating serenity stabbed it's way through my defences.

'I freed you and fed you, my lords.' Timur's Adam's apple vibrated against my blade.

The lamiaes' laugh was like rocks falling in a gravel pit. 'You have ssserved your purposssse. Now you die.'

'Couldn't agree more,' Terens said, his words slurred.

Timur growled. 'You ungrateful pack of—'

'What did I say?' I pulled Timur's head back, straining the sinews in his neck. It took all my strength to keep focused. He grunted but dared not touch my blade, his nails digging into the carpet as I kept him on all fours.

'If you wanted me dead, I already would be,' he said.

We needed to get out of here. 'You're going before the Eldership. Whether alive or dead is up to you.' I glanced at Terens. My next words had to get through; shake the lethargy settling over him. 'I think Terens would prefer you dead.'

It worked. Terens growled, and his lip curled back in a sneer as he glared at Timur. 'Let's do it now.'

The lamiae hissed, stood to full height and unfolded their leather wings. 'Our sssstrength returnssss.'

Timur snickered. 'Hear that? Not good news for you.'

'Sssssoon will we fly again.'

'—hunt—'

'—and feed our fill.'

'Pity it won't improve your looks.' Terens smirked.

They screeched and inched closer, their extended talons as lethal as swords. 'You die firsssst!'

Terens chuckled, dropped Rasputin and unsheathed the second sword on his back. 'Do your damnedest, you ugly bastards!'

Cal swore when the shrieking lamiae flew at Terens. 'Just once, I wish you'd keep your mouth shut!' Dagger held aloft, he attacked.

'Where's the fun in that?'

Their blades danced in unison, the lamiae no match for their superior speed. Yet no matter how many times they struck at the creatures' necks, their thick hides deflected every stroke. The creatures refused to fall.

Timur's body shook with suppressed laughter. *How I itched to end him, but I wanted to bring him back him alive. The Rebels needed to see him publically put down.*

With a shout, Cal darted to the side and plunged his sword into one of the creatures' soft underbelly – its only vulnerable soft. The lamia's eyes widened, its mouth opening in a silent screech as smoke and flame rose from its body. Within seconds, nothing remained but a stinking pile of brown ash.

'Huh! It works.' Cal stared dumbfounded at the smoking mess.

'What'd you do?' Terens gaped at Cal.

'Bit of Laura's blood. Scraped it along the blade.'

'Hell! Good thinking.'

The remaining lamiae howled and retreated then turned and fled, darting high into the rafters, leaping from beam to beam like spider monkeys. Almost instantly my energy returned. Cal set off in pursuit.

'No, leave them,' I said. 'We need to get away from those things. Doubt they'll attack us again, and they're too weak to venture out.'

'You sure?' His gaze darted around then his shoulders relaxed. He threw Terens his dagger. 'Here, take this in case they come back. Got Laura's blood on it, too.'

Rasputin stirred. Timur tensed beneath my grip. *Was he expecting Rasputin to rescue him? He'd be disappointed.* I threw him against the wall next to his monstrous juvenile, the edge of my sword poised beneath the throats of both.

Cal and Terens crouched eye-level with the two.

Terens held the point of the dagger directly beneath Rasputin's nose. *Nice touch.* Rasputin blinked then stared at the knife. 'That's it. Take a good whiff. Recognise it? Ingenii blood,' Terens said.

Rasputin's eyes widened. He gulped as he stared at the dagger. Fear and anger emanated from him.

'Not so brave now, eh? Yet you planned to spill that blood. I should make you lick it!' I barely controlled my rage. If Terens hadn't shown up, I hated to think what he would've done to Laura. I owed him.

'Good idea.' Terens grasped Rasputin's chin and placed the flat of the blade a whisker from his mouth.

Rasputin inhaled sharply, sucked in his lips and tried to draw away. I wanted him dead, a slow tortuous death. Unfortunately, Laura's blood was too efficient. 'What kind of sick son of a bitch does that to a woman?'

My fists begged to connect with his face. Hell, I'd punish the son of a bitch now.

'Cal, swap.' In an instant, Cal held Timur down, his dagger poised at his throat.

I indicated for Terens to lower his knife. I slammed Rasputin in the face, a small measure of satisfaction sinking into my gut. His head rebounded against the wall. I hit him again, my serpent ring leaving an indentation on his cheek and mouth.

His eyes narrowed as he glared at me. He raised his handless arms and through bloodied lips mumbled, 'Vvvengeance.'

'You were a priest once! Didn't you used to preach that vengeance belongs to God? Or have you abandoned that, along with your humanity?'

Rasputin stared at me defiantly, blood trickling down his chin. 'Your kind made me that way. You turn us into monsters then bind us with your rules. You want us to be like the humans when there is nothing human left in us!'

'Wrong. Attempting to murder an innocent girl then seeking retribution against the one who saved her? Only a diseased mind thinks like that.' I struck him again and wiped the blood from my hand onto his shirt.

'And you' —I speared a look at Timur— 'wanted to send her back in pieces!' I backhanded him. He licked the trickle of blood from the cut on his lip and grinned at me. Sick son of a bitch. 'Let's see how you like it.'

'Alec, we don't have time for this. We need to get out of here,' Cal said.

'I know,' I panted, bracing my shoulder.

I asked Terens for his dagger since mine was smeared with Laura's blood. It wasn't Timur's time to die, yet. I glanced at Cal. 'Get him down.'

Cal pushed Timur's head to the ground with his foot and held him there as I bound his arms behind his back with my belt. I grabbed his ringed finger. 'That ring isn't yours.' He struggled and roared when I sliced off his finger, removing the ward ring. 'You're lucky I didn't saw it off!'

I tossed the dagger back to Terens, who cleaned it on Rasputin's coat before sliding it back into his boot.

Timur angled his head and glared at me, spittle trickling from the side of his mouth onto the carpet. 'How does it feel to be so self-righteous, you and your elite daywalking group?' His words spewed out from between clenched teeth. 'At least I've accepted what I am, not fighting against my nature. I'm not the one living a lie!'

Ripping a section of his jacket, I wrapped both ring and finger in it then pocketed it. The ward ring wasn't mine to wear, but I hoped it would be enough to lift the protective ward from around Timur's fortress.

I indicated for Cal to haul him to his feet. If my hunch was correct, my bloodvault key, and Luc's, would be somewhere on him. Buttons flew from the old military jacket he wore as I tore it open. There it was, round his neck, still dangling from my chain, including Luc's key and my mother's crucifix. 'Mine, I believe.'

'We deserve to walk in the daylight, too,' he said as I threw it around my neck and tucked it beneath my shirt.

'I agree. Which is why we distributed the Ingenii blood among all Principate prefects. I'm surprised you haven't been informed.

Didn't your human underlings mention the number of Brethren enjoying the daylight when they kidnapped Laura?'

His sneer turned into a wide-eyed stare and he swallowed. 'All of it…?'

'Seems you missed out. How does it feel knowing your rebellion was all for nothing?'

Timur's face turned ashen.

My phone buzzed – message from Karl. Laura was safe and he was sending the jet back – with reinforcements. 'Karl's sending backup.'

Timur's eyes narrowed, and he swore at the mention of Karl's name. 'You're presuming you'll leave here alive.' His eyes darted to the rafters.

I didn't sense the return of the lamiae, but something else. Growls, snarls and shuffling feet came from all around us. Brethren appeared from behind closed doors, wall panels and the top of the stairs. At least two-hundred pairs of pale lavender eyes were levelled at us.

We were surrounded.

Cal shot me a look. 'Too much bloody talking!'

Timur laughed.

The Rebels edged closer, fangs extended.

Two choices darted through my mind: kill both, make a run for it and still risk being overwhelmed. This place was crawling with Rebels. Or, use Timur and Rasputin as hostages – they'd slow us down – and get to the jet. We'd do this. I doubted Timur's minions would risk an attack.

'We need these two alive as leverage. We're taking them with us.' I speared Terens with a look and indicated the nearest tall, narrow window. 'Cal, you first.'

Terens and Cal exchanged glances and nodded.

The remaining lamiae reappeared, screeched and flew into the rafters directly above us.

'Now!'

Cal dove out, dragging a reluctant Timur with him. Crashing glass heralded their exit. Terens with Rasputin followed while I brandished my sword at the converging group of Rebels. 'Who wants a taste of Ingenii blood?'

They hesitated; then five charged me at once. I struck at two. The others registering their screams and the smell of burnt flesh gave me enough time to scramble out the window. Glass cracked beneath my feet as I landed. Terens and Cal sprinted just ahead of me, the crunch of their boots on the hard ground loud in the winter silence. Behind us came the horde, hissing and wailing, threatening to flay us alive and rip us to pieces.

They'd never catch us. The Ingenii blood made us faster and stronger, but Timur and Rasputin deliberately dragged their steps, slowing us down. I caught up and snapped their necks. We hoisted their bodies and ran, zigzagging through the woods, deliberately brushing against trunks and leaves to confuse our scent. But the lamiae flew above us, swinging from branch to branch, once or twice attempting to land in our path only to be thwarted by the low-hanging branches.

A jet zoomed overhead. The initials LLE – Lucien Lebrettan Enterprises – on the tail. It circled and landed close by, on the road we'd used as a tarmac. An expanse of field lay between. Here among the trees, at least there was some shelter.

No choice but to risk it. We darted from the relative safety of the trees and raced across the field. Weighed down by their burdens, Terens and Cal's boots sank into the muddy snow. I'd seen men drown in such mud, exactly a century ago, and the memory sickened me. Even now, the site of untilled fields made my stomach turn.

The flickering lights of the jet and screeches of the lamiae, as they attacked from overhead, merged in my mind with the flashes of exploding mortar shells. Their repeated dives, cutting into my shoulder with their talons, burned like shrapnel. I could almost smell the cordite. Again, a sense of tranquillity came over me, the desire to stop running, that safety lay with the lamiae. I slowed.

Blood streamed down the side of Cal's face. His stride slackened, and each step seemed to suck him further into the mud. Next to him, Terens swore. 'Damned lamiae! They're ... getting stronger.'

From the hisses and cries behind, the Rebels were gaining on us.

'Fight it!' I trudged ahead, dragging any image into my mind to counter the drugging influence of the lamiae.

Cal growled, shook his head and picked up his pace. Terens followed.

The jet's lights winked as the engines started. We reached firmer ground and raced toward it only to find ourselves encircled and cut off.

'Back-to-back!' Terens called out.

With Timur and Rasputin's bodies flung over each shoulder, Cal and Terens stood back-to-back. I joined them, our swords at the ready. The lamiae edged closer.

'Ssssubmit to ussss, and you will live.'

Laura in my bed, ready for me. Her sweet body.... 'Ah!' Not real. I tore the image from my mind and focused on the grotesque faces before me. Terens's sword hand trembled, the blade dipped. I nudged him. 'Timur took your arm. Remember the pain. Get angry!'

He grunted, and the sword swung a wide arc as the lamiae pounced. So close but out of sword reach. They feared the Ingenii blood. Gaping mouth, fangs extended, one leapt over me, the tip of his wing gashing my chin. I smelt blood. Another one leapt over us, and another. We spun and swiped at them, our swords clashing as they met in mid air.

Behind me, Cal panted. 'Bastards! In my head ... my wife ... my son ... can't fight this!'

'Yes, you can, bro. Keep them alive in your memory. Stay with me.' Terens breathing was laboured.

As the lamiae did another pass over us, the Rebels attacked. I punched at faces and hacked off the limbs of those who attempted to drag their unconscious masters from Cal and Terens's shoulders.

Talons ripped my coat. Wings tore my scalp. 'Ssssurender to ussss, and all will be well.'

Weakening … a shout. Screams. Part of the circle broke as Rebel bodies spontaneously combusted. Several black-uniformed men hacked their way through. The rest of the Rebels scattered into the woods, leaving their charred companions behind. The lamiae, the winged demons of nightmare, cringed and fled back to the fortress.

A black-uniformed leader approached us. 'Count Karel von Czernin sends his compliments.'

I smelled Ingenii blood on his sword. For a moment my heart stopped.

'Do not fear, my lord. Lady Laura is safe. She generously donated a few drops of her blood.'

I breathed again. 'Make sure you clean it thoroughly.' He understood – Laura's blood was deadly to every vampire, except me.

Terens grinned and clapped him on the shoulder before striding to the waiting plane, Cal by his side. The man's Nordic-blonde eyebrows rose seeing Rasputin and Timur's bodies dangling down each one's back.

'I'll convey my thanks to the count personally,' I said as we followed them in.

'Are you stopping there, my lord?'

'Yes, your master is protecting a priceless treasure for me. Can't go back to D'Antonville without her.'

He smiled broadly. 'No, indeed. We have orders to stay and secure the fortress and prevent the lamiae from escaping, and to take any further instructions from you.'

There was only one way to achieve that. 'Burn it down. Let no one escape. They chose their side.'

'Yes, my lord.'

Cal and Terens would most likely drop me in Prague then fly the Rebels back to Marcus in D'Antonville, to be held in custody until their executions. This time, there must be no slip ups, no unexpected fires, no escape from a locked cell.

I turned to look at the fortress, as we ascended. From the windows, flames leapt into the night sky. Those who tried to flee were cut down. One lamia attempted flight only to be seized by Karl's men and thrown into the blaze.

Surely no rebellion could survive this?

## CHAPTER 26 – PRAGUE

**LAURA**

A dozen black-uniformed men, the insignia of a crowned black stag on a silver background emblazoned on their jackets, waited for us on the tarmac. Karl had arranged for us to be collected from an airstrip just outside Prague. He spoke to them rapidly in Czech. Twice I heard the word "lamiae." I could guess what he was saying. Only my blood could kill those creatures.

I unwound the handkerchief from my hand – it had stopped bleeding more than an hour before. A thin white scar lined my palm where an ugly scab should have been. My body's healing rate had accelerated. Just as well, for I was about to administer another cut.

'You'll need this against the lamiae.' I withdrew my dagger.

Karl laid his hand over mine. 'Sure? You've already cut yourself tonight.'

'How else can they fight against those lamiae? Besides....' I showed him the white scar. 'I heal as quickly as you now.'

He gave me a lopsided grin. 'That you do. *Dobre!* He nodded. 'Just as long as Alec doesn't get the wrong impression when he smells your blood on their swords. I can't afford to lose my best fighting men.'

Six stepped forward, and I smeared a few drops on each man's sword tip. They bowed their heads and uttered a word of, I assumed, gratitude. I looked to Karl for confirmation. '*Dekuji mockrat*, means thank you.'

'What does "dobre" mean?'

He chuckled. 'You caught that? It means "good"'.

After a few words to them, they boarded the jet and took off. Karl and I climbed into the back of one of three black SUVs. Escorted by his men – one car in front, the other behind – we drove through the streets of Prague. I kept glancing at my ring, my thoughts focused on Alec. As long as the serpent's eyes remained red, I could breathe. Once or twice they darkened to near black, and my chest constricted. All I could do was whisper a prayer.

'I'm sure he's doing fine.' Karl lowered his phone and turned to me. 'Besides, my men'll be there soon.'

I nodded, watched my ring and wiped my sweaty palms on my coat. In spite of the biting cold outside, I craved fresh air and rolled down the window, just a smidgeon. The streets thronged with people. New Year's Eve was only a few days away. Market stalls lined the streets, and leafless tree branches were strewn with fairy lights. The aroma of fried potato pancakes and roasting chestnuts hung in the night air. Believe it or not, my stomach rumbled.

'I've arranged supper for you.' Karl lit a cigarette.

Karl had no idea I was pregnant, nor could I tell him. I wound the window further down to avoid inhaling the smoke. Somewhere in the distance, the clang of a tram and music drifted on the night air. 'Thanks. I didn't think I'd be hungry after everything that's happened.'

'Adrenaline's been driving you, and now it's wearing off. I prefer to eat after a fight, find a pretty girl and enjoy some horizontal pleasure.' He grinned from ear to ear, his lavender bedroom eyes almost shining in the dim light.

'Wearing a mask?' I laughed when I recalled the Venetian mask he'd worn to hide his identity when he, Luc and Cal had gone to Alec's aid.

He laughed, too, and wriggled his eyebrows. 'Best way.'

Some silly, innocuous banter to lighten my mood – just what I needed.

Soon the road gave way to cobblestone streets. This must be the old part of town. It was quieter here. Windows were dark. Old-fashioned street lanterns provided the only light. I guessed everyone was in the busy part of town enjoying the food and winter entertainment. The buildings looked older, painted in shades of yellow, red and ochre with some in grey or dark blue. Many boasted decorative stonework, gables, gothic-style inscriptions and animal and bird figurines high above the doorways.

We stopped next to one with the figure of a black stag wearing a winged crown, its snow-covered antlers reaching out to the windows on either side. It was identical to the image on the jackets of Karl's men, so I knew where we were.

'Welcome to my home, Lady Laura.' He flicked his cigarette butt into the gutter and offered me his arm as we stepped from the car. Snow crunched beneath our boots as he led me through a set of reinforced iron doors.

'Just Laura.' I gazed up at the ornate façade. 'How long have you lived here?'

'Over four-hundred years.'

'And nobody has noticed in all that time that you haven't died? Your neighbours?'

He chuckled. 'People see what they want to see.'

A vine-covered well stood in the centre of a large courtyard, ringed by bare-branched rose bushes and classical statues. To my right, a spiral stone staircase led upwards to separate apartments. Small busts of famous composers sat serenely within niches carved into the wall, their glazed eyes staring into nothingness. I peered at the names – Bach, Mozart, Corelli, Zelenka, Neruda, Smetana, Dvorak, Liska.

Had Karl known any of them? Prague was the favoured city of many famous musicians through history.

'Did you know any of these composers?' I trailed my fingers along the heads as we walked up.

'This one, this one and … this one.' He patted Dvorak's head last of all. 'He wanted to write an opera about a vampire. Was crazy about that Irishman's book, Dracula.' He rolled his eyes. 'I suggested a water nymph.'

'Dvorak wanted to write an opera about Bram Stoker's Dracula?' My head swam. 'Well, I guess it's not every day a vampire persuades a famous composer to write an opera about another mythical creature.'

Karl chortled and opened a door nearest the top of the stairs. 'Here we are.'

He ushered me into a warm salon, with an ornate floor-to-ceiling tiled stove at one end, scattered furniture and a table laden with supper. I caught the whiff of freshly baked bread and brewed coffee. My mouth watered.

'First, let's rid you of this monstrosity.' He threw my coat on the floor by the door. 'I had to endure Timur's scent till now. No more!'

Two Brethren servants stood nearby. Karl spoke in Czech. They smiled, nodded, retrieved my discarded coat and left.

I was glad it was gone, too. The room was warm enough, and I nearly ran to the table, filling a plate with a little of everything.

'Delicious,' I said with a full mouth. Never had a roast chicken, gherkin, mustard and cheese sandwich tasted so good. Next to the tray, the wonderful aroma from freshly brewed coffee tickled my nose. I sat and poured a cup.

While I ate, Karl chain-smoked and paced the room issuing orders on his mobile. Every few minutes his men would enter, receive orders and leave. He stubbed out the last cigarette, looked at me – a curious expression on his face – and strode to a cabinet at the other end of the room, well away from the tiled stove.

'You like music?' he asked.

'Love it.'

He smiled, and from the cabinet extracted a honey-coloured cello. He sat, raised the bow and began to play. Whether it was the warm notes that rose from Karl's fingers, the scrumptious meal, the cosy ambiance of the room, or a combination, my spirits lifted, and a comforting peace settled over me. I recognised the piece: The Swan by Camille Saint-Saens – one of my favourites.

With coffee in hand, I left the table and settled on a red leather sofa near the tiled stove, letting the music drift over me.

'Another?' he asked.

'Please.' I laid my head back and stared at the stuccowork on the ceiling as he played Dvorak. Fat, smiling cherubs playing musical instruments grinned down at me. As I looked closer, references to music appeared everywhere, from the wooden music sheets that decorated the cabinet, to the chair backs carved to resemble a musician's stand.

Karl played for what seemed like hours, eyes occasionally closed as immersed in the music as I was, his fingers and bow dancing over the strings. I imagined him in eighteenth-century costume entertaining the greatest musicians of the day. Who knew how many famous names played in this very salon.

'You could be a concert cellist,' I said after he completed the last piece.

He dipped his head in a bow. 'Unfortunately, it's impractical for one of my kind. I play to calm myself ... when I want to kill.'

I preferred bubble wrap. 'Timur and Rasputin?'

He nodded, his face grim. 'I want to be there when Alec exterminates those vermin.' His phone buzzed, and he checked the screen. 'Speak of the devil.'

I sat upright, tension coiling in my body like a taut spring. The eyes of the serpent ring shone bright red. I released a breath. 'Alec?'

Karl pocketed his phone and grinned. 'On his way. My men picked him up just now.'

I lay back against the sofa, spread my arms along the top and released a loud sigh.

Soon, Alec was in the doorway. I ran into his arms. He crushed me to him and whispered into my hair. 'It's nearly over, darling. They're in custody, on their way to D'Antonville.'

I cupped his face in my hands. 'I don't care about them. Only you.'

His kiss seared my mouth, arousing a hunger in me only he could satisfy. I heard a click as the door closed. We were alone. Alec picked me up and carried me to the sofa and sat down with me on his lap. Our tongues hungrily entangled as he took possession of my mouth. Neither of us spoke as our breaths mingled and my hands tangled in his hair, drawing him closer. He was here in my arms, and that was all that mattered.

Alec caressed my face, gently running his thumb along my chin and jawline before his lips followed. My body trembled, as it always did whenever he touched me. His hand trailed to my breast causing my nipples to peak through the soft woollen dress.

'I'd have that dress off in a flash if we were somewhere more private,' he said between ragged breaths, his eyes a deep purple pool into which I could gaze for eternity.

My breathing was just as uneven. 'Here? One of Karl's rooms?'

His smile dazzled me. 'Why not.' A sudden pained expression crossed his face. 'Ah, I forgot. Dominik.'

'Who?' I nibbled his chin hoping he'd forget whoever this Dominik was.

'A kid. I promised to mentor him. He'll be here soon.' Between kisses, he explained the situation and the task he'd accepted. 'I had to, darling. These youngsters are lost … a danger to themselves as well as to humans. Since this was the nearest Principate safe house … I sent them here. Karl's going to find them new sires.'

'He's going to be your responsibility for the next one-hundred years? Like Luc was with you?'

'Exactly.'

'How soon do you think they'll get here?'

He looked at his watch. 'An hour, maybe two.'

I smiled and straddled his lap. 'Plenty of time.'

Alec's eyes darkened further as he slid my dress up and gripped my thighs. 'Karl, don't let anyone in here for the next hour or so.'

Wherever Karl was, he'd hear. There was a chuckle and a click as the door was locked.

# CHAPTER 27 – PARTING

**LAURA**

Marcus threw his arms around me and squeezed me tight. 'Terentius gave a full report. Deus! I'm proud of you for the way you fought back.' He kissed my brow.

'I owe Lucinda. If it hadn't been for her....'

'When this is over, I promise she'll be suitably rewarded.' His lavender eyes were grave. Until this rebellion was quashed, even with Timur and Rasputin imprisoned, her life was still in danger. It was best she stayed in hiding until then.

We had returned to D'Antonville a couple of hours before dawn. The entire household was there to greet us as we stepped from the car, including some of the prefects and Elders. The Brethren servants clapped and congratulated Alec, and Kari whistled and whooped. Luc and Judy enveloped me in double hug. I sensed Luc's tension, and from the concerned glances of those around him, I wasn't alone. He must have received news of my kidnapping badly. I was sure I'd soon hear the story.

One face was missing. 'Where's Jen. Is she okay?'

'Had to give her a sedative,' Jake said. 'She's traumatised.'

'Oh no!' Guilt weighed heavily on me as I sprinted to her room. I thought she'd be safe here, away from danger. Instead, she was right in the thick of it.

I stood outside her room. Should I, shouldn't I? She may still be asleep, depending on how high a dose Jake had given her. Sunrise was still a couple of hours away. I leant my head against her door, and whispered, 'I'm sorry, Jen. So sorry.'

There was movement from within, the opening and closing of drawers, and rapid breathing. I rapped gently. The movement stopped.

'Jen, you awake? It's me.'

Hurried footsteps. The door was flung open and Jenny threw her arms around me. 'Thank God. Thank God, they didn't hurt you.' A shudder went through her. 'Terens told us what they'd planned to do to you. To think if he hadn't gone….' Tears welled in her eyes as she gazed at me. 'Here I was, balling my eyes out like a selfish sod that he'd gone away, yet…. Oh God, Laura!'

I suppressed the dreadful memory as we closed the door and sat, hand in hand, on the ornate couch. 'I used my dagger on them, but that wouldn't've been enough. When Terens appeared, I nearly kissed him!'

She gave a tearful laugh and clung to me as she sobbed, taking great gulps of air between words. 'I just froze. They stuck a gun in my face. I'm so sorry. I should've done something… I, I didn't know what to do. I should've used my knife ... anything.'

'And get yourself shot? Like Kari? No, there was nothing you could've done. Stop saying that before I shake you! They were commandos, professionals. They would've killed you, Jen.'

We clung to each other, until Jenny's breathing slowed. 'I couldn't sleep until I knew you were okay. Even then, Jake gave me something, so I think I crashed for a few hours.'

'I'm so sorry, Jen. Sorry for bringing you here.'

She pulled out of my embrace. 'What? This isn't your fault, silly goose. I wanted to come, remember?'

'Luc and I persuaded you—'

She shrugged. 'I kind of wanted to come, you know?' She took a deep breath. 'The danger's over now. The bad guys are caught, and … I want to go home. I need to go home.'

Her words punched me in the stomach. Over her shoulder, I saw her suitcase open on the bed, partially packed. Other clothes were strewn around it, ready to be folded and thrown in.

I swallowed the painful lump lodged in my throat. 'You're leaving.'

She wiped her eyes and drew away, pulling her knees up to her chin. Dark circles marred the skin under her beautiful eyes, and the laughter that usually shone from them was gone. 'I can't stay, hon. Can't go through that again. I don't belong here.'

I perched on the edge of the bed. Selfishly, I didn't want her to leave me, yet what right did I have on insisting she stay? Would she have been in danger if she'd remained in Sydney? Was it a monumental mistake bringing her here? I had no answer.

'I can't stop you going. Look, if it's any consolation, the bad guys have been caught and the rebellion *has* to fall apart.' It must, I thought. 'It's over, Jen. Our guys proved they're stronger. It's pointless for the Rebels to continue.'

She lowered her chin onto her knees and swiped her nose with the back of her hand. 'It's not just that. When Jake got Alec's call to lock up the housekeeper, Luc had just woken up, and … he went crazy. Trashed their apartment looking for her. Threw her husband – the manager guy – against the wall. I thought he'd killed him.' Her face paled. 'Sam and Jake had to restrain him. Marcus threatened to lock him up if he didn't get a grip. Judy suggested I stay in my room.'

My hand flew to my mouth. Although I could understand Luc's anger, to nearly kill his faithful estate manager was extreme. Even Jenny felt unsafe. No wonder she wanted to leave. 'Oh Jen!' I lowered my head into my hand. 'Where is Madame Thierry now?'

'Gone. She must've had an extra key or something. No one can find her. Mrs bloody Danvers, all right!' She pulled a face. 'Cal told us you said Luc's ring and key were sewn up inside your coat, and I remember her giving it to you. Bitch!'

'If Luc finds her…'

'He'll burn her alive like he wants to do with the Rebel guys— stake 'em out in the sun.' She shook her head. 'No way can I watch something like that. I'm going home, hon.'

It struck me that I could easily condemn Timur and Rasputin to such a horrific death. After what I'd seen in his fortress, they deserved no less. But Madame Thierry was a different case. She was human. He couldn't possibly judge her under Brethren laws, yet, knowing Luc, I feared he would. Perhaps Jenny was right.

'I'll miss you.'

'Same, hon. I'll email you, keep in touch. Besides, I've got stuff to get ready for the new term.' She gave me a wan smile. 'Oh, before I forget….' She pulled her phone out. 'Here, take a look at this.'

It was a message from Matt. I hadn't given my ex-boyfriend a thought since leaving Sydney. He was out of my life, and I hoped he felt the same. Looked like I was wrong. He was asking after me – if I was okay. 'Why send this to you? How'd he get your number?'

'He's a cop, Laura. He can get anyone's number. And I reckon he's not game to use yours.'

Mmmm … probably not. 'I hope he's not up to anything where I'm concerned. If he asks about me again, don't tell him I'm pregnant. He doesn't need to know. Actually, don't tell anyone. You never know, it could get back to the Brethren, and we're trying to keep it secret until all the Rebels are caught.' I handed the phone back to her.

'Sure.' She rose and strode to her bedroom, pulling the rest of the clothes from the wardrobe and dumping them on the bed. I joined her. 'I was kind of looking forward to shopping in Avignon with you, or sampling some amazing pastries in Lyons....' She laughed then promptly burst into tears.

I hugged her. 'I was, too. This isn't fair.'

'It sucks. But I just can't stay here.' She released me and placed her hand against her nose. 'I need a tissue.' She tore several tissues from the box on the dresser, blew her nose and dabbed at her eyes. 'Can you get someone to drive me to the airport? I want a regular flight ... be among people, you know?'

I knew she meant humans. 'I'll tell Alec. We'll see you off.'

'Appreciate it, hon.' She turned from me and resumed packing.

I rose from the bed and headed for the door.

'Laura, you don't need me here with you. You've got Alec. I'm only in the way.'

'Rubbish!'

'You know what I mean.' She smiled then pointed at my belly. 'Don't forget, I'm the bub's auntie, so you can't be away too long. Besides, everyone knows Australia's the best place to raise a kid.'

'Sure is.' I left, crossed the hall to my suite and closed the door behind me before I completely broke down. The gems in the blue Faberge egg on the coffee table near the window glinted in the light thrown from the chandelier. It was probably worth millions. Probably belonged to the last of the Russian tsars, and that reminded me of Rasputin. I picked it up intending to smash it against the wall. But I couldn't do it. It was too beautiful, too precious. Instead, I hid it in the drinks cabinet and hurled a coffee cup into the wall. Pity it wasn't Rasputin's head.

# CHAPTER 28 - CAGED WOLF

**LAURA**

Sunrise wasn't too far away. My hand clasped in his, Alec leaned back in the Alabaster Throne and surveyed the gathering. Prefects and Elders mingled with one another in the Great Hall, their voices subdued. They were gathered for one grim purpose – to sentence Count Timur and Rasputin. Although both had been proscribed during the Pledging, more crimes had been added to their tally, my kidnapping being among the most serious.

Their death sentence had been pronounced – this court convened to decide whether it was slow and torturous or quick and merciful.

Marcus, wearing the same golden hooded cloak he'd worn to the Ritual, stood with two other Elders at the foot of the dais.

'Who are those two?' I indicated a tall man with long dark hair pulled back in a ponytail and the woman next to him. From their features, I guessed they'd be American Indian.

'Grey Bear. He and Maira represent the Brethren in North and South America.'

'Maris's replacements?'

He nodded. 'They should've been chosen in the first place.'

And perhaps the problem with Alec's ex-girlfriend, Maris may have been avoided? Still, she'd been so determined to regain Alec as her lover and take her place at his side, I believe nothing would've stopped her.

I buried that painful memory as Marcus strode to the centre of the hall and gave three sharp raps of his staff on the stone floor. 'Bring in the prisoners.'

My mouth went dry. Alec squeezed my hand. Leaning against the pillar next to my chair, arms folded across his chest, stood Luc, a forbidding smile on his face. I had no doubt Luc wanted the worst type of death for them. Had my mother ever taken part in these events during her time as Ingenii?

I touched Luc's arm. 'Why isn't Judy here?'

He leant down and whispered, 'She's no longer Ingenii. Not allowed to be here.'

Oh.

Jake swung open the massive double-doors of the Great Hall. Candles fluttered in the invading draught while the flames in the fireplace shot high into the chimney. The crowd of prefects and Elders parted, as Terens and Cal wheeled in two cages. Slumped, bare chested, both men's heads drooping, were the wretched figures of Timur and Rasputin. Timur's right arm and left hand had been removed. Rasputin was missing his forearms. Burns along their skin marked where a flame had been applied to cauterise the wounds, which had already begun to heal.

Neither would live long enough to regenerate their lost limbs.

My stomach heaved. Alec had prepared me for this, but still, I had to turn my face away. Yet I couldn't deny the fairness of their harsh punishment.

Timur shuffled forward on his knees and pressed his face against the bars. He stared straight at me. Trembling, he gritted his teeth as he tucked his handless arm beneath his armpit. The pain must be agonising, the same he'd been ready to inflict on me. Yet I couldn't gloat. All I felt for him was pity.

Alec's voice whispered through my mind. *Don't pity him. They were going to do this to you, Laura. They've only been repaid in kind.*

*I know.* I blinked back tears.

Alec lifted my hand to his lips. *So tender hearted, my darling.*

*Brethren justice is new to me.*

I glanced up at Luc. His green-eyed serpent ring had been returned and glinted in the firelight. He leant down and whispered, 'We dealt with those two Rebels no more and no less than what they'd planned to do to you, ma petite – and what Timur had done to Terens. I could've treated them far worse, but I chose not to.'

'Was that for my sake?'

He gave a barely perceptible nod, and I swallowed.

I gazed around at the crowd – at the golden-cloaked Elders who'd gathered together at the foot of the dais, faces stoic, betraying no hint of emotion, like cold stone statues, unblinking and unmoved. The prefects, in contrast, were animated. Some objected to the treatment of the prisoners, saying their high office still accorded them respect, while others hurled insults, calling them traitors and a disgrace to the prefecture.

On either side of the cages stood Terens and Cal, tall and noble, their faces schooled into expressionless masks. Only the movement of their eyes, as they surveyed the crowd, hinted at their tension. A camera was in position, filming proceedings for the prefects who couldn't attend.

Timur kicked the bars of his cage. 'Hypocrites! You crawl to the Principate because you finally get what you want. Would Lucien have shared the Ingenii blood if he'd had any other choice? No! I forced him. I. FORCED. HIM. You all owe me! Have the guts to admit it – secretly, most here wanted to join me.'

Shouts of "wrong", "no", "you're delusional", rang throughout the room.

Karl stepped up to Timur's cage and crouched down to face him. 'I've waited a long time for this, you fucker!' He stood and faced the crowd, raising his hands for silence. 'Brethren, I confess I was shocked and angry when I first heard of the hidden Ingenii blood store, but I understand why. All these centuries, Lord Lucien has collected and secreted those vials. It's been for *our* protection, *our* benefit, for a time when danger should arise from which only the power of Ingenii blood could save us.

'Do we face such a crisis now? I don't know. I only hope a greater one won't arise in the future when we really will need those blood vials. But because of *this man*' —he jabbed a pointed finger at Timur— 'the stock had to be shared out now. Because of the false accusations of *this man*, this precious commodity has been depleted.'

Stomping feet reverberated through the hall. Some prefects nodded, while others stared at the prisoners with narrowed eyes.

*Karl should've been a lawyer. He missed his calling!*

I bit down on my lip trying not to smile at Alec's comment.

One prefect, O'Toole, from Hibernia, stepped forward and joined Karl. He slapped him on the back and faced Timur. 'Speaking for myself, I object to your rebellion. For if we were all to do as you, and drain every human every time we feed from one, within a generation, there'd be none left. Then what would we eat? Each other?' His strong Irish accent ended his question on a lilt, which brought a smile to some faces. 'Frankly, since when do we need to drain a human to fill our need? What's wrong with you, man?'

Sweat glistened on Timur's moustache. 'You lie if you say you never wanted to daywalk. Why shouldn't we share in that? Don't we all deserve that right?'

His evasion of O'Toole's question resulted in another round of shouted protests and accusations. If Timur's aim was to divide the hearing, he was succeeding. Or was it to buy time? Was he expecting a rescue?

'Is the Principate on trial here, or this criminal?' Luc said.

Timur's lip curled. Was he smiling?

Rasputin shifted and aimed his gaze at the Elders. 'You know my master has only the good of all his Brethren at heart. Don't believe the lies spread about him. Join together against the injustice of the Principate.' His voice was velvet, yet his eyes no longer held their power.

Cal rapped the cage with his sword. 'Silence, snake!'

'Good try, but you're powerless over us.' Alec lifted his hand, and the eyes of the serpent ring glowed faintly.

Rasputin flinched, and his face blanched. He stared at the serpent ring and uttered a string of curses before falling quiet. Timur turned and yelled at him, in what sounded like Russian.

Grey Bear spoke. 'My Lord Marcus, our laws have always held that a juvenile should not be held accountable for the crimes of his sire.'

I nearly leapt from my chair. Was he about to suggest they let Rasputin off? He had to be kidding! Alec squeezed my hand. *Wait.*

'I believe that rule does not apply in this instance. There is undeniable evidence Rasputin initiated some of the offenses, and in others he was fully complicit.' Marcus's voice held the power of conviction, but Grey Bear pressed on.

'May we know the evidence?'

Marcus glanced up at the windows. Sunrise wasn't too far away. 'Very well.' He turned to face me. 'Lady Laura, please tell us exactly what you heard while you were held prisoner by Count Timur.'

I rose, clasped my hands in front of me and speared a look at the two crouching, caged men. Word for word, I revealed what Rasputin had planned to do to me, recalling every vengeful threat made against me. I omitted nothing, so indelibly was it etched in my memory.

Timur glared at me, his eyes blazing. His hatred was palpable. What had I done to him to deserve it? Rasputin remained strangely quiet, staring at the ground, every so often raising wild eyes. It chilled my blood.

'Deus! Have you heard enough, my friend?' Marcus clapped a hand on Grey Bear's shoulder.

Grey Bear gave a curt nod. 'I'm satisfied.'

Behind me Luc murmured, 'About time.'

Marcus unfurled a scroll and read. 'Brethren, this is not a trial. These prisoners have already been proscribed and condemned. Their crimes are: Rebellion against the principate; attempted assassination of Prefect Count Karel von Czernin; planned assassination of the Princeps, Alexander Munro; kidnap and torture of the Ingenii, Lady Laura.' With a sweep of his hand, he indicated the prisoners. 'The horrendous injuries they intended to inflict on Lady Laura have been dealt to them. For that alone, Count Timur has lost the privilege of his high office and the dignity normally accorded a prefect.'

Many in the crowd stamped their feet. I looked at Alec. *That means they approve,* his thought whispered.

Marcus continued. 'To these crimes, Prefect Count Timur has added three more – trafficking in human blood slaves, turning underage humans, and finally, failing to declare his juvenile, Jose Luis Rodriguez Gonzalez, had transformed a human, one Lucinda Ortiz.'

Timur's eyes widened. He stared at Marcus. Just as quickly, he sneered. 'You can prove nothing.'

Luc snorted.

'My Lord Marcus, if I may?' Alec released my hand, rose from the Alabaster Throne and signalled to Jake, who stood by the doors. 'Bring in Dominik.'

Alec had introduced me to Dominik, and the others with him, soon after he'd arrived in Prague. I was shocked: not only at his bedraggled physical condition, but that he was only a boy – not yet sixteen. Karl had cleaned him up before we'd left. Shy at first, because of his broken English, he'd eventually relaxed, and we'd spoken on the flight back. One of three children, his mother was a pastry chef, and he missed her terribly.

A crease appeared between Timur's brows. Like everyone else in the room, he faced the doors, angling his body in the tight confines of his cage.

Dominik's thin, slightly hunched figure appeared in the doorway. He scratched his shaggy brown hair as his head swerved from side to side like a wary bird. On seeing the cages, he paled and took a step back.

'Don't be afraid, Dominik. Come up here,' Alec said.

The boy's face relaxed and he started forward. Timur whispered to Rasputin who called out to the boy in Russian, his voice low, hypnotic. But it no longer held the power of command. There was a tremble in it.

Cal clanged the cage with his sword. 'Shut it!'

Dominik didn't respond. Rather, he shielded his eyes as he hurried past the cage on his way to the dais. He smiled and gave me a clumsy bow before returning his attention to Alec. His wide-eyed gaze didn't waver. I hid my smile at the boy's obvious hero worship.

'Tell the Elders you're age, Dominik.'

*'Patnac.'*

'Face the crowd, and speak English. Not everyone here understands Czech.'

'Oh.' The boy swallowed, and wiping palms down his sides, turned to face the gathering. 'I am fifteen. Nearly sixteen, in ... how you say, *v lednu*,' his brow puckered.

'January,' Karl called out.

Dominik grinned and nodded. *'Diki.'*

Some smiled at the boy's lack of Brethren etiquette when addressing a prefect, but from the rest arose angry murmurs against Timur. It was because this boy would never grow up. Even if the Brethren aged one year in every five-hundred, it would still take two millennia for Dominik to be free of puberty – and zits. Poor kid.

'Now tell them how you came to be transformed. Leave nothing out,' Alec said.

'I … um…. A man grabbed me when coming home from concert. He threw me into dark cell. It smelled.' His voice squeaked; it must have only just begun to break. 'Many other kids like me there. We were scared. Some kids crying. They took us out when he' —he pointed at Timur— 'and he' —his finger moved to Rasputin— 'were hungry, or to get rid of bodies.' He dropped his head.

Luc growled.

The mood in the great hall grew darker. Each person gazed at Dominik.

Marcus pointed his staff at the prisoners. 'Did they ask you if you wished to be turned?'

He shook his head. 'No.' Alec whispered in his ear. 'Oh. No … milord.'

Marcus's mouth cracked into a half-smile. 'One more question, son. Did all those who were with you remain in Count Timur's castle?'

The boy glanced at Alec, who gave him a nod, before he answered. No one moved. Dominik shook his head. 'No, milord. Others came. Picked out ones they wanted and took them away.'

There was uproar. Some prefects openly called for the most extreme execution to be carried out – staking out in the sun. Some rushed the cages and hammered on the bars. Those who were close enough managed to reach in and pull the prisoners' hair and tore at their bodies until Cal and Terens intervened and pushed them back.

'There we have it.' Luc stepped down from the dais and fronted the prisoners, both bleeding from their wounds. 'Blood slavery of human children! The lowest act to which any Brethren can stoop.' He extended his arms to the gathering. 'What say you, my brethren? What punishment is due for such a crime? Tell me.'

Shouts of 'Let them burn! Stake them in the sun!' were repeated through the Great Hall.

As horrific as the sentence was, it was what Timur and Rasputin deserved. My stomach churned as I recalled the countless bones of murdered children I'd seen in the tunnels of Timur's fortress.

Alec stood and took a step down from the dais toward Marcus just as Luc grabbed the staff from his hand.

'You have spoken. To the sun. I lead the way!' Luc raised the staff, and the gathering parted as he strode toward the doors.

My father wanted to see them suffer. And perhaps Alec did, as he didn't oppose him. Yet I sensed frustration in Alec. His mouth was a tight line, hands curled into fists.

'I will not burn! I will not burn!' Timur threw himself against the cage bars and bashed his head until blood flowed. His attempt to render himself unconscious failed, for his wounds healed immediately.

Luc, without a backward glance, threw open the doors and triumphantly led the way out. Cal and Terens had to stand aside as much of the crowd surged after him taking the caged prisoners with them. The sun posed no threat to the gathering as they'd been gifted vials of Ingenii blood.

'This isn't over!' Timur banged the cage with his feet and shouted as they were wheeled outside. 'Lucien Lebrettan, as I burn this day, so will you! We will meet in hell!'

From Rasputin's cage came a low hum, which grew into a melody. His deep bass baritone chanted a hymn in the style used in Russian Orthodox churches. Louder and louder. Did he see himself as some martyr?

It was madness.

Alec drew Dominik back. 'Go to your room. Rest.'

The boy fidgeted, glancing at the departing crowd. 'Can I, too, get that snake tattoo?' He pointed to Alec's chest.

'We'll see. Go.'

Dominik waved and sped off. Alec dropped into the throne, his fingers crushing the stone as if it were putty. A muscle ticked in the side of his jaw as he glared at the doors.

Was he still angry with those two Rebels? I lay my hand on his.

'We need to be present,' he said, stony faced.

'I know.' I stood, willing myself to see this execution through.

A small group waited by the doors. Alec looked across at Karl, who jerked his head toward the doors.

Yells came from the courtyard.

'It's a horrendous punishment, yet I can't feel any sympathy for them,' I said.

A blood-curdling scream flowed into the hall.

'Timur and Rasputin need to be made an example of. If seeing this doesn't sway the other Rebels, nothing will. But I believe it will. Such an execution is a powerful deterrent.'

'I hope so.' I brushed my hand across my forehead and eyes, and my knees sagged. I was drained, but determined to be present. It was important the Brethren see me there.

'Ready?' He grasped my hand.

I breathed in deeply and we left the Great Hall.

The sickening odour of burnt flesh assailed my nostrils as soon as we stepped outside. My stomach turned. Timur screamed and threw himself around in his cage as the flames consumed his body. Rasputin remained in a kneeling position, his loud humming giving way to shrieks as the sun destroyed his flesh. Soon, he keeled over.

Within a few minutes, it was all over. The weak winter sun had done its work. A great pall of black smoke rose into the morning sky, rising high until caught by the wind and dispersed. The two monsters who had murdered and terrorised so many, and threatened to bring down the Principate, were no more than a couple of blackened corpses. None of those present had jeered or hurled insults once they began to burn. All had stood silently, some with bowed heads, others with backs turned.

I wanted to be sure they were truly gone. 'Alec, please, pass me your sword.'

Holding a hand to my nose and mouth to stop me from retching, I swung the sword down through the bars of the cage and sliced off Rasputin's carbonised head then flattened it to ash with the sword's broadside. I did the same to Timur's remains before passing the sword back to Alec.

Keeping my sight fixed to the ground, I strode into the house and up to my suite, just making it to the bathroom before I threw up.

## CHAPTER 29 – UNHEALABLE BREACH

**ALEC**

No one spoke. Every eye followed Laura as she re-entered the house. Her courage amazed me. It took guts to destroy the Rebels' heads the way she did. Making sure they were dead? I'd ask her, later.

Luc stood in the centre of the crowd, smiling after Laura. He and I had words due. My gaze locked on him. 'A word. In the library.'

Not waiting for his response, I re-entered the house. This matter had to be settled. I spun the ancient globe in the centre of the library so strongly it spun off its hinges and went careering onto the floor, smashing into a bookcase.

'Damaging my possessions?'

I faced Luc. 'What the hell were you trying to prove?'

He raised his eyebrows. 'Don't know what you mean.'

I laughed and shook my head. 'Unbelievable! You can't let go, can you?' His face darkened. 'You still have to takeover. Still see yourself as princeps. Snatching the staff from Marcus's hand proved it.'

'Ah, so that's it. You resent me interfering.' He crossed his arms and stared at me.

'No. I resent you for undermining my position and authority; for taking over the Principate whenever it suits you.'

'How dare you!'

'I thought we'd settled this. But it seems you're incapable of keeping your word.'

His eyes flared. 'Take care, Alec. I'm your sire and an Elder.' The threat in his voice was unmistakable.

'And I'm princeps, so show me the same respect. It's my arse on the Alabaster Throne, not yours.'

He took a step toward me. His pupils narrowed into slits, and he bared his fangs. 'Not another word.' His breathing quickened. I knew he could best me in a fight, but I pressed on.

'I can only assume you did it to assuage your wounded pride, because you were fooled by your housekeeper.'

He sucked in a breath, and I felt the back of his hand. 'Remember who you're speaking to.'

Luc had never struck me before. I licked the blood from my lips and pounded him, sending him flying into the wall. He snarled and tackled me to the ground. Bookcases toppled, manuscripts crashed to the floor as we wrestled. Luc's rage blazed in his eyes. Would he kill me?

'Stop!' Marcus tore us apart and held us at arm's length.

My chest rose and fell, anger seething. For a juvenile to strike his sire was death. Although my century had been brought forward by five years, if Luc wanted to stick to the letter of the law, I was still a juvenile.

'I could have you killed for that.' Luc's nostrils flared, and blood dripped from the cut above his eye.

'I'm no longer a juvenile, nor your servant.'

'Enough! Deus! You're bonded by blood and by kin. This should not be.' Marcus released us and we stood apart. 'Everyone hears your exchange.'

I massaged my knuckles. 'It needed to be said.'

Luc paced, rubbing his face and kicking a book out of his way. 'You presume too much of yourself.'

'What's that supposed to mean?'

He took a step toward me, and Marcus intervened. 'I made you princeps for one purpose – to end the curse. Now that Laura is with child and the rebellion is over, you're no longer needed. I can protect my own. I'm taking back the Alabaster Throne. Where you go, I don't care.'

'Luc, I forbid this.'

My gut hollowed out. Was he mad? 'The Ingenii's your daughter. There's no way you can be princeps.'

Luc and I had been close friends. How it had it come to this? We'd had our disagreements in the past, and our friendship had remained intact. But this … I could see no way to heal this breach. His words cut too deep.

A sob had me spinning around. Laura stood in the doorway. Tears streamed down her cheeks

Behind her, faces pale in the early morning light, stood our men.

\* \* \*

## LAURA

'How could you, Papa?' Luc blinked at me, and his fangs retracted. 'Alec's done everything for you, whatever you asked of him. And you treat him like … like….' Words failed me. My hands shook, as did my voice.

Behind me, Jake ushered the others away and closed the door.

Alec's lower lip, swollen and bloodied, dripped onto the navy shirt I liked so much. It was ripped in several places. He swallowed and ran his hands through his hair. 'I'm sorry you heard that, Laura.'

My face tensed in a grimace. 'Saw it all, too. Heard the shouting. Came to see what the heck was going on.' I wiped away my tears. 'The two men I love at each other like rabid dogs! Do you know how it feels?'

'Ma petite.' Luc's face softened, some of his rage dissipating as he wiped away the blood from the cut above his eye. 'This is between me and Alec.'

'Whatever involves Alec' —I slid my hand in his— 'involves me.'

'Into the study.' Marcus indicated with a flick of his head. 'It's private.'

Judy entered, still in her slippers and pale-green robe. 'Luc, what's happening? People are saying—'

Luc groaned and threw up his hands. 'I don't give a dog's balls what people are saying. This is – argh! I've had enough.' He stormed from the room, slamming the door behind him so violently it came off its hinges. 'Wash out those cages!' he roared after banging the front doors as well.

'Oh dear.' Judy sighed. Her fading red hair drifted about her shoulders as she stared after him.

Marcus strode to the door and set it upright. 'I should go after him.'

'Let him be, Marcus. He'll come back when he's sorted himself out.' She turned to Alec. 'He hit you?'

'We hit each other.' Alec's voice carried pain.

She tucked her hands into her pockets and glanced at the collapsed bookcases, broken table, scattered books and manuscripts, and the remains of what was, probably, a rare antique globe. 'I see. Care to tell me why?'

There was no accusation in her voice as she pinned him with her gaze. I remember her giving me the same look many times when I was growing up. I always knew I'd get a fair hearing from her.

Marcus found two unbroken chairs on which Judy and I could sit. He stood behind her with folded arms as Alec told us what had transpired.

Judy sighed again and shook her head. 'Oh, Luc, Luc! I thought as much, from what Kari told me. No wonder he thundered out of here.'

'Because he doesn't want to hear the truth.' Alec's voice carried a bitter tone.

'Do any of us?'

'Are you defending him?' I swivelled to face her, my voice tight. 'I'm so angry, I could leave on the first flight for home.' With Timur and Rasputin dead, and the Ingenii blood distributed, the Rebels had nothing against which to rebel. I no longer needed the protection of the chateau. I missed Sydney's sunshine. I missed my friends, and most of all I missed the smell and feel of familiar things. With Alec, we'd start anew.

'If I'd done that every time your father and I had a disagreement, you would never have been born. Remember what the Bible says about love covering a multitude of sins?' She raised her eyebrows.

In other words, none of us is perfect. We all stuff up, and I shouldn't let this incident wreck my relationship with my father. I knew she was right. 'I'll think about it.'

'That's all I ask.' She returned her attention to Alec. 'You made him feel ashamed, and he lashed out. He was wrong to hit you. I'm sure he realised it right after, and that's why he left.'

Alec huffed. 'Sorry, Judith. I find that hard to believe, and I've known him longer than you have.'

'But you haven't lived with him as I have. I know him.' She smiled and patted his hand. 'Alec, dear, find it in your heart to forgive him. He didn't mean those words. I know that he loves you as a son.

He's proud of you – he told me. We all say and do things in anger, which we later regret.'

Marcus shifted. The sadness I'd first seen at the Ritual was there in his eyes. A split-second decision prompted by a moment of anger – he knew the consequences for he'd spent nearly two-thousand years paying for it. Did he still carry the guilt of the day he and his troops massacred that Pictish village? Or had time lessened the weight?

His eyes connected with Alec's. 'I won't defend my son. He was wrong to have disgraced you before the entire assembly … and for striking you when you confronted him with the truth. That's something he will have to live with. But you, my boy' —he pointed at Alec— 'are princeps. Luc may have manoeuvred you there, but you have since earned that right, and it was confirmed the night of the Ritual. The ring doesn't lie.'

Alec's hand squeezed mine. Perhaps that was what he needed to hear. 'I want to hear that from Luc's lips.'

Judy smiled. 'Give him a few days. He'll calm down.'

'A few days?' I rolled my eyes. 'And in the meantime we … what? Walk on eggshells? Stay out of his way?' I had no intention of locking myself in my suite – no matter how luxurious – to avoid bumping into my father, or fearing I'd provoke him in some way. Why should I?

'You won't see him,' Marcus said. 'If I know my son, he's probably out looking for Madame Thierry. She's the one responsible for your kidnapping and the theft of his key and ring … and the cause of his rash action.'

Judy's face tightened. Her eyes took on a flinty edge. 'I never trusted that women from the start.' Her mouth was a hard line. 'I caught her staring at Luc a few times, fawning over him. If she hadn't been a Thierry, I would've sent her packing.'

I'd noticed the tension between Judy and the housekeeper. On our arrival, Madame's gaze had lingered on Luc while her husband had fussed with our luggage.

Marcus and Alec exchanged glances. 'I smelled her arousal when we arrived,' Alec remarked. 'I assumed it was to do with Terens.' He shrugged, a lame smile on his face.

I nearly laughed. Terens certainly had that effect on woman. I saw it in Jenny. 'Papa never noticed?'

'Not that I saw.'

I shook my head in puzzlement. 'You think she's in love with him? It makes no sense. Why on earth would she do that to him – and me? I mean, if you love someone, you don't betray them to their enemies.'

Judy exhaled. 'I can't begin to understand her motive.' She spread her hands. 'What complaint can she have? The Thierrys are well paid, well treated – as are all the staff. It's her own little domain when we aren't here.'

Judy's words hit me like a hammer. I was certain now that Madame Thierry resented our presence. 'Maybe that's what she wants – this.' I indicated the chateau. 'Her and Luc. Kill the wife and daughter; make it look like a Rebel attack.'

'Laura, you can't possibly—' Judy's eyes widened. Her normally pale complexion blanched.

Marcus placed a hand on her shoulder. 'Judith, there may be some substance in this.'

'Think about it.' I was on a mission as Madame Thierry's goals crystallised to me. 'Timur took no care to hide Luc's key hidden in the lining of the coat Madame Thierry handed me. As his prisoner, who would I have told? And with the chateau defences down, a Rebel raid would have killed everyone, leaving her – and Luc, of course.'

'Except the raid never took place, because Terens rescued you,' Alec added.

'Exactly.'

Judy stared, open-mouthed. 'But, but … she can't possibly think Luc would return her silly infatuation?' She grimaced.

'Remember that movie, about the psycho woman, Fatal ... something? Who knows what's going on in there.' I tapped my head. Another idea sparked, which, sadly, was too late to verify. 'Pity we can't ask Timur what she expected in return for helping him. She didn't hand me and those things over to him for nothing. I'd love to know.'

Marcus raised his eyes. 'The pieces are coming together. I was willing to consider she may have been forced to betray us.'

'Why run if you're innocent, Marcus? Laura's right. That woman has her own agenda, and she's using the Rebels to achieve it,' Alec said.

Judy shot to her feet. 'Bitch!' It was one of the few times I'd ever heard her swear. She searched her pockets. 'Blast! Luc needs to know this. I left my phone in my suite.'

Alec handed her his. I wasn't surprised he didn't want to speak to him yet. 'Use mine.'

'You think he can find her? What then?' I asked.

'I hope he rips her to pieces!' The violent words were at odds with her elegant gesture. Smoothing down her hair, she waited for Luc to answer.

Something niggled. Madame Thierry was human, and not youthful anymore. In order to be with Luc, she would have to be immortal. 'She wants to be turned.' They all faced me. 'I'll bet you anything, that's what Timur promised her in return.'

Marcus stroked his chin. 'I agree. That means there must be a Rebel nest either in Avignon or Lyons, even Orange, somewhere close. She must be able to contact them since there's been no sighting of unknown Brethren in D'Antonville.' He and Alec exchanged glances.

'She could be hiding out with them.' Alec smiled. 'It's daylight, and if Luc finds their resting place....'

Marcus chuckled.

'In that case, Luc needs to know.' Judy pressed the phone to her ear and waited.

# CHAPTER 30 – PUNCHING BAG

**ALEC**

The leather punching bag nearly flew off its hinges as I pounded it. Son of a bitch backhanded me.

Jake steadied the bag and held it in place. 'Again.' He grunted as I pummelled it. 'Get it all out.'

'Damn it!' Sweat poured from me. Judy had called using my phone. Luc hadn't answered. Probably saw my name on the screen. Son of a bitch.

'Pretend it's Luc.' Cal strained at the weight machine, pushing with one leg then the other.

Jake shot him a look.

'Only a suggestion.'

'Not pretending.' I panted, and he laughed. I kept pounding until my knuckles ached.

He laughed.

I gave Jake a nod and removed my gloves. I stripped and dove into the gym pool. The water revived me. A few laps helped rid me of the remaining fury.

Jake sat on the bench, towel draped over his lap. I climbed out, grabbed it and joined him.

'Feeling better?'

'Somewhat.'

Weight plates clanged against each other as Cal cranked up the machine. I almost asked if he'd ever hit his sire, when I remembered he'd never had one. Did Luc infuriate them too? I closed my eyes and leant my head back against the wall.

'We've all been tempted to do what you did.' Jake's quiet voice was beside me.

'Reading my mind?'

'I've known Luc from birth.' He grunted, the bench straining as he leant back. 'Midwife was late. I was there … Marcus begged me, scared he was going to lose her. I held Luc in my arms, covered in blood, and handed him to his mother. Two minutes later his sister, Antonia, came out.'

I eyeballed him. 'Why are you telling me this?'

'There are things about him you don't know. Yeah, he can be pigheaded, tyrannical and a pain in the arse, but, overall, he's a good man.'

'I don't discount that. Despite this, I'll still respect him.'

Jake stood. 'I'm not excusing him, but try to remember Luc's always been in charge. Control was his way of coping with the curse's grip on his life. With the housekeeper's treachery and Laura's kidnapping, he felt he'd lost control and it scared the shit out of him.' He pressed my shoulder. 'When you've lived as long as we have, you'll see how much harder it is to change.'

He went to the bench press, giving me time to think. Would I have done anything different? No. Time Luc learnt to trust me with the office of princeps.

I stared at the water in the pool. Calm, placid, the opposite of my own raging thoughts. Even if Luc apologised, nothing would ever be the same between us. He was obsessed with ending the curse.

All I wanted was a life with Laura.

Even if we wanted to return to Sydney, I doubt he would let us go. Luc needed control, to steer everyone around him to fulfilling that one ultimate end: his family's freedom from the curse.

Damn, could I blame him for that?

I rose and walked to the shower. Somehow we had to work through this. For Laura's sake. The rebellion may be just about at an end, but the real battle, as to who was princeps, was far from over.

# CHAPTER 31 - ORANGE

**LAURA**

While I'd slept through most of the day, Judy had trawled through the list in her notebook and chased down her favourite kitchen staff.

'Looks like I'll have to find someone local, in Orange.' Judy sighed and dropped her head into her hand. 'Madame Thierry rang the extra kitchen staff a few days ago and cancelled their services. Told them the masquerade ball on New Year's Eve was not taking place this year.' She slammed her notebook closed. 'It'll be a miracle if we can find anyone from either Lyons or Avignon who's free at this time of year. Cook can't possibly be expected to cater for so many people on her own.'

Judy, Kari and I were seated in the kitchenette of her suite. New Year was only two days away. Luc and Alec had, as yet, not reconciled. We'd heard Luc had cleaned out the Rebel nest in

Avignon, but the estranged housekeeper was not there. He was now on his way to Lyons in search of her. To make matters worse, her husband, Serge Thierry, the estate manager – in hospital with several broken ribs – had resigned.

'I'd checked with her months ago to make sure we had the cooks, and she'd confirmed it.'

'That was before she knew about me. Like everyone else, she probably believed you to be childless – the last Ingenii. When she heard I was your and Luc's daughter, she must've flipped. Especially if I'm right and she's got the hots for him.' I raised an eyebrow as I sipped my late afternoon coffee.

Kari's eyes were downcast. She rubbed the spot on her chest where she'd been shot. 'She had me so fooled.'

'She had us all fooled, Kari, dear.' Judy picked up her mobile phone and pressed another number. 'I'll try just once more, and if he can't help … Ah Monsieur duPont….'

Judy's fluent French was too rapid for me, but the disappointed expression on her face gave it away. He'd taken a job somewhere else.

Kari nudged me. 'You know how to cook?'

'I don't think my lasagne for two would go very far.' I could manage a small dinner party, but a formal event for hundreds of people was way out of my league.

Judy thumped the phone down on the kitchen bench and poured herself a scotch. 'I could kill that woman.'

'Not if Luc does it first.' Kari hopped down from the kitchen stool and gazed out the window at the expanse of lawn.

She probably wished she were out there. Like the others, Kari had a supply of Ingenii blood, but it would only last for a few short months. And although there were thousands of vials still stored in the bloodvault, if the Principate continued to share them out, it wouldn't be long before nothing remained. No more daywalking.

Judy glanced at the clock. 'Three pm. The restaurants that are open this time of the year are now between shifts. If I'm really lucky,

I might get to talk with someone,' she began, as if speaking to herself. 'I know one or two…. C'mon girls, we're going to Orange. Face-to-face, I just might be able to get someone.'

'Yes!' Kari clapped her hands.

'And if that doesn't work?' I asked.

'Cook will probably resign.'

I grinned. 'Oops, there goes the masquerade ball.'

'Not funny, Laura!'

Less than forty minutes later, our car was manoeuvring through the narrow two-lane streets of the old part of Orange, the nearest town to D'Antonville. A scattering of snow covered the ground. A strong wind blew at people's coats, whipped hats from heads and tossed around the decorative lights strung across the street. Pedestrians hurried to the shelter of a warmly lit café – the only one open. Others along the boulevard were closed, their shutters rattling in the icy draught.

'Marcus, stop here. That's it.' She pointed to the café. 'Wish me luck.' Kari's fingers were crossed behind her back as she and Judy alighted from the car. Too many visitors would overwhelm, so Judy had suggested Marcus show me the Roman theatre, which just happened to be across the road. 'There's something there you'll find interesting.' She winked at Marcus.

Marcus chuckled and swivelled around in the driver's seat. 'Still up for it?'

I nodded, even though in the gloom of a wintery afternoon, the imposing ancient three-storey stone building with its windowless façade resembled more a prison than an ancient theatre. My curiosity was piqued, despite the cold wind.

'Did you see it being built?'

'It was already two-hundred years old when I watched performances here.'

'Don't think I'll ever get used to that.'

He laughed, parked and with my coat collar up and my woollen cap pulled low on my head, we ventured out. Marcus linked my arm through his, and we strode through the metal gates. 'Don't let the exterior fool you. Wait till you see inside.'

It took my breath away. Set into the side of a hill, the semi-circular tiered seating faced a massive stage edifice that would have once been covered with slender marble columns and frescoed panels. Only a few remained, their fading and chipped surfaces a sad reminder of its past glory.

'Wow!'

'In its day, it was stunning,' Marcus said.

How had it survived so long, through the rise and fall of empires and history's most tumultuous events? If only these walls could speak. I glanced at Marcus's profile, at the sad little smile tugging at his mouth, as he stared at the stage. *He* was living history.

'What are you remembering?'

'My father first brought me here when I received my toga virilis. I was sixteen. The play … I don't recall the name anymore, but it had a young actress. She appeared naked on stage.' He laughed and shook his head. 'My father thought it was about time I got acquainted with the female sex.'

'Oh my!' I laughed with him.

'Come, I'll show you something.' We wandered down to the front rows of seats. At the beginning of the third row, Marcus pointed. 'Take a look.'

Carved into the stone were letters and numbers, EQ GIII. 'What does it stand for?'

'"Equites Row 3". This row was reserved for the cavalry unit stationed here.'

'Front row seats? Why were they so lucky?'

Marcus pursed his lips. 'Mmm … let me see. We defended the empire, kept the city safe, built the roads and aqueducts….'

'Okay, okay, I get it.' I laughed. I'd forgotten Marcus had been a military commander of a cavalry unit. Had he sat here? Had he known some of the men?

'Move along four seats and look closely.'

Along one side of the stone seating, smoothed over by age was a barely visible scratching: MAR. ANT. PUL. I gasped. It could only be the abbreviated letters of Marcus's name. 'Your seat?'

He nodded. 'I got bored during one pantomime. A few days later, I was assigned as commander to the Frisian Cohort in Britain.'

And his whole life changed.

I blinked up at him. 'Do you wish you never received that command?'

'No. The only regret I have is that one particular day.'

He fell silent. As the wind howled through the columns, I fancied I heard the whispered voices of long ago – the excitement of the crowd, voices calling out greetings; the shuffling of feet on the stone steps, their centres worn by the weight of thousands over the centuries; the laughter and banter of soldiers in the front rows. All beneath a statue of the emperor, whose sightless eyes surveyed the crowd from his niche above the stage.

'Too much?' Were the memories of the past painful for him? Or had time dulled the ache?

His gaze flickered to me, and he smiled. I knew he had understood. 'Sometimes. But not today. Wait here.' He strolled onto the stage.

I sat on the stone bench and ran my fingers along my grandfather's name, the eighteen-hundred-year-old young man who now bowed to me. 'They still give performances here. Operas, plays….' His voice reverberated off the back wall to the audience, clear and loud.

'Let me go right up the back.' I raced up the steps to the topmost row.

'In ancient times' —Marcus called— 'this is where the women, slaves and prostitutes sat.

Nice. 'Now say something,' I cried.

His voice rang out clearly. Two-thousand years old and the acoustics of this building were still brilliant. A gust of wind blew at my cap, and I caught it in time. In a blink, Marcus was beside me.

'Enough of the past.' The barely detectable trace of sadness I'd seen in his smile earlier was gone. He wrapped an arm around my shoulders and pulled me into his warmth. 'Come. Let's get you into the car.'

'Are there any ruins in D'Antonville?' Surely there must be something, since the Roman presence here was so prominent. 'You had a villa, didn't you?'

'Indeed. It was demolished long ago to make way for the chateau. We reused the stones, dug up the mosaic floors and relaid them elsewhere. Some went into the flooring for the chapel.' He opened the car door for me. 'You haven't seen that yet, have you?'

'I didn't know there was one.'

He glanced at his watch. 'We still have another hour of daylight left. I'll show it to you if you like?'

My face split into a grin. I'm sure it rivalled that of the Cheshire cat. Who else could boast their guide through an ancient site as old as the site itself? He knew what he was talking about.

Judy and Kari walked out of the café just as we pulled up. Judy gave us the thumbs up. 'Cook has two extra helpers,' she said as she climbed into the front seat.

'The chef was free?' I asked.

'Not really. I offered to pay her more.'

Marcus laughed. 'Deus! Some things don't change.'

* * *

Marcus and I strolled through a wooded area to the north of the house. On a small rise overlooking the vine-covered hills lay a non-descript, honey-coloured building with a fusion of architectural styles. Three rounded apses with conical slate roofs – one flew the D'Antonville standard – formed one end, while the other end had a squared-off columned entrance.

'When was it built?'

'Let's see....' He rubbed at his lower lip. 'It was the same year Avitus was murdered ... about the mid four hundreds. But it's been restored over the years.'

'What a memory you have.'

He chuckled, and the cobweb-ridden wooden door scraped the ground as he pushed it open. Dust and bits of masonry flew about, hitting my eyes and nostrils. I coughed and fanned the debris away, brushing thick dust from my coat. 'How long since anyone was here?'

He sniffed the air. 'Many years.'

The tiny entrance porch gave way to a mosaic-tiled floor, the colours as fresh and vibrant as the day they were laid. Lines of waves, meanders and zigzags interspersed with flowers, figures in Roman dress and mythical creatures paraded across the floor.

'It's magnificent.'

'Part of the atrium, originally. Would've been a pity to have dumped them with the other building debris.'

I shook my head as I tiptoed around the images, careful my heels didn't land between the tiny coloured squares, some of which were loose. 'You know how many museums would love to get their hands on this?'

'One day ... perhaps.' He shrugged and walked to one of the two bathtub-shaped sarcophagi in the centre of the main space.

Light slanting in from the stained-glass windows bathed it in pale watery hues, highlighting the ornate carvings decorating the sides. Sculpted flowers, what looked like cherubs, and the image of a woman bouncing two babies on her knees stood out in high relief. On the top, reclined the figure of a smiling woman, her eyes crinkling at the sides, a bouquet of flowers in one hand.

Marcus stroked its face, his fingers lingering on her cheeks. 'My wife, Gallia, your grandmother.'

My head spun. I gripped his arm. Here I was face-to-face with my direct ancestor, yet more than eighteen-hundred years separated us. 'She was beautiful.'

He smiled and nodded as his gaze scanned her features. 'She had so many suitors, but she chose me. I miss her every day.' He swallowed hard, the emotion raw in his voice.

After all these centuries, he was still in love with her. I blinked away tears at the cruelty of the curse that condemned a man through countless aeons of existence without the one he loved by his side. I slid my hand beneath my coat to clutch the precious blood vial Luc had given me, and prayed Alec and I would not share the same fate.

Marcus sniffed, and rubbed his nose and turned to face the other sarcophagus. 'That one' —he waved towards it— 'is my daughter, Antonia, your aunt.'

The unknown sculptor managed to capture the women's likeness without losing their distinctiveness. I sucked in a breath. It was as if I was looking at an image of myself – the same high cheekbones, arched brows, fuller lower lip and straight nose. 'She looks….'

'Like you. Yes. It struck me at the Ritual.'

I thought back to that night, to his exact words. *So much like Antonia.* Was there a reason for that? 'A genetic throwback?'

'Perhaps. Or, as she and Luc were the firstborn of the curse and you being the last, carry her image.'

I took a deep breath as Marcus's words sunk in, my hands straying to my belly. My child would not have to experience the Ritual, would not have to wonder about a guardian, nor fear being manipulated by rival Brethren factions. He or she will be free to live a normal human life.

I glanced around. Set in niches into the walls, were many other sarcophagi. Some had lids like pitched roofs, some were flat, while others had recumbent figures in armour, their hands joined as if in prayer. I looked closely at some of the inscriptions to confirm my suspicions. They were all D'Antonvilles.

This was the last resting place of the Ingenii. 'A family vault,' I said quietly.

He looked around. 'Yes, yes it is. There's more down in the crypt.' If there was one word in the English language that conjured images of mummies, zombies and all manner of scary creatures, that was it. But then, what could be scarier than vampires? 'You want to see it?'

'Sure do.'

Towards the back of the chapel, a set of narrow twisting steps led down into the dark. He took a candlestick from a small box nailed to the wall, blew the dust and cobwebs from it before he lit it. 'No electricity, I'm afraid.'

Narrower than the chapel above it, but longer, the crypt was lined with more stone coffins, each set into their own niche. Marcus held the candle aloft. Faded scenes of shepherds, biblical characters and early images of Christ and the apostles came into view. He lit a few more candles and placed them into wall-mounted holders in the shape of a closed fist. Stalagmites of candlewax hung from their bases, their drippings leaving a hard yellowing lump on the ground. Soon the smell of burning candles drifted on the air, their slender flames illuminating walls, whose every spare inch was decorated with Judaeo-Christian images. One panel showed Daniel in the lion's den. Another displayed the resurrection and ascension of Christ. It was like being in a small-scale version of the catacombs in Rome.

'When did the family become Christian?'

'Same time as the emperor. Political correctness is nothing new.' He grinned and tapped his finger against the side of his nose. 'Only much later did I personally believe.' Marcus lowered the candle to one inscription: SECUNDUS LINUS. 'Linus, your second cousin. He's among the first Ingenii. Their remains were brought here when I had the chapel built.'

He read out a few more names until we both turned at the creak of the entrance door opening. Soon, Alec's face peered down at us.

'Judith told me you'd be here.' He dropped a light kiss on my lips and wrapped his arm around my waist. 'Have you shown Laura the secret passageway yet? The one that leads down to the caverns?'

'Another? I thought you said there weren't any others?' This estate must be honeycombed with secret underground tunnels.

'Not from the chateau. To be honest, I'd forgotten about this one. If Judith hadn't mentioned you coming here….' He shrugged.

'Never been used. It's an emergency exit.' Marcus strode a few metres ahead and pressed a carved rosette on a section of wall between sarcophagi. 'It's stuck.' He tried again using both hands, and slowly it moved. With a grinding noise, that part of the wall slid aside to reveal a passageway. The candles flickered at the sudden updraft, throwing shadowy images across the ceiling and walls. Marcus smiled. 'Glad to see it still works.'

I wrinkled my nose at the dank scent and squealed as a rat scurried across my foot. 'Eww!'

Marcus stepped across the threshold and peered in. 'I should check … make sure it's still clear.'

'You can get into the vault from here?' I'd be surprised if that was the case.

'No, no. It can only be opened from within the vault, like an emergency exit.'

'Sam checked this one lately?' Alec asked.

'I know he upgraded the security in the chateau passageways. Not sure about this one. And I haven't been here since 1940. when the Nazis—' Marcus's gaze panned to me, his brow creased. 'Has Luc told you anything about that?'

'Nazis here? No. What happened?'

'The Germans wanted to commandeer the chateau; make it their headquarters in this region. Luc got a message to me at the monastery…. Five of them showed up spewing their orders.' With a flick of his head he indicated the interior of the tunnel. 'We dumped their bodies in there. Their vehicle we drove into the lake.' He smiled grimly. 'Best feed I'd had in years!'

I should have been shocked, but I wasn't. On the contrary, I was proud my family had done their bit to fight one of the world's greatest evils. 'I'm glad you got rid of them,' I said softly.

Marcus entered the tunnel and disappeared into the gloom. I closed my eyes and focused; heard the thud of his boots, the swish of his arms sweeping away cobwebs, even the scuttling of spiders and other insects that scampered at his approach. Next came a thwack, then another, as if he were kicking something aside. The remains of the Nazis?

'I can hear everything,' I whispered to Alec.

'Good. Me too.'

Soon Marcus stopped. A second later, his figure emerged from the tunnel, brushing dirt and insects from his hair and coat. 'Deus! It's filthy in there. Sempronius'll have to oil these rusty hinges and remove the skeletons. They're clogging up the passage.'

Marcus was the only one who called his men by their original Roman names. I liked it. He dropped something into my hand. It was a Nazi insignia – a silver badge in the form of an eagle with outstretched wings. In its claws it held a swastika emblazoned shied.

'Perhaps use that in your classroom. Tell them it's a replica.' He gave me a wink before depressing the rosette and closing the tunnel entrance.

A dull ache gripped my chest. I missed my teaching. Not until the rebellion was truly over, the curse ended and we were back in Sydney, would I consider returning to it. In the meantime, I thanked Marcus and pocketed the medal.

'Want to go?' Alec asked.

'Yeah. Glad to have seen this, though.'

We strolled back through the woods and into the clearing behind the house. The clouds had lifted, and the last rays of the weak, winter sun were dipping behind the vine-covered hills.

Sam appeared. His light brown hair shone almost russet in the late afternoon glow. 'Good news. The Rebels are giving up – those who've seen the video, that is.'

'Luc'll be happy.' Alec's voice was deadpan.

Sam's mouth crinkled into a smile. 'It's *you* they want to surrender to, not Luc.'

'Ha! What did I tell you?' Marcus slapped Alec on the back as he strode past him toward Sam.

My heart leapt. Perhaps Alec's position as princeps had not been compromised after all. I needed to dispel the shadow of doubt in his eyes. 'They saw you didn't hesitate to hand out the death penalty and it made them fear you. And the fact it was you who captured Timur and Rasputin, not Luc, earned their respect.' I faced him and took both his hands in mine. 'You're the princeps the Brethren need. The Rebels surrendering to you is proof of that.'

Alec exhaled slowly and folded me into his arms. 'How did I exist before you came into my life?'

'With great difficulty?' I smiled.

He chuckled as we continued up the path to the house. Marcus and Sam walked in front, heads bent in private conversation. Alec tapped him on the shoulder. 'Sam, tell the Rebel prefects to get here by tomorrow night. We'll hold them in the dungeons till the masquerade ball, where they'll be stripped of their offices and made to take the Bloodpledge.'

'Done.'

Alec continued, 'Marcus, how about we send Sam and Terens to collect the Keepers of the Lamiae. I want to confirm they were mesmerised.'

Sam's eyes brightened as his gaze flicked between Alec and Marcus. I recalled him struggling against Rasputin's taunts, trying to stir his resentment against Luc for not including him in missions. He was the stay-at-home boy, forever stuck to the computer.

'Sounds good to me. What about security monitors?'

Sam's face dropped.

'I can take over for a while,' Alec said.

Sam's face lit up in a broad grin. 'Owe you, man.'

'Try to get them here before dawn.'

Sam clapped him on the arm. 'Done.'

It was nearly dark when we re-entered the house. The Brethren staff were turning on the lights. They bowed their heads in deference as we walked past. What was their employment future should Luc and Marcus choose death when the time came? What would happen to the chateau? I recalled Judy's words about plans she and Luc had made, that she had at least another fifty years ahead of her. Did that mean Luc had decided to choose to remain as vampire? My mind was abuzz with questions, and my heart ached at what the future held for them.

# CHAPTER 32 – MASQUERADE

**LAURA**

'Whatcha think?' Kari's entry into my room was like a whirlwind. She twirled causing the skirts of her midnight-blue gown to billow. She'd tamed her short, spiky Nordic-blonde locks into some semblance of order with a matching ribbon, the ends trailing down her low-cut back.

'You look gorgeous!' If Jake didn't notice her tonight, he was blind.

Her tinkling laugh rang out as she put her glittery blue-feathered mask in place, twirled and curtsied. 'Now let's see you.' She grasped my hands and pulled me from my dresser chair.

Judy had stocked my French wardrobe the same as she had in Sydney. I had a plethora of the latest designer dresses. One caught my eye, a beautiful red gown with velvet black trim and off-the-shoulder bodice that perfectly hugged my curves. It contrasted perfectly with the voluminous scarlet taffeta skirt.

I chose it in honour of Alec, whose clan tartan was black and red.

I'd curled the ends of my long hair, gathered a section and pinned it at the back.

'Ooh….' She cooed and clapped. 'And your mask?'

I opened my palm to reveal a red-lace mask, trimmed with rhinestones and held it to my face. I, too, did a little pirouette.

'Alec won't be able to keep his eyes off you,' she said.

'I already have trouble doing that,' Alec drawled, his deep voice sending little tingles scooting down to my nether regions. He leaned against the door, arms folded, gaze raking the length of my body, his eyes twinkling behind his tartan mask.

I wanted to purr.

He looked utterly delicious in his clan kilt – the red-and-black Munro dress tartan and black velvet jacket with silver buttons. The cropped jacket emphasised his broad shoulders, and the smile he gave me hinted at later pleasures.

'Why can't I go?' Dominik stood at his elbow, his jaw dropping as he gazed at Kari.

Since coming to live with us, Dominik had practically become Alec's shadow, following him around and even mimicking his mannerisms. If Alec twirled the ring on his finger, so did Dominik, even though he didn't own one. And if I didn't lock the door to our suite, he'd be there all the time.

'Two reasons: first, you're too young, and second, it's an Elders and prefects ball only.' Alec ruffled his hair as he stepped past him into the room.

'Not fair.'

'Life's not fair, Dom.' Alec took me in his arms, spun me around and dipped me low to the ground. *I'll enjoy untying that bodice later,* his voice whispered seductively through my mind.

*Make sure the door is locked first.*

He chuckled as he lifted me up, and formally offered me his arm. 'May I escort you, my lady?'

'You may.'

Jake stuck his face in the doorway. 'Ready to go, kid—?'

His jaw dropped seeing Kari. I enjoyed his stunned look. Surely he'd seen her in evening dress before? Recent balls she'd forgone. What had stopped her? He swallowed and offered her his arm, his eyes never leaving her face. I gave her a wink over my shoulder as Alec and I went to the door.

We started up the stairs to the ballroom; soon the guests would arrive. Several rooms on this top level had been opened for their comfort and convenience. One was a banquet room for the donsangs, where they could eat and meet other humans. Cook and her helpers had excelled. Earlier in the day, I'd peeked at the bustle of activity in the kitchen. The food was a feast for the senses: tiny triangular white sandwiches, a range of colourful salads, roast meats of every kind and delicate mouth-watering pastries and desserts only the most hardened dieter – or vampire – could resist.

In the driveway, fairy lights blinked on the trunks and leafless branches of the trees, while a million tiny bulbs twinkled in the windows and the front doors of the chateau. The candelabras in the entrance hall had been polished to a mirror sheen, the candles' flames dancing and swaying on the ebony surface. Illuminated garlands twisted their way up the staircase that led to the ballroom.

We took our seats on the dais next to Luc and Judy. Swathes of entwined green and lavender silk – the D'Antonville colours – hung from the canopy and pooled on the floor. Five gold sashes lay draped across the arm of my chair. I knew their purpose, as Alec had briefed me earlier.

My mother, resplendent in a rich jade-green dress, acknowledged each guest as they were announced. Her silver-streaked auburn hair was caught back in a chignon and crowned with a white-gold tiara of intertwining leaves and flowers adorned with a single emerald. Her eyes shone behind her butterfly shaped mask.

She leant across and whispered in my ear. 'You look stunning, dear.'

'As do you. Nice bling.' I grinned at her tiara.

'Your father's gift at your birth.' She beamed and placed her hand over his. Luc drew them to his lips and kissed her fingertips.

Earlier, my father had approached Alec and formally apologised, ending several days of tension between them. The entire household breathed again, now they were reconciled.

This night, the Elders discarded their gold cloaks for formal attire. Kwome, Grey Bear and Zhao wore their traditional dress, while Maira came in an exquisitely embroidered gown with a fringed hem. They bowed to us and then mingled. They, and a few more of the most prominent prefects, were the only Brethren who stayed in the chateau grounds. Even with multiple guest rooms and cottages, the chateau wasn't made to accommodate over four-hundred extra people, especially as many Brethren were accompanied by their donsangs.

The ballroom was a sea of colour. Elegant women in dazzling gowns of electric blue, silver-grey, apricot, sunny yellow and turquoise swept the room, greeting friends and chinking glasses. Lavender eyes glinted behind feathered, lace and rhinestone masks shaped like butterflies, cats and flowers, some covering only the eyes, others half the face. The men, likewise, many in tuxedos with long-nose masks or in traditional costume, added to the magnificence of the occasion.

'Have I told you you're the most beautiful woman here?' Alec whispered in my ear.

I turned to face him, my mouth barely a breath away from his, and inhaled his intoxicating scent, drawing it deep into my lungs. 'Not yet, but you can if you like.'

His heart-stopping smile had my insides twisted tighter than the flavours of my favourite candy cane – and just as sweet.

The announcer struck the tiled floor three times with his brass rod. 'My lords, ladies and gentlemen. Sieur Marcus Antonius Pulcher. Arch Elder and High Lord of the Brethren.'

The crowd knelt as Marcus, in black bow tie and gold mask topped with a crown, entered. We stood as he took his seat next to Luc.

Alec spoke. 'Brethren, welcome to our New Year's Eve Masquerade Ball. This year, we have double reason to celebrate. First we welcome our new Ingenii, Lady Laura, whom many of you have already met.' They bowed, and I inclined my head. Karl, standing near the front with Milena, cheekily gave me a wink.

I couldn't help smiling back.

'Second, we celebrate victory over the rebellion.' At this, the crowd cheered. 'Tonight we see the surrender of the traitorous prefects.' He turned toward the door. 'Bring them in.'

The crowd parted as Jake, Cal, Sam and Terens ushered in five chained men, dressed in sackcloth, their heads bowed in shame. Alec's men carried no swords, but I guessed Terens, at least, hid one or two daggers strapped to his legs.

'Weren't there nine, my lord?' O'Toole called out. Like Alec, he wore a kilt, but in dark green plaid.

Alec's voice rang out. 'Correct. But we found four to be innocent. Keepers of the Lamiae, step forward.' Two men and two women entered. 'These, your brethren, are exonerated. Rasputin mesmerised them into gaining control over the lamiae. Their minds are free again.'

'And the lamiae?' a few asked.

'Ash, like Lord Timur and his castle.'

A general murmur of assent and nodding of heads greeted Alec's pronouncement. The four prefects – ex-keepers of the lamiae, now – bowed and joined the assembled guests. Some slapped them on the back. Others handed them flutes of champagne.

Alec addressed the Rebels. 'Kneel.' They did so, unprompted. 'Before your brethren, I relieve you of the Office of Prefect. You are unworthy. You will swear the Bloodpledge.'

At this point, I rose and, with him, extended my ringed hand. The eyes of the serpents began to glow, and a warm tingle raced up my arm. A hush settled over the room, not a swish of fabric, not a tinkle of a glass.

'On the serpent ring of D'Antonville, do you solemnly swear to pledge your allegiance on pain of death, to the Principate – to myself, Lord Alexander Munro; the Ingenii, Lady Laura D'Antonville and all future Ingenii born from her body?'

One by one they swore allegiance and kissed our rings. As they did, light flared from the serpents' eyes, swirled around each man and merged into their bodies. A communal gasp arose. Perhaps, like me, few had ever seen the Bloodpledge take place.

The four Rebel prefects jerked upright then collapsed, their heavy breathing audible in the silence.

'You and the serpent rings are now bonded. Any treachery and the serpent will erupt in flames, reducing you to ash. Now, you are free to go.'

They stood with heads bowed, and, after having their chains removed, exited the ballroom. Cal, Jake, Terens and Sam then took their places behind us. We remained standing as Luc handed Alec a scroll. I glimpsed a list of names. Alec called each one and, as they stepped forward, appointed them the new prefects. I presented each with a golden sash while Alec placed the prefects ring – the Praefectus black enamelled P against an iron shield – on their fingers. After the crowd's acclamation had ceased, Alec signalled to the orchestra in the upper gallery.

'Let the festivities begin.'

Alec led me from the dais, and we swayed to the romantic strains of a Strauss waltz, weaving in and out with other couples. I floated on an idyllic cloud beneath the blue and gold rococo ceiling that gleamed in the light of crystal chandeliers. The troubles of the last few days were forgotten as I lost myself in his arms and was drawn into the lavender depths of his eyes.

*It's time we were wed.*

I glanced around just in case anyone, somehow, overheard Alec's telepathic message. We'd discussed this before. Initially it was to have been after the Pledging, but circumstances intervened. *When?*

*Day after tomorrow, after the guests have gone. Private ceremony. I want you as my wife, Laura, not just as my lover.*

My heart melted. *Sounds good to me.*

His eyes darkened, and with a flourish, he spun me around and caught me tightly. As far as we were concerned, we were the only couple in the room. Everyone else disappeared as the music and the beating of my heart drowned out every other sound.

'Oops, excuse me.' Karl grinned as he bumped into us. Milena gave me a warm smile.

'Yes, Karl?' Alec rolled his eyes.

'Great party. Entertainment's not bad either.' His eyes sparkled beneath his black Venetian mask.

'Is that why you interrupted?'

I laughed.

'Karl, stop teasing and tell them,' Milena said. No mistaking the serious note in her voice.

Karl's expression sobered, and he lowered his voice. 'I've been hearing some interesting gossip. You might want to eavesdrop and find out for yourselves. Tell me later if it's true.' With that, he and Milena waltzed away.

'What did he mean?' I had my suspicions and hoped I was wrong.

'Not sure.' *Let's listen in.*

Closing my ears to all other sounds, I concentrated on the couples who danced by us, picking up snatches of conversation.

'… his daughter all right. Same face.'

'Think he can breed, too?'

I assumed that last comment referred to Alec. His smile faded.

'… a couple, for sure. Heard she had a boyfriend.'

'…O'Toole's right and she is the Child of Light and Darkness? Could he be…?

Alec's eyebrows rose.

*It won't take them long to work it out,* I sent the thought to Alec.

He nodded.

After a few more similar comments, I'd heard all I needed to. Would it be so bad if everyone knew Alec was the witch's descendant? That we were the Destined Ones? These people were all loyal Principate supporters. They understood the value of maintaining a system of government that protected them and their food supply. I doubted the ending of the curse could adversely affect that.

*You think we should still keep it secret?*

Alec's face hardened, and he gripped my fingers. *There could be pockets of rogue elements we don't know about. I'm not taking a risk with your life.*

*Or yours.* If there were Rebels who hadn't surrendered, Alec's life was as much in danger as mine. What really concerned me was how close the Principate came to losing its supporters: firstly because Luc had kept my existence a secret, and then over the hidden Ingenii blood vials. Five prefects had defected. And from the bit of information I'd gleaned from Alec, even Karl has been upset. We couldn't afford that happening again. *At least share that knowledge with Karl, and maybe O'Toole. They supported you at Timur's hearing. If anything, Karl convinced the prefects to side with us. You owe him that. He's risked his life for the Principate to bring you news of Timur's treachery, cared for me while—*

*You've convinced me.* He exhaled. *I hate keeping secrets from him. But it's not up to me.* His gaze flicked over my shoulder, and as we spun to the music, I glimpsed Luc and Judy dancing on the other side of the ballroom.

My mother laughed at something Luc said and looked so happy. Another pang of sadness seared my heart at the unfairness of their situation – one immortal, the other not. The blood vial Luc had given me nestled between my breasts. Just a few drops each of his, Antonia and Marcus's blood and my life span would equal Alec's. My father ensured I would not suffer the same fate as he and my mother. Blast! This was not the time to be morbid. Not tonight, I told myself. This was a joyous occasion.

*Talk to him. Karl could be a good barometer to gauge how the Brethren might take the news about us.*

Alec's stern expression gave way to a smile. *You really would make a good diplomat.*

*It's a skill I honed as a school teacher.* I shrugged.

'Mmmm … he needs to know.'

I glanced at my serpent ring, it's eyes shining a glorious red indicating all curious looks and remarks were harmless. 'Later. A few hours won't make any difference. Besides, I don't want to miss the fireworks and my New Year's kiss.' I beamed up at him.

Alec's mouth curved into a smile, and his eyes took on an impish gleam. 'Must I wait till then?'

He manoeuvred us from the ballroom and into the hallway behind one of the marble pillars. The stone cooled my back as his mouth claimed mine in a searing exchange of lips and tongues that ignited a fire in every cell in my body. Our ragged breaths mingled, and through the thin fabric of his kilt, I felt his arousal.

'Maybe we should get a room,' I said, breathless.

Alec touched his forehead to mine. 'We'd be there the rest of the night. You'd miss the fireworks.'

'I can think of other fireworks.' I pressed myself closer to him.

His eyes darkened and he groaned. 'Darling, don't tempt me.' The Scottish lilt in his normally Australian accent, more pronounced. 'Too many awkward questions if we were to disappear,' he murmured as his lips nibbled my earlobe and brushed the side of my neck.

My pulse quickened at his hot breath on my skin. I missed the sting of his bite, the total surrender, as I entrusted my life into his hands. It was euphoric, which had surprised me.

I lifted his head to meet my eyes. 'Do you miss it?'

'Every day.'

Movement caught my eye. A figure in a sable cloak with hood pulled low strode by us. It was a vaguely familiar scent, but I couldn't place it. 'Who was that?'

'Who?' Alec's eyes were glazed as he looked around.

Another figure, mask held up to her face, giggled and raced past our hiding place. A young man followed, caught her in his arms and they disappeared into a darkened room.

'Never mind.' I wrapped my arms around his neck, ready for another kiss, when Kari found us.

'Aha! Knew I'd find you smooching somewhere. C'mon, need you.' She grabbed my hand and Alec's and pulled us into the ballroom. 'They're doing a quadrille, and we're short a couple. You can kissy kissy later.'

A quadrille? 'I don't know how to do one of those.' I pictured myself bumping into other couples, stepping on toes and being a total embarrassment.

But Kari was determined. 'Easy peasy. Just do what I do.'

Easy for her to say. Alec had the temerity to laugh. I sent him a filthy look, which had no affect. 'Don't worry,' he said. 'I'll lead you. You'll be fine.'

I needn't have worried, for we partnered her and Jake, Karl and Milena, and Luc and Judy – my family and friends. They made sure to guide me. Just before the fireworks were due to start, I'd muddled my way through at least three to four new dances.

Luc left us and strode to the dais. 'Madames and monsieurs, the fireworks start in one minute. Please make your way to the balcony.'

Several-hundred people surged onto the wide verandah that ran the length of the upper floor, its white tiled floor and stone balustrade gleaming in the light of a full moon. The cool air hit my face and bit my cheeks. Unlike many of the donsangs, I had no wrap. Alec removed his jacket and draped it over my shoulders as we made our way through to the front the crowd. He stood behind, wrapping me in his warmth, as the countdown began.

'Ten, nine, eight … two, one. Happy New Year!' Everyone cheered and clinked glasses, others were locked in passionate embraces.

'Happy New Year, darling.' Alec lifted my chin to meet his lips just as the first explosions sparked in the sky. Those fireworks couldn't compare to the touch of his mouth on mine. Behind my closed eyelids, I was vaguely aware of splashes of light and colour, and the "oohs" and "aahs" of the crowd.

If the Brethren had questions about our relationship before this evening began, they certainly wouldn't have now.

'Hey, you're missing it.' Kari thumped my arm.

About to tell her to go away, I saw red tears glistening in her eyes. She swiped at them. Next to her, Jake appeared shell shocked – rubbing the back of his neck, eyes wide as he stared at the fireworks. Milena hung onto his other arm, a smirk on her face. Karl's expression could've curdled milk. He turned and pushed his way out through the crowd.

What'd happened? Although I could guess.

'Back in a minute.' Alec went after him.

I missed the sudden loss of his warmth and pulled his jacket tightly around me. Kari rested her head on my shoulder. 'What's wrong? Want to tell me?'

She sniffled and shook her head. Above us, the sky exploded in brilliant hues, and the smoke and the partly burned paper casings from the fireworks floated down to us. Kari whispered, '*She* kissed him.'

I didn't have to look to know which *she* Kari referred to. What was Milena up to? Poor Kari. She'd dressed to impress, hoping tonight she might win a kiss from Jake. Milena stole that moment. How cruel of her, and then Karl had stormed off.

From behind, a familiar pair of arms encircled me. 'I asked Karl and O'Toole to meet us in Luc's office, right after the fireworks.'

'Us?'

'I'd like you there. After all, this doesn't concern just me.' He kissed the top of my ear. 'Time we ended this boys' club.'

I angled my head up at him. 'If you're not careful, you'll become one of those sensitive new-age guys.'

'Have to keep up with the times.'

We both chuckled.

'How was Karl?' I couldn't care less if Milena overheard.

'Angry.'

I glanced at her. It was hard biting my tongue, especially seeing how she clutched Jake's arm. Didn't she care he was Kari's escort?

The last of the fireworks burst above us in a dazzling shower. The smell of the pyrotechnics lingered in the air as the music began and groups drifted back into the ballroom. Kari lifted her head from my shoulder and strode away. Jake didn't follow.

I was sorely tempted to slap him in the back of the head but resisted.

Alec waltzed me into the centre of the room. 'Let them work it out, Laura.'

I sighed. I hated seeing Kari so unhappy, but she was an adult, and older then me by a few-hundred years.

On the dais, we joined Luc and Judy.

My mother's face was flushed from dancing. She plucked a drink from a passing waiter. 'Another successful ball.' She fanned herself with an exquisite Venetian fan. 'To think how that wretched woman tried to sabotage it.'

'She lost.' I raised my glass, and we toasted.

Alec leaned close to Luc. 'We need to talk. Heard the scuttlebutt?'

Luc lifted an eyebrow. 'Like what?' Alec repeated some of the comments we'd heard earlier. Luc shut his eyes and growled low in his throat. 'Ah! Let them talk.'

'Will it cause problems? I need to know.' Alec glanced at me before returning his attention to Luc. 'I asked Karl and Derek to join us in your office.'

Derek? Was that O'Toole's first name?

'Why?' Luc's brows snapped together.

'In your office.'

Luc opened his mouth then closed it again. Alec twisted the serpent ring on his finger and waited. My father inhaled deeply and gritted his teeth while Judy placed her hand over his. He gave a curt nod, fished a key from his pocket and tossed it to Alec. 'You're princeps. You want a meeting; we'll have one.'

Yes. I wanted to do a fist pump. Instead, I smiled and sipped my drink.

'I'd like Marcus there, too.' Alec took my hand. 'Let's hope this won't take long … an hour, maybe, and we'll be back.'

Jake joined us. Was he required? Or was facing a possible angry Luc preferable to being caught between two women?

As we left the ballroom, Alec approached Marcus, who stood with three others, laughing and drinking near one of the refreshment tables. From the dark red stain on his lips, it wasn't wine he swirled in his goblet. As Alec whispered in his ear, I looked around for the other men.

Cal and Sam both had dance partners, yet their gaze never strayed far from Judy and me. Even at an occasion such as this, and within the relative safety of the chateau, they were still on guard. Where was Terens? There he was, towering above everyone else, a chequered harlequin mask on his face, weaving through the crowd to sit next to Judy. Guard or companion? Maybe both.

This was going to be an interesting meeting, I thought, as we traipsed down the stairs and through the library to Luc's office. How was he going to react to Alec and me sharing the family secret with Karl and O'Toole? We might see another sort of fireworks.

And then there was Karl. He was already angry because of Milena. How would he take this latest news?

# CHAPTER 33 – TRUST

**LAURA**

Karl paced the floor outside Luc's office, cigarette between his lips. He spied Jake. 'You can have her. I'm done!'

Not a good start.

'What the hell you on about?' Jake walked up to him.

'Protecting her lands, looking out for her ... and she chooses you!' He spat out the cigarette and ground it beneath his foot.

Jake groaned. 'Listen—'

'Not now. There are other matters. Karl, if you and O'Toole don't mind waiting a few minutes....' Alec unlocked the door and Luc and Marcus went in. 'I'll call you in.'

Karl scowled. I wished the library included a cello among its acquisitions – he could play a few notes to calm down, as he had when we were in Prague. I squeezed his arm before entering.

Alec closed the door and pulled out a chair for me. He chose to stand.

'So, what's with…?' Luc waved his hand toward the door as he sat behind his desk.

'Exactly why we're here, Papa,' I said.

His eyebrows shot skyward. 'You're in on this?'

'My idea.' I grinned.

Marcus perched on the end of the desk. His mouth twitched as his gaze roamed the three of us. 'Modern times, son.'

Luc leant his elbows on the desk and steepled his fingers. 'I'm listening.'

I was aware Alec had tensed. Probably remembering their last nasty confrontation. None of us wanted a repeat performance. If I spoke carefully, there might be a chance my father wouldn't react too strongly. He may even agree.

I touched Alec's hand. 'Let me ask him.'

'Go ahead.'

'Papa, how would you reward your most loyal Principate supporters?' Luc gazed at me and brought his fingers up to his mouth. He was listening. I pressed further. 'Those who stand up for you in public, support your policies, justify them.'

His eyes glittered, and I had the distinct impression he knew where this was leading. 'Those two out there have anything to do with it?'

'Mmm … could be.'

'How is this related to the gossip Alec's so worried about?'

'We don't want to alienate our most loyal supporters by keeping more secrets from them.' I gripped the arms of my chair. I remembered something Alec had said. 'Wasn't Karl your informant against Timur? He risked his life to get you that information, didn't he?'

Luc gave a slow nod.

I crossed my fingers. 'Would it be so bad to share with him and O'Toole that Alec and I are the prophesied ones? That I'm carrying the child that will break the curse? Their reaction will be a good indicator of how the rest of the Brethren feel.'

I held my breath and waited.

I jumped as Luc slammed his palms on the desk. 'Do you know what you're asking?'

'Yes, Papa, I do,' I said quietly and firmly. 'Karl risked his life for you, came to Alec's aid with you when he was attacked by Stockton and his bikie gang. He then helped Alec rescue me and protected me in his house while Alec took on Timur and Rasputin. And he and O'Toole had your back at Timur's hearing. I reckon their testimony influenced everyone for our side. Surely all this has earned them the right to share in our secrets? We need them on our side, and they've proven their loyalty.'

Luc rubbed his eyes and exhaled. His gaze swept to Marcus. 'What do you think?'

Marcus picked up the glass paperweight on Luc's desk and spun it around in his hand. 'Very persuasive argument, to which I'm inclined to agree.'

'You do?'

'Laura and Alec are adults. They've weighed up the risks and believe Karl and O'Toole worthy of their trust. Maybe we should too.' He tossed the paperweight to Alec. 'Am I right?'

'Absolutely.' Alec handed me the paperweight, a beautiful glass ball of millefiori. Venetian? 'And what better way to repay their loyalty.'

'Jake?' Luc turned to him.

He stood with his back against the door, hands in his trouser pockets. 'Karl may get on my nerves but' —he tipped his head in my and Alec's direction— 'they're right. We owe him ... and O'Toole.'

Thank you Jake.

Luc leant back in his chair and stroked his chin. If he agreed, it would be another monumental step for him. Relinquishing the Principate was one thing, but trusting such an enormous, and long held, family secret to a non-family member was something else entirely. Especially as one from his household had recently betrayed him. Were we asking for too much?

'Luc, let me ask you this,' Alec said. 'Can the Principate survive without the Ingenii?'

Such a simple question, yet it encompassed the entire argument.

'Yes.' He paused. 'As long as we have the prefects on our side.'

'They're waiting outside.' I tossed the paperweight back to Luc.

He caught it and spun it on the tip of his finger as his gaze locked on mine. I could see every concern, every precaution he'd taken over the centuries to ensure our family's survival written in his eyes. And now he was being asked to compromise that. I prayed I wasn't wrong.

Exhaling long and slow, Luc set the glass weight back atop a pile of books on his desk. 'All right.' He pointed at Alec. 'But this is your responsibility. I take no part in it. Bring them in.'

This was momentous. I released the breath I'd been holding.

Jake opened the door, and with a jerk of his head, indicated the two men enter. I rose and moved my chair against Luc's desk so I faced the men. Alec stood next to me.

'What are you going to say?' I whispered to him.

He said nothing but squeezed my hand.

Karl stubbed his cigarette out in his gold cigarette case and rammed it into his pocket. O'Toole cracked his neck and adjusted his tie. Their gazes landed on each of our faces.

'Karl, O'Toole,' Alec began. 'The Principate owes you a debt of thanks for your loyal support. We acknowledge this by sharing with you information known only to Clan D'Antonville.' Their eyes widened, and they exchanged glances. 'Before I do so, I must have your word that this information will not be divulged to anyone. Not even to your life mates.'

'I swear,' they said in unison.

Alec grasped my hand. 'The rumour about Laura being the Child of Light and Darkness is true. You know the prophecy – she must bear a child with a descendant of the witch who uttered the curse in order to end it. I'm that descendant. And Laura is with child – our child – a few weeks gone.'

I nodded.

'Holy shit!' Karl ran both hands through his hair.

O'Toole stood dumbfounded, mouth open, his eyes darting between Alec and me. 'Sweet Mary and Joseph! I was right!' He grinned slowly and slapped his thigh.

'You can understand why this cannot be common knowledge,' Alec added.

'Ain't that a fact! Don't reckon our brethren are ready for this, yet. You can trust me to keep the sweet colleen's condition a secret.' O'Toole's Irish brogue rang through the room.

'You know for sure you're of the witch's direct bloodline?' Karl asked.

'There's no doubt. I smelled her blood on him the day we met.' Luc's gaze panned to Alec. 'So much for me not taking part in this,' he muttered.

'My sword carries the stain of her blood, the scent still strong. There's no mistake,' Marcus said.

Karl's brow creased, and he rubbed the side of his mouth with his finger. 'Wait a minute.... If you knew who he was way back in...?'

'1918,' Alec answered.

'Right ... then why didn't you get together with Lady Judith?' His face brightened, and he looked from me to Luc. 'Ah, I got it. The child of darkness bit refers to her being half vampire. And since Lady Judith's not.... But then why turn Alec? Did you plan—'

'No.' Luc shook his head. 'Alec was dying. Owen, the idiot, shot him.'

'It was an accident,' Alec added quickly.

'Remember him.' O'Toole grimaced. 'Unpleasant fellow.'

Luc snorted.

From what I remembered of my grandfather, I was inclined to agree. We didn't find out till later that he'd had an affair with a

French girl while stationed in France during the First World War. She'd had a child by him, a boy. The only reason he returned to Sydney, and his wife, was because mother and baby died of the influenza epidemic after the war. Who knew if he would have stayed permanently in France? It would've caused problems for the clan, dividing half their time protecting the Ingenii in one country and his heir in another.

'How convenient that his child would be a female.' Karl's eyes narrowed.

Jake briefly closed his eyes and shook his head.

O'Toole paled and he licked his lips as his gaze flitted between Karl and Luc. 'Sure you can't be serious?'

Luc shot from his seat. 'What are you implying?'

Karl stood his ground. 'You have to admit it looks a remarkable coincidence—'

'I married Judith because I loved her, and our daughter was conceived in that love. If you think I used her to end the curse, then you couldn't be more wrong!' There was no doubting the passionate truth in my father's voice. 'Yes, I want it to end; I won't deny that, but for her.' Luc pointed to me. 'Not for myself. You think I want to see my grandchild go through the Ritual? To be in constant danger from the rogue elements?' He slammed his fist on the desk. 'Why do you think I lobbied the Eldership to allow Alec, while still a juvenile, to sit as princeps? Because he was the only man I trusted not to take advantage of my daughter since I couldn't be her guardian. And by virtue of his blood, the seat belongs to him, anyway.' No one uttered a word as Luc sat back down and massaged his forehead. 'My only regret is not stepping back sooner.'

I glanced up at Alec. His lips were a tight line as he rubbed my fingers. Did he regret his altercation with Luc the other day?

Karl lowered his head. 'Please, accept my apology. I'm honoured that you're trusting me with this knowledge.'

Luc waved his hand in dismissal and jerked his head in Alec's direction. 'You have Alec and Laura to thank for that, not me.'

Both men bowed their head in deference to us, and Karl mouthed a silent thanks to Alec.

O'Toole folded his arms, his gaze darting from face to face 'I take it, this is the end of the curse. But what does that mean exactly?'

'We don't know. There are no specifics,' Alec replied. 'Will Laura's blood retain the power of the Ingenii gene? Or will it revert to human? Your guess is as good as mine, but were hoping it's the latter.'

'Me too. If there's no Ingenii, there's no reason to rebel. My blood benefits no one,' I pointed out. Halleluiah to that, I wanted to add out loud.

'Precisely. It places everyone on an even keel. Nobody will be able to daywalk once the Ingenii blood vials run out. We'll all be in the dark together.' Karl pulled out his gold cigarette box, glanced at me, and closed the lid. Instead, he stuck a toothpick between his lips and chewed on it.

'It's the killin' some are after. That I can't abide.' O'Toole grabbed a chair from against the wall and straddled it. 'I enjoy a good hunt like any of my brethren, but not murder. That fool, Szechenyi, just didn't get it.'

It took me a moment to recognise that was the late Count Timur's surname.

'Why should we all be so worried?' Karl tucked his hands into his pockets and leaned back against a bookshelf. 'You saw how united the prefects were at the Pledging. We could've all used the opportunity of the fire to run, but we didn't. What does that tell you?'

'It's not the prefects that concern me. It's the rogue elements which could still be out there.' Alec preferred to err on the side of caution. I was with him on that.

'There'll always be rogues as there'll always be criminals. It's the nature of things. When they arise, we'll find them.' O'Toole shrugged. 'Even without the Ingenii blood, our age still gives us the edge.'

I liked his confidence.

'The Principate will survive the transition. Got no doubt there, but not if you keep secrets. Brethren loyalty will only stretch so far; you know that.' Karl lowered his voice and he glanced at Luc.

I recalled the shouted protests at the Pledging when Luc was forced to reveal he and Judith were my parents. That could've gone badly, especially as Luc struggled with his temper. Alec had stepped in and salvaged the situation.

'I agree,' O'Toole said. 'Let them know. Don't wait for them to find out. It won't go well.'

Luc rose and, with his hands clasped behind his back, stared out the window at the darkness beyond. 'We thought to keep Laura's pregnancy a secret for as long as possible. Even after the babe's birth, we hope to keep it confidential. The Principate would continue and nobody would be the wiser.'

'Aye, you can take that gamble.'

Alec gripped the back of my chair, his fingers curling into the cushioned leather upper. I reached up and placed my hand over his. He grasped my fingers. 'Laura's safety is my primary concern. I'm not going to compromise that. I say no.'

Marcus bowed his head and stared at the floor as if the answer lay there. 'If we agree to share this with the prefects, it may or may not affect their loyalty. Yet, a government that keeps secrets from its people earns its distrust, and that we cannot risk happening. We're at a knife's edge.'

Karl rolled the toothpick around in his mouth, his sharp eyes roaming between each of our faces. 'Correct me if I'm wrong, but once an Ingenii conceives, has a babe ever died or miscarried? Would the next carry the gene?'

'I have no idea.' I spun in my chair to look up at Alec.

He shrugged and looked at Marcus. 'It's never happened.'

Luc turned to face us. 'Until Judy's birth, all the Ingenii have been men. Their wives never miscarried. Why ask?'

Like the proverbial light bulb, I knew what Karl meant. 'I never thought of that!' He gave me a cheeky grin, the toothpick sticking out from the corner of his mouth. 'Were I to lose the baby, there'd be no other Ingenii because the cursed gene is only passed on once, right?' I'd be of no use to the rogue Brethren.

Luc sat back down and raked his fingers through his blonde hair. 'I don't know, ma petite. Only the firstborn inherited the cursed gene. Not those who came after.'

'And if the firstborn died before they came of age ... say an accident or something...?' I looked at him, automatically flattening my palms over my belly, protective of my unborn child.

'Never happened.'

'So nobody knows if the gene would be passed onto another child?'

He shook his head.

My heart sank. I didn't want to be the one to find out. If there was any possibility the gene could skip to the next child should the firstborn die, then I was in danger. If the rogues were to learn of Alec's bloodline and that I was carrying his child – the Child of Promise – I feared what they would do. There was now no chance of us sharing this information with the prefects. If only Karl had been right.

'Too risky. I'm with Alec on this,' I said, as he gripped my shoulders. 'If there are still Rebels out there and they find out Alec's bloodline, they'd kill him and our baby for sure, and use me to breed the next Ingenii.' My stomach crawled at the thought. 'The less people who know I'm pregnant the better.'

Karl gave me a sad smile. 'Good thing I asked.'

'That'll be settled then. A secret it remains.' O'Toole retrieved a pipe from his back pocket and knocked it clean on the back bar of the chair. 'But what'll you do when the Ingenii blood vials run out? We've all been given a taste of the day, the extra speed and strength an' all ... won't be easy to give up.' He pointed the pipe at Luc before placing it to his lips. 'You've opened up Pandora's box, and you know how that ended.'

Alec nodded grimly and hissed.

Evil was released into the world.

'The Ingenii blood is what kept your family in power. With that power base gone, the Brethren might demand a new princeps – one less concerned for humans.'

O'Toole made sense. The Principate would remain, but would the Brethren still want a D'Antonville as its leader? No more Ingenii blood also meant no more Ritual and the power of the serpent ring to choose the next princeps. The whole Brethren world was about change, and not necessarily for the better.

'Unless....' Alec's fingers dug into my shoulders. I sensed excitement from him. 'Jake, I've an idea. How about we create a synthetic version of Ingenii blood? Identify and isolate the gene responsible, then replicate it?'

'That'd be brilliant!' I spun in my seat to look up at him.

Alec's face broke into a dazzling smile.

Jake's eyes lit up, and he punched his fist into his palm. 'Yes! Done it with white-oak why not with Ingenii blood?'

The mood in the room shifted. Jake moved away from the door and stood between Karl and O'Toole, who bombarded him and Alec with questions: how soon could they produce it? Would it be for everyone? Would its effects wear off? O'Toole practically bounced in his seat.

'We'd need a proper lab setup,' Jake said.

'Easily arranged. We can convert one of the stables.'

As they became engrossed in the possibilities of producing a synthetic version of Ingenii blood, my father and grandfather remained strangely silent. Their stern expressions, unnoticed by the others, worried me.

Eventually, Marcus pursed his lips and shifted where he sat on the edge of Luc's desk. 'Alec, you can't replicate magic.'

Conversation ceased, and heads turned in his direction.

'Magic uses nature. It manipulates it. Two-hundred years ago, the mobile phone would've been considered magic,' Alec said.

Marcus and Luc exchanged glances, but from their silence and the subtle shake of heads, they were unconvinced. Their non-committal attitude puzzled me.

'If Alec's idea works, don't you see what this means? All the Brethren would be able to daywalk. It could end your dependence on humans. You could lead normal day lives.'

Karl whistled, and O'Toole grinned, the dark wooden pipe a striking contrast against his white teeth. 'Sweet Mary and Joseph! A never-ending supply of daywalking blood. Can you imagine it?'

The silence from Marcus and Luc grew like fog around them. Marcus licked his lips. Was that fear on his face?

'I wish it were that simple,' he said. 'We're not dealing with something Alec can manufacture in a test tube. Deus! This thing is an entity. You mess with it, and there may be repercussions.'

I'd heard that somewhere before. A chill coursed through me. 'Repercussions?'

Marcus shrugged. Luc picked up the paperweight and rolled it around on his desk. 'We want to get rid of it, not patent it.'

Alec folded his arms, his jaw set as he faced them. 'We don't need to replicate the gene, just the chemical composition of the blood. What is the problem?'

Jake moved to his side and nodded.

Luc seemed mesmerised by the paperweight he rolled around. I sensed his agitation, and the fog around him thickened, like a gathering thunderstorm ready to break. In their excitement, Alec and Jake were oblivious to his darkening mood as they tossed around ideas. Only Karl noticed. He glanced at Luc and Alec before exchanging a look with me, eyebrow raised. Last thing I wanted was another confrontation between the two most important men in my life. Before I could grab Alec's attention, Marcus stood, hands on hips and paced a few steps away from the desk, his posture rigid.

'I would rather you didn't pursue this. There's too much at stake.' It wasn't a request.

Alec's body tensed. His lips thinned into a tight line, yet from the set of his jaw, I knew he was about challenge him. No, no, no … not again. I touched his arm. 'Are there enough blood vials to last the next nine months?'

'More than enough. They're still in the vault.'

'So you don't need to make a synthetic batch right away, do you?' *Luc's about to blow. Can you shelve the idea for now?*

He breathed deep and twisted his serpent ring as his gaze landed on Luc, then me. 'No. It's not immediate. We could wait. Maybe … till after the curse is lifted.' *Thanks for the warning.*

I squeezed his hand.

Marcus smiled and thumped Alec on the back. 'Wise decision.'

Luc stopped rolling the paperweight ball and looked up, relief clear in his eyes. 'Once the curse is lifted, you can do whatever experiments you want.' He rose from behind his desk and adjusted his evening jacket. 'We're finished here for tonight. I promised Judy dancing, and that's what I'm going to do.'

He strode out the door leaving us staring after him.

'I believe that's a none too subtle hint,' Karl said. With a flourish, he whipped his black mask from his top pocket and tied it on, bowed low and followed Luc.

O'Toole shook his head and grinned. 'Aye, he's got style that one.'

The rest of us re-entered the ballroom, and Alec swung me into his arms. For the rest of the evening I lay aside future concerns … surely all would turn out well? One has to have hope, I reasoned, otherwise it didn't bear thinking about. My dress swished over the parquetry floor as we twirled to yet another waltz. I shivered at the feel of Alec's arms about me, his deep-purple eyes drawing me into their depths. I tuned out to the conversations around us, letting the timeless melodies engulf me, cocooning me in a blissful bubble from which I didn't want to emerge. Yet, a thought niggled, that come sunrise, the bubble would burst and the world would intrude again.

I sighed.

I hadn't deliberately shared my thoughts, but Alec must have guessed. His eyes shone behind his mask, as he pressed me closer and whispered in my ear. 'The rest of this night it's just you and me. No one else exists.'

And so it was. We danced until my feet ached, until the guests drifted away, until the sun's weak rays peeked through the lower branches of the trees on the far side of the estate. I yawned. Alec scooped me up and carried me back to our bed, enfolding me into his arms. He curled the ends of my hair around his fingers and brought them to his lips.

I drifted off, and somewhere between sleep and dreams the hooded figure I'd glimpsed in the corridor crept through my consciousness. She turned and lowered her hood. Madame Thierry.

I woke with a start. Was it a dream, or something more? The half-familiar scent still lingered in my nostrils. Madame Thierry. I was sure of it. My heart hammered at the thought she was near, that she may have been at the ball. With so many Brethren present, her scent may not have been detected, and with the magical wards down to allow the guests to enter, she could have snuck in easily. Was she still here? With the Elders and perfects gone, her scent should be easy to detect.

'Alec?' It was dark, and the other side of the bed was empty, the sheets cold. A moment of panic seized me.

'Here, darling.' Light streamed into the room as he opened the bathroom door. His hair was wet – damn he looked good in jeans and a tight-fitting, long-sleeved T-shirt.

Did he have to be such a distraction? I blinked and cleared my thoughts. 'Madam Thierry was here ... last night ... the hooded figure who passed us in the corridor.' I pointed upwards.

His seductive smile faded. 'How can you be sure? Everyone was masked, and I would've detected her scent.' His eyes rounded in understanding. 'Of course ... her scent would've merged with the other Brethren.'

I nodded. 'When we first arrived, her perfume impressed me. Last night, I smelled it again.'

Alec's expression darkened. He angled his head toward the door. 'Sam?'

'Yo!' His voice came from the other end of the chateau.

'Check all the passageways. Madame Thierry could be hiding out in any one of them.'

'Why would she return? Luc would kill her.' I jumped off the bed, peeled off my ballgown, pulled on jeans and a cashmere sweater, and tied my hair back into a ponytail.

A shrill beeping filled the air. I heard Sam swear. 'Breach in the tunnels.'

'It's her!' My voice was sharp. What was she doing in the tunnels? Didn't she know they were booby trapped?

Luc's voice, from his suite on the floor above us, cut through the commotion. 'Judy's missing!'

# CHAPTER 34 – HELL HATH NO FURY

**LAURA**

Blood drained from my face. Yet I couldn't bring myself to believe there was a connection. 'Surely she's in the garden, or somewhere on the grounds?'

'No. I can't sense her presence anywhere in the house. Her mobile phone is here, and she never leaves it behind.'

My stomach cramped, like I'd swallowed rocks. 'Alec, she's got Judy.' My voice shook.

'Jake, Terens, Cal! Head to the tunnels!' Alec grabbed his sword and headed for the door. 'Laura, stay here.'

'No way! My mother's in danger and you're asking me to stay here and wait?' I strapped on my belt and dagger, leaving behind my sword. The dagger was easier to handle. 'Not on your life Alec Munro.'

Ripples crossed his face – annoyance? Worry? Or admiration? Maybe a combination of all three. 'Once in the tunnel, stay behind me. That's not open to debate.' We raced downstairs. 'It doesn't have to be her,' he grunted.

'Wanna bet?' I could think of no one else who'd want to hurt her. Was this revenge – unrequited love for Luc? I swallowed down bile. If that bitch hurt her….

'Who's got her?' Luc joined us on the landing, his pupils narrowed into slits.

'Madame Thierry. She's here. I know she is.'

He growled, and his fangs slid down from his upper jaw. In a flash, he flew down the staircase, threw open the doors to the Great Hall and disappeared inside.

Alec picked me up and dashed after him. Everything blurred at his burst of speed, and I had to close my eyes to stop the dizziness. He slowed to squeeze past the narrow opening of the Alabaster Throne, which then closed with a snap behind us. Darkness. Icy air … and snarls up ahead. Another burst of speed before we reached the others.

Ahead of us stood Luc, the men by his side, swords drawn. What they faced had me reaching for my dagger. Six vampires – four men and two women – stood barely metres from the flamethrower trap. One of them, a large man with a military-style buzz cut, held Judy's limp form. A dread cold seized me. I homed in on her heartbeat – it was there. She was only unconscious. When his other hand closed around her throat, a memory resurfaced – when Russell once had me in such a neck-breaking grip.

One of the women whimpered and slid to a crouch against the tunnel wall. I gasped when I recognised her sable cloak from last night. Madame Thierry, her once-perfectly coiffed hair lay in dishevelled strands down her shoulders. Dried blood smeared her mouth, and her wild lavender eyes looked up at Luc in hopeless adoration.

'Let her go,' my father said. 'Whatever you want, it's yours. Just don't harm her.' He lowered his sword to the ground and raised his hands.

'That's it, or one twist and I'll snap her neck like a dry twig.' Buzz-cut grinned.

'No! Please.' I couldn't hold the cry back and itched to throw my dagger, see it embedded in his miserable heart. But I couldn't risk it. He could break her neck in a nanosecond.

Buzz-cut's Rebel pals laughed and mimicked me. I sensed Alec's anger, his hands curling into fists.

'This cow' —he sneered at Madame Thierry— 'provided us with a nice map of this place. But where's your secret little blood vault? So here's the deal. You lead us there. We take what we want, and you can have Lady Judith back.'

'Alors. I'll do what you want.' Luc paused. 'Let me first switch off the booby traps. You're too close to the first one.'

'Careful,' buzz-cut said, eyeing Luc and angling Judy's neck a fraction more.

I sucked in a breath.

Luc slowly pulled out his mobile, pressed a few buttons and pocketed it again.

'The rest of you, swords down.' Buzz-cut said.

Metal clanged against stone as the men dropped their swords. Alec, too. Buzz-cut was tall, and Judy's feet dangled off the ground as he took a few steps back. In a way, I was glad she wasn't conscious to see what was happening. Had she been drugged or hit? My fingers clenched around my belt buckle, which hid my dagger.

'You,' he said to Luc. 'Lead.' Buzz-cut jerked his head toward the tunnel exit.

Luc strode past him, and, as he did so, gazed down at Judy's face. His chest rose and fell, and he swallowed hard. 'Harm her and I swear I'll hunt you down and roast you alive!' As he took the lead, Luc glanced at Madame Thierry. 'Traitorous bitch!' He spat on the ground near her feet.

Her lips quivered, and she turned her head away from him.

'Get up!' Buzz-cut kicked her.

She whimpered again, and his female companion grabbed her by the arm and hauled her to her feet. 'Do as your master says. Help pick up the swords.'

It was pitiful to watch. The once-proud housekeeper now a slave to a Rebel. Had she not known the price of transformation meant a century of servitude to her sire?

A drop of water splashed into a pool and echoed through the vastness of the caverns as our reluctant party marched behind Luc. One of the Rebels held a sword to the back of Luc's neck, while Madame Thierry shuffled behind. The other Rebels held us at sword point.

Once or twice I turned to see if Judy had woken. Buzz-cut still held her in a vice-like death grip. *I thought Ingenii blood made you faster? Can't you do something?* I sent the thought to Alec.

*His grip on her is too delicate ... thumb's right on her spinal cord. A sudden move from any of us, and she's dead.*

My poor father ... anger, fear and frustration must be raging through him. As it was through me.

In front of us, the massive smooth rock face that hid the vault loomed. Luc approached and slid aside the locking panel. 'I need three keys to unlock this.'

'Get them,' the man said from behind.

'One is around my wife's neck.' Luc spun to face him, his pupils narrow, pale reptilian slits, and his grimace revealed fangs.

'You, housekeeper, come here.' Madame Thierry slunk past us, her eyes low. 'Get the key.' He lifted Judy's chin without lessening his hold on her neck. Madame Thierry unclasped the chain and brought it to Luc.

He raised his hand, and for a moment, I thought he would strike her. She cowered. But he snatched the chain and turned his back on her. 'That's two. The princeps has the third.'

Alec nodded. Moving slowly, he removed his key and tossed it to Luc.

All three keys in the lock, Luc inserted his serpent ring, gave it a twist and the vault swung open. The Rebel group gasped at the scarlet glow of the Ingenii blood vials. They inhaled deeply, eyes glazed in ecstasy.

'The Holy Grail,' one of the Rebels uttered, his tone reverent.

'Leave the ring and keys in the lock. Drop the phone. No activating of the traps afterwards. Get inside,' Buzz-cut said.

We'd emptied many of the niches previously, but enough remained to make a sizable haul for the Rebels. They surveyed the vault with open mouths.

'Fill up the bags,' Buzz-cut ordered his group.

From within their cloaks they produced a dozen or so plastic garbage bags, which could hold several-hundred vials each. The looting began.

*They'll be nothing left! We've got to do something.*

*Not while he's got Judith!*

Terens's fingers twitched. I knew he had a dagger strapped to the inside of his wrist besides one he usually carried inside his boot. Would he risk using it? I'm sure all the men had considered taking either of the women hostage to use in an exchange – if the man holding my mother had any regard for them. I guessed his type would sacrifice anyone to obtain the Ingenii vials. He probably considered his accomplices expendable.

'Throw me one,' he called to Madame Thierry. Buzz-cut dropped to a crouching position, which allowed him to maintain his death grip on my mother with one hand, while catching the blood vial with the other. Without letting his gaze stray from Luc, he downed the contents. His eyes widened, and he howled like a wolf in heat until the stone walls vibrated with the sound. 'Another one.'

We stood there helpless, as he downed another two. The others did likewise, and as Madame Thierry brought one to her lips, the female Rebel snatched it and backhanded her.

'Not for juveniles.'

Madame Thierry uttered a cry, and just when I thought she would cower, her expression changed. She snarled and threw herself at her tormentor. The impact sent them hurtling toward Buzz-cut.

My heart stuttered at a sickening crack of bone that echoed around the chamber. In that split second, I knew Judy was gone – Buzz-cut's thumb had snapped her neck.

My mind went numb, and the world slowed on its axis. Like an enraged animal, Luc roared and sprinted toward my mother's body, which, now freed from Buzz-cut's grip, had rolled to the side. Terens and the men attacked. Loud growls filled the vault as heads were ripped from bodies. Alec panted, the head of one Rebel clutched in his hand.

My father, on his knees, cradled my mother's body, his cut wrist dripping blood into her lifeless mouth. 'Judy, please! Please!'

Hot tears spilt down my cheeks … I spied Madame Thierry, on all fours, crawling toward the exit. Blood roared in my ears as all-consuming heat coursed through me. *Oh no! Bitch!* I palmed my dagger and chased her.

She spotted me, rose up and ran, discarding her sable cloak at me. I dodged it, and she put on a burst of speed. A flash of silvery hair just ahead of me as she sped past the oldest of the recessed stone bays. I knew I couldn't catch her. As a vampire, her speed was far greater than any human's. Unsheathing my dagger, I aimed and threw. She screamed as it sunk between her shoulder blades.

*Damn! Why did I wipe my blood from it?* She stumbled and clawed at the weapon protruding from her back. Yet she kept moving and made it to the exit slamming the door shut in my face.

No! I hammered and scratched at the solid rock until my nails bled, trying to find an opening. The keys and Luc's ring were still in the lock – on the other side.

'Laura!' Alec twisted me around to face him. 'Are you hurt?'

'No, but she got away.' I banged his chest with my fists. 'The bitch got away!'

'Luc needs you now.'

I looked over his shoulder. Luc hadn't moved. He hunched over my mother's lifeless body, rocking back and forth on his knees, stroking her hair and calling for her to come back to him. A dark trail of red tears flowed down his devastated face. His shoulders drooped, and the cavern shook with his sobs. Jake, Terens, Sam and Cal knelt by him, the headless and dismembered bodies of Rebels strewn around them.

A dagger thrust into my heart could not have hurt more. Each breath burned in my lungs and caught in my throat until I could contain the pain no longer. It burst from me in an agonising wail. A fog shrouded my eyes, and I stumbled to my father's side, threw my arms around his neck and sobbed.

How had this happened? I never got a chance to say goodbye. I took her hand – already cold – and lifted it to my cheek. Every memory I had of her played in my mind, like a scattered collage of videos on a screen: here smiling proudly at my graduation, there laughing at a joke or cheering me on at a high school softball game, or kindly reproving me the few times Mum and I had a tiff. Never again would I hear her soft voice, laugh along with her … so much I still wanted to enjoy with her. This was too soon, too soon….

My heart shattered.

Shrill beeping.

'Shit!' Sam's voice. Pause. More swearing. His voice louder now. 'We need to get out. The failsafe's gone off, and I can't override it.'

'How the hell…?' That was Terens.

'Luc's phone. Someone's tampering with it. Set off the failsafe.'

Alec grasped my elbow. 'Laura, we need to move. Now!'

My legs shook, actually, my whole body did. I leant on Alec. 'What's happening?'

'C'mon, Luc. We need to move. Take her with us. This place is gonna blow.' Jake's gentle voice nudged Luc from his grief.

'Blow?' The words were lost in the pall of grief that clouded my mind.

With his arm around my waist, Alec hurried me to one of the bays. Antonia's, I think. 'Self-destruct mechanism has been activated. We've got less than five minutes to get out.' I must have worn a blank expression. 'Three tries at a password and you're locked out of a site, right?' I nodded. 'One false try on Luc or Sam's phone to get in here sets off an alarm. Two tries and we have sixty seconds to override the self-destruct. Three tries, no override.'

'Oh lord!' It had to be Madame Thierry. Luc was forced to drop his phone outside, and that's where she was.

'We need to get into the crypt tunnel.' Alec scoured the bay, his fingers looking for whatever mechanism unlocked the entrance to the tunnel Marcus had shown us.

Four minutes left.

At vampire speed, Cal, Terens and Sam collected as many blood vials as time permitted and added them to those in the sacks the dead Rebels had collected. Jake stayed by Luc, who tenderly lifted Judy's body from the ground and carried her toward us.

'C'mon open, open.' Alec kept pushing a stone block that refused to budge.

'Two minutes. Get it open!' Sam called from the back.

Alec thumped it with both hands. 'It's stuck!'

Sam dropped the sack, and he and Alec tried to prise it open. Running footsteps from the other side. 'Marcus? Is that you?' Alec called.

'It's me.' Marcus's voice was muffled. How thick was the rock?

'Open it!' Terens and Cal had crowded around us, trying to depress the stone slab. Slowly, it disappeared into the rock face and the entire bay swung open.

A cool draught of air fanned my face. Marcus and Kari stood there. His brow creased in concern on seeing Luc. 'Is everything…? Deus!'

'Run! We've got two minutes before the vault self-destructs.' Alec picked me up and ran into the tunnel.

I looked over his shoulder. Kari ran behind. Her lower lip quivered. I extended my hand, and she grasped it. Luc, with Judy in his arms came next, followed by our men. Marcus slammed the door shut.

'One minute. Go faster!' Sam yelled.

Alec charged ahead at dizzying speed. Light up ahead. The chapel. Boom! Boom! The walls shook, sending dust sprinkling down on our heads. Another boom, a flash … light ahead … the chapel crypt. Crashing noise behind us and shouts. Part of the tunnel ceiling had collapsed. I kept a tight hold of Kari's hand as she ran with us.

'Keep going,' Jake shouted.

I couldn't see as dust and debris rained down on us. Alec rounded a corner, and I lost sight of Luc and Marcus. A gust of fresh air.

'Nearly there,' Alec panted.

We emerged in the crypt, stone sarcophagi around us. Alec took the stairs three at a time. The chapel resounded with the booms from far below. Would it withstand the force of the explosions?

We burst through the chapel doors. Trees all around us. The ground shook, and a deep rumble came from below the earth. Flames shot from the chapel ceiling into the night sky.

Part of the roof crumbled and fell into the burning ruins. The acrid smoke assailed my nostrils, further fuelling the tears that streamed from my eyes. Alec stopped at a small copse of trees and set me down.

Where were the others? Soon, blackened figures emerged. Cal, Terens and Sam raced up the hill and joined us, still carrying the bundles of Ingenii blood vials.

Jake appeared from nowhere, his eyes wide as he scanned the fiery scene.

'Luc. Where's Luc? And Marcus?' *Please, please may they not be dead.*

'They were behind us.' Terens lowered the sack and shook debris from his hair. 'He's still in there. Won't leave Judy. Marcus is trying to drag him out,' he said.

I bunched Alec's shirt in my clenched fist as I squinted to see past the flames, and … there! Luc stood in the chapel doorway, silhouetted against the flames. His face blackened by smoke, blood-red tears left a dirty crimson track down his face, and agony was etched into his expression.

My heart shattered. 'Papa.' I could only whisper it.

Marcus appeared, grabbed his son's arm and they raced toward us. They crashed through the trees, and in the blink of an eye, Luc had caught me in his arms, crushing me to him.

'At least you're safe, ma petite.' He kissed the top of my head.

'And you.' Some of the tension left my body, but returned the moment I didn't see my mother's body. 'Where's Judy?'

'… In the chapel. With Antonia.' His voice broke.

Marcus placed his hands on Luc's shoulders and bowed his head.

'Why did you leave her there? Why?' I could've seen her one last time before … her burial … say goodbye.

'It's where she … belongs. Among her ancestors … her funeral pyre.' His shoulders quaked.

I sucked in great gulps of air as the pain threatened to overwhelm me.

'I'm so, so sorry my darling.' Alec's voice wavered.

Luc and I clung to each other. This was too much, the loss, too great.

Another, smaller, figure emerged from between the trees a few metres from us. My heart caught in my throat. How had she found her way out of the tunnel?

Jake growled. 'There's that creature.' The venom in his voice fuelled the anger in mine. He sped after her, caught her, and she struggled in his grip as he dragged her back.

'You killed her! Why? Why did you do that?' My voice came out as a strangled sob. My mother's beautiful body lay in that burning wreck. And the ancient chapel that had been my family's final resting place was now a fiery pyre surrounding her remains. 'I want her punished! I want her dead!' I twisted out of Luc's embrace and pummelled Madame Thierry with my fists.

She cowered, and I saw my dagger sticking out from between her shoulder blades. I pulled it out, ready to plunge it back in. Luc grabbed my arm.

He looked like a wild man as his gaze settled on the one who was the cause of his deep anguish. A snarl rumbled free from him. In a blinding move he seized Madame Thierry by the hair. 'You bitch! Judy was my life.'

'I love you,' she screamed.

'You don't know the meaning of it,' he hissed. 'Love does not kill. You tried to murder us in the vault. Judy is alone in there, but not for long. I will not leave her alone in death – and neither will you.'

'No! No, have mercy, milord!'

'Mercy? As you had mercy on her, who showed you only kindness? No. I want to see the flames lick your flesh, consume you slowly, make you suffer as I'm suffering now.'

She screamed and clawed at him, struggling to be free of his grip – all to no avail.

'Luc! Stop! Don't do this!' Marcus seized his arm, but Luc only threw him off.

'If not for her, Judy would still be alive. You know I ...' —he swallowed. 'I choose this way. I'm not afraid. Let me go, Father.'

My gut churned as I understood what he meant. Time seemed to stand still as Marcus and Luc faced each other, until Marcus dropped his hand and bowed his head. A great wrenching sob broke from him.

'Papa!'

Luc stopped and looked at me, a faint smile on his lips. 'Goodbye, ma petite. I go to join your mother.'

'No! Not like this.'

A pained expression crossed his face, and he shook his head. 'You don't need me anymore. A better man is by your side.' He glanced at Alec, gave him a slow nod before turning away.

'No!' I tried to claw off Alec's hands, to grab my father, reason with him, but he held me fast. 'Let go!' How could I stand by and let my father take his own life in such a horrific way?

'Laura! It's his choice. You have to let him go. He can't live without Judy just as … I couldn't live without you.' His words crashed through the turmoil in my brain. If something were to happen to me, would he…? 'I would want to follow you into eternity.' Alec cupped my face and brushed away my tears with his thumbs.

I sucked in a shaky breath. He would do that for me? Staring back into the lavender depths of his eyes, the certainty of his words frightened me. 'Promise me you won't ever do that. Life is too precious. Only God determines when it's our time.'

He kissed my brow and wrapped me in his arms. 'Promise.'

I turned my head into his chest, clapping my hands over my ears to lessen Madame Thierry's shrieks as Luc dragged her into the raging flames.

I looked up at the sound of creaking leather. The men had sunk to their knees, heads bowed. Not one tried to stem the flow of tears down their cheeks.

Marcus's broken voice boomed out. 'We honour you, Lucius Antonius Pulcher, Lord of D'Antonville, Chief Elder of the Brethren … and my son. No father had a greater. And you, sweet Lady, Judith Anne Dantonville, child of the Ingenii. May your souls find rest in the lap of God.'

The men rose and gave the Roman salute. 'Hail Lucius Antonius Pulcher.'

In that moment I was never more proud, never more hurt nor angry. My emotions were as tumultuous as the writhing flames that twisted and hurled themselves into the clear dark sky. Was it a heroic deed, momentary insanity brought on by heart-wrenching grief, or had it all been pre-arranged? I would never know.

Alec's arms tightened around me. For a few minutes – or was it an hour? – we stood until he whispered. 'It's over.'

He wasn't referring to the fire. I lowered my hands and turned to see two of the conical roofs collapse as the flames roared. Sparks flew upwards, lighting up the darkness. Two people whom I had come to love, so dearly in a short time, were gone. Now they were no more. How could that be? I reeled beneath the pain of the searing loss. It threatened to crush me. If Alec hadn't been holding me, I would've collapsed beneath its weight. It would've been merciful for my heart to have been ripped out and thrown into the flames with them.

'The old Principate is dead,' Cal muttered.

For a few seconds no one spoke. It was as if a death knell had been pronounced. The conical roof – bearing the D'Antonville standard – collapsed into the flames, adding weight to his words.

We stood in silent reverence until the last of the flames died down and the smoke that had obscured the stars drifted away on the night breeze.

'Goodbye,' I whispered.

# CHAPTER 35 – LAST FAREWELL

**LAURA**

'Luc asked me to give you this.' Marcus handed me a CD. His red-rimmed eyes gazed into mine, filled with such sadness as to make my heart shatter again. 'You can watch it in his office.'

His office. How could I enter that room and not see my father sitting behind his desk? 'Not there. I'll use Alec's laptop.'

He gave a slow nod and pulled something from inside his jacket: a small enamelled box. 'This is for you, too.'

He turned to walk away. 'Don't you want to see?' I asked.

He swallowed. 'Luc showed it to me. I'll be in the library if you want to talk afterwards.'

I set the box on the coffee table. The silver disc burned in my hand as I fed it into the laptop. Alec had given me his password. He and the men were at the chapel, clearing the burnt debris to set up a monument to my parents.

The screen fired up, and Luc's face appeared. My heart lurched. I touched the screen, traced the lines of my father's face.

'Ma petite, if you're seeing this, it means your mother and I have passed on. Please, do not mourn us. When you were a babe, Judy and I made a pact to leave this world together. Whomever of us died first, the other would follow.'

As he spoke, Judy appeared and sat next to him. The smile they exchanged brought a lump to my throat. The few silver strands in Judy's auburn hair showed the CD had been made recently. Perhaps only in the last few days. 'Laura, dear, your father and I knew this day would come. We've led a full and rich life, and now we are together in eternity.' I tried to blink away tears. 'I know you'll be sad. Please don't be. I wish for you to be happy and to know the same love in your life your father and I shared. My dear, you've grown into a beautiful, bright and caring young woman, and we couldn't be more proud of you.'

Luc leant forward. 'We've made all the necessary arrangements for your future. As our only child, you inherit this estate and all its contents, your mother's personal assets and the monies in my account. I've left provision for my men and for Alec. That information is on a separate disc in Marcus's possession, as are all the legal papers. You should also have the Aeternum Box. Please open it.'

I cracked open the lid. Inside lay five glass vials. They glowed red in their blue velvet casings.

'Each of those little glass bottles contains a few drops of our blood.' He took Judy's hand and kissed her fingertips. 'Enough to ensure your children a long lifespan should they so choose.' He paused. 'Ma petite, you have been the joy of my life, my light, my precious jewel. Now live your life and carry us in your heart. One day we will meet again. Until then, au revoir.'

The screen went blank. It took me a few seconds to tear my gaze away. I lifted the box to examine it more closely. Luc and Judy had thought of everything. Five vials. I certainly never counted on having that many children. But I guessed they added that number as a precaution. I closed the lid and placed the box in the bottom drawer of my dresser. The D'Antonville Estate was mine, yet all I wanted was to go home – to Sydney, Australia.

Marcus said he'd be in the library. I found him standing in the open doorway to Luc's office. He turned and gave me a sad smile. 'This room will now have a new occupant.'

I steeled myself to look at it. Was it only last night Luc had been sitting there? 'Are you taking that position?'

His eyes widened. 'Deus, no! I relinquished it to Luc. It goes to his heir – Alec. He's the new lord of D'Antonville.'

My stomach did an unpleasant little twist. Was he, and by extension me, expected to stay? 'I … thought to go home.' To see my family – John and Eilene, my foster parents – and my friends. To sit at a beachside café sipping cappuccino and watch kids jostle each other at a gelato bar. To give my heart the time it needed to deal with the grief that clung to me like a shroud.

'This is your home. You and Alec are now Lord and Lady D'Antonville. Too long has this house been without a permanent occupant. Ever since Robert D'Antonville forced the clan to move to Australia in his quest for adventure has it lain as if asleep, waiting for its lord and lady to return.'

Oh my! How could I extinguish the spark of hope in his eyes? 'Does Alec know?'

'He does. I gave him his CD earlier today, while you were sleeping, mea neptis.' His eyes softened.

Without the sedative Alec had given me, I probably wouldn't have slept at all, as the haunting images of that dreadful night kept replaying in my mind like a bad dream. 'Mea…?'

Marcus smiled. 'It means "my granddaughter" in Latin. You're all I have left of my family. They're all gone – Gallia, Antonia and now Luc.' He swallowed hard. 'I didn't think … I would outlive my son. So close to the end.' He took a deep breath, blinked rapidly and turned his eyes upward.

What could I say? No words were adequate to fill the gaping hole in his heart. I ran my arms around his neck and hugged him.

His arms encircled me. 'You are my comfort,' his broken voice rasped in my ear. We stood like that for a while until Marcus pulled back. 'And now, mea neptis, I must notify the Elders and prefects.' He kissed me on the brow and left.

If they came to pay their respects and acknowledge Alec as the new lord of D'Antonville, did that mean another huge gathering? What did I know about the organisation and planning for such an event? Judy knew. But she wasn't here. I rubbed my chest at the ache that had taken up residence there. I wasn't prepared for this.

What would she have expected me to do? The answer was simple – I was my mother's daughter, and there was a job to be done. I was now the new lady of the house. But what did that mean in this instance?

I sighed and entered the entrance hall, glancing around at the magnificence of the ancient chateau, knowing the centuries of tradition practised within its walls now rested on my shoulders. Was I up to the task? The enormity of it scared me. I sank onto the bottom step of the staircase and dropped my head into my hands. A small voice in my head whispered that I could do this. Hadn't I been doing it for years? Organising events, allocating tasks, dealing with large gatherings, preparing programs and implementing them? It was part of a teacher's job description.

I can do this, the small voice whispered again.

I squared my shoulders and, for now, shelved the idea of going home. But, I couldn't tackle this on my own – I needed some professional help.

'Kari?' I knew she was somewhere in the house. 'We need a new housekeeper. How do I look for one? And a new estate manager, too.' A new chapter entirely.

'You're staying?' She appeared at my side in a flash.

'Yes, and I'll need lots of help as I have no idea what a lady of the manor is supposed to do.'

She clapped her hands, some of the sadness leaving her eyes. 'I have a few suggestions … but it can wait for a bit.' We linked arms and started back up the stairs.

The afternoon sun glinted through the great stained glass window on the first landing. A cascade of jewel-like colours spilled down the stairs and overflowed onto the floor and walls. I stood transfixed. Whether it was my imagination, or something else, but I caught the faint whiff of Judy's perfume on the air, and comforting warmth that enveloped me like a soft blanket. A sense of peace settled over me, and I knew with absolute certainty that I was home.

# EPILOGUE

## Three Months Later

Jenny Callan stacked her dishwasher then prepared herself for a late night. A pile of marking sat on her living room floor. Why did I take up teaching, instead of some cushy nine-to-five job? she thought for the umpteenth time. She poured herself a cup of coffee – mug size – set it on the coffee table, grabbed a nice thick cushion from the settee and dropped it on the floor. Some mood music and she was ready to start.

The doorbell rang.

'You're kidding me!' She wanted to shout, 'Go away! I'm working.' Instead, she stomped to the door and peeked through the spy hole. What does he want? Laura's ex-boyfriend, Police Detective Matt Sommers stood on the other side.

She debated whether to open the door. Was he still curious about Laura? Did he hope to find out from her? She'd promised to say nothing. He was a good-looking guy, and as far as she knew, he wasn't dating anyone else. Why couldn't he just get over her the way she got over Terens? The punch in her stomach put a lie to that. Being back at work was good – kept her mind on more important things.

The doorbell rang again, and she jumped.

'Okay, okay, don't get your knickers in a twist.' She cracked it open.

'Hi, Jen. Mind if I come in?' His gaze went to her black and white, fluffy panda slippers, and his mouth curled at one end.

She sighed. 'I bought them on eBay. They're comfy.' Meaning: one derogatory word and you're out on your ear. His smile widened as she stood back to let him in.

'Working late?' He pointed to the paper pile on the floor.

'What teacher doesn't?' She indicated for him to sit.

His six-foot frame dominated the normally spacious living area, and he easily dwarfed her two-seater sofa. Ages since a guy had sat there, she thought. Just as quickly, she dismissed it. Men are nothing but trouble, especially this one. She once liked Matt, until Laura had told her what he'd been planning to do to the vampire side of her family.

Jenny sat on the opposite sofa and picked up her mug of coffee. 'So?'

Matt Sommers's smile disappeared. 'Did Laura ever mention a man by the name of Jean-Philippe Reynard?'

Guy didn't beat about the bush. Yeah, she knew about the creep who tried to rape and murder her best friend. 'She told me about him.'

'Everything?'

Jenny weighed up her answer as she sipped her coffee. No way was she going to incriminate her bestie, or her man. 'Depends what you mean by that?'

He crossed one leg over the other and let out a deep breath. 'Look, Jen, I know you're protecting Laura. Commendable, but not helpful. I know what this piece of shit tried to do to her, and we both know Munro killed him in probable self-defence.'

She slammed down her coffee mug. 'No *probable* about it. It's the truth. Alec saved her life.' Oh bullcrap! She shouldn't have revealed that. By not reporting it to the police, it made her an accessory. Her hand shook slightly as she raised the mug back to her lips to stop herself saying anything more. She stared at him over the rim of her coffee mug. He hadn't reported it either. He must still care for her.

'The guy was officially listed as missing presumed dead. Now it's gone to Homicide – my desk.'

'Why tell me?'

'A reliable witness saw a man matching Reynard's description climbing up the side of Alec Munro's building and smashing through the window into his apartment. Saw the whole thing. They're both wanted for questioning.'

Jenny dropped the mug, coffee splashing over the pile of marking. She swore and dashed to the kitchen to retrieve a towel to mop up the mess.

'Here, let me help.' Matt collected some of the papers and wiped them down with another towel.

'You've done enough! Why did you come here and tell me that?'

He rose and pulled a folded piece of paper from his back pocket. It showed a group of people standing next to a large stone monument. Laura and Alec were among them. It was taken in France. Her gaze was drawn to another tall figure with them – Terens. Her heart gave a little kick. They'd had no communication since she'd left France just before the New Year.

Mustn't think about him.

She knew the occasion – Laura's parents' memorial service. She'd rung and they'd both cried. That was three months ago. Still, she couldn't quite believe Luc and Judy were dead.

'I have an extradition order to bring them back here for questioning.' His voice roused her back from her musings.

Jenny looked up at him. Did he expect her to warn Laura? Is that why he was here? 'You're going over there?'

'Flying out tomorrow morning. Interpol's expecting me.'

Her stomach dived. Got to tell Laura.

'Let her know I'm coming.' He stood and let himself out.

Jenny jumped to her feet and reached for her mobile. After three rings, Laura answered. 'Hon, we got a problem.'

## END OF BOOK THREE

## LETTER FROM TIMA

I hope you enjoyed reading Laura and Alec's continuing story and the dangers they face trying to bring her family's curse to an end. Please don't hesitate to contact me if you did, as I love hearing from my readers.

If you enjoyed BloodVault, I'd be grateful if you could write a REVIEW. That is the best gift, you as a reader, can give an author. Please, share it with others, so they too, can be introduced to this series. RECOMMEND it to friends, and reading groups and clubs or other online forums.

To find out more about the world of Dantonville and be the first to find out about new releases, giveaways and teasers, please subscribe to my mailing list:
http://timamarialacoba.blogspot.com.au/p/books.html

You can also keep in touch with me at:
Facebook – https://www.facebook.com/TimaMariaLacoba?fref=ts
Twitter – http://www.twitter.com/timamarialacoba
My website – www.timamarialacoba.com
Amazon author page -
http://amazon.com/author/tima_maria_lacoba

# GLOSSARY OF CHARACTERS, PLACES AND TERMS

**Alec Munro** – Vampire, Princeps and together with Lucien Lebrettan, leader of the 'Brethren', a community of vampires living in Sydney, Australia. Originally a doctor, he had enlisted in the Australian Infantry Forces (AIF) soon after the death of his wife and child. He was later transformed by Lucien while serving in an army medical field hospital in northern France in 1918. He owns and manages a private hospital in Sydney dedicated to blood disease research.

**Antonia Pulchra** – Daughter of Marcus Antonius Pulcher, twin sister to Lucius. Antonia was the first to carry the Ingenii mutation. She lived for 218 years and was the mother of Paulus, the next Ingenii.

**Bloodgifted** – Term given to certain members of the Dantonville family who carry the cursed gene, giving them unnatural long life and youthfulness. Their blood alone provides vampires with superior strength and heightened senses, and the ability to daywalk. The Bloodgifted – Ingenii – are much coveted by the Brethren community and were the epicentre of two previous rebellions, the first taking place in the tenth century, resulting in the deaths of two of Luc's men – Galen and Martius – and another in the seventeenth century.

**Blood Vault** – A secret vault hidden deep beneath the foundations of Chateau D'Antonville in a series of underground caverns in the Rhone Valley. It contains thousands of vials of Ingenii blood collected by Luc through the centuries. Those who drink Ingenii blood experience superhuman strength, enhanced senses and the ability to daywalk.

***Bonne matin*** – French (fem.) for "good morning."

**Cal** (Calixtus) – Vampire, former Roman soldier, First Frisian Cavalry Regiment, stationed at Vindobala (Rudchester) on Hadrian's Wall, northern Britain. Part of Marcus' Antonius Pulcher's cohort, he was cursed (along with his comrades) by a Pictish witch into vampire form. Cal is also a widower, having lost his wife in childbirth. Currently, he is bodyguard to the Ingenii, friend to Alec Munro and he owns an Armagnac distillery in France.

**Chateau D'Antonville** – The ancestral home of the Dantonvilles, and built over the ruins of Marcus Antonius Pulcher's original Roman villa. It is located in the Vaucluse Department of the Provence-Alpes-Cote D'Azur region in southeastern France. The Romans first settled there and produced the earliest wines. The area is littered with Roman ruins, the greatest of which is the Roman Theatre at the town of Orange (pronounced O-ronje), just a ten minute drive from the chateau. The closest cities are Lyon, to the north, and Avignon, to the south.

***Comment-est ce possible, mon chouchou?*** – French for, "How is that possible, my little cabbage?"

**Constans Thierry**, **Madame** – Human and housekeeper at Chateau D'Antonville, a position of honour in the village of D'Antonville. She is a direct descendant from one of the First Families. Constans Thierry fell in love with Luc when a young woman, and married her husband, Serge, in order to serve in the household and be close to Luc. She betrayed the family in order to have Judith and Laura killed so she could claim Luc and be mistress of D'Antonville.

***Dobre*** – The Czech for "good".

***Doña*** – Spanish for "Lady".

**Dominik** – 16 year-old vampire, recently turned by Timur after having been kidnapped by him for the illegal blood-slave racket. Originally from the Czech Republic, Dominik joined the Principate side and becomes Alec's juvenile.

**Elders** – Group of the world's oldest vampires, who set the rules by which all blood drinkers must abide in order to keep their presence hidden from the human world. They have power over life and death in the Brethren community. They also officiate at every Coming-of-Age ceremony and induct the new princeps. They are among the oldest living creatures on earth.

**Eilene Dantonville** – Human, wife of John Dantonville. Her first child, a baby named Katie, died of SIDS aged three months. She and John accepted the infant Laura in place of their deceased daughter, in order to help out Lucien and Judith. She loved Laura as her own child.

**Eithne** – A Pict witch and high priestess of the Caledonian goddess of retribution, Melusine. She cursed Marcus Antonius Pulcher and his men for killing her people in the mid 3rd. century, effectively turning him and his men into vampires. She used kidnapped Roman captives as human sacrifices in bloody religious rites.

**First Families** – Humans descended from the original slaves, then servants, at Marcus Antonius Pulcher's villa in Gaul. They make up the bulk of the villagers in D'Antonville, and only they know the secret of the Lords of Chateau D'Antonville.

**Grey Bear** – Vampire and newest elder, elected to replace the Rebel, Maris. Originally chief of the North American Indian tribe, the Shoshone, he was transformed by a medicine man, during a time of war, to protect his people.

*'Il est un cadeau du princeps. Est-il pas marveilleux?'* – French for, "It's a present from the princeps. Isn't it marvellous?"

**Ingenii** – Latin term for "Bloodgifted".

**Jake** (Caius Justinius) – Vampire, former Roman soldier and physician to the First Frisian Cavalry Regiment, stationed at Vindobala (Rudchester) on Hadrian's Wall, northern Britain. Along with his comrades, he was cursed by a Pict witch into becoming a vampire. He is a close friend and colleague to Alec Munro, and loves sports cars and racing horses. Currently, he is bodyguard to the Ingenii.

**Jean-Philippe Louis Auguste de Reynard** – Vampire and 18th century French nobleman who once fought for Napoleon. He was Lucien's illegitimate son and Laura's half-brother. His mother was the Duchess D'Orleans. He was a well-known portrait artist who met Laura in Italy where he fell in love with her unaware he was her half-brother. Jean introduced himself to her by his second name, Philippe. Lucien broke up the relationship. Their romance is the subject of the short story **Laura's Locket.**

**Jenny Callen** – Human, Laura's best friend and work colleague in a primary school in Balmain. She's had several failed relationships and is currently single, although she is romantically interested in Terens.

**John Dantonville** – Human, Laura's foster-father and maternal uncle. He is Judith Dantonville's younger brother and Eilene Dantonville's husband. He and Eilene adopted Laura as a favour to Lucien and Judith, but came to love her as his own. His pet name for her is, "baby".

**Judith Dantonville Lebrettan** – Human, thirty-third Ingenii. Pressured into marrying her first husband, William Allerdyce, by her father, Owen Dantonville, to clear gambling debts. Only meant to be a business arrangement, he raped her on their wedding night. Judith met Lucien some time after and they became lovers. Later she divorced William and secretly married Luc after giving birth to their child, Laura.

**Kari** (Karelia Anakeinen) – Born in Finland in the late eighteenth century, Kari's family moved to France when her father was offered the position of chief stonemason on the D'Antonville estate in the Rhone Valley. She had been transformed by Jake when the rest of her family died in an epidemic, which swept the region. Kari is Judith Dantonville's best friend, and unofficial bodyguard to the current Ingenii, Laura Dantonville. She is also secretly in love with Jake.

**Karl** (Karel von Czernin, Count) – Vampire, Czech Prefect and principate spy who befriended Count Timur Szechenyi, the Hungarian Prefect, in order to infiltrate the Rebel ranks and learn of their plans. His easy-going nature hides a sharp mind and decisive character. He is friends with Alec Munro, and secretly in love with the Baroness Milena Flaks.

**Kwome** – Vampire, and one of the Elders. Originally, Kwome was king of the ancient African kingdom of Benin. He was transformed by his teacher and mentor.

**Laura Anne Dantonville** – Part human/part vampire, thirty-fourth – and current serving – Ingenii, and Lucien and Judith Dantonville's biological daughter. She is a primary school teacher and former girlfriend of Police Detective Matthew Sommers. Laura was raised by John and Eilene Dantonville, who she believed to be her parents. She was also Jean-Philippe's half-sister.

**Lucinda Ortiz** – Vampire, and daughter of a minor Spanish nobleman, transformed by Rodriguez, a juvenile sired by Timur. As a result of being turned by a juvenile, Lucinda is slightly mentally disadvantaged. To some, she is known as Loco Lucinda. While a juvenile herself, she found Jean-Philippe dying on the battlefield and turned him. She gifts Laura a beautiful antique dagger as thanks for her kindness. Currently living in hiding in Uruguay.

**Maira** –Vampire and newly appointed elder. Originally a princess of the Incas, she was transformed by an outcast priest of Supai, the god of death.

**Marcus Antonius Pulcher** – Vampire, former Roman legionary cavalry commander – Praefectus Equituum – stationed in Vindobala (Rudchester) in the 3rd century AD. It was his actions, which led to him and his men into being cursed by the Pict witch, Eithne. Marcus Antonius is the father of the twins, Lucius and Antonia, and husband to Gallia. He departed Britain after being turned into a vampire and went into hiding at his villa in Gaul (France) – Villa Antonii.

**Matthew Sommers** – Human, Police Detective Inspector. He was Laura's boyfriend and rival with Alec Munro for Laura's affections. He was attacked and nearly killed by rogue vampires while trying to protect her. Laura broke of their relationship at the end of Book 1 when she learnt of his plans to kill the vampire side of her family in a misguided attempt to protect her. He hates Alec Munro and does not want to let Laura go.

*Mea Culpa* – Latin for "My fault."

**Milena** (Baroness Milena Flaks) – Vampire, the Slovakian Prefect and Principate supporter. Her concerns over Count Timur's ambitions – and threat to her territory – lead her to approach Jake into becoming her consort, and thus her protector. Like other aristocrats of her generation (eighteenth century) she believes in the superiority of her noble blood, although Brethren laws discourage class discrimination. Her old-world attitude leads to clashes with more-recently turned Brethren.

**O'Toole, Derek** – Vampire and Prefect for Hibernia (Ireland) and loyal principate supporter. He was transformed in prison while awaiting execution for leading a rebellion against Cromwell's forces in the mid seventeenth century. His sire, tired of living, walked into the sun three-hundred years later, happy he'd seen Ireland gain its independence from the hated English.

**Princeps** – Latin term for First Citizen and the origin of the English word, prince.

**Principate** – The Brethren political system established by Marcus Antonius Pulcher and his son, Lucius (Lucien Lebrettan) to control the Brethren and protect humanity. It is composed of the Elders – Kwome, Zhao, Grey Bear and Maira – as well as Marcus, Luc and Alec. As a result of the death of Maris Quesnel, Grey Bear and Maira were appointed to the office.

***Prokleta svine!*** – Czech for "cursed swine!"

**Rasputin** (Grigory Rasputin) – Vampire and former confidant of the last Russian royal family, the Romanovs. He was transformed in 1917 by the Hungarian noble, Count Timur Szechenyi, the Brethren prefect. Many blame Rasputin for the demise of the Russian monarchy, and his sinister influence over the royal family. Before his execution, he had the ability to mesmerise humans as well as vampires, and he used that to further his master's ambitions to overthrow the Principate.

***Regardez-moi madame!*** – French for, "Look at me, madame!"

***Sacra*** – vulgar Czech oath.

**Sam** (Sempronius) – Vampire, former Roman soldier in the First Frisian Cavalry Regiment stationed at Vindobala (Rudchester) in northern Britain. Along with his comrades, he was cursed by the Pict witch, Eithne, into vampire form. He is also the former lover and sire of Maris Quesnel. Sam is a techno-wiz and responsible for security in the Lebrettan household. Currently, when not hacking into rebel communications, he is one of the bodyguards to the Ingenii.

**Serge Thierry** – Human and trusted estate manager at the D'Antonville estate. He is a direct descendant of one of the First Families. His family has served as stewards at D'Antonville for over a thousand years. It is regarded as a position of honour among the villagers. One of his ancestors rode to the crusades with Lord Lucien Lebrettan.

**Serpent Ring** – Ancient artefact created by Marcus Antonius Pulcher on the instructions of the Pict witch, Eithne. It is in the form of a golden serpent with blazing red eyes – symbol of Melusine, the Caledonian goddess of vengeance or retribution. It renders the wearer invisible to vampire senses, as well as burning the fingers of imposters and shooting fire from the serpent's eyes destroying those who physically threaten either princeps or Ingenii. In times of danger, the eyes turn black. Every fifty years the ring is passed down to the next Ingenii.

*Sieur/Seigneur* – French for "Lord."

**Terens** (Sextus Terentius) – Vampire, former Tribune attached to the First Frisian Cavalry regiment, stationed at Vindobala (Rudchester), northern Britain. Along with the rest of the cohort, he was cursed by the Pict witch, Eithne, into vampire form. Although he has a reputation as a ladies man, Terens is also a deadly swordsman and is known to have fought off eight armed Rebels in the last rebellion. He has always wanted to try skydiving. Currently, he is one of the bodyguards to the Ingenii.

**Timur** (Count Timur Szechenyi) – Vampire, Hungarian Prefect and leader of the rebellion to overthrow the Principate by kidnapping the Ingenii, Laura Dantonville, and breed her with a human to produce the next generation of Ingenii. He used his family crest – a snarling wolf's head – to create the outlawed wolf's head rings, which contain a deadly white-oak spike. He is also the head of the illegal blood-slave racket, which traffics in selling underage humans to the Brethren. Timur is Rasputin's sire.

***Toga Virilis*** – Ancient Roman tradition celebrating a young man's coming of age, usually between the ages of fourteen and sixteen.

**Zhao** – Vampire and one of the Elders. Ancient Chinese warlord turned philosopher. His sire is unknown.

# AUTHOR BIO

Tima Maria Lacoba is a former ancient historian and archaeologist who accidently smashed a 3,000 Egyptian vase while on her first dig! Her supervisor made her glue it back together again. It took a week. From there she went on to specialise in late Roman-British archaeology, and the military forts along Hadrian's Wall, because buildings don't smash as easily. Now Ms Lacoba's combined her love of history with another passion—story-telling—to create a dark tale of Roman soldiers cursed by a British witch.

Tima Maria has always been a storyteller, but it wasn't until five years ago that she seriously ventured into writing. The result was *Bloodgifted*. In 2011 it was shortlisted in the Atlas Award and eventually came fourth place. In 2012 it was listed among the top ten in the Choclit Search for an Aussie Star Competition. In 2013, she was offered a publishing contract but declined in favour of going indie, preferring the idea of being in charge of her own creation.

*BloodGifted* is just the start of a four-part series entitled, *The Dantonville Legacy*. Book 2, *BloodPledge,* Book 3, *BloodVault* and Book 4, *BloodWish* are all available for purchase.

She also intends to satisfy her fans requests by writing individual books on the other characters in the series. So Terens, Cal Jake and Sam will each have their own story.

Tima Maria currently lives on the Central Coast, an hour's drive north of Sydney in Australia. Her little house is surrounded by bushland, possums and seed-dropping Rosellas on one side, and waterways on the other.

Between bouts of writing, she can be found in the kitchen baking yet another chocolate recipe. This activity is responsible for forming more gothic, urban fantasy stories in her mind for future books.

# ALSO BY TIMA MARIA LACOBA

## The Dantonville Legacy series:

Laura's Locket: A Dantonville Chronicle (Prequle to BloodGifted)

1. Bloodgifted

2. Bloodpledge

3. BloodVault

4. BloodWish

# CONTACT INFO

Tima Maria Lacoba
Visit me at my website:
**http://www.timamarialacoba.blogspot.com**

If you enjoyed reading this book, I'd love you to share it with others, RECOMMEND it to friends, family, and reading groups or clubs, or online forums. You can also REVIEW this book at the site where you purchased it. That is the best gift, you as a reader, can give an author. And if you happen to do that, email me at, fatimamarialacoba@gmail.com and I'll send you a personal message of thanks.

**You can also connect with me at:**
Facebook – http://www.facebook.com/TimaMariaLacoba
Twitter – http://www.twitter.com/timamarialacoba
Goodreads –
https://www.goodreads.com/book/show/14760394-bloodgifted

# BloodVault

## The Dantonville Series - Book 3

# Tima Maria Lacoba

www.ingramcontent.com/pod-product-compliance
Lightning Source LLC
Chambersburg PA
CBHW020659110726
47901CB00001B/254